THE BA

By the same author

To Harry Chapman Pincher

Author's note

This is a work of fiction writen against a background of historical fact; where the fact ends and the fiction begins is for the reader to decide. Charles Baring and the other fictional characters are not based on any real persons living or dead.

The
BARING FAULT

John Stonehouse

JOHN CALDER . LONDON
RIVERRUN PRESS . NEW YORK

First published in Great Britain, 1986, by
John Calder (Publishers) Ltd
18 Brewer Street, London W1R 4AS

First published in the USA, 1986, by
Riverrun Press Inc
1170 Broadway, New York, 10001

British Library Cataloguing in Publication Data
Stonehouse, John
  The Baring Fault.
  I. Title
  823'.914[F]   PR6069.T6/

  ISBN 0-7145-4069-2

Library of Congress Cataloging in Publication Data
Stonehouse, J.
  The Baring fault

  1. World War, 1914-1918—Fiction. I. Title.
  PR6069.T597B37 1986   823'.914   86-4861

  ISBN 0-7145-4069-2 (Riverrun Press)

Set in 11pt Plantin by Margaret Spooner Typesetting, Bridport, Dorset
Printed in Great Britain by Heffers Printers Ltd, Cambridge

BOOK ONE

To Eton and Beyond

CHAPTER 1

Yesterday, and again this morning, Sarah was sick. It was not the same as the diptheria four years earlier when her whole throat had been inflamed and she had felt at death's door. In a way it was similar to the food poisoning after Mary's last birthday party that had made her weak all day. This time it was bad, very bad, when she first woke up. The uncontrollable retching made her gasp for breath. But, unlike the food poisoning, it soon cleared up and for the rest of the day she was fine.

It was a day of great excitement. Sarah's father had completed his round of calls earlier than usual.

'Are you children ready?' he called up the stairs. 'Make sure you bring parasols. The sun is very hot today.'

While they were getting ready, Old George, the groom who was also the gardener and the general handyman around the house, came to the front drive with the Belvoir phaeton drawn by the family's other two horses. It was well polished and the harnesses were gleaming. George liked the master to have the smartest carriage in the county and had collected it himself only a month before from Maythorn's of Biggleswade. The cost of thirty-five guineas had shocked him. George had worked for Doctor Tallen, and his father before him, for forty years, had watched two generations of Tallens growing up and was proud to be serving such a well respected family.

Inside the house Mary came down the stairs, clutching a large white bonnet which matched her long frilly white dress.

'Where's Sarah?' asked her mother.

'Still lacing her corset' said Mary. 'She's having trouble with it.'

'Go and help her then. We can't be late. I'm on the committee you know,' said Dr. Tallen. 'What's wrong with Sarah anyway?'

'She hasn't said anything to me,' said her mother. 'I 'spect it's just the time of the month.'

'I'll have to talk to her 'bout it, said Dr. Tallen. 'We can't have any more illness in the family, 'tisn't good advertisement for the practice.'

'She's alright, I 'spect,' said Mrs. Tallen as she went to the kitchen to collect the second basket of cakes.

Before long they were all sitting in the phaeton: Dr. Tallen holding the reins, his wife with a basket and the two girls behind on the narrow jump seats with the picnic box between them.

'Goodbye then, George,' said Dr. Tallen 'sorry you can't be coming with us.'

'Sor'right, Sir' replied George giving a respectful tap to his cap with a right finger. 'I've seen 'nough excitement in my day to last a journey, though fairly said, I nowt 'spected the dear Queen, bless 'er, to see her Diamond.'

'We're glad Edith is going to be there. She can tell you all about it,' said Mrs. Tallen anxious that George should appreciate his wife's afternoon holiday.

Edith was the Tallen family cook and she had left earlier in the trap with the maid, Mabel. The Committee, of which Dr. Tallen was vice-chairman, had asked all employers to give time off, even to the domestics, and it would not have looked well if his own servants had been kept at home.

They trotted steadily for the three miles into Saxmundham and saw only a few workers in the fields.

'Should be a big crowd there then,' said Mrs. Tallen.

''Tis a day everyone will want to remember,' said her husband. 'Can you imagine what it's like in London? There'll be a fine spectacle there.'

At Saxmundham there was a veritable jam of carriages and two motors which, as they attracted sightseers, made it all the more difficult to get through to the Market Place.

'Look' said Mary, 'there's a Benz.'

'So it is,' said Sarah. 'Let's go and see it.'

'Don't be long,' Dr. Tallen ordered 'and don't get caught up in that bunch of yokels over there. We'll wait for you here.'

'Those things should be banned from the country roads' said Mrs. Tallen after the girls had slipped into the crowd but still within sight, 'they make an awful lot of dust and dirt. The other day one passed me going at speed — at least twelve miles an hour — and I was covered in the muck it threw up.'

'They're a dreadful nuisance since the four miles an hour law was dropped last year' added Dr. Tallen. 'I hear there are lots in Ipswich. If this goes on the Government will have to ban them or bring in strict controls. They will soon be a serious danger to public health and that'll wake people up.'

The girls came back and they walked together into the crowded Market Place where the trestle tables were already being laid for the tea. Dr. Tallen and Mrs. Tallen joined the other local dignatories and their ladies, who had gathered to dispense growing mountains of donated food. Today was an unusual day. The gentry were serving the lower classes. It was ten years since they had last done it; ten years since the last Jubilee.

Sarah and Mary waved to friends, found some seats on the benches and put up their parasols. Dr. Tallen greeted patients soliticiously. Most of Saxmundham had been through his, or his father's, hands and he remembered their ailments quicker than their names. Everyone treated the doctor with respect. They never knew when they might need him and many had dark secrets they needed him to keep.

Dr. Tallen was sitting with the Saxmundham seeds wholesaler and his brother, a manufacturer of tools in Colchester, who often visited the area to drum up business. The brothers were portly, wore coloured waistcoats under their frock coats and had long, greying whiskers sticking out below their hats. Everyone could see they were men of substance and rumour had it that the second brother — the older of the two — was buying the local manor house on the strength of his profits. The shopkeepers were fawning and scraping in the hope of picking up some useful trade from the newcomer. He was enjoying the attention, and pontificating to all and sundry on the occasion they were celebrating.

'Never thought we should see another jubilee for Victoria,' he was saying, 'when she lorst Albert no one thought she'd have the stamina to carry on. Now look at her, she'll outlive us all.'

'She's trying to cheat Bertie of the Kingship,' said the local haberdasher, mischievously, 'at the rate the rake's going he'll die before his mother.'

Dr. Tallen, who enjoyed scandal as much as anyone but did not like to admit it, tried to change the course of the discussion. 'I still think the Prince will make an excellent King although no one could match the Queen's achievement. The monarchy is so popular now. Look how people have flocked to the Jubilee celebrations. They all love her.'

'It's because the country is so successful,' said the Colchester man. 'We're the richest nation in the world and the sun never sets on the Empire. No Englishman can fail to be proud of that.'

'Our industries dominate the world' said his brother 'because we're more inventive, industrious and enterprising than anyone else. We set the standards and the rest follow.'

'It's our control of the sea that does it,' said the Colchester man not willing to lend too much of the stage even to his brother. 'Do you know that four-fifths of all the steamships on the high seas are British and that last year our shipyards launched a thousand new ships?'

'I was in the Navy,' piped up a new voice. 'If it weren't for the Navy we couldn't control the seas or our colonies. We've got the continental powers boxed in.'

'I know, I know' said the Colchester man. 'We've got over three hundred big ships in the Navy — destroyers, battleships and all. No one else has more than a hundred and America, who thinks she's so great, has only got fifty.'

The tea was now in full swing with the magistrates, members of the Board of Guardians and some of the local landowners carrying plates of cakes to the townspeople and trying at the same time, successfully, to look superior. They had to make it clear without words that this once for all event could not invalidate the class structure of Suffolk. The maids, farm labourers, shop assistants and petty clerks, who were enjoying the service from their betters should not be allowed to get ideas above their station. Tomorrow all would be returned to normal as everyone slipped back into their natural places in society. The Jubilee had to be marked by an exceptional demonstration of the oneness of the nation under the great Queen. All her loyal citizens understood that. But it could not mean the order could ever be changed.

CHAPTER 2

The tea over, with volunteers doing the washing up in the back parlours of the nearby shops, people moved back to the tables and turned round on their benches to watch the pageant. The children of the Board school played the roles of brave Boadicea, who defended East Anglia against the Roman overlords — 'She burnt Roman Colchester and killed 70,000 Romans' the Colchester man was heard to say — then brave King Harold against William the Conqueror, Clive conquering India, Admiral Nelson, who was proudly shown as coming from East Anglia, and the Duke of Wellington defeating Napoleon Bonaparte at Waterloo. A specially poignant moment was reached when a small boy, in rags and completely blacked with charcoal was led on in chains which another boy carrying the name William Wilberforce proceeded to break whilst brandishing an imitation cutlass against children made up as Spanish, French, Americans and Arabs. The people cheered Wilberforce's success against all the foreign odds.

The headmaster of the Board school then brought on the grand finale with children carrying high above their heads symbols of contemporary British success: copies of the Morning Post and the year-old Daily Mail, a huge map of the world with big areas of red stretching from New South Wales to British Columbia, a cardboard model of a Lancaster motor, followed by a girl on a Townend bicycle.

A group of Morris dancers came down the street stamping their feet, with jingling bells on their ankles and clanging their staves against each other's. The gossipers stopped to watch.

The girls sitting further down the Market Place were transfixed by the performance. Mary at fourteen was three years younger than Sarah, and had never seen them before. 'They're wonderful,' she said. 'Why don't we form a group and do it?'

'You're not allowed to,' said her older sister, 'it's for men and boys only. It's a tradition going back to medieval times. You'll never change it.'

'I think girls should do more things' said Mary. 'Why should boys have all the fun and get all the interesting jobs when they grow up?'

Because they're stronger than us, I suppose' said Sarah.

'Not cleverer, then,' said Mary.

'I didn't say they're cleverer. I don't think they are. But girls can't learn so much as they have to have babies.'

'I don't want to have babies' said Mary emphatically. 'I want to do more interesting things than having babies.'

'Unless you're wrong inside, you've got to have babies,' said Sarah. The exchange was cut short as the dancers were parading again, to the music of a violin and a flute, fluttering white handkerchiefs from outstretched hands and lifting their heavy booted feet high in unison. The audience gave them a warm burst of applause.

The sun, high and strong all afternoon, had dropped towards the West and so to one side provided a comforting shade. The ladies who had taken down their parasols, stacked them against their legs and adjusted their wide-brimmed hats as they could now use both hands. Some people were already leaving. The Tallen cook, Edith, and the maid Mabel, were among the first to go. They knew their place was in the kitchen preparing supper and they did not want to take liberties. Dr. Tallen was a very understanding and generous employer but they could not afford to jeopardise their jobs or the four shillings a week they each earned. Edith considered she was extra lucky as Old George had a job too which brought in six shillings a week — way above what he could get elsewhere. With the combined income of ten shillings a week and their board they felt very prosperous.

One of Sarah's friends was pulling at her sleeve. 'There's a performing bear at the end of the Market Place. Let's go and see it. The showman will only want half-a-penny.'

'Oh I don't think we could go, Lily, father will want us to keep near him and mother. He always gets worried when we wander off.'

'Why you're seventeen now,' said Lily.

'You don't know my father' said Sarah sombrely.

'I do, he's my doctor and he often comes to our house.'

Doctor is one thing, father is another.'

'Come anyway, risk it this time. It is the Jubilee. There's a woman on the throne and we should have some rights.'

'Alright then, but we'll have to come back soon,' said Sarah following Lily as Mary tagged along.

Along the side of the road some itinerant traders had set up rough stalls selling knick-knacks and baubles for a farthing or halfpenny and various patent medicines for a penny or twopence. Some gypsy women were telling fortunes by reading palms in little lean-to tents and a group of uncouth youths were jeering at a man who had gone into one. Further along they could hear the rattle of the showman with the bear and they hurried to see him.

A group of about twenty adults and some children were looking apprehensively at the huge beast which stood on its hind legs almost twice the size of its owner. He was an Italian-looking man with a bright blue shirt in felt, which looked as though he slept in it, and a big beret of the type painters wear. He was calling to the bear in a foreign language.

'Isn't he huge?' said Mary.

'Don't get too close' cautioned Sarah.

'He's got a muzzle on. He's quite safe.' said Lily.

'But look at those paws. They could knock you sideways,' said Mary. As they looked, the bear, sensing he was the centre of attention, started to jump up and down in a lumbering

dance. Then under directions from the owner he held a long
pole and twirled it round and round. A few boys who had
crept too near had to run away for fear of being hit.

The owner took the pole and prodded the beast on his
backside. On this signal the bear leaned forward on his knees
and did a series of fantastic somersaults, getting dust all over
its dark brown coat and scattering the crowds to shrills from
the women. The showman persuaded the bear to stand
upright again and it gave a little bow.'

'Only a ha'penny each please,' said the owner in a thick
accent. 'Give a ha'penny for the big Russian bear' and a tiny
girl of about seven ran from behind him holding up a
collecting tin to all and sundry. Some people put a halfpenny
in and others sauntered off, shrugging their shoulders as
though the show was not worth that much.

Lily took a halfpenny from her purse which was dangling
on her arm. 'There, I said I'd pay, didn't I?' and dropped it in
the tin with aplomb.

'I'm going back,' said Sarah. 'Come on Mary.' Lily
reluctantly joined them.

In the Market Place which was now practically deserted
except for the volunteers clearing up, they soon met an angry
Dr. Tallen and a near distraught mother.

'Where have you been?' they asked.

'To see the sideshows.'

'With all those gypsies, tinkers and diddicoys' expostulated
Dr. Tallen. 'They're filthy people, covered in lice and they
cheat you. If I had my way they wouldn't be allowed in the
town. It's a respectable place. Let's get home before you get
up to more mischief.'

Sarah was about to remonstrate but Dr. Tallen was a
disciplinarian of the old school and no one — in the family at
least — could afford to cross him. Men made all the decisions
and ruled the family. It was as inexorable as the British
Empire.

CHAPTER 3

After supper Dr. Tallen called Sarah into his study and asked her to sit on the sofa whilst he took the commanding seat at his large mahogany desk. Behind him the bookshelves were filled with medical books — forbidding tomes which the children were forbidden to read. Sarah by now was apprehensive as her father only ever talked to his daughters in this way when he had something serious to impart. The atmosphere of gloom was not dispelled by the gaslight even though it was turned up high. The room was — for Sarah — the most depressing in the house with its fusty smell of old books, stale tobacco and leather chairs. The dark walls were not relieved by the two engravings of Landseer in their huge gilt frames which dominated the room. Sarah hated these pictures as representing the worst in modern art: cold, static and masculine; she preferred Millais.

'Now, my dear,' her father was saying in his pompous, putting-down way, 'you know I don't like admonishing you but you must understand I have your best interests at heart. Soon you will have to be thinking of marrying — your mother and I will arrange some coming out parties for you so you can meet some suitable young men, but it won't help you to get a good husband if you have a reputation for gallivanting around the town with the rabble.'

'It was hardly that, father,' Sarah defended herself. 'I only went to see the fair.'

'You went with Lily Mitchell. I shouldn't tell you this, but I know she's a very naughty girl. If you're seen around with her people will think you're the same.'

'She's not so bad, father. She has lots of ideas about women's freedom but it's not a crime to have ideas is it?'

'She's much worse than that. She's an immoral girl and could be a very bad influence on you. No decent man will want her for a wife and I don't want you to be looked at in the same way.'

'Oh, father.'

'It's for your own good Sarah. A woman's life depends on getting a good marriage — there can be very few Florence Nightingales, you know — and your chances will be ruined if people think you are as immoral as that Lily Mitchell.'

Sarah tensed up and gripped her hands tightly on her lap sitting bolt upright on the uncomfortable sofa. Her father sensed the tension and tried a more conciliatory tone.

'Please Sarah, I am your father and I want to help you, you know that. In any case I've been concerned in the last few days about your health. You haven't been looking your usual self. Has anything been wrong with you?' Sarah did not reply but gripped her hands even tighter. 'If so we should nip it in the bud. A healthy body means a healthy mind and is worth caring for.'

Sarah said nothing as the Monarch of the Glen looked on.

'Come Sarah, you can confide in me. I am your doctor too. What has been wrong?' Dr. Tallen was, by now, certain his daughter was hiding something from him. He left the desk and strode over the room to the sofa. 'I'd better examine you. Stand over here in this light and let me see your tongue. Now, say "ah"', he added as he looked down her throat. 'Let's see your eyes,' but before he could do that Sarah suddenly crumpled on her feet and fainted. Her father held her from falling and helped her to the sofa where he stretched her out with her legs on the raised end and her head below. 'Rest there a few minutes' he said solicitiously, 'the blood will soon flow to where it's needed and you'll feel better. I'll go and bring some cold towels — and your mother.'

When her parents returned Sarah's colour had already

returned to her cheeks but her father still applied the towel to her forehead. 'That will help,' he said. 'I'll get some medicinal brandy but first I think we need to know what's really wrong with you.'

'I suppose it's nothing' said Mrs. Tallen, 'just the excitement of the day.'

'No, it's not only that. Sarah's been unwell for some days and she hasn't confided in us.' He lifted his daughter's legs on to the floor, sat her up and said firmly 'Now Sarah tell us how you've been, we must get to the bottom of this.'

'I was sick this morning,' she admitted, staring at the floor.

'Why didn't you tell us?' said her mother, now very worried. 'You could have stayed home today and rested.'

'I didn't want to worry you. Anyway I was sick yesterday too, but it goes off very quickly and I feel alright afterwards.'

Her father was now looking extremely concerned and not a little angry.

'Tell me more about this sickness,' he demanded.

'It's nothing, father. I'll soon get over it.'

'When was your last monthly?'

'I missed last month's and this month's a week overdue.'

'I thought so, you're not ill, Sarah. I think you're pregnant,' said her father with disgust.

'Heaven's no!' said his wife.

'You've got some explaining to do my girl. The sickness you have is known in medical terms as 'hyperemesis gravidarum'; it's a nausea felt by pregnant women and it usually begins in the fifth or sixth week of pregnancy. Who have you been with?'

Sarah said nothing but looked disconsolate.

'Come on,' insisted her father 'you can't get pregnant all by yourself. There's no such thing as immaculate conception for ordinary mortals.'

'It was George Baring,' Sarah said reluctantly.

'My poor child,' exclaimed her mother, suddenly becoming aware of the full enormity of the situation.

'"Poor child" fiddlesticks,' said Dr. Tallen, '"silly child" more likely, giving herself away like that for nothing. Now she'll have to marry him. I presume that's the George Baring at the Hall?'

'Yes, yes, yes' said Sarah, she knew that if 'George Baring' had been a shop assistant or a farm worker her father would not have wanted her marriage but would have banished her to some distant aunt's where she would have had to have the baby secretly so it could be adopted with no stain on the family.

'I don't think she should marry him unless she really wants to,' said her mother bravely. 'Perhaps he doesn't want to marry her.'

'There are no "wants" about this, only duties' said Dr. Tallen, 'that young Baring must do the honourable thing. I'll go and see his father in the morning about it.' Sir Tuke Baring, who was the fifth baronet, was one of his patients and Dr. Tallen thought he knew exactly how to handle him. Arrangements for the wedding would have to be rushed and that might raise a few eyebrows but it would be better than delaying the inevitable and having to give away an obviously pregnant daughter at the altar.

'I don't want to marry George' said Sarah petulantly, 'I don't love him, I hate him.'

'Are you suggesting he took you against your will, Sarah?' Dr. Tallen asked angrily, 'that's rape and he can go to prison for that.'

'No, no, no' said Sarah in alarm. 'It first happened six months ago. I loved him then but he's been horrible to me for the last three weeks since I told him I missed my monthly.'

'The things you modern girls discuss,' said her mother in disgust. 'Why didn't you tell us?'

'I was hoping it would turn out alright.'

'You mean you wanted a miscarriage,' said her father, 'that's very dangerous; girls have been known to bleed to death with that, especially when they go to those filthy gypsy abortionists.'

Sarah started sobbing and her mother tried to console her. 'Don't worry child you'll be all right, girls have had babies before and you're healthy enough.'

'But I don't want to marry George Baring. I hate him. He has other girlfriends now. I haven't seen him for two weeks. He won't want to marry me.'

'He'll have to,' said her father firmly. 'Now off to bed with you. I'll get you a sleeping draught. No talking to Mary about this. She's too young to understand.'

After Sarah had gone upstairs Dr. Tallen turned to his wife and said sternly 'I wish you would not contradict me, least of all in front of our own daughter. There is no possible alternative to marriage. That young Baring won't be the ideal husband and he won't inherit the baronetcy, that goes to the eldest son, but at least there's money enough in that family. Sarah will want for nothing.'

'Think we should consider her happiness,' said her mother, who sometimes regretted her own marriage.

'I'm doing just that,' said her husband, 'you don't think it's just my practice and our reputation I'm considering do you. It's Sarah's interest I've got at heart. She'd be terribly unhappy if the baby had to be adopted. I had a patient last year who hanged herself after her baby was taken away.'

'But what if George Baring refuses to go through with a wedding. It definitely sounds, from what Sarah says, that he's not very keen on her.'

'He'll just have to. That's all there is to it. His father will see to that. Remember the young George has no separate income. His father could cut him out of the family estate if he doesn't cooperate. I'll ride up to the Hall in the morning and make sure the old man does what we want.'

'What you want,' said Mrs. Tallen in a rare burst of independence.

'It'll be for the best,' said her husband. 'It'll be for the best.' He was too tired for arguing.

CHAPTER 4

Sarah's father could not see Sir Tuke on the following day. The baronet was still in London, attending the Jubilee celebrations, but as he was due to return to the Hall at the weekend Dr. Tallen arranged to see him on the following Monday morning.

When he arrived he handed Dobbin over to a groom who was waiting at the front entrance and was taken, by an appropriately attired footman, through the magnificent entrance into the library where Sir Tuke was sitting reading a copy of the *Illustrated London News*.

'Good morning, doctor,' said the baronet jovially, 'or should I say "good afternoon" as I see it is past midday.'

'It's good to see you looking so well Sir Tuke, as I am sure you do any time of the day' said Tallen. 'Did you enjoy the Jubilee?'

'Indeed I did,' replied Sir Tuke. 'It was wonderful to be at the heart of our great Empire on such an occasion. The heart was beating well — if I may use a medical metaphor, doctor,' he added. 'All the young blood we've sent to those distant places has sent back reinforcements of strength through the arteries.'

'Yes, I see your meaning' said Tallen, humoring a man who never failed to pay his medical accounts on time.

Motioning Tallen to sit on a settee and calling the footman to get a couple of whiskies, Sir Tuke went on: 'The Queen looked so regal in her black moire dress. The Prince of Wales rode immediately behind her in his most resplendent uniform and plumed helmet.'

'It must have been magnificent' said Dr. Tallen.

'It certainly was. There was a splendid display of troops under the command of Lord Roberts in the Queen's procession. There were Canadian Hussars, the Zaptiehs from Cyprus, the Cape Mounted Rifles, the Jamaican Artillery,' the Baronet rattled the names off with pride, 'the Trinidad Mounts, the Borneo Dyak Police, troops from New South Wales and a score of other places. It was inspiring to see their loyalty, doctor. With those men — and thousands like them — the Queen's peace can be kept in all our possessions and there's no reason why our Empire shouldn't go on forever. We live in great times, doctor and what a better world we are leaving to our British stock.'

'Yes, indeed' said Tallen who had never left England in all his fifty-one years but was as proud of the Empire as any of the intrepid adventurers who had carved it out of pagan backwardness.

'The Irish are the only blemish on this great occasion,' went on Sir Tuke, 'their refusal in the Commons to support the loyal address to the Queen was a treasonable act, although I see it was passed in the end by 411 votes to 41.' He went on with emphasis. 'That traitor Parnell has a lot to answer for. Gladstone should have left him in prison. The fact that he can do this to the Queen shows he has no moral standards. I thought that divorce business would have ruined him completely. Won't the Irish ever learn to get themselves some respectable leaders?'

'I read in the *Times* that the Lords and Commons went personally in their hundreds to pay their respects to the Queen to make up for that snub' said Tallen trying to make a positive note.

'That's so' said Sir Tuke. 'It was a superb demonstration of a loyal Parliament and certainly helped to cover up the awful Irish lacuna. But look here, my dear doctor, I have the *Illustrated London News* which shows the whole celebration in graphic form.' He picked up the copy and showed it to

Tallen. 'Isn't it a miracle of modern technology that they can produce these illustrations so quickly!'

'It's very impressive' said Tallen.

'I wish I were a young man again,' said Sir Tuke with feeling 'there will be so much to look forward to in the twentieth century and *anno domini* will take care I only see a few years, if any, of it however you fine doctors strive to preserve me. Eh what!' Sir Tuke Baring had not married until his mid-forties, was already approaching his seventies and sometimes felt his age.

'You've still got a good innings left before you're bowled out, I'll warrant,' said Tallen.

'Will you put that in writing for my dear lady wife, doctor? She's always complaining I do too much for my years but she doesn't realise how she keeps me young,' he added with a twinkle in his eye. Lady Baring was twenty years his junior and the heirless baronet had surprised everyone by marrying her just when they thought he was well past it and that the baronetcy would be extinguished on his death. Instead he had confounded them all by producing two strapping sons. 'Anyway, I've been talking far too much. I'm sure you haven't come here on a merely social visit,' he said abruptly.

'Indeed not' said Tallen. 'I've brought some very important, and in some ways disturbing news for you, about your son George.'

'George!' said Sir Tuke, 'what's the young lion been up to?' He looked over his spectacles quizzically. 'He's not caught some frightful disease like poor old Randolph has he?' Lord Randolph Churchill had died only two years before, and the circumstances of his death had shocked all those who were privy to the lurid details.

'Oh no, nothing like that!' said Dr. Tallen, 'as far as I know he is in absolutely perfect health.'

'That's good,' said Sir Tuke, 'we don't want the line to be broken now I've started it off again, do we?'

'In a way that brings me to what I have to say,' said Tallen, getting up courage. 'George is going to be a father.'

'What! George a father!' exclaimed Sir Tuke. 'Well he's not even married!'

'Truth is, he's made my daughter Sarah pregnant,' said Tallen, hoping against hope that the crusty old baronet would not take it too badly.

'Your daughter!' said Sir Tuke, 'why she's no more than a slip of a girl. She was in pigtails when I saw her at that garden party we held here last year for the Tories.'

'Actually she's seventeen and old enough to get married,' said Tallen.

'Now I see what you're on about,' said Sir Tuke with a knowing look at his guest. 'This calls for another whisky I think. How about you, doctor?'

'Well I shouldn't, not in the middle of the day,' he hesitated, 'but Dobbin will see me safely home so I will be pleased to join you.' Tallen felt a relief that Sir Tuke was taking the news so equably.

Sir Tuke pulled the cord to summon the footman who duly dispensed two large whiskies and served them on a silver platter. When he had left the library the two men resumed their conversation.

'Don't misunderstand me, doctor, but are you quite sure the male responsible for your daughter's condition is in fact my son George?'

'Yes,' said Tallen firmly. 'Sarah has been with no other man.'

'Of course I take your word for it,' said Sir Tuke, who for all his inexperience and late-developing in sexual matters, knew there could be no certainty about anything and that Dr. Tallen could not possibly know the truth which only Sarah knew. 'Which leaves us with a problem eh, if we are to be the grandfathers of the baby-to-be,' he added, taking the rest of his whisky in a gulp.

'I think the best solution would be for Sarah and George to be properly married as soon as possible,' ventured Tallen.

'Do we know if George wants to marry her?' asked Sir Tuke.

'I don't think they've discussed it and he certainly hasn't asked me for her hand in marriage,' Tallen said a little pointedly, 'but it would be the honourable thing for him to do.'

'That's true' said Sir Tuke 'and Sarah would make him a lovely wife.'

Tallen smiled at this compliment but what he did not know was that Sir Tuke Baring had his own reasons for wanting his second son safely married to a local girl. The eldest son — and heir to the baronetcy — had left the family seat to join a firm of stockbrokers in the City, and there were indications too that he wanted a political career. Consequently, and as the youngest son was destined for a commission in the Army, it was important for Sir Tuke to get George to tie himself down to running the estate which stretched for 25,000 acres around the Hall. George had been reluctant to do this for his own ambition was to join Cecil John Rhodes in South Africa, and to make his fortune there. The old baronet had successfully stymied this move in the previous year when Rhodes had been forced to resign as Premier of Cape Colony, after the notorious Jameson raid, but George was still chaffing at the bit like an unbroken stallion. Marriage might be the solution to keep him in Suffolk, the wily baronet thought.

'How do you think we should go about it?' asked Tallen, deferring to the older man now he knew they were in agreement.

'The first thing we've to do is to confront George,' said Sir Tuke 'and the sooner that's done the better. He's out riding now but before long he'll be back for luncheon, then we'll see what he's got to say for himself. If he agrees he's the father, then there's no alternative, he'll have to marry Sarah. We'll get the bans announced as soon as the vicar can attend to it.'

Sir Tuke's firm pronouncement was music to Dr. Tallen's ears. The interview had gone much better than he had dared to hope. It was now safe for him to finish the remainder of his whisky and to relax.

The baronet pulled the bell for the footman, who appeared quickly, and he ordered another two whiskies. What the two men did not know was that the servant had been listening throughout to their animated conversation from behind the door to the lobby hall. There were not many compensations in being a poorly paid flunkey to an employer who could spend more on buying a horse than a servant earned in a lifetime. But one of them was to know all the gossip before the rest of the village and the footman was satisfied that this time he had heard his money's worth.

Sir Tuke, now he had firmly reconciled himself to the prospect of the two families being linked through marriage, turned his attention to making his guest, who was also becoming a co-conspirator, feel at home. He did this by sharing confidences about his other sons.

'You know John, of course, don't you doctor, although it must be some years since you treated him for his childish ailments?'

Dr. Tallen nodded, he was feeling mellow from the effects of the whisky and remembered affectionately the boy who had been laid up fifteen years before with mumps. 'How is he?'

'John is doing very well in the City. He's been promoting those new railway shares and made a packet on them. Can't go wrong with British industry — there are some fortunes to be made.'

'Personally I think we should beware of competition,' said Tallen 'things might not always be so easy for us. I read in the *Fortnightly Review* that only twenty years ago our textile industry was selling eighty-two percent of the cotton imported to Hong Kong, China and Japan but that's fallen now to under fifteen percent. That's a big drop and our mills in the north country are feeling it.'

'I agree' said Sir Tuke 'and I know the reason for it. It's

those Nips. They've stolen our ideas. Only twenty years ago
they started spinning cotton for their own consumption and
already they're destroying our export trade in the Orient. But
what I feel is so wrong is that we have allowed cotton spinning
to start in India too. That's the silly thing. What's the point of
having a colony if we can't dominate its markets? They
should be producing the raw materials for factories in this
country not setting up industries to compete with us.'

'Yes,' said Tallen, 'we're allowing them to buy the same
machinery we have in Lancashire but the Indian workers
who use the machines are paid a tenth of what our own people
get. It's no wonder they can produce more cheaply out there.'

'Trade Unions are killing the goose that lays the golden
egg' said Sir Tuke, getting into his element, 'they don't seem
to realise that if our workers get too much no one will be able
to afford to buy our goods. Those rabble rousers Ben Tillett
and John Burns should be banished to van Diemans land
along with the other criminal classes. They're a danger to the
nation,' he added. 'John feels very strongly about it. He's
going into politics to help strangle the Trade Union demon
and we're going to get him a seat at the next election. It'll cost
me a bit but it'll be worth it. I'm told Lord Salisbury is very
keen to have him in the Commons to strengthen the number
of backbenchers who understand financial affairs. John's firm
handles the Prime Minister's investments and he's met him
on business once or twice. That's done him no harm.'

'Has George ever shown an interest in politics?' asked
Tallen.

'Not at all. He's the playboy adventurer of the two; no
nose to the grindstone for him, though I think he might
reform when he gets married,' he said, remembering
suddenly. 'He had ideas of going out to Africa but I've been
trying to stop that. His place is here at the Hall, I'm getting
too old to run this estate and it's becoming more difficult
dealing with the tenant farmers, That's why I need George
here.'

There was a noise of shouting coming from the stables. 'That'll be George coming' said Sir Tuke and within minutes the young man strode into the library flicking his riding stick against his mud splattered breeches in a constrained temper. George resented his old father, with whom he had so little in common as the gap in their ages was so wide, and doubly resented being summoned to the library by a footman. Sir Tuke had previously told the servant to ask his son to join them but what he did not appreciate was that the flunkey would have a smirk on his face when he did so.

'Did you want me, father?' he asked in an arrogant tone, barely looking at Dr. Tallen.

'Yes, George, this is Dr. Tallen as you know, we'd like you to join us for a drink.'

'Good day, Dr. Tallen' said George in a peremptory way. He sat heavily on the low leather chair, which had an old blanket permanently thrown over it so riders could sit without soiling the furniture. He stretched his long legs and scraped his filthy boots on the Persian carpet. Sir Tuke's middle son was no respecter of property — particularly his father's. Dr. Tallen had often observed that inherited wealth created such benign disdain in some offspring in every second generation. George was totally unlike Sir Tuke, who was fastidious in his concern to protect the inheritance, but quite like his grandfather — Tuke's father — who had been a spendthrift in his day. I'll have a whisky' he announced to the footman who had been summoned again. It was considered bad form for anyone to help themselves to drink, that was servants' work.

'Did you enjoy the ride?' asked Sir Tuke of his son.

'It was superb. I took him for a canter down to Snape and on the moor to the estuary. It was a beautiful day for it. I wanted to come back through Aldeburgh but there wasn't enough time.'

'You mustn't work the horses too hard,' said Sir Tuke.

'They love it,' said George, 'just like the men, the harder

you work them the better they like it. They respect a tough master.'

'Dr. Tallen has come to see us about something most important' said Sir Tuke broaching the awkward subject.

'What's that?' answered George already on guard, suspecting what was coming.

'His daughter Sarah is expecting a baby and she says you are the father.'

'That could just about be right dead on target,' said George, too much of a braggart not to own up.

'Dr. Tallen thinks you should get married and make the child legitimate,' said Sir Tuke.

'What does Sarah say?' asked George quickly.

'She would be very pleased and happy,' said Dr. Tallen equally quickly, so Sir Tuke had no time to throw any doubt on the matter.

'I must be honest with you and say I'm not very keen,' said George. 'I know it's the ungallant thing to say but frankly I don't love Sarah and I never have done.'

'You're a cad,' said Tallen, unable to control his feelings. 'You took my daughter when she was barely sixteen, took advantage of her youth and her immature emotions and now you say you didn't love her. She thought you did or she would certainly never have given her virginity to you.'

Sir Tuke did not like the way the situation was developing and tried to calm things down.

'Now, now,' he said briskly 'that's not the way to speak to your future son-in-law, doctor. I've known George a few years longer than you and I know he likes to speak his mind but it's better than dishonesty isn't it?' He raised his eyebrows towards Dr. Tallen and turning towards his son added, 'He hasn't said he wouldn't marry Sarah, after all. He'll soon learn to love her especially when they have their own offspring — my first grandchild — to draw them together, won't you George?'

'I haven't yet made up my mind what to do, Pater. This has

come as a big shock to me. Sarah never said anything about being pregnant,' lied George, 'and I haven't seen her for weeks.' George was gently reversing his engines as he could see the way his father's wishes were leaning. He was inclined to be hot-headed, obstinate and selfish, but he also had a practical streak. Although he had fantasies of fortune-making in Africa, he knew that he had no real career in sight and was completely dependent upon the goodwill of his old father who could cut him out of his will as easily as saying 'William Shakespeare'.

Dr. Tallen wisely kept silent as he could sense the way Sir Tuke was handling his difficult son and Sir Tuke pressed home his advantage.

'It's for you to decide, George my dear boy, but it would please me greatly if you did marry Sarah, a sweet girl as I remember her. I could make a very useful marriage settlement and, if you settle here, you will inherit the Hall.'

This was an offer George was loathe to refuse. He had always been insanely jealous of his older brother who was brighter and more energetic. Taking over the Hall would be a single victory in their long-running feud. Marriage seemed a small price to pay.

'Can I think it over?' George pleaded, although his mind was already made up.

CHAPTER 5

The wedding took place a month later in the Saxmundham church with both families putting a brave face on the hurried arrangements. The bride wore a white satin dress with a cape of Brussels lace, which had been worn by her mother twenty-two years before. Fashions had hardly changed in that time and few would have noticed that it was that old. The bridegroom wore a long morning coat of the newest cut from tailors in Savile Row, striped trousers and a large glossy top hat. Sarah looked radiantly happy but George, to anyone who did not know him well, looked faintly churlish as if he had wandered in to the wrong party by mistake.

Outside the church after the ceremony there was great difficulty in persuading the bridegroom to stand still long enough for the photographer to creep back under his cloth to get the shutters working properly. Sir Tuke Baring who had paid him to come out from Ipswich to take the historic record was visibly annoyed with his son for messing up the arrangements. George was behaving like a frisky horse who would not get into harness. His father knew the reason; others put it down to the bridegroom's exuberant good spirits, although the sour look on his face confirmed that this was a charitable interpretation.

Walking down the steep path towards the carriages waiting on the road below, Sarah had an effort to keep up with her husband. He was rushing past the grave stones as if he desperately needed to put as much space and time as possible between himself and the events which had just overtaken him.

At the reception, he became so drunk that he could barely respond to the toast and had to be carried to a settee in the library where he eventually recovered after an hour's snoring sleep and a vigorous application of cold towels by the servants. The new Mr. and Mrs. George Baring were very late leaving for their honeymoon at Great Yarmouth and those few guests who waited to see them go did not think it an auspicious start. George, hardly revived from his drunken slumber was in a flaming temper and treated his wife worse than he would a servant girl, screaming at her with foul expressions even as the carriage went down the drive. The bride could scarcely hold back tears as she attempted a feeble wave to the small knot of friends standing by the entrance to the Hall. They waved back relieved, at least, that the couple had got away.

The honeymoon was a disaster. George was moody and morose without his friends and Sarah felt lonely and isolated in the big hotel where she knew no one and felt out of place. Every evening she was left alone whilst her husband went drinking in the taverns, mixing with dubious sea-going characters, and usually ending up in one of the town's two brothels for mariners.

During the afternoons, when George had partially recovered from the ravages of the night before, he took Sarah for a promenade and tried to repair the damage. It was a hopeless exercise as he had no heart in it and she was only too painfully aware of the artificiality of their relationship. Her husband had not attempted to make love to her; she was affronted by this neglect but could not find the words to raise it with him. She wondered if he held back because of her pregnancy but as he exercised restraint in no other area of his conduct she rejected that idea. One day she made an attempt to get through to him.

'George, darling, why are you so unhappy?'

'I'm not exactly unhappy; I'm restless. There's so little to do here.'

'I'm here, you can enjoy my company. Why do you have to go out every night? Can't you stay with me sometimes? I thought that was what wives were for. Companionship and that.'

'Don't be ridiculous. There'll be enough time in our lives for that sort of thing' he replied callously. 'You can't expect me to be hanging about waiting for you to have the baby, do you?'

'That's the reason for it isn't it? You don't want me because I'm pregnant. It's your baby as much as mine, you know. There's no reason to avoid me as if I had the plague.'

'Alright, it's my baby. You don't have to go on about it. I've had enough of that rammed down my throat by your father, I don't need more of it from you.'

Sarah pricked up her ears. 'What did my father say then?'

'He made me marry you. That's all,' George said defiantly. 'In most languages it would be called blackmail.'

'I don't believe it' Sarah sobbed, feeling tears welling in her eyes. 'I don't believe it. Father could never do that.'

'He did! He wanted to protect his little girl from nasty little rumours and his respectable practice. That's why he did it!'

'I thought you really wanted me. You were so kind when you came round to ask for my hand' she cried, sobbing uncontrollably, 'why didn't you tell me how you really felt?'

'My father held a pistol at my head, that's why,' George replied callously.

'You didn't mean anything then?' she said through her tears as she sat on a bench overlooking the harbour. She hardly saw the beautiful four-masters in her own despair.

'You wanted the truth and you've got it,' said George. 'I married you because you'll be having our baby and for no other reason. It's better that you know. I don't want to be tied down in this marriage. You must know that. I will take care of you and the baby but don't expect anything else.'

'Oh dear, oh dear,' sobbed Sarah, knowing that she had no escape.

The honeymoon could not have been more of a disaster and it set the pattern for their future life. Until the birth of their child the parents contained a truce. George cut himself off with rude, thoughtless behaviour and Sarah retreated as best she could into a world of petty domestic arrangements and pre-natal preparations. In their new home, which Sir Tuke had provided just outside the estate, they occupied separate bedrooms and saw little of each other except at meals.

One day after dinner, five minutes after the servants had left the room to clear up the dishes, George toyed with his port glass and looked pensively at his wife.

'How are you feeling these days Sarah?' His concern for her welfare was so rare she was surprised more than flattered.

'I get more tired nowadays but there seem to be no complications,' she answered.

'I wondered if you would like to spend Christmas with your family. It would be better for you to have some cheerful company,' he said with unusual concern.

'I hadn't thought of it' she said 'wouldn't my people think it somewhat strange if I leave you over Christmas?'

'It would be the last time you could be with them for the festive season. I'm sure you'd enjoy it better than staying here. Anyway I was thinking of going to Paris with some old chums of mine.'

'Really' said Sarah haughtily 'one of your drinking orgies, I suppose?'

'You know I like my freedom,' he said, 'I live for it. Paris is getting back its old *joie de vivre.* It took the Frenchies a long time to recover from the decay of the third Napoleon and I'd like to see it again. Next time, I promise, I'll take you with me.' He had not been so forthcoming before about the future and Sarah was expected to be grateful for such crumbs. 'In any case you're in no condition to travel now. It's better you rest up a bit with your family.'

'You've made up your mind, so you do it' Sarah said resignedly.

'I want you to take good care of yourself so nothing happens to our baby' he said. This concern was a new feature in his conversation. 'I've great plans for our son.'

'You're sure it's a boy then?'

'It'll be a boy, I know,' he said. 'My father will be so pleased there won't be anyway I could lose the Hall then.'

'That's all you think about — your inheritance' she said scathingly.

'I want our son to inherit it. Don't you see the importance of that?'

'What difference does it make if he's unhappy and we're unhappy. What's the point of inheritance and material things if you don't have happiness?'

'You can't begin to be happy without possessions. Have you seen those miserable people who work on the estate? They have nothing. We might have the biggest Empire but it's not much good unless one has a share of the property, and I want our son to have his rightful share.'

'He might be a better man if he worked for it,' said Sarah.

'Work!' said George derisively, 'work didn't do anyone any good. You can work yourself silly and get nowhere. The secret of success is to get others to work for you and you get them to work for you if you've got property, power and prestige. I want our son to have all these advantages.'

'I want him to be happy,' said Sarah weakly, knowing she could never win the argument.

'Happiness will follow as day follows night,' said George. 'and by the way, I'm putting him down for Eton.'

'Eton? Already? He isn't even born yet.'

'There's a big waiting list. It's better to get in early.'

'But Eton's miles away. Can't he go to a nearer school?'

'He'll go to a prep when he's young but he should go to the best.'

'You didn't go to Eton and nor did your father. Doesn't it usually go in families?'

'I went to a rotten minor school and I haven't forgotten it.

As a result I know I've missed out. At the top schools you make friends and that helps in future life. Anyway my uncles went to Eton so that will be a good recommendation,' he said, finishing the subject.

We'll have to wait and see if it is a boy, won't we?' said Sarah.

'That's settled then. You go to your parents and I'll go to Paris over Christmas.'

'If you say so,' she sighed, thinking she would at least be spending the 'festive' season in a happier environment.

CHAPTER 6

On the 13th February, 1898, the baby was born at home without complications. It was a boy of eight pounds two ounces. That night the father celebrated by going to Ipswich and getting blind drunk with his riding friends. Sarah, at least, had her parents and her sister Mary with her. They all knew by this time that the marriage was a disaster and wanted to give Sarah all the comfort they could. Perhaps, they thought, there was some hope that George would reform after he had sown his wild oats and that the child would draw his parents together, but their vain hopes were short-lived. The boy — christened Charles after the Restoration King — became yet another source of quarrels between the parents.

Before the baby was even toddling, George was taking him riding over the estate — not at a gentle pace but at times hell-for-leather, with the father clutching his son to his breast with one arm as the other tried to control the racing stallion. The poor nanny, whom Sarah had recruited, left in disgust and in tears after the second of these incidents, declaring that she had never seen a child exposed to such danger and that the master must be mad.

One evening Sarah tried her best to reason with her husband.

'George, can't you see that it's very dangerous to take such a small child on your rides — Charles is barely eighteen months. He can't hold on and you could easily drop him, especially if the horse runs out of control.'

'My horses don't go out of control,' George said firmly. 'I know what I'm doing for my son. I'm putting character and strength into him. He will know no fear.'

'But the poor little chap has been so distressed'

'Not always, yesterday he didn't cry at all and we went for ten miles.'

'He is too young for it. Sometimes when you bring him back he cries uncontrollably for ages and I don't know what to do for him.'

He's getting used to it and its toughening him up when it really counts. The Red Indians put all their babies outside the wigwams at night so that only the strongest would survive. The earliest years are the best testing times.'

'You'd kill our baby then, would you, just to prove your point?'

'Charles won't die so easily,' George exclaimed in anger at his wife's arguments. He had no patience whenever she attempted to express a point of view. 'He will grow up to be the strongest man in the county — if not the country. I will have my way with him. If we have a girl child you can bring her up in your way. The man child is mine.'

'The chances of us having any more children are very remote when you hardly ever come to my bedroom,' said Sarah with a note of despair. She could count on the finger of two hands the number of times George had had sex with her during the past year and he had left her alone for six months after Charles was born.

'Some women have to be grateful for small mercies,' said George. 'You want to show a little gratitude. I married you, didn't I? Most men would have just let you get on with having the baby put away somewhere, but I wanted a son.'

'You wanted a son so you could get the estate. You only wanted to upstage your brother' Sarah shouted. Sir Tuke had already, a year before signed the papers ensuring that George would inherit the Hall on his father's death. The stockbroker son — the eldest and the aspiring politician — was still unmarried and showed no signs of being so.

'True, true. I don't deny it. I want the Hall. I will get the baronetcy if my brother dies without an heir and Charles will get it after me. We are helping the Baring line. That's why father loves me so much.'

'I don't understand all this worship of blood lines,' said Sarah. 'It's happiness in this life that matters. You're absolutely obsessed with a myth.' In two years, the pressures of unhappy marriage and the responsibilities of running a home and controlling ten servants, had matured Mrs. George Baring beyond recognition. The carefree young girl of Jubilee year had been moulded into a strong, determined woman. She knew her husband had most of the power, and would have even more when Sir Tuke died and they moved into the Hall, but the one card she could play in the constant manoeuvering with her errant husband was the knowledge that he could never divorce her. After the birth of his grandson Sir Tuke had stipulated that the Hall would pass to him through George as trusteee during his own lifetime. George had tried to persuade his father to leave the estate to him without strings but the canny old man would not fall for it, for he knew only too well George's weakness.

'You call it a myth, do you. Let me tell you, wife, something you will never understand. This country's greatness is based on myths. Look at Queen Victoria. She's a myth in her own lifetime and she holds an Empire together. That's the strength of a myth. We can dominate the world because other people's myths aren't as powerful as ours.' George was taking Sarah out of her element. In national and international affairs she had to acknowledge she was lost.

'I certainly don't know what that has to do with our problem here,' she said.

'A great deal' George expostulated. 'You live well don't you? You wouldn't like to live in one of those miserable hovels with a farm labourer would you? Look at some of those girls you were at school with; they have to skivvy around for a living while you stay here in luxury, wanting for nothing. That's what the myth's about. I have the property — and will

have even more when father dies — because people believe
we are entitled to it. Call it a myth if you like but it sounds
more like money to me.'

'Your father owns this estate and his father before him.
That's legal title not myth.'

'That shows how much you know about it, woman. That
legal title is only a piece of paper but it means something
because years ago a King gave all the land around here to one
of my ancestors for services rendered. People respect that
royal decision right down to the present day. It's a myth but
it's how you can live here in comfort whilst others are poverty
stricken.'

'I hadn't thought about it like that.'

'Because you don't think and you don't learn. And you
don't realise that there are socialist agitators who would
overturn everything we believe in and substitute their own
myths. Then we would have nothing. What we have we must
protect with everything we've got — myths and all,' George
declared, striding out of the room. It was a long time before
Sarah dared to raise the subject again.

The following Christmas George surprised Sarah by
staying with his family rather than gallivanting with his
drinking friends. It was a relatively peaceful occasion.
Christmas trees had become the fashion and a huge one was
put up in the sitting room, festooned with candles and
baubles. It looked very pretty and Sarah — still a girl at heart
— was delighted. Charles too seemed to realise it was a
special occasion and gurgled with pleasure at the pretty
flickering lights.

George bought presents from London for his wife —
perfumes imported from France and silks from Italy which
the new departmental stores stocked in abundance — and for
Charles a box of carved wooden soldiers dressed in the
uniforms of Wellington's and Napoleon's troops at the battle
of Waterloo. They took cigars to old Sir Tuke at the Hall. He
had been poorly for months suffering from gout and

grotesquely swollen legs which confined him to a wheelchair. Nonetheless he was still mentally vigorous and was able to play with Charles on his knees and give him rides in the wheelchair pushed by a footman. Sir Tuke clearly adored his grandson and George was astute enough to realise that the boy was the key to all his fortunes. His father, who was becoming senile, had little time for his other son as he had produced no offspring. George knowing that the old man could not have long to live was careful not to offend him or disturb the prospects of the inheritance. The fact that he would be trustee rather than owner did not bother him now as his possession and control would be just as effective.

After Christmas, and having done his duty, George left for Paris. Sarah suspected him of having mistresses there but did not complain as she preferred him to engage his dalliance as far from home as possible. Paris was far enough away to undermine the capacity of local gossipers to spread stories of Baring the Suffolk rake. Sarah had already dismissed two scullery maids George had seduced and she hated the frequent confrontations with him about his adulteries in the village.

Sarah went to her own parents to celebrate the arrival of the twentieth century. She always had warm hospitality from her father who had been mellowed over the years by feelings of guilt over his daughter's enforced marriage. Dr. and Mrs. Tallen were entranced with Charles and always made a great fuss of their only grandchild. Mary, unmarried, was still at home, but Edward had been shipped to South Africa with his regiment as the Boers under Kruger had broken out of the Transvaal and invaded the British territories of Natal and Cape Colony. The Tallens thoroughly approved of the Government's action even though it meant their son could not be with them. Like most English Tories they thought that Gladstone's Liberal policy in giving virtual independence to the Transvaal had been a terrible blunder. Dr. Tallen held no respect for Gladstone, whom he had considered to be a humbug and a prostitute chaser. When the statesman had died two years before he had refused to wear black in mourning.

The nineteenth century passed quietly away in this tranquil corner of England. The older people who recalled the temptestuous earlier part of the century from the stories of their parents, were thankful that under Victoria so much progress had been achieved in the later years. The twentieth century promised prosperity, stability and peace in Europe and an ever improving life for everyone. Good had triumphed over evil and there could be no looking back. British concepts of property and justice were conquering the world.

CHAPTER 7

Queen Victoria died at her Isle of Wight home on the 22nd January, 1901. She had reigned for nearly sixty years and her death signalled the passing of an era, plunging the whole nation into deep mourning. Charles Baring was not yet three and remembered nothing of the events, but in later years his mother gave him vivid descriptions of the carriages and shops swathed in black and the piles of floral tributes that were collected in every town and village to be sent to Windsor. She also told him how people came from all over the globe to pay respects to the great Queen, how her grandson, the German Kaiser, rode with the new King Edward behind the gun carriage and how they were followed by the Kings of Portugal and Greece and dozens of Princes and Dukes, all on horseback.

The boy lapped up the stories with relish as he had an intuitive sense of history. By the age of seven he was already taking a keen interest in the brilliantly unfolding saga of the new century. He searched the *Graphic* and the other illustrated magazines for pictures of Zeppelins and the new heavier than air machines which the Wright brothers had flown in a big country across the ocean called America. He graduated from reading the stories in the Boys Own paper to the 'Invisible Man' of H.G. Wells and any news he could pick up about the exciting world outside England he found totally absorbing.

His childhood was sometimes unhappy because of the constant rows between his parents. As a small child he could not understand why his father was always shouting at his mother. He loved them both as they each gave him warmth and attention. But they never did this together as other children experienced. He hardly ever went out with both parents and in the Hall it was obvious to him from an early age that father and mother lived separately.

Charles had two sisters, Emma, four years younger, and Edith who was born when he was six. As he grew up he noticed that his father had nothing at all to do with them. He never visited their nursery and they never ate with him. It was as if the father had disowned them. Charles' mother doted on the girls so much that Charles might have been excused had he felt jealous, but in fact was so sorry at his father's cruel indifference to his sisters that he never resented the maternal love they received.

Charles soon became aware that many of the arguments in the Hall were about his father's long absences from home. The rows were so normal that little effort was made by his parents to keep any secrets from him. Father indeed would not even curb his temper in front of the servants. Sir Tuke Baring had died the year after Queen Victoria and George had inherited the Hall and estate — albeit subject to conditions; he no longer had any restraints on his behaviour. He revelled in his lack of inhibitions and the family simply had to put up with his boorishness.

One day Charles, from behind the sitting room door, then aged eight, heard his parents arguing vehemently.

'Don't you have any respect for me?' he heard his mother say.

'Yes, of course I do. You're the mother of my children aren't you?' his father shouted.

'Can't I mean more than that?' she sobbed 'why can't I be a wife to you too? Why do you always have to go off with other women?'

'Don't be so puritanical, Sarah. You're out of your age. These are modern times and men expect to have their freedom and to have it openly. In the old days it had to be furtive' — this was a word Charles did not understand, 'but nowadays everything can be open and above board.'

'It would be different if I went with another man wouldn't it?' his mother answered. 'It seems to be one rule for men and another for their wives.'

'You won't change that in a thousand years,' his father sneered, 'the male has always been superior and always will be.'

'Not all husbands have other women, otherwise there wouldn't be enough to go round,' his mother said with a logic her son could understand when he thought about it later.

'I don't intend to change my ways. You knew the terms of our marriage and why I had to marry you and we can't change those terms now. You should be philosophic about it. Alix accepts Bertie's need for Lily Langtry and all his other women.' Charles, straining his ears, guessed Alix and Bertie were the Queen and King. Many times he had heard them referred to in such a familiar way, as if they were distant relatives.

Once there was a ferocious row about the administration of the estate and this time Charles took his mother's side. One of the ploughmen who had worked for the family for at least thirty years had fallen ill with some awful wasting disease. The estate manager found a replacement — who was actually a second cousin of his wife's — but as the new man was coming from the other side of Lowestoft accommodation had to be found for him. George decided to evict the ploughman from his tied cottage and give the place to the recruit, but Sarah was horrified.

'Do you mean to say you would throw a man out on his neck when he's worked all those years?' Charles heard her argue.

'It's the only thing to do. The cottage belongs to the estate, the man has no rights there,' his father answered.

'Not after thirty years!'

'Thirty years, three years or three months. It doesn't make

a blind bit of difference. There would be no way we could run
this estate if we gave cottages to non-workers. My! We'd have
no one to work the land if you had your way.'

'It's only one man.'

'Once you give in on principle to one, they'll all expect the
privilege of staying in their cottages. Supposing one of the
dairymen got a job for two shillings a week more in
Saxmundham, would you let him stay in our cottage at our
expense?'

'That's a different case.'

'It's a principle on these estates that you keep your
labourers by tying them to the soil. Once you gave them
freedom of tenure they'd be moving from job to job, wanting
more money and creating chaos in the labour market.'
Charles was completely fascinated by the discussion though
he could not understand some of the words like 'tenure'.

'But surely if a ploughman falls ill you're honour bound to
let him stay? The man's fifty and won't get a job at that age
and in his state of health,' his mother was saying, and Charles
could see the morality behind her plea.

'You've said it! He's good for nothing now. Supposing he
lives to sixty, am I expected to provide him with a cottage all
that time? Who's going to pay the rent?'

'The man has a wife, doesn't he; can't she work?'

'She can but it wouldn't justify a cottage. The decision's
made Sarah, the man'll have to go. Charity is not the job of
this estate; it's the job of the parish!'

When Charles took the problem back to his own room and
thought about it he became quite perplexed trying to find the
right solution. In the end he firmly agreed with his mother,
not because of any moral argument she might have put
forward but because he calculated that over the thirty years
the ploughman had worked he had created enough wealth for
the estate to be entitled as a right to live in the cottage until he
died. Charles had seen that the land was worthless without
men to plough and sow it and to harvest the crops and to care

for the animals. It seemed to him — even at eight years old — that it was only fair for the man who did the work to own a bit — if only a little bit — of the value built up. Charles felt guilty that his toys and books cost more in a week than a man's weekly wage.

Charles had grown into a sturdy youngster. He still had his mother's soft good looks which were enhanced by his curly blond hair but his limbs and big frame were definitely his father's. Apart from some childish ailments, measles and influenza, he had avoided debilitating illnesses such as meningitis and typhoid. His grandfather, Dr. Tallen, took a great professional interest in the wellbeing of all the family and Charles much looked forward to the old gentleman's visits, when after prodding his chest and legs with sounding instruments and peering down his throat to see the tonsils, he would laugh and say, 'Nothing much wrong with you Charles, my boy, which won't go away. I wish all my patients were as healthy' and then get down on the floor to play with the soldiers or wooden model cars Charles had acquired, as if he were eight years old himself instead of nearly sixty. Sometimes they would play word games, which Charles liked best of all, especially one they had invented together. It needed one of them to write words on pieces of paper which were put in a pile whilst the other wrote verbs on other pieces. They thought some of the results like 'cat swallows camel' or 'retriever dog reads bible' hilarious but for Charles the best bit of the game was when the one who had drawn the sentence had to make up a story on the spot in which it would appear most naturally. He had great fun doing this and hardly ever any difficulty.

As time went on both of the protagonists became more proficient in creating complicated sentences such as 'countries slide downwards' or 'books drink lessons' and the stories which had to be invented became more and more interesting. Occasionally Charles's mother was persuaded to join in, but quickly became tongue-tied which amused her son. His father never participated as he never got on with Dr. Tallen. Many years later Charles was to find that these experiences helped him enormously when he had to make impromptu speeches about strange subjects, just like playing games with grandad.

Since four years old Charles had had tutors to visit the Hall and teach him basic subjects. Apart from a young graduate of Cambridge university who was a wizard at mathematics they were a string of dour, uninspiring old codgers. Charles was a patient student and pumped them for all he could get — apart from Latin and Greek which he hated — but in some subjects, especially English literature, they regarded him as presumptuous. Once it was obvious that the understanding the boy had of Spencers 'Fairie Queene' was much deeper than the tutor's but the man would not admit it and complained to Mrs. Baring that her son had been cheeky.

After this incident the parents had a discussion — one of the few amicable ones they had ever had — and decided to send Charles to a preparatory school where he would board all week and come home every weekend. The latter arrangement was a concession from the usual term holidays but as the school was only a few miles distant at Aldeburgh it seemed the sensible thing to do. George was anxious to keep up his son's riding and his interest in the estate, while Sarah wanted to see as much as possible of the boy, who was fast growing into a little man with a personality and character of his own. She was often surprised by his innate wisdom and firmness in argument. She could see more in Charles of his grandfather than of George and, secretly, she was relieved.

The two girls, Emma and Edith, who were also blossoming, were not sent away, of course, and their mother was glad to have their companionship. Her husband continued to provide little of that.

At first Charles was apprehensive about leaving home as he had few friends of his own age and did not know how he would get on with other boys. In the book he had read about

Rugby public school, life for boarders seemed tough and although he was no coward Charles considered the cruelties boys had to put up with a silly waste of time.

It was late January and bitterly cold when the fateful day came and Charles had to climb on his own into the carriage wearing his new school uniform and with his box of clean clothes to wave goodbye to his parents. This time, unusually, they were together and united in the one emotion of sadness at his going. It was a moving occasion for a boy of almost nine years who had never known his parents to agree about anything. It had been a particularly happy Christmas with the grandparents coming over loaded with presents and father's elder brother coming and staying a few days. He had been elected to Parliament in the previous January as a Conservative and considered himself lucky to do so in a General Election which produced a Liberal landslide. Charles had lapped up all the political gossip he could follow about a Prime Minister called Campbell-Bannerman and strange people called 'suffragettes'. He was fascinated to hear that they were women fighting for what they considered were their rights and doubly so when he discovered that his mother actually supported them. Charles felt he was on the threshold of exciting new discoveries and they all happened at the Hall. It seemed a great shame to be leaving it for some dreary, dull old school. As the carriage went down the drive he waved vigorously to the fast disappearing figures of his parents, trying at the same time to force back his tears.

The Aldeburgh School turned out to be heaps better than he had feared. He was ushered into the headmaster's cosy study and sat on a stool as the tall, whiskered man who looked old — as old as forty — stood with his back to a roaring coal fire. His name was Mr. Rumbles and he greeted the new scholar with a hearty joviality.

'So Charles Baring you've come to join us at Aldeburgh have you?'

'Yes Sir.'

'Welcome, my boy, welcome. You've come a little older than most of our new boys, they come here from seven years old, but better late than never. I'm told you've done well with your tutors and we'll just have to see how much catching up you'll have to do, won't we?'

'Yes Sir.'

'We have only three Houses here as it is really a small school, but we still like to have the House traditions and the House rivalry in games. The competitive spirit is good in sports, isn't it Baring, teaches loyalty to the team and this great country depends on that doesn't it?'

'Yes Sir.'

'The Houses are named after ancient Kings of England: Edmond, Harold and Canute and we're putting you into Edmond. It's a fine House and you'll like the master, Mr. Keate. Now is there anything you want to ask me?' He looked quizzically as though no sane boy would so dare to at this early stage of his school career.

'Well Sir, I was wondering if you have a library here,' said Charles tentatively.

'Library!' said the headmaster in surprise as if it was the last thing in the world any boy would want to ask about. 'Of course we have a library. It has all the great classics, Aristophanes and Socrates and all the Shakespeare and sensible novels like Thackeray and Jane Austen.' Charles had heard of Shakespeare but none of the other authors.

'Is there any H.G. Wells?' he asked innocently.

'H.G. Wells!' said Mr. Rumbles 'good gracious no. You can't expect to see socialist writers displayed in this school. I'm surprised at you coming from the home you do. Have you actually read any?' he asked in disbelief.

'Only *The Invisible Man*, Sir' said Charles who was extremely confused by the headmaster's outburst.

'Well that's not so bad, I suppose. Not so bad as some which are only tracts for socialism.' Mr. Rumbles shook his head. 'What you have to understand Baring is that you come from the very class of people which Fabians like that H.G. Wells are trying to destroy. With their ideas they are encouraging the lower orders to envy what you have. They'd like to destroy our society, which depends on the class into which you were born.' The headmaster considered himself a High Tory and worthy enough to be a coopted member of the aristocracy, although his background was merely lower middle class. In his position at Aldeburgh School he had a comfortable living and frequently met the Lords and squires in their great houses, where he felt he belonged.

'No, my boy,' he continued 'you won't find H.G. Wells in our library and nor will you find Charles Dickens. I want my boys to have a good grounding with the respectable authors; there's no time to read that other rubbish.'

'Yes Sir,' said Charles making note of 'Dickens', a new name to him.

The Aldeburgh School was situated in a large house in the middle of the town. It had been built a century before by a prosperous Dutch merchant who had developed a big trade through Aldeburgh before its decline as a port. The facade of the house was in the Flemish style with distinctive gables set off with coloured bricks. Inside, the rooms were spacious and clean, if sparsely furnished. Charles was shown around by a senior boy — a year older — who took delight in explaining all the tricks of the place.

'Old Rumbles is alright — by the way we call him "Thunder", but for goodness sake don't let him hear you say that! The master to beware of is old Brassington who teaches Geography and History. He's a terror. They say he was speared by the Dervishes in the Sudan when he went there in the army in '98 and he picked up their madness.'

'He had some adventures then,' said Charles whose world was already widening, for he had never heard of the Sudan.

'Oh yes. You'll hear all about the battle of Omdurman in your lessons, and he'll be as pleased as punch if you ask him more about it.'

In the Edmond wing of the school Charles was shown the bed and study room he was to share with four other pupils. It was about the same size as his own room at home and seemed terribly small for five boys. His clothes box was stacked in one corner with the four others which made the place even smaller. For the first time in his life Charles felt cramped and claustrophobic; it was as if not only his body but also his spirit had been ensnarled.

There were compensations however in his three years at Aldeburgh. It turned out that the standard of educational performance of boys who had been there since seven was no better than his. In most subjects he was streets ahead of them and in Latin and Greek, his weakest, he had no trouble in catching up. It was fun too being with boys of his own age and he revelled in the pranks and games and the stories they told. Inevitably — helped by his wide reading — Charles was the best story-teller of them all. Every night after 'lights out' at eight o'clock, when all candles and lamps had to be dowsed, the five boys would exchange tales for an hour or so but it was Charles who was always in demand. The room-mates loved his exciting stories about robber barons who stole from the rich to help the poor (a variation of Robin Hood) and adventurers who sailed the seas to South Africa and other far away places to conquer the Boers and other backward people and create better countries where everyone could live in happiness. There was always a moral in the Baring stories and never cruelty for its own sake. Baring — the boys were all known by their surnames and Christian names quickly faded from neglect — soon established a reputation and a following. The four or five bullies in the school who thought intelligence and learning were the marks of pansies who had to be put down, tried to 'discipline' the newcomer but Baring held his own in the fisticuffs and they learnt to leave him alone.

It was a rule that no boy went out unaccompanied by one of the masters which meant, in practice, that only groups of boys went out at all. Charles enjoyed the botany trips to the nearby forests and the dinghy sailing on the Alde to Orford but he longed for the solitude he had been used to at the Hall. He could never escape from other boys and masters, they intruded on his thoughts and prevented him from reading the books he had borrowed from the library. It struck Charles very forcibly that most boys' lives were filled with silly activity and even sillier thoughts. He knew he was different.

His weekend visits to the Hall were a godsend; they helped to wash away the ennui of too many boys living in crowded conditions and the oppressive 'Yes, Sir' 'No, Sir' to the masters who expected the children to be the mere receptacles of their teaching, never to have ideas of their own nor to answer back.

He obtained a forbidden copy of Wells' *In the Days of the Comet* from one of the other boys in his room who had brought it from home at his suggestion after the winter holidays. He was transfixed by the book, could hardly put it down and read snatches of it in every spare moment he could find. Although it made a bulge he was able to hide it under his coat, held up his left armpit, which made his movements very awkward. Fortunately no one noticed as Thunder would have broken into a vindictive temper if he had discovered a forbidden tome by H.G. Wells.

The story Charles read was as written by a character he found most engaging, known fictitiously as Willie Leadford, a young office clerk. In the beginning there was much chaos in the way Willie described England as being run. There was suffering and injustice for the ordinary people and frequent industrial crises with confusion of thought on all sides and looming large was the prospect of war with Germany. Charles remembered being told by his mother that the king was the German Emperor's uncle and that the Kaiser had ridden in Queen Victoria's funeral cortege. He could not understand how anyone — even an imaginery Willie Leadford — could predict a war between Britain and Germany, but he read on. To conquer the chaos and the injustice Willie can see a salvation only in practical socialism and calls on his fellow wage-slaves to rise up. But other events supercede. Willie has a girlfriend called Nettie but she is stolen by the son of a great landowner who is also her father's employer. In the anger of the wasted passion and class hatred Willie buys a gun to pursue the couple but before he can do any damage the green vapours of the comet envelop the globe and put everyone into a transforming sleep. When mankind awakens all is transformed into reason; war and cruelty are no more and the world is reorganised on a sane and socialist basis.

The book had a profound influence on Charles. He dreamt about the green vapour which would turn ogres into kind men and fools into wise ones, and in the morning recalling the dream, he wished it could one day be true.

CHAPTER 8

In 1910, soon after Charles's twelfth birthday, preparations were started for his admission later that year to Eton. His father went to the College to see the housemaster of Evans's, the House to which his son had been booked before he was born, and to check on the admission arrangement. He also ordered the Eton jacket and trousers to be made at Manley's the tailors of Windsor, and bought the special collars. Charles, himself, could not go to the College until the day of his induction but by then he had to be properly kitted out. Boys could feel awkward if their uniforms were not correct in every particular.

At Aldeburgh School Mr. Rumbles was proud that one of his boys was going on to Eton that year and two to Harrow and he found ways of giving them special cramming. Although there was no possible doubt about the admission, which depended on money and position and not educational attainment, Rumbles knew that an entrance examination held on the day after arrival at Eton would decide which form his boys entered and he wanted the credit if he scored high marks.

In July, just before school broke for the summer holidays, the three boys were put through a week of mock examinations taken from various public school entrance papers. It was harsh but Rumbles had discovered that it was always effective in preparing his boys for higher things.

When the time came for term to break up, Charles had mixed feelings about leaving Aldeburgh: the three and a half years he had spent there was a big slice of his young life. In that time his understanding of people and situations had grown considerably. He could even make allowances for Mr. Rumbles' strange attitudes, having realised that the headmaster was locked into a quaint class-layered world where if you did not actually have the good fortune to belong to the top, serving the cause of aristocracy was the next best thing. There had also been the companionship of other boys, all the greater as they shared and suffered the idiocies of institutional discipline together. Charles discovered that there was nothing like common adversity to create group loyalty and friendship.

At the end of July — at the beginning of the long holiday before Eton — Charles was given the treat of a lifetime with a trip to London. It was a reward for doing so well at preparatory school. Sarah remained at home with the girls as her husband saw little point in having all the females in tow. George had recently acquired a brand new Armstrong Whitworth motor of eighteen horsepower for which he had paid the princely sum of £415. He was keen to try it out on a long run, having enjoyed driving it around the estate. It gave him a tremendous sense of physical power and now he wanted to steer it through the traffic on the streets of the Metropolis, as proud as a peacock.

Charles, at twelve and a half, felt he had graduated to a new stage in his life. Rumbles, and all the petty tyrannies he stood for was behind him and London, the centre of the Empire, was ahead. In a few months he would be at the best school in the country. He saw it as the stepping stone to shape destiny, the chance to change people's lives for the better and to use the force of reason to defeat backwardness. His big regret was that he could never discuss his ideas with his father. Mother, although more kindly and encouraging, was also unable to see what he was striving for. Charles could feel the impatience and frustration building up inside him, until at times he could bottle it up no longer. If only, he often wished, he had just one person he could talk to. It surprised him that all around

everyone accepted life as it was without question, as if the
state of things was God-given and unchangeable. Each adult
Charles knew was self-opinionated; his father at least was
honestly boorish about it, whereas the others clothed their's
in a cloud of humbug. Charles wanted desperately to be a
man so he could do something to blow all that deceit and
humbug away. His ideas were locked inside a child's body and
like all imprisoned creatures they screamed to get out.
London, the stage on which one day it could all happen,
would be a wonderful place to see.

They stayed at the Langham Hotel in Portland Place,
mainly because George did not want to run into his gambling
and whoring friends who used the Savoy and the Ritz. The
Langham became a central base for exploring all the sights:
Buckingham Palace, The Tower of London, the big museums
with their feasts of exhibits, and for tripping down to
Hampton Court Palace and the fantastic Kew Gardens. On
Saturday when they were walking in Hyde Park they saw a
huge crowd of women — thousands of them — parading
about with banners. As demonstrators they looked
incongruous in their long tight dresses and large hats. George
wanted to take his son away from the scene as he did not
approve of women behaving in this unseemly way but
Charles begged.

'Can't we just see what they are doing, Father?' and
George who wanted his son to understand, as he did, how
ridiculous women could be, agreed that they could stand on
the bye-lines for a while.

'Alright Charles,' he said, 'but let's keep well back. Those
policemen on horseback over there might have to charge and
we don't want to be caught in that. It would be messy.'

The crowd was milling about a number of carts used as
platforms for speakers who were addressing — in high
pitched voices — all who were near enough to hear. Most
women were pressing around a speaker who clearly
commanded a great deal of authority.

'Who's that Father?' asked Charles.

'Mrs. Pankhurst. She's quite crazy,' he said.

On one side a large number of women were shackled together inside a stockade of bars.

'What are those women doing over there?' Charles asked, very curious as it appeared there was no one guarding them.

'They're women who have been in prison. They're just trying to make a propaganda point,' said his father. 'Just shows how foolish they are and how wrong it would be to give tham any share in running the country. They'll be wanting to be MPs next. Women's place is in the home, they don't have the intelligence for politics,' he added with a snort.

As they walked away towards the Serpentine the noise behind them grew as thousands of voices cried 'Votes for Women, Votes for Women.'

On Monday they called at the Birkbeck Bank in High Holborn where Baring Senior had some business to conduct and went on to the Palace of Westminster. For Charles this was the highlight of his holiday and he felt a surge of excitement as they passed through the ancient Westminster Hall, where Warren Hastings had stood trial, and through Saint Stephens, which his father explained was the site of the Royal chapel where the House of Commons had met for over three hundred years. They entered a vast hall where people were talking, or arguing, on all sides and in the wide corridors which led from it.

'Are all these MPs, Father?' Charles asked.

'Oh no! They're mostly visitors on deputations. There are a lot of Irish here today. You can tell from the gabble.'

Charles's uncle, Sir John Baring MP, a tall distinguished figure, with prematurely greying hair, and the patrician good looks of Sir Tuke, came to escort them along the corridor to the dining room. They had luncheon in the visitors room among the famous and the powerful and as it was considered bad form for the host to give the names of the other diners, Charles had to curb his curiosity. He longed to ask, 'Is that

Mr. Asquith?' but knew he could not dare.

During the meal the brothers spent much of the time discussing family affairs and the news of relatives but Charles was far from bored. The atmosphere of bustle and animated conversation was intoxicating to him. He did not want to leave and when his uncle asked 'Would you like a seat in the gallery, young man?' he jumped for joy. 'Yes please, Uncle,' he gasped, nearly spilling his lemonade.

George looked unhappy and Sir John, who sensed his younger brother's moods added quickly, 'He'll be alright with me, George. I'll take care of him and bring him back to the hotel tonight. He'll be safe in my hands.'

'Do you really want to stay here all day?' George looked at his son in disbelief, for he found more than ten minutes of politics extremely tiresome.

'Oh, yes please Father, I'd love it,' said Charles.

'That settles it then,' said Sir John smiling broadly, 'we'll make you MP for the day for the younger generation!'

George who wanted to visit some places where his son certainly should not go, willingly agreed to the arrangement. In the Great Hall they had to wait for several minutes, and Sir John explained to his nephew that they could not go to the gallery until the Speaker had made his procession, proceeded by the Sergeant at Arms carrying the mace.

'Can we see them?' asked Charles.

'No,' said Sir John, 'the procession passes from the Speaker's House along by the Library and into the Members' Lobby which is down that corridor. All that area is for Members' only and you can't see it from here which is a pity as it's a charming ceremony.'

As Sir John had no questions on the order paper for oral answer he sat with Charles in the front seats of the gallery to explain, in a low voice, what was going on.

'That's Mr. Speaker Lowther in the long wig. He sits up there on that high chair to keep order and to call the Members who are chosen to speak.'

'Why is he called Mr. Speaker?' whispered Charles.

'Because he's the only Member of Parliament who doesn't speak I suppose,' Sir John said confusingly. 'No actually it's because years ago one of his predecessors was chosen to speak for the Commons against a King who wanted to close the place down.'

They watched as more members crowded into the chamber until there was a sea of top hats and heads below.

'That's Mr. Asquith and he's about to reply to a question from Mr. Fell,' said Sir John, 'listen carefully and you might hear the answer which is more than the reporters can. They've been complaining about the acoustics.'

Charles concentrated on the elegant figure standing at the despatch box and heard him say that an advisory committee on aerial navigation was sitting and that Mr. O'Gorman superintendent of the balloon factory had been made a member. Charles was totally absorbed. For him this was history in the making. Bleriot had flown the channel last year and now the Prime Minister himself was talking about navigation of the air ways. Charles had visions of heavier than air machines carrying passengers in all directions to all places.

'That's Mr. Lloyd George, the Chancellor of the Exchequer,' said Sir John, referring to a younger man who had given an answer about unemployment insurance which Charles had found less interesting. 'I have to go to a committee meeting, but I'll come back to see you later. Will you be alright here?'

'Yes, Uncle, yes,' said Charles who felt he never wanted to leave.

He was in the gallery for hours but the time did not go slowly as the constantly evolving scene had him completely absorbed. He was almost sorry when his uncle took him off for tea on the terrace.

In the evening Sir John came back for the third time and said 'Have you had enough yet?'

'No Uncle. I'm not tired at all.'

The debate was on a proposal to reduce the tea duty on Colonial tea and Charles could not hear or follow all of it. Sir John quietly explained what was happening. 'Mr. Bonar Law is in favour of the Empire and the Tories who you see sitting on the Opposition side want Colonial tea to be cheaper. The Government over there are against it. They have the majority as the Liberals won the last election so the proposal will be voted down.'

'What's the point of the debate then?'

'The Tories want to show the country we're for Imperial Preference.' There was a burst of shouting below, a chorus of 'ayes' and then of 'noes'.

'There's a Division now,' said Sir John, 'I'll have to go down and vote but look, you can see all the Members trooping to the lobbies to cast their votes. There's Mr. Churchill, the Home Secretary, and Mr. MacDonald — the Labour man — going to vote in the same lobby. They're both against the Empire. And there's another of them, that Mr. Benn from Tower Hamlets, watch him he's a treacherous little man.'

'Why Tower Hamlets?' asked Charles.

'In debate we call the members by their constituencies because their actual names can be very confusing when two have the same name,' said Sir John, 'can't stop now, have to rush before the doors are locked.'

There were several more Divisions expected that night and Sir John could not leave the Palace so Charles was packed off to the Langham Hotel in a hansom cab. He felt extremely important as the policeman saluted as he left New Palace Yard.

Next day George greeted his son at breakfast.

'How did you like your day as an MP?'

'It was marvellous, Father.'

'Didn't you think they were a lot of windbags? It would be better for the country if they all got on with running their businesses,' he added answering his own question before his son had a chance. 'Anyway today, as it's your last day, we have a treat — a visit to the theatre.'

'That's wonderful, Father. Where are we going?'

'We've got a choice,' he said picking up *The Times*. 'I don't suppose you want to hear Madame Melba in *La Traviata* at Covent Garden and nor do I, but the Arcadians are at the Shaftesbury, and let's see, something called the Ri-Tchave troupe are doing a show at the Alhambra.'

'I don't mind. Anything will do for me' said Charles.

'*The Importance of Being Ernest* is on at the St. James's with Allan Aynesworth, they say, in the original part, but I think that Wilde stuff will be a bit heavy for you,' said his father, who did not go much on plays.

They chose — or rather George chose — the *Dollar Princess* at Daly's and the head porter was summoned to send a messenger to the theatre to get two best seats.

Over toast and marmalade George read bits of the paper for his son's edification. 'Some dago has tried to kill the ex-Prime Minister of Spain, President Taft has sprained his ankle playing golf in Maine, there's unrest in India and Japan is trying to stop our textile imports. Not much to disturb Pax Britannica.'

'What's Pax Britannica?' asked Charles who thought he knew but liked to flatter his father.

'The peace we British give to the world' said Baring senior without any hint of irony.

CHAPTER 9

It was a hot summer and Charles enjoyed it to the full like a thirsty traveller about to trek on a long dry journey. At Eton there would be no home leave at weekends and he knew he would be surrounded by other boys day after day. After Aldeburgh Charles no longer feared the company of his contemporaries although he still loved the quiet times of solitude when he could think out ideas for himself without abrasive intrusions.

His father was often away in London, Paris or Monte Carlo but when he was home, Charles would enjoy riding with him over the estate and visiting the tenant farmers. They showed a great respect to the 'young master'. They knew he would one day inherit the Hall and then be the arbiter of all their lives. The feudal relationship died hard even though many of the labourers or their sons had been liberated by finding work in the new engineering industries in Norwich and Ipswich.

Charles also had the joy of books as his father, who was sensible enough to recognise his son's ability at reading although he did not share it, had made him a substantial allowance to spend as he wanted at a booksellers in Woodbridge. George would have had a fit if he had realised that some of the novels his son was ordering were written by socialists. Charles was able to read Richard Whiting's *No. 5 John Street*, Maxwell Gray's *The Great Refusal* and Robert Blatchford's *The Sorcery Shop* with impunity and no one at the Hall, except he, knew what revolutionary theses were lodged between their covers. Charles had learnt enough cunning to protect his secret world of thoughts which he could not dare to share.

The holiday — which included a fortnight's stay at Walberswick for swimming — was soon over and September, the time for Eton, came. This time George drove his son to College, for, in truth, he was proud that a new generation of Barings was to be represented at Britain's premier public school. In the motor he basked in the reflected glory. 'You are going to a place which has produced half the country's Prime Ministers,' he said 'it has a reputation which will stand you in good stead whatever you do in life.' By now George had come to realise that his son's intelligence and drive might take him further than merely running the estate.

'How did it become the best school?'

'Henry VI set it up over 450 years ago and over the years it established good traditions, especially the traditions of fierce competition with others but keeping loyalty to one's own group.'

'How did they do that?'

'From the first days, they tell me, there was a tradition of helping the poor — actually in the beginning there was even an almshouse — and places were kept for seventy scholars who had to pass stiff examinations to get in. They paid no fees and came from the lower classes but by golly they had to be clever,' George said with emphasis. 'The rest of the boys came from rich and aristocratic families and they didn't have to be so bright because they were paid for. All the boys were dressed the same and taught the same but the rivalry between the scholars and the Oppidans, as the others were called, was intense. The rich Oppidans had to be clever too. You see they could not afford to be put down by the lower classes.'

'Are the scholars still there?'

'No, not in the same way. After the Board Schools were started forty years ago the poorer children had somewhere else to go and didn't need Eton's charity. But they left the tradition with tough examination entry for boys who were put down for entry at birth as you were. I think they are still called scholars or Collegers or something like that.'

'I'll be an Oppidan then?'

'Yes because you were put down for the Evans' House. I chose it because it has a famous tradition and a lot of character,' his father said proudly as if he had lived there himself. 'It was set up by William Evans. In those days even the men who ran the boarding houses were called Dames and he was the most famous Dame of them all. His daughter, Jane Evans, ran the House after him and was every bit as good. She was the last surviving Dame and only died four years ago. She was eighty but still ruled the roost, I understand.'

'Who runs it now?'

'All the Houses are run by Housemasters. We pay the fees for Eton to them and they pass on a proportion to the College. They say that old William Evans died without a penny because he put all his profit back into the House. The housemaster there is Mr. Ramsey, you'll be meeting him soon, he's a nice man. I hope you like him because you will be in his House for the next six years. You can't change Houses, you know, only if you're expelled for bad behaviour and that could never happen to you could it?' George was teasing his son as he knew, to his secret relief, that Charles's behaviour took after his brother's more than his own.

In Eton they booked in at the Bridge House Hotel, parking the Whitworth in the new garage for motors. George was exhausted after the long drive, made hazardous by the large number of farm carts on the roads in the haymaking, and was relieved he had arranged to stay overnight. After a hot bath and when Charles had changed into his Eton clothes and admired himself in the long wardrobe mirror his father said:

'Put your hat on. Let's see the full works' and Charles obliged with the top hat at a slightly jaunty angle.

'That's magnificent,' said George as proud as any father could be. 'By the way do make sure your collars are always turned down. They're only allowed to stick up when you get into Pop,' he added, anxious that Charles should observe all the Eton etiquette.

They strolled the five minutes to the College, turned into Keates Lane and found Evans's House where the housekeeper was already receiving two other new boys who looked chastened by the experience. Charles's courage perked up when he realised others were going through the same ordeal as himself and from all appearances were not bearing up as well.

'You'll be young Baring,' said the housekeeper cheerily. She looked seventy and was wizened with a starched white head-dress which made her complexion look even paler. 'I remember two Baring boys years ago,' she said with a knowing wink in her good eye, 'could they be relatives of yours?'

'They were my uncles,' said George amazed that this woman could be old enough to remember them for it was nearly sixty years since they had been at Evans's.

'I was only a girl then,' said the old woman, 'but I remember those two lads as if it were yesterday, proper terrors they were. Do I understand from what you said they are not passed away?

'Yes they both died,' said George.

'How sad,' said the woman, adding in a mournful voice, 'Strange isn't it. I can remember what happened all those years ago when dear old Mr. Evans was here as if it were yesterday but ask me what went on last week and I'm completely flummoxed.' She wandered off in a distracted way as if she had seen a ghost.

George turned to Charles and whispered 'She must be over eighty to have been here with your great uncles. Perhaps she had a frolic with them to remember them so well!'

Mr. Ramsey the housemaster came to greet them and to show the new arrivals the dining hall with its oil portrait of Jane Evans looking on as if she still presided in spirit if not in person. Tapestries, antique armour and crossed guns decorated the walls giving the place a distinctly regimental air.

'At mealtimes you will sit at the lower end of the tables,' he motioned to the boys 'and year by year you will move up to the top positions. That was the Evans's tradition which, of course, we keep.'

Charles thought of all the venerable bottoms which had polished the benches and which were now sitting in the High Courts handing out death sentences to murderers, in the driving seats of great businesses or running the country from behind huge ministerial desks, whilst lesser mortals who went to lesser schools, were doing their biddings.

Up the poky stairs along a tiny corridor Mr. Ramsey showed Charles his room. 'All our boys have rooms of their own. They can study harder then,' he nodded to George. Charles was left with the other new boys while his father had tea with the housemaster and a porter was despatched to fetch his ottoman from the hotel.

In the placing examination held next day Charles did well but in view of his age was still placed in the junior form in the Lower School.

The following morning began in a great rush with First School at 7.30. The housemaster checked the boys names and took in their overnight essays. Breakfast of porridge, eggs and bread and jam followed before the boys trooped in strict lanes towards the chapel.

Charles was taken aback by its impressive beauty. Father had said it was superior to Kings College Chapel in Cambridge but he had not believed this possible. He was wrong. The high fluted columns and the light filtering through the stained glass windows gave a sense of solemn grandeur. Charles felt very small and insignificant at this first daily service sitting amongst the new arrivals as the Collegers and Oppidans walked sedately in, holding their top hats carefully in front of them. The Collegers diverged to the side whilst the Oppidans walked to the middle and the masters in their gowns sat in ranks of their own. The great spiky organ towered up towards the far-off timbered roof and when the whole College was gathered in let out its glorious sounds in the first hymns. Charles's spirits were lifted by a sense of belonging which he now felt suffusing through his veins.

Before the week was out he had been invited into many of the Eton rites, designed over the centuries to curb the arrogance of the recruits whatever their aristocratic backgrounds. The little Marquesses and Honourables suffered the same treatment as the sons of the newly rich industrialists. They were all learning that joining the élite involves certain penalties and that the vigours of mindless discipline is the best training for a lifetime of applying discipline to others.

All the boys in the first year had to be fags to the Collegers in the Upper School and the members of Pop, the self-elected Eton Society, to which a select twenty-eight senior boys belonged. Charles discovered that the system was confusingly haphazard. When a Pop member called out 'Boy' or 'Lower Boy' all the fags in hearing distance would be expected to scramble to do his bidding. Sometimes a boy would be called by name which made life much easier. The chores involved making coffee, clearing up, polishing shoes and delivering notes. The Captain of the Oppidans, a very senior boy, was the fagmaster and he had the authority to cane anyone who did not behave according to the rules.

Charles was taught the importance of being on time for the absence, when names were called three times a day in the School Yard and Cannon Yard. The system ensured that no boy could possibly be missing for more than three hours and a Bill, which allowed a boy off absence, was only granted in the case of illness or some approved activity such as practice rowing which might overlap absence times. He learnt how to be properly dressed: to turn up the bottom of his trousers and to leave the bottom button of the waistcoat undone; how to touch hat when passing a master and how not to remove one's top hat when delivering messages as a fag; to walk on the right hand of the pavement when going into town and if carrying an umbrella never to roll it up.

The rituals followed in the sports were every bit as important as in the school. When watching games on the playing fields a cap was worn instead of a top hat and an ordinary coat instead of the tail coat, but Norfolk jackets could only be worn by members of Pop. In the summer straw hats or land-and-waters were worn.

By the end of the first half— or term as other schools called it — it had dawned on Charles that Eton was a microcosm of society but with its own strict rules binding its members together in a sense of belonging which gave them an immense confidence in their later dealings with the world at large. The traditions were as important as the lessons for they gave the boys the stability on which motivation could be built.

On St. Andrews Day it was non-dies and no early school, so everyone could watch, if they wanted, the annual wall game between Collegers and the Oppidans. It was held on a pitch 120 yards long but only five yards across by the long brick wall to the east of Fifteen Arch bridge and, as Charles had learnt to his cost, it had curious unique rules of its own. There had been only a few opportunities to play it as Oppidans were allowed to play only once a week on Fridays after twelve noon. The Collegers, however, were allowed to play at virtually any free time, which gave them an advantage in contest with the Oppidans although there were only seventy of them from which to choose a team.

It was a cold November and rather than hang about stamping his feet or cheering to keep warm Charles went for a walk. It was relatively peaceful on these playing fields but with distant cheering at the wall game and the noise of the football on nearby Agar's Plough, Charles could not forget he was at Eton. He longed for the solitude of East Anglia. It would be Founders Day — 6th December — in a week and not long to the end of half and then Christmas leave. Over a year at Eton had gone quickly; he was generally happy but there were still many thoughts and ideas which troubled his conscience.

He often worried about justice and concepts of fairness which no one in the College seemed in the least concerned about. The Eton philosophy was unquestionably of the existing order in Britain: the monarchy, aristocracy and the present ownership of property could be expected to go on forever; the grateful proletariat would always willingly accept the leadership of O.Es. and Old Harrovians and other such privileged people. The state of society was never in question, although most workers and labourers were paid so little they were unable to save in a lifetime what a rich man might spend on a horse in a week. But it worried Charles who remembered the farm worker evicted from his cottage on the Baring estate after years of hard work. The injustice of it still saddened him, grieved him and stimulated a deep energy in his soul. Instead of accepting conditions as they were Charles felt that the leaders of men should attack evil wherever it was and change society for the better. The complacent attitudes of the other boys — and indeed of the masters — appalled him. They could see as well as he that in Britain, even with its industrial revolution, there was misery and want. The trades unions were trying to do something to protect their own members but Charles felt in his bones that trade unionism with its emphasis on strife and confrontation could not be the whole answer. There needed to be a wise, beneficent leadership which could dictate from the top a new and just order which would give everyone a share in property and the full fruits of labour.

It amazed Charles that no one else could see the need for change. Their only concern was to take from society as much as they could get in the way of wealth, with servants to do the work, and the devil take the hindmost. At Chapel every day they paid lip service to the Christian doctrines but in reality it was a sham. The words of the prophet Isaiah still rang in Charles's brain. 'From the sole of the foot even unto the head there is no soundness in it, but wounds and bruises and putrifying sores: they have not been closed, neither bound up, neither mollified with ointment.'

Charles had read in the newspapers about the seething unrest in India and had wondered just what right the British had to conquer it. The rape of its wealth by Clive and all who followed him was, Charles felt, in moral terms not much less evil than the slave trade which now everyone condemned. He thought perhaps one day everyone would condemn colonialism too, but not if the reform were left to Old Etonians. Proud as he was of being part of Eton Charles suddenly had a spasm of shame that the College could never be a vehicle of reform.

He was so lost in his thoughts that he was hardly aware of three other boys coming up behind him, laughing and joking. 'Hey,' one called out, 'Baring! Are you dreaming of Christmas turkey at home?' It was Radcliffe major, in his own house.

'No,' said Charles, 'I was thinking of weightier things than that.'

'You know my friends,' said Radcliffe introducing his two tall companions, smart in their greatcoats, 'Eden and Dugdale.'

'Pleased to meet you,' said Charles who remembered seeing the older boys before at Chapel.

'Like you, they're keen on books and politics,' said Radcliffe.

'Oh,' said Charles, 'are you Liberal or Conservative?'

'Tory,' said Eden, 'and so is Tommy here. The Tories are for a strong British stand in the world, no one in his right mind would support Asquith, the Liberals would give it all away.'

'What about Churchill then, he's for a strong foreign policy,' said Charles.

'Churchill's an opportunist,' said Eden, 'he'd cross the House if it suited his career.'

'I'm not so sure, Robert,' said Dugdale, 'do you think the Tories would have him?'

'Bonar Law wouldn't, but he won't last forever,' said Eden.

'Your uncle's in Parliament, isn't he?' said Radcliffe major to Charles.

'Yes, I went there to see him last year,' said Charles.

'Did you hear a debate?' asked Eden now very interested in what Baring could offer.

'Yes,' said Charles 'it was on colonial tea.'

'And our side lost, of course.'

'Yes.'

'Who did you see?' asked Dugdale.

'Practically everybody,' said Charles nonchalantly.

'Keir Hardie?' asked Eden.

'No he wasn't there that day,' said Charles.

'Out, rabble-rousing, I expect,' said Dugdale.

'They should watch that man,' said Eden, 'rabble-rouser or not he's building up a lot of support in the country. The Liberals should beware he doesn't steal their votes.'

'Split votes should help the Tories though,' said Dugdale knowledgeably, as the four boys sauntered down the path towards the footballers.

'Are you going into politics like your uncle?' asked Eden turning to Charles.

'I hadn't considered it,' said Charles who would have liked to have blurted out his innermost doubts about both the Tories and Liberals, but restrained himself. 'I hadn't considered it,' he repeated, although the germ of ambition was already stirring. 'Are you?'

'Yes,' said Eden, 'as soon as I decently can.'

CHAPTER 10

Of all the sports at Eton, Charles preferred rowing as it fully
represented teamwork and cooperation in the use of energy.
He was definitely a wet-bob but he also played the Field
Game where he learnt to rouge and ram and he occasionally
tried Fives when the courts were free. The dry-bobs included
a lot of bullies and it seemed appropriate that the Field Game
had an official place in its terminology for the 'bully'. There
was altogether too much bullying at College for Charles, who
was particularly upset by the harsh treatment given out to
many new boys, indiscriminently and inaccurately called
'Jews'. Some of the real Jews suffered from ragging
throughout their whole College careers. Although the
authorities did their best to discourage the nauseous practice
it never completely ceased.

Charles was all for seeing the other fellows' point of view
and often found himself in hot water for defending minorities.
The inane rivalry between the wet-bobs and dry-bobs also
annoyed him. However hard he tried he never did succeed in
reducing the rivalries which were endemic to the Eton
system.

In the Spring and Summer Charles enjoyed swimming. As
a lower boy he had been restricted to the Cuckoo Weir under
the railway arches, but by now he had graduated to Boveney
Weir, a much better place, which the older boys reserved for
themselves. The Henley Regatta was also a great treat which,
of course, all the wet-bobs — Charles included — attended.
Most of all they looked forward to George III's birthday on

the fourth of June when visitors came, the Sixth Form select
had their speech day in the Upper School and the boys could
show off.

Charles was hoping his parents would come. He wrote
several times imploring them to do so, but fearing that, as
usual, his mother would be left at the Hall. When the day
came he had a wonderful surprise for not only did both
Father and Mother come but they brought Emma and Edith,
now ten and eight years old and dear grandfather Tallen who
was soon retiring from his practice and could afford to take a
holiday. It was wonderful for Charles to have all his people
with him and he showed them off proudly. George Baring
had acquired a twenty horsepower Napier and amongst the
carriages in the park this attracted most attention from the
motor buffs. During the long warm afternoon Charles had
another surprise: his uncle Sir John Baring arrived from
Parliament. 'Had to come to see all these aspiring politicians,'
he said jocularly, 'I hear there's great competition in store for
us old fogies from down here. We'll have to be watching our
laurels, won't we,' he added, eyeing Charles with the pride of a
bachelor uncle.

Charles showed them Evans's House, spic and span for the
occasion, and the Chapel. 'It is better than King's College,
isn't it John?' said George.

'Far more splendid,' said Sir John.

The visitors met Mr. Ramsey, the Housemaster and one or
two of the 'beaks', and all commented favourably on the
young Baring's school work.

'We're all hoping he'll get an entrance to Christ Church,'
said Mr. Ramsey, 'though it's early days and we don't know
yet what he will read. I expect it will be history, he's showing a
real aptitude for it.' The parents beamed and Sir John added,
'A good grounding for our nascent politician, eh?'

Mr. Ramsey looked curiously at Charles. 'Have you
ambitions to go into politics?'

'I haven't made up my mind, Sir.'

'It's a worthy career for a Tory,' said the Housemaster, who knew Sir John's party affiliations.

Charles escorted his people through the College buildings. In the Lower School they admired the bronze statue of Henry VI, the founder, and on the shutters studied the inscribed names of scholars elected to go to King's College, Cambridge, as far back as the sixteenth century. In the Upper School designed by Wren they fingered the carvings of the boys who had left in the last two centuries, Fox, Shelley and Gladstone among them.

'Doesn't this sense of history overwhelm you?' asked Sarah.

'Oh no, Mother' said Charles, 'it gives one a greater sense of belonging to the stream of history. We know we are following on some great personalities, so we have to try better.'

Later that year Charles was allocated a new tutor in history. It proved to be a turning point in his whole Eton career. The master, Mr. Cordell, took a great interest in the work of his new pupil and encouraged him to write essays on the economic developments of the nineteenth century. This was in addition to the usual curriculum.

It was the custom of masters to give dinner occasionally to their senior boys and when the invitation came from Mr. Cordell, Charles was prepared. He had read all the hints in the College magazine and knew the rules. Even in such relaxed surroundings the guests should, it advised, never refer to another master except with the prefix 'Mr' and never by nickname. Never revile the school stores or the Library in case the host was on the Committee. Never praise the wine 'hysterically' as good wine is treated as a matter of course at Eton entertainments. Never talk as grace is being said and above all never ask one's host to repeat 'bon mots' which have to be understood first time round to be effective.

There were five boys in the master's dining room and it was rather cramped and stuffy. The room was lined with shelves, crammed with books, and it was obvious the room doubled as a study. Mr. Cordell, tall and lank with receding hair highlighting his large forehead, had a College reputation for being extremely erudite although he was still only in his thirties. Some boys had said he was earmarked to be headmaster one day, but others countered it would be impossible as Mr. Cordell had never been an Eton boy himself.

The meal was excellent: soup, roast beef and Yorkshire and a delicious plum pudding. There was claret to drink. It was very civilised and the boys soon developed a very mellow feeling. The master lit up a cigar. The boys, some of whom smoked Ogden's golden guinea cigarettes in secret in their Houses, were tempted to bring out their tins and light up but discretion proved the better part of valour. The conversation ranged from the prospects of the annual match against Beaumont, the importance of the new plays by George Bernard Shaw and the dangers of German naval rearmament. Mr. Cordell clearly enjoyed guiding the delicate game and drawing each boy into the exchange of views. It was part of the Eton training to teach the social graces including the art of dinner talk.

At the end of his cigar the master rose to indicate that the time had come for the boys to repair to their separate Houses and their beds. At this stage of intoxication they could hardly be expected to do any prep. He motioned to Charles to stay behind, and when the others had left, he said, 'Baring, I've been thinking of giving you a sent for good for your economic history essays. You seem to have a deeper understanding of the issues than most boys. Have you been reading any special books?'

'No, Sir.'

'But who have you been discussing the subject with?'

'Only m'tutors, Sir.'

'I wondered if you talked to any family people. You have a deep moral sense that is most unusual to say the least. In fact I have not come across it in any of my pupils in five years of teaching here.'

'I've read novels, Sir.'

'Whose?'

'Well, H.G. Wells for instance,' Charles said cautiously remembering old Thunder at Aldeburgh, not knowing whether he was being led into a bog.

'That's excellent.' said Mr. Cordell, 'a fine man. Did you read his latest *The New Machiavelli?*'

'No Sir.'

'I must get it for you. Come and see me tomorrow after Third School.'

Next day Charles went happily to Mr. Cordell's. It was a new experience to find a master who approved of H.G. Wells and he relished it.

'I've been thinking since last night about some other authors you should get acquainted with,' said Mr. Cordell. He went to his bookcase and took down carefully a beautifully bound volume tied in yellow ribbons. 'This is a first edition,' he said handling the book lovingly, 'only three hundred copies were printed. I got it from Reeves and Turner in the Strand when I was a student in '93. They're already collectors' items.'

Charles admired the workmanship. It was the most beautiful book he had ever seen. The printing was exceptionally clear and set off with individual blocks at each chapter heading.

'It's William Morris's belief that the arts should flourish in all fields, including publishing,' said Mr. Cordell. 'He produced this himself at the Kelmscott Press in Hammersmith as an example which all other printers should follow.'

'It is a beautiful book,' said Charles with genuine admiration.

'I would like you to read it and come back to discuss it, say' — he hesitated for a moment as though something else was on his mind which he needed to unburden — 'next Tuesday directly after Third School. By the way please don't show the book to other boys or mention it to other masters,' he added.

Every night, in his room at Evans's, when he had finished his ordinary prep, Charles turned avidly to the book Mr. Cordell had lent him. It was *News from Nowhere*, a quaint story of a utopia as described by an old sage called Hammond who talked to a visitor about an England being transformed 'into a garden where nothing is wasted and nothing is spoilt'. In a perfectly ordered society it became possible 'to meet the real demands of each and all and for everyone to work for livelihood instead of working to supply the demand of the profit market.' At first old Hammond explained it would be necessary to use authoritarian means 'to organise unwasteful production and exchange of wealth' and 'the State would be the only employer of labour', but eventually the State would wither away.

Charles was fascinated by what he read, *News from Nowhere* subtly undermined all the assumptions of contemporary society. Money, for instance, although necessary in the beginning would become unnecessary in an age of abundance. According to old Hammond there would be beauty in everyday life and people freed from the shackles of an exploitive system would be able truly to fulfil their lives.

On Tuesday as soon as School was over Charles strolled with a jaunty step to Mr. Cordell's rooms. He felt immensely happy. He had found in *News from Nowhere* so much of his own philosophy, but this time too he had a friend with whom he could discuss it, and who appeared to share his enthusiasm. And 'He's m'tutor' thought Charles with joy 'what luck to come across a master — no less — who can help me cut through the barrier of present day thinking.'

Mr. Cordell, smoking a cigar when Charles arrived, was in an expansive mood and seemed to have thrown off the inhibitions of the previous meeting. 'Did you enjoy the book?'

'Yes, Sir very much.'

'You understand that William Morris is attacking the

whole basis of our capitalist society — the property, the privilege, the ugliness, the squalor — all that has to go in favour of the new order. Some people who have an unfair share of the nation's wealth would lose but the great majority would gain in a more equitable distribution.'

'Do you think, Sir, that such a society can really be achieved or is it just a figment of imagination?' Charles asked, anxious not to make too many assumptions about his tutor's views.

'Yes. It can be achieved if the people really want it, but it will probably need a revolution. The privileged classes will do their damnedest to keep their wealth,' Mr. Cordell said with vehemence.

'How could it happen?'

'Firstly through the spread of ideas, so there can be more understanding of the benefits of socialism and less animal-like acceptance of life as it is. That means more and more books — like Morris's — are needed to wake ordinary people from their torpor. Socialist newspapers would help. Fleet Street is controlled by capitalist tyrants like the Harmsworth brothers,' said Mr. Cordell, 'who do their harm's worth alright, peddling their daily propaganda.'

Charles had never heard an adult — least of all a master — express himself so strongly and he wondered what was coming next. It was almost unbelievable that here in Eton, the bastion of privilege, he was hearing such revolutionary talk.

'Do you believe, Sir, that novels help to spread moral ideas?'

'Yes, I think they are the most effective. Charles Dickens revealed the evils of Victorian times in Britain and, in the United States Upton Sinclair has shown the immorality of the American capitalist system in *The Jungle*.'

The tutor and his pupil talked for an hour and a half and for Charles it was not long enough. He savoured every sentence of the seminar. It was like a revelation for it confirmed so much of his searching over several years. Before Charles left, Mr. Cordell explained the importance of discretion. 'What we have been discussing is socialism and in this College it's a forbidden subject. As you gather I totally disagree with that rule. I believe that our society is sick, is based on the wrong principles and that we need to think — and act — our way out of this malaise. In my way, Baring' he said pensively, 'I am a revolutionary and sometimes I wonder what I am doing here in Eton. I suppose I thought ideas could prosper in a great centre of learning. Instead I find this place is dedicated to keeping ideas under wraps and preserving the existing order — however bad — in aspic.'

Charles nodded sympathetically, intrigued that an adult should speak so frankly in his presence. The confidence shown in him was a new experience which made him feel mature.

'In this situation,' Mr. Cordell went on, 'we have to show extreme caution. If the authorities thought we were exchanging ideas on socialism there would be ructions. I would lose my post. Will you help me by keeping quiet about our conversations?'

'Of course, Sir, you can trust me,' said Charles, delighted to be enrolled as a co-conspiritor.

'Excellent,' said Mr. Cordell, 'then we shall meet again.'

Charles looked forward immensely to the weekly meetings with his tutor. Most of the time was spent in academic discussion and in analysing Charles's essays which were improving in range and complexity under Mr. Cordell's guidance but often they would break off and discuss their mutual interest in socialist ideology. One evening Charles was enboldened to ask, 'How did you become a Socialist, Sir?'

'As a young man,' replied Mr. Cordell, 'I was angry that there was so much cruelty in this country and so much exploitation of workers. I never suffered myself as my family is quite prosperous — my father is an estate agent and developer on the South Coast.' He hesitated as if unsure about unloading yet another confidence to a thirteen year old, but went on, 'I suppose it was my father's activities that made me think. He borrowed money from the banks to buy agricultural land which he sold to builders when it was agreed by the local authorities that housing could be built.'

An expression on Charles's face indicated a lack of understanding of his tutor's point and seeing it Mr. Cordell emphasised, 'You see Baring my father made an immense profit because the land as building plots was worth ten times what it had been as farming land. My father took the benefit which should have belonged to the whole community. Public roads and public bridges paid for by public funds had opened up the land for development. I tried to discuss this with my father but he wouldn't listen.'

'But surely your father, as developer, was providing a service for which he should be paid?' said Charles entering a defence for Cordell senior.

'Yes, any labourer is worthy of his hire, but my father's profit was extortionate and you can see it happening all over the country. Immense profits are being made by developers and builders on the new estates. That wealth should belong to everyone not just a few.'

'Do you think all the land should be State owned?' Charles asked.

'Yes it would be the fairest way but much of the damage has already been done and the profits taken away. It was my disgust that it had been allowed to happen that first turned me into a socialist. The people who hold political power seemed only concerned to allow their kind to make more money. They're not worried about the workers, and worst still the unemployed, who are all suffering while the rich live fabulously. I went off to Oxford to read history,' he went on, 'and that was an eye opener too. The dons are complacent to a man. The lessons to be drawn from history all point towards a violent convulsion when the common people are no longer prepared to put up with oppression. It will be the French

Revolution all over again but the dons can't see further than their own high table.'

'But surely, Sir, the French conditions — of the peasants I mean — were far worse in 1789 than conditions in England today.'

'That's where you're wrong, Baring. The influx of farm workers into the towns, putting them into hovels so they can service the needs of industry is producing a proletariat ripe for revolution. Uprooted from the land, and without enough to live on, they are worn out and spiritually destitute. The possibilities of organising them to create a new order are really great. The Labour Party is a beginning but I doubt if they can achieve socialism through democratic means; the enemy needs to be overturned first and its power removed.'

Charles was surprised by his tutor's fierce partisan attitude and excited by the opportunities he could see for that revolution which could reform society. Mr. Cordell did not pursue this line but reverted back to his personal history. 'You asked how I became a Socialist. Well, I think the biggest influence on me was a remarkable man I met after I came down from Oxford. My parents were living at the time in Hastings and I got a post as a teacher in a small private school. It was a dreary place and to find stimulating company I joined a local literary circle. It was an odd bunch of people: some Fabians, some retired Indian civil servants living on their pensions and one or two teachers like myself. And there was this chap who was actually a worker — a housepainter by trade — and naturally all the others humoured him, as the middle class are inclined to do when they want to prove their own superiority.'

Charles nodded, he knew what his tutor meant. Mr. Cordell went on. 'I became very friendly with the housepainter — his name was Robert Noonan, he came from Dublin and was born illigitimate. I admired the man's frankness for telling me that. And what a social conscience he had. It would put all the sanctimonious Christians in this

place to shame. When we became close friends Robert
Noonan showed me a massive book he had written. It was still
in manuscript and a thousand pages long but what a book!
Robert had put into it all his revulsion at the dreadful
conditions the workers suffered in and around Hastings.'

'I thought Hastings was a middle class, prosperous place,'
said Charles.

'It might appear so on the surface but underneath the
comfortable society on top is a layer of people who have a
constant struggle to make ends meet.' Mr. Cordell's voice
cracked with the emotion of it and Charles thought for one
horrified moment that his tutor was going to break into tears.
'Robert wrote about their struggle in a very poignant way. He
called the book *The Ragged Trousered Philanthropists* and the
town they lived in 'Mugsborough'.

'What a strange name,' said Charles.

'He chose it deliberately to make a point. They were ragged
trousered workmen, but philanthropists because they
donated the surplus value they created by their work to their
employer. If only people would read that book they would
then understand how terrible a life it is for skilled painters
and plasterers. They work only when jobs are available so
there's no security and for forty hours at sixpence ha'penny
an hour they get only £1.1s.8d. a week. How can they bring up
a family on that pittance with rent alone taking six shillings a
week?' he added in desperate tones. 'Robert reveals all these
sordid facts but what is best about the book is its analysis of
the problem. There's a character he invents called Frank
Owen who tells his fellow workmen how they're being
exploited and shows what needs to be done about it. I think
Frank Owen is actually Robert's *alter ego*.'

'Did Robert Noonan ever publish his book?' asked Charles.

'No. The poor fellow died. He left Hastings about three
years ago, went to Liverpool and died there of tuberculosis. It
was a tragedy. Such a loss. He was only forty.'

'Has the manuscript been lost?' asked Charles who would

have liked to read it.

'I think it's with Robert's daughter, Kathleen. Perhaps she will be able to get it published. I certainly hope so,' he added.

CHAPTER 11

The months passed quickly by. There was always so much to
do. St. Andrews Day, with its wall game, Founder and
Visitors Days all came and went. The winter season of the
Field Game Football and Fives finished and cricket on the
Mesopotamia pitches was the choice of the dry-bobs as the
wet-bobs took to their rafts. The new boys came and were still
bullied as 'Jews' and those graduating, or 'taking leave' as it
was called, were presented by the headmaster with a volume
of Gray's poems. The pattern of events seemed pre-ordained
but an explosion was coming which would shake even the
stability of Eton.

The summer of 1914 was exceptionally hot. In the middle
of the hottest week Charles went to see the Eton eleven play
Harrow at the Marylebone Cricket Club's ground at Lord's.
It was a glittering occasion with the ladies in high fashions
carrying parasols and the men in top hats and morning dress.
Charles's parents weren't there but he was pleased that his
bachelor uncle, Sir John Baring, joined him to watch the
match. There were advantages in having an MP in the family;
he seemed to know everyone. Between the strawberries and
cream and the cakes at tea, uncle and nephew circulated
amongst the masters and the celebrities. Charles introduced
Mr. Cordell to Sir John and was pleased to hear his tutor
saying, 'Your nephew shows a remarkable grasp of history.
He would make an excellent politician' to Sir John's evident
delight. They caught up with an Eton boy called Boothby, a
year or two younger than Charles, who was talking to Sir

John Jellicoe. Charles heard the Admiral confide to Boothby's father: 'You have a fine son and he should go far and people will hear a lot of him.' At Lord's that afternoon all was calm, sedate and mutually congratulatory but the distant shots at Sarajevo could not long be ignored.

After the assassination of the Archduke Franz Ferdinand, the powerful Austro-Hungarian Empire delivered an impossible ultimatum to the tiny state of Serbia and the Russians mobilized to stand by their fellow Slavs. The Germans declared that they would back Austria and the French that they would support Russia. Like a house of cards the fragile structure of Europe's nation states was collapsing at the first angry breath.

The boys at Eton watched the unfolding of violent history with fatalistic fascination knowing it would soon engulf them as well.

Winston Churchill commandeered a Turkish warship, newly completed on the Tyne, and the Germans replaced it with two other ships to ensure the Turks' support. German admirals went ashore at Constantinople wearing fezzes. The German army invaded Belgium and Britain was soon in the war to support its allies.

At Eton Charles joined the Officers' Training Corp and at about the same time he had the distinction of being enrolled in the select Eton Society. At one fell swoop he had grown into the privileges of the coloured waistcoats and carnation button holes of Pop as well as the khaki uniform of the OTC. He could wear stick-up collars, sit on the long wall, walk arm in arm with a friend, have a fag to do his chores and, he hoped, shoot rifles with real bullets at the weekends. It was a curious mixture of the inane and the insane. In those turbulent times Charles valued his regular meetings with Mr. Cordell all the more, because he represented a sense of certainty when everything else seemed to be collapsing into madness.

Mr. Cordell became more urgent and insistent in his advice. 'This conflagration,' he said, 'could be the beginning of the end of capitalism.' He begged Charles to find time to read Karl Marx who had, he said, 'done for economics what Darwin did for biology in stripping away the falseness and showing the reality.' He lent Charles a copy of *Das Kapital* and a student's guide to Marx by Edward Aveling. Charles made the time to read them for he was discovering that Marx gave theoretical justification to all the ideas which had been bursting inside him since his first days at Aldeburgh School. It was like being initiated at last into a powerful religion to which he had been instinctively drawn for years.

Under Mr. Cordell's patient tuition, Charles learnt the Socialist formula for the rate of surplus value and the function of money in Marxist economics. The tutor explained that the symbols of wealth in capitalist society were not always of real value — there were myths about gold which had to be exploded. 'Remember,' he said 'that even Sir Thomas More in *Utopia*, four hundred years ago, saw through those myths and proposed that gold should only be used for chamber pots.'

After a few months Mr. Cordell prepared to leave to join the war. 'I could never be a conscientious objector,' he confided to Charles, 'not when we're up against a militaristic tyranny such as Germany. They must be defeated before we can have the revolution. A new world can rise from the ashes.'

On their last evening together he became blunt in his advice to a pupil who had become both his friend and his acolyte. 'Charles,' he said reverting to the Christian name as a mark of friendship, 'I think you can play a great part in transforming England from its class-ridden backwardness into a free and equal society. Communism will be a wonderful liberator and you can help to create it. Don't ever be put off by all the propaganda against Communism; it comes from people with a vested interest. Of course they don't want Communism. It would spell the death knell of their privilege. Remember that William Morris said he was a Communist without qualification and what better standard bearer could you hope than him? If only his ideal of society can be achieved, this damn war would be worthwhile. But please take my word of warning to heart. In your position you can do better by waiting. Don't reveal your ideals to anyone you cannot trust — and that means practically everybody. Keep your ambitions a secret and then you can get into power to do something effective. Reveal your secret and the establishment will manoeuvre against you and destroy you. Your's will be a special task. Others can fight on the barricades, if there have to be barricades, but you — with your background — can get right to the middle of the power structure in this country and from there you can destroy it.'

They grasped hands, and embraced like men, and vowed to meet after the war. It would, they thought, be over within a year. But Charles never saw his tutor again. Lieutenant Alexander Cordell was posted as missing, presumed killed, after the battle of Vimy Ridge on 25th September, 1915. When Charles heard the news he went to the solitude of his room and wept unashamedly.

The remaining six months at Eton were no longer the happy carefree days he had known before. More time was spent on military training and less on dead languages. The Eton Officers' Training Corps was affiliated to the 1st Bucks Regiment which sent a ferocious Sergeant to train the cadets in weaponry. On the playing fields of Mesopotamia, instead of cricket, they were instructed in games of a lethal kind. Dummies were set up for bayonet practice and there was much screaming and shunting as the trainees vied with each other in bloodcurdling calls. The N.C.O. gave them no respite. 'Come along there you lazy lot,' he yelled, 'get the bayonet into the stomach. Don't hesitate. You'll be dead if you do.' One morning a rifle was produced. It was the only one the cadets had seen in weeks — all their drill had so far been with wooden ones as the real things had been sent to the front. 'This morning,' barked the sergeant, 'I am going to show you the Mark VII Lee Enfield rifle. You will learn all the parts by heart and you will in turn repeat this instruction word for word, because one day — God help us — you will be doing it for men in the field. Their lives will depend on you. So make sure you get it right.'

The headmaster called the cadets to Chambers to give them another sort of pep talk. 'We did not choose this war. It chose us,' he said. 'We have to win it for the sake of civilisation that we all believe in. Remember the great Sterry who said "the purpose of Eton is to teach the higher patriotism". He did not have war in mind but he would recognise that war in our country's cause is the highest patriotism we can possibly achieve. Many of our old Eton boys have already given their lives and more will have to follow until the Hun is defeated. But defeat him we must. It is ironic that our enemy, the Kaiser, came here to inspect the Eton College Rifle Volunteers back in '91 and his words then would equally apply today. He said "If ever you are called upon the serve the Queen I am sure you will show that courage and manliness which are the characteristics of the British soldier." When you are over there,' added the headmaster with feeling 'let the Kaiser know that his words are as true today as they were then and Eton will be proud of you.'

Charles carried on with his general studies in a desultory way and attended the Pop debates in the old Christopher Inn every Friday, but though his brain functioned perfectly his heart was no longer at Eton. There was no possibility now of going to Oxford or Cambridge for the degree course and entrance examinations were postponed. Normality would be resumed later when the world was saner.

At the end of the final half he had a brew of champagne in Evans's for a few of his closest friends. They knew the arbitrary postings of the services meant they might never meet again. The evening was a sombre and sober occasion with little of the revelry and boisterous fun of previous farewell parties. Next day Charles received a volume of Thomas Gray's poems on taking leave from the head who quoted '"Know, one false step is ne'er retrieved, and be with caution bold".'

As he walked to the station to catch the train to Paddington the last words of Mr. Ramsey, Housemaster at Evans's rang in his ears. 'Good luck Baring, Floreat Etona Floreat Etona.' The College would always survive however many of its boys might be snuffed out in the prime of life like Alexander Cordell. 'Floreat Etona'. There would always be the Wall Game and Pop. 'Floreat Etona'. There would always be the swimming at Athens and Boveney Weir. 'Floreat Etona'. There would always be the Gray on leaving. *The Curfew tolls the knell of parting day* filled Charles's mind with renewed meaning as his eyes watered involuntarily. Ahead the porter had his ottoman on the cart. There was no turning back.

CHAPTER 12

At the Hall, Charles found much had changed. With Sir John Baring's help his father had found a job in London at one of the Ministries, thinking it would create the least dislocation to his life. His mother had joined a Committee in Saxmundham to collect comforts for the troops. Emma, now fourteen and growing prettier with adolescence, hoped to be a nurse, but her mother discouraged the idea. 'The war will be over long before you'll be old enough,' she had said. Edith was too young to have any wartime ambitions but was following the awful unfolding events in France with a scrapbook, an activity of which her mother heartily disapproved. Many workers on the estate had joined up and the manager was finding it difficult to achieve last year's quotas for wheat production. The Ministry of Agriculture wanted more home production to replace the wheat no longer available from the granaries of North America and the estate was expected to play its part.

Charles did what he could to help on the estate, but apart from giving encouragement he felt his contribution was useless. The education at Eton had nothing to do with the land and the 'young master', as the workers still called him, was like a fish out of water. He rode around the countryside, exercising the horses and filling his lungs with clean Anglian air. He also learnt to drive the Armstrong Whitworth, after making it serviceable with the blacksmith's help, and took it to Saxmundham and down to Woodbridge. He was restless waiting for the posting for further officers' training and was unable even to put his mind to his beloved books.

There had also been a sharp awakening interest in girls which disturbed him greatly as he had been able to do nothing about it. At Eton there had been a lot of sex talk and vain boasting by lads who claimed the conquests of parlour maids. Charles had eschewed it. He felt instinctively that sex was precious and deserved something better than dark fumblings with servants under the stairs. Nor had he shared in the homosexual liaisons at Eton; they nauseated him. All he had learnt about sex had been picked up through College chatterings and from the few medical books in the School Library. There had been no formal sex education and his father had never raised the subject.

He felt his burgeoning every day. It would not go away and had to be satisfied. On his second trip to Woodbridge he saw a girl in a shop whose well curved figure and Viking blond hair made his blood flow all the quicker. His own physical condition was superb. At eighteen he stood five foot ten with broad shoulders, brown hair and a smooth fine complexion. He shaved every day and kept himself extremely smart. Being modest he did not realise what a stunning figure he cut on the streets of Woodbridge. The girl had noticed him too.

Next day Charles went into the shop — an outfitters next to the Post Office — on the pretext of looking at some ties. The girl he admired bustled over to serve him and he was practically dumb-struck with embarrassment. He bought a tie he did not like just to be able to retreat gracefully. It was a waste of 1s. 3d.

On the following Wednesday he was again in Woodbridge using the Whitworth, which was running on petrol allocated to the estate and he went to the bookshop to browse. After fifteen minutes, to his astonishment, he found the blond girl standing by his side, flipping through some novels. 'Hello,' she said smiling at Charles, 'didn't I sell you a tie the other day?'

'Yes' he said nervously.

'You're not wearing it,' she reproved.

'No, I'm keeping it for a special occasion,' he improvised.

'What's that for instance,' she demanded coquettishly.

'Like my farewell party,' he countered.

'Are you going away?'

'I'm going in the Army.'

'My brother Henry's in the Army, in France,' she said. 'When do you go?'

'Soon,' said Charles. 'I'll be going to France too, perhaps I'll meet your brother.'

The shop manager came over and Charles bought a dusty second-hand copy of *Endymion* by Benjamin Disraeli. It cost 4s. 6d.

They walked out of the shop together. 'Aren't you working today?' asked Charles to keep the conversation going, not realising that the girl was suffering the same dilemma.

'No, it's my afternoon off,' she said gaily.

'Would you like a ride in my motor?' he blurted out, surprised by his impudence.

'Do you have a motor?' she exclaimed. 'I've never been in one. I don't think I should.'

'They're quite safe you know.'

'That's not quite what I meant,' she said, 'but I will come providing you promise to bring me back here by six. I have to be home for supper.'

They walked to the motor parked around the corner. 'Isn't it huge?' she said, her eyes large with admiration.

'It's pretty old now,' he said disparagingly, not to appear boastful, 'but at least it still works. Look, let's run down to Aldeburgh. I used to be at school there and I know a place where we can have tea.'

'That would be marvellous,' she replied, her synthetic apprehensions now entirely dissipated.

Charles got the motor going at first try and edged the Whitworth past the vehicles and traps cluttering the Woodbridge streets on to the Tunstall road. Soon the road was their own, apart from the occasional farm cart. Passing through Rendlesham Forest he picked up speed until he reached thirty-five miles an hour. 'This is so fast,' the girl shouted. 'I've never been so fast in all my life,' and Charles took it as encouragement and went faster.

They reached Aldeburgh in a little over an hour and it seemed a record. The place was exactly the same as Charles remembered it: a sleepy, dreamy backwater. The girl, who had never been there before, was delighted. She was amused when Charles showed her the outside of his old Aldeburgh School and told her about Thunder.

They went to a tea shop called The Old Barn and ordered a pot of tea, buttered scones, teacakes and strawberry jam. The place, as so many in the country — even in wartime — had its stock of home-made supplies but they overcharged the couple at a shilling each.

'I don't even know your name,' said the girl.

'Sorry,' said Charles, 'we should have been introduced. 'It's Charles Baring.'

'Mine's Mary Hudson.'

'Mary's a nice name' Charles said shyly.

'And Charles Baring sounds very distinguished,' said Mary. There was an embarrassed silence, which was broken by the welcome tinkle of teacups.

'Did you go to another school after Aldeburgh?' she asked.

'Yes I've just finished at Eton.'

'Isn't that a famous school?' said Mary in awe.

'We think so,' said Charles proudly, 'at least we try to keep its good reputation.'

'Do you have to be rich to go there?'

'It helps,' said Charles.

They ate all the scones and tea cakes and drank all the tea but did not exhaust the conversation. Charles drove the Whitworth slowly back to Woodbridge but he did not have the courage to stop. He had never been out with a girl before, except with his sisters which did not count, and he had no idea what was expected of him. He dropped Mary in

Woodbridge and arranged to meet her on her next half day. As he drove the lonely road back to the Hall he felt it was a long time to wait.

Next day a thick, long buff envelope marked O.H.M.S. arrived at the Hall by the first post addressed to C.E. Baring Esq. His mother brought it to him at breakfast in some trepidation for she could guess what it was. He ripped it open impatiently. It contained a letter informing him that King George V had been pleased to grant a Temporary Commission in His Special Reserve of Officers' in the Third Battalion of the Essex Regiment. 'Hurrah,' said Charles. 'I'm an officer,' and his mother kissed and hugged him in pride. The envelope also contained the information than an account had been opened for Second Lieutenant C.E. Baring at Cox's Bank with the standard £50 allowance for the purchase of kit and a schedule of what the War Office considered it should be spent on, including uniform, binoculars and a prismatic compass. There was also a letter saying that Second Lieutenant Baring had been chosen for a special Young Officers' Course of one month which would be held at Oxford beginning on the 1st April 1916 and that he would be billeted in Worcester College. 'I'm going to Oxford after all, Mother,' he cried out in nervous excitement.

As the first of April was only five days away there was a lot to do — a uniform and kit to be bought — and they agreed it was no good trying to do the shopping in Suffolk. Charles would have to go to London to see his father's tailor and get priority for the uniform. He left that afternoon to catch the train, for there was no time to be lost. His mother and sisters saw him off on the slow train from Lowestoft to Ipswich where he would pick up the express. They all waved frantically, animated by a mixture of pride and fear.

Before he arrived at Liverpool Street, Charles remembered his date with Mary which, in his excitement, he had completely forgotten, but fortunately found the receipt for the tie. He would write her at the shop. She would understand.

In London he went back to the Langham Hotel which he had not seen since his visit as a small boy before Eton. It seemed that an age had passed, schoolboy to Second Lieutenant, peace to war. Everything had changed.

He had sent a telegram to his father at the Ministry and called to see him at his club where they had dinner. Baring senior was in an expansive mood. 'The war will be over before the end of the year. I have it on good authority that the morale of the Boche is collapsing and our trenches are holding firm. Our next big push will finish them off.'

Charles had already heard of appalling British casualties and was not so sure, but his father was adamant.

'We've got the measure of the Hun. He's suffering a lot from our blockade. He can't get his supplies. We'll starve them out.'

'Do you think the Americans will come into the war?'

'No chance of that. The damned Yankees are too busy making money out of both sides. They won't want to spoil that. They're a chicken-hearted lot and we can win without them. When we do, we can take over all of Germany's colonies in Africa. We don't want America interfering with that.'

Charles felt his father had not fully grasped the awfulness of the situation despite his position in the Ministry, but he did not want to argue with him. Their meetings were too infrequent for that. He turned the conversation to the affairs of the estate and his father said, 'I was sorry we didn't have some time together. I was coming home this weekend and hoping we could do some riding. Do you remember the old times?' Charles, whose earliest memories were from the back of a horse, said, 'Yes Father, there'll be time for more when I get back from the war.'

George's tailor in Savile Row made the uniform for Second Lieutenant Baring within two days as military orders had top priority. Charles bought all the required kit in shops in the West End, called at Cox's to make himself known to the

Manager and went to the music hall to see Harry Tate and Shirley Kellog. It was soon time to go to Oxford. He had written to Mary Hudson apologising that he could not meet her and gave his Worcester College address. In great daring he signed 'Love Charles'.

At Paddington carrying his new uniform in a cardboard box, he was pleased to find two O.Es from the O.T.C. also going to the Oxford course. 'A bit of luck,' he thought, at least he would not be entirely among strangers. They shared a crowded taxi to the college. It had only two cylinders and chugged reluctantly through the streets whilst the three O.Es admired the Oxford stores.

'It's one way to get an Oxford degree,' said one, puffing on a cigarette, 'even if one only graduates in bayonet practice.'

'Perhaps they'll call it Bachelor of the Martial Arts,'said another.

At Worcester College he was shown into a shabby room up a winding staircase. There was little time to reconnoitre as they had to report in an hour's time. He set about mastering the secrets of the Officers' Sam Browne belt, an incredibly complicated affair. It had a sword frog attached, which was not used, and two shoulder straps, only one of which was used. It was important to get it over one shoulder but was it the right or the left one? The struggle was hair-raising and Charles hoped it would not always be as bad.

In the street as he walked towards the reporting centre a private passed him and saluted smartly. Charles tried to return the salute equally smartly but it seemed too clumsy. It was all very strange for the fresh O.E. just one month and two weeks after his eighteenth birthday.

After the training at Oxford which was more effective than anything at Eton, Second Lieutenant Charles Baring joined his regiment at Colchester. The officers' rooms in barracks were full and the newly arriving subalterns were shown into bell tents which had been erected on the football fields. He was surprised to be allocated a batman, a soldier in his mid-forties, who saluted respectfully and proceeded to make up a camp bed and wash-basin and to sort out the kit. Charles was a little ashamed to be taking up the time of a man old enough to be his father, who could be doing more useful work for the war effort than polishing an officers' shoes and other such menial tasks.

For Mess Charles changed into mufti and sallied forth to meet his fellow officers. They were a motley bunch, mostly young subalterns who had been recruited from the middle and educated classes without any particular regard for their qualities of military leadership, but there was a sprinkling of hard-bitten regulars, clearly determined to keep all the traditions of the regiment. At the weekly Guest Night they wore their full mess uniform at the head of the table, relishing the impeccable service by smart mess waiters in khaki and good service stripes. On the long table stretched a long row of the first, second, third and fourth battalions' silver centre pieces, which had been gifts of colonels long since retired. They had intricate designs showing battlefield scenes and must have been worth a fortune. The regimental band played music as the dinner proceeded while the waiters, who seemed to equal the officers in number, deftly removed dishes in unison.

The meal over, two decanters of port were passed down the table from the Colonel who had ceremonially unstoppered them as if performing a ritual. Once all glasses had been charged the call rang out, 'Gentlemen the King' and the band immediately crashed into a loud rendering of the National Anthem.

Charles found he was torn between feelings of alarm that so much time and effort was put into ceremony when a deadly war was on and admiration for the *sang froid* with which the regulars carried it off. It was clear that the process of instilling loyalty into the regiment was more complicated than mere military training or providing a strong motivation. Meanwhile everyone enjoyed themselves, including the waiters who probably drank the dregs.

Colchester lasted two months and then Charles, considered good material by the Captain in charge of subalterns, was transferred to Hayling Island for a gunnery course. All training was being speeded up as the front in France decimated officers who had to be replaced quickly. It was a hot June and the subalterns were able to creep through the barbed wire on the sand dunes and cool off in the sea. The war was getting closer and they would soon move to France. They learned that Lord Kitchener had been lost at sea on his way to Archangel for a conference with the Russians and everybody felt a fateful foreboding that if the Secretary of State for War could be killed so easily then their own chances of surviving were that much less.

The German assaults at Verdun that Spring had taken a heavy toll of the French allies and Haig, the British commander, made plans for a British-led offensive on another front. The Somme was chosen and a new army of volunteers — the best men Britain could provide — were being prepared for the attack which, it was believed, would split the German forces and defeat them *en masse.* The young officers at Hayling Island were to be part of this force: raw, untrained officers to lead raw, untrained men. The war Cabinet, in panic desperation, was preparing to sacrifice the flower of Britain's youth on the altar of an ill-conceived plan. At Hayling Island, sunbathing on the sand dunes, the sacrificial victims being prepared for the slaughter were unthinking and unaware of the horrors ahead. The war propaganda machine still had them mostly believing in the infallability of their generals.

One morning in mid-July, a fortnight after the Somme offensive had begun, Second Lieutenant Baring left Hayling Island with twenty other officers to join a troop ship at Southampton Docks. It was the kind of bright, sunny day which shows England's summer at its best. The Hampshire Downs above Portsmouth stood out clearly without a hint of mist to obscure them and the fort projected a beacon of

British defiance. Beyond Porchester and Fareham the fields looked green and lush. The people they saw en route were happily going about their business. The air of normality was deceptive as if the whole scene was a moving stage deliberately contrived to lull the cannon fodder into a sense of security, like the calming of cattle on the way to the abattoir.

Very little truthful news about the Somme had filtered through. The official line was that a successful offensive backed by artillery had been launched and that good advances were being made. In fact, on the first day alone, twenty thousand Britons were killed and another forty thousand were wounded or missing. The British casualties for Day One of the Somme were eight times as many as Britain had suffered at the Battle of Waterloo. As the ships sailed down Southampton water bound for Le Havre, the thousands of volunteers on board could not know they were about to be thrown into an inferno.

Charles, standing on the poop deck reserved for officers, watched Hamble on the port and Calshot spit on the starboard disappear as they steamed into the Solent, as the slow twilight crept in from the East. He saw the escort destroyers appear from Portsmouth passing two Dreadnoughts lying at anchor. After four tantalising months of dreary waiting for action, he was at last tasting the flavour and excitement of a war which he had only read or heard about at secondhand. His hand felt the bulge in his tunic pocket made by the letters Mary had sent. It was a comfort that contained a few memories he cherished and a promise of a reunion.

Mary had written to Worcester College with stilted banal phrases in her large childish hand and this had led to their meeting again during his brief pre-posting leave. More letters had followed, each getting more relaxed and expressive, reflecting the confidence the seventeen year old Mary was developing. She was a romantic and could not fail to be drawn to the tall handsome officer who had so much charm and an elegant poise in his smart subaltern's uniform. He was completely unlike the rough local boys she had known with their course hands and beer-drinking, who crudely tried to persuade her to do what they said all the other girls did.

Charles's thoughts of Mary were broken by a subaltern at his shoulder who said nervously, 'Are they expecting trouble then? Why do we need two escorts?'

'Damned if I know,' Charles answered, who did not want to be someone else's nursemaid. The pasty faced little man next to him was renowned as a funk and was the poorest of the hastily-enrolled officer material. 'I suppose with a couple of thousand men on board we'd make a good target for a Boche torpedo. A fine way to end the war,' he ventured, 'drowning in the Channel without even setting foot in France.'

The nervous officer lit a cigarette and remained silent as if he had heard his death sentence and the next puff would be his last. A Lieutenant leaning on the rails called over, 'Don't worry so much, if it's got your number on it you'll get it.'

Eventually the small convoy was underway, passing the Isle of Wight and heading for Le Havre in the deepening dusk. Charles went below to find a corner where he would get a few hours fitful sleep. Next day would be a long one.

As soon as they arrived in France Charles's company was packed into trucks for the journey to Amiens where, it was rumoured, they were to have battle training before going on to the front. But within two days the officers were told they had already been allocated to platoons which were being sent forward to strengthen the British attack. No one spoke of the enormous carnage that was taking place, but the facts could not be denied; the wounded filling the rear hospitals were enough evidence. Defeatist talk was strongly discouraged and emphasis put on whatever seemed positive. England's sacred weapon — the tank — was being brought into the attack. Rumour had it that it had been developed by Winston Churchill through the Admiralty as the War Office would have nothing to do with it, but now at last the Army had ordered a hundred of them. Talk in the Officers' Mess at

Amiens was optimistic that the new weapons could turn the tide after the initial setbacks on the Somme. Others spoke admiringly of the Royal Flying Corps at Vert Galand on the road to Doullens. The older officers were clearly awestruck by the flexibility of the De Havilland scouts which gave enormous support by their reconnaissance and artillery spotting and bombing missions over the Hun lines. Everyone believed that British superior air power together with the tanks would defeat the enemy, and convinced themselves that the casualties so far suffered were acceptable. Even though the war had been going on for two years the jaunty devil-may-care, all-over-by-Christmas, spirit still prevailed, as if a whole generation had been afflicted by a silly irresponsibility bordering on madness. The foolhardiness in the conduct of the war could not be blamed on the generals or the War Cabinet alone. The officers, almost to a man, were unquestioning and later, looking back on the horror, they would say that they had no alternative. Second Lieutenant Baring found himself drawn into looking on the optimistic side. 'What was the point of doing otherwise?' he asked himself. In all situations one should put a brave face forward, never be defeatist and certainly never question orders from the War Command. Loyalty came first.

On the first day in the front line he began to have his niggling doubts. The conditions were as atrocious as they possibly could be and worse than anything he had ever anticipated. The men in his platoon were in trenches armed with rifles and Lewis guns but some of them could not work through lack of overhaul. The machine guns mounted on the enemy trenches did work and were murderous and any movement in the British trenches was greeted with a fusillade of shots. Only a few of the men present had been on the front since the beginning of the Somme Offensive on the 1st of July. The months had taken their toll of the rest who were dead, wounded or missing. The battalion, to which the new arrivals had brought reinforcements, had started with nine hundred

men and was now down to sixty-five. Charles had heard talk
of decimation but the word he thought more appropiate was
elimination. People back home had no idea but should they
be told? Charles swallowed his doubts and did his best to
cheer up his troops.

One of the first jobs was to ask for the supply lines to be
improved so the rations and ammunition got through. One of
the bitterest complaints had been that tins of bully-beef had
run short on this sector due to a cock-up by transport.
Charles was determined that this would not happen again.
His men would, at least, not die hungry.

The worst enemy was not the Hun but the mud. The
trenches were full of it and slithering about between them a
man was a perfect target for the sharpshooters from the other
side as he could not crouch and run as he had been trained to
do. It was impossible to control one's movements. Charles
soon found that much of his training was useless and that
improvisation was the order of the day: the Commanding
Officer, a newly promoted Colonel, turned a blind eye to
many practices to which his battalions had to resort. The
mud was almost impossible to deal with after heavy rain,
when water flowed down the trenches in cascades, producing
a glutinous mess which men wallowed in up to their hips.
There was a trench sense of humour, which must have saved
many a mutiny; the men calling themselves the P.B.I. (Poor
Bloody Infantry), made crude jokes about Fred Karno's
Army and sang war songs to rude words.

Charles found the N.C.O.s an excellent bunch, including
the sergeant majors with their clipped way of talking and
their pointed waxed moustaches. They had style which he
came to respect, and with it went incisiveness and courage.

The platoon waited for days on end, exchanging infrequent
shots down to no-man's-land, watching the observation
balloon and the occasional aircraft fly over the lines, followed
by puffs of anti-aircraft fire, as if they belonged to another
distant war, and wondering when the boredom of it could be

swopped for some action. The stench pervading the whole scene was a constant reminder of the lethalness of the conflict. There were dead Germans in no-man's-land that no one would dare to bury. Putrefaction had long since set in and when the wind blew towards the British trenches it made even the strongest men puke. Worse than gas some of the old lags quipped: 'Must be Jerry's secret weapon!'

Charles's 'quarters' were in a dug-out in the middle of the Battalion's position. He shared it with other officers and in theory was entitled to a bunk but often did not get one as the junior officers — and he was the most junior of all — did not get priority. Sleeping on the hard ground was extremely painful and Charles looked forward to night duty when he could chat to the sentry and peer out into the dark night. Apart from the occasional shell exploding on the horizon and the rattle of machine gun fire from a distant position it was relatively quiet and the best time for reflection. The war was not what Charles had expected. It seemed completely deadlocked, neither side anxious to make a move which would expose it to the dreadful casualties of the earlier offensives. Perhaps, he thought, the Generals have learnt their lesson and will find a better way than human carnage to end this crazy conflict. It seemed ludicrous to him that men could have allowed themselves to sink to such conditions of degradation and that civilised nations allowed millions of men to sit for weeks on end in the mud.

At dawn the battalion 'stood to' for an hour as this was the time of possible attack, after which the trenches settled down to inspections, rifle-cleaning and meal preparations. Charles was instructed by the Captain to inspect the men's feet regularly to seek for signs of 'trench feet' — a swelling which would soon incapacitate a soldier if it took hold. A few cowards had been known to tolerate the malady in the hope it would get them sent to Blighty and even the threat of amputation did not deter them. Hence the regular inspections to eliminate the risk. Censorship of the platoon's letters back home was another of the young officer's duties. At first it seemed a stupid ritual to Charles, as it was fairly evident that the P.B.I. in the trenches had no useful information it could possibly pass back for the enemy. But then it became clear what the censorship was about. As the Colonel told Charles: 'Our job is to stop the civilian population losing hope in this war. If they hear just how bad it is they'll give up backing our men in the field and then morale would collapse. The homefires have to be kept burning bright.'

'But surely,' Charles asked, 'the wounded going back to Blighty are going to tell the story as it is?'

'I don't think so,' said the Colonel. 'Things always look better when a chap's on English soil, even if he is a stretcher case. If you come across a disloyal letter just tear it up and burn it. Don't tell the man, but make a note of his name. When the time comes for us to go over the top make sure he's one of the first. Understand?'

'Yes Sir.' Charles had learnt it was better not to argue with superior officers. Rank always before reason.

In September, after weeks of waiting, the officers were alerted that a big offensive was soon to come and that tanks — for the first time — would spearhead the British attack. Charles's spirits rose. This could be the breakthrough they were expecting; the tanks could break the stalemate and perhaps dent the German morale. The Huns had no idea what was about to hit them.

As Charles was the most experienced horseman in the Company he was ordered to ride over the trenches with another officer to check the best terrain where the tanks could advance. It was a risky enterprise but necessary as the reconnaisance planes could not fly low enough to get a proper look. It was essential that the tanks should get through to the German lines. If they became bogged down before they saw action it would be a flop of the greatest magnitude.

Cutting through the barbed wire the two horsemen rode

out in the late afternoon when things were generally quiet —
the Jerries were thought to sleep at this time — and made a
good hundred yards before they were spotted by a sentry on a
machine gun outpost. The horses were exceptionally calm
under fire and by weaving through clumps of trees the officers
were able to gallop them back safely to the British lines. The
Germans must have thought them mad Englishmen on a
hunting party. It was not unusual for a hare or two on no-
man's-land to be shot for the pot and the horsemanship could
easily have been an extension of that folly.

That night in the dug-out Charles was commended for
bravery with Cognac which had been requisitioned from
shops in Montauben taken on the last push and kept in
reserve for special occasions. The brigade's task was
identified as an advance on a broad front with the town of
Flers as the objective. In mid-September a heavy
bombardment started; it was a signal to the enemy that an
attack was coming but they were not prepared for the tanks.
The strange lumbering machines caught them by surprise,
but they were not nearly as effective as everyone had hoped.

Charles took his troops over the top behind the tanks but
two of them got stuck and a third began firing at British
troops who were spreading out the attack. Charles was
incensed by the idiocy of the gunners in the tank and,
ordering his men to lie low, he crept towards it to try to signal
the man inside to stop firing. By good luck more than
prudence, and after frantic battering on the vehicle for what
seemed ages, the firing ceased. Charles, remarkably, was
unharmed. It transpired that the tank crew had been given
the wrong orders and once mobile it was virtually impossible
to communicate any change to the crew.

The offensive pushed the British lines forward by a mile
and a half and Charles's platoon captured the town of Flers
which it entered with one of the surviving tanks. Although
the military uses were limited the new weapons had secured a
psychological advantage over the Germans. Some terrain

had been secured for the price of revealing a secret to the enemy. To Charles's eyes the cost of the attack in British dead was horrifying. From Flers back to the original trenches was a distance hardly bigger than the length of the Eton grounds and it was full of the dead and dying. Many of the walking wounded had found their own way to casualty stations and stretcher bearers were doing their best to cope with the others. Charles wondered how he should help, but his orders had been to bring a fresh detachment of troops back into Flers to secure the town against a probable German counter-attack. It was distressing to pass the men lying in the mud with their arms shot off or pumped full of shrapnel and moaning for help, but Charles had lost half of his own platoon in the attack and he owed it to the fallen to safeguard the small advance they had paid for with their young lives. Corpses were everywhere, German and British together at last in death, a scene out of Dante. Charles fought back his feelings of revulsion and physical sickness, but he knew he had to keep a brave façade for the servant who accompanied him everywhere and the two escorts. It would be fatal to morale if officers showed any weaknesses.

The new line was successfully consolidated and another long wait for an offensive began. This time Charles felt battle-hardened; a different sort of steel had been inserted into his backbone. He had been through a trauma for which none of the training courses could possibly have prepared him. It was as if ten years had been put on his life, as if all the nightmares of a normal lifetime had been concentrated into one short horrific event. No books he had ever read — or ever would read if he survived — could convey the hell of unreason through which he had just passed. The smell of needless death all around was bad enough but for Charles the worst aspect was his mental incapacity to grasp any rationality behind the wanton slaughter. It worried him deeply. Was he going mad? How could he be the only sane one among so many? The other officers seemed to take it in their stride, enjoying the spoils of war from the wine cellars of Flers and the caches of Cognac found in the magnificently deep, well constructed, German dug-outs, while making jokes about the next lot of Jerries they would blow to smithereens on their way to Berlin. Even the exhausted P.B.I. seemed happy in the relief of surviving the holocaust; their unquestioning acceptance of a war strategy which could kill or wound half their mates for a mile and a half of useless territory amazed Charles who had never conceived that Englishmen could be so bovine. Unlike him they had never learnt to think and human feelings had been cauterized.

The wait for the next offensive was shorter than anyone expected. Within a fortnight, with fresh troops, they were on the move again, but the weather grew steadily worse, the mud deeper and bitter cold added to the general misery. The rats were not deterred by the weather and were very active, huge beasts which ate the corpses which no one could bury in no-man's-land and attacked the troops sleeping in their trenches. One man woke in the morning to find a rat had eaten right through his webbing. He stood up and his equipment just fell off.

On 12th November the order was passed down from General Gough to attack on both sides of the Ancre River. At dawn the next day Charles led his weary men against the German lines. Miraculously for five days they made progress but then a blizzard broke; they were blinded by the driving sleet and snow, knowing that pockets of Germans in hasty dug-outs were all around them. Charles suddenly felt a searing pain in his legs, as if red hot needles were being plunged into him, and the same almost simultaneously in his shoulder, with the sound of the rat-tat-tat of a machine gun. He collapsed in the mud and saw two of his men falling with him just as he lost consciousness.

Second Lieutenant Baring would have been taken for dead and left on the battlefield — priority was always given by the stretcher gangs to those obviously wounded — had it not been for his faithful servant who, although wounded himself, dragged his officer's body back to the trenches in the hope that there was life left. Charles revived sufficiently to remember being carried back to a casualty clearing station and receiving a morphia injection. It relieved his pain and put him into a vivid hallucinatory sleep.

When he awoke he could have been forgiven for thinking he was still in a nightmare for he found himself in a huge factory-like building with hundreds of camp beds full of men groaning, drugged or dying and as many on the floor between them. The wounds of the men in the nearest beds were awful. It was a miracle they had survived with faces half blown away with shrapnel and great holes in their sides. Nearby others were dying and their bodies quickly carried out by orderlies making room for the newly wounded cases. The stench of septic limbs was overpowering.

After an hour a V.A.D., looking like an angel in a white uniform, came to his bedside to comfort him and offer a mug of tepid tea.

'You were a lucky one,' she said, 'those bullets grazed your chest and tore through these letters in your pocket.' She held up a bundle of envelopes with a hole through them. 'Never know,' she added, 'they could have saved you.'

Charles wanted to reply but felt too weak for words.

Later a surgeon — looking wan — came and said, 'We'll have you as right as rain soon. Some urgent cases to deal with first but then I'll remove those nasty bullets. You'll feel better without that extra weight.' He laughed merrily. 'You'll be for Blighty then. Lucky fellow.' Charles said a weak, 'Thank you,' and sank back into another fitful sleep.

Charles was transferred back to England for convalescence and found himself in a school in Chelmsford which had been converted into a temporary hospital. The clean sheets, the pleasantly antiseptic smell and the smiling, unharassed nurses, were a heaven after four months of horror. Years later Charles realised how lucky he had been to survive intact for the odds on death or permanent disablement had been incredibly high. On the Somme there had been 475,000 British, 200,000 French and 500,000 German casualties. A terrible toll of well over a million dead and wounded men for an advance of only eight miles.

CHAPTER 13

After two weeks Charles was discharged from hospital to continue rehabilitation at home. His parents who had seen a boy go to war, welcomed back a man. He wore an arm in a sling and had a limp from the leg wounds. He was their hero. Baring senior dropped his work at the Ministry and came up from London and Sarah and the girls made excited preparations for a Christmas celebration. There was a lot to be thankful for. The news had come through that Charles had been promoted to full Lieutenant and had been Mentioned in Despatches.

As soon as he was well enough he arranged for the estate manager to drive him to Woodbridge to find Mary Hudson. Her letters had ceased soon after his arrival in the Somme and he had assumed they were not getting through. Many men had complained to him as censor that letters from home had dried up. It was not an unusual experience at the front. In the outfitters, which had not changed, he had a rude shock. One of the girls answered his inquiry pertly: 'Miss Hudson? You mean Mrs. Horrocks. Mary married the manager three months back. He insisted she stopped work at Christmas. They're expecting a happy event,' she winked. Without replying and stunned Charles got back to the car and slumped in a seat before faintness overcame him. The sharp disappointment was equalled by his self-disgust as he realised what a damn fool he had been. As soon as he could he tore the already bullet-mutilated letters into shreds and burnt them, vowing never again to make a mistake over a woman and never again to let his fragile emotions affect his judgement.

Charles nineteenth birthday came on 13th February, 1917, and was made an occasion for a big family reunion. Sir John Baring arrived at the Hall from Parliament. Doctor and grandmother Tallen brought Sarah's sister Mary. She was still unmarried, had become the headmistress of a board school and was well known locally as a campaigner for women's rights. Charles was in a deeply melancholic mood as his place was not at the Hall but at the front. He felt guilty knowing what the men of his brigade were suffering. The people around him would not, or could not, fathom the sheer horror of what was happening on the continent. It annoyed him greatly when they tried to act — for his benefit mainly — as if everything was fine. The trivialities of life were a crushing burden and the family's inane and happy conversation a terrible strain on his temper. He did not even feel stimulated when Mary Tallen and Sir John Baring started discussing politics and the role of women in the new society which would emerge after the war. It struck him as totally irrelevant to the slaughter still going on and he felt a bitter impatience that even intelligent leaders like Sir John were so protected by propaganda or a blithe arrogance that they could not understand that Germany might easily win the war.

For his birthday present he had wished that the Regiment could have sent his posting back to France. This was impossible until the hospital passed him as fit and it was to be another six weeks before the doctors at Chelmsford did that. The posting when it eventually came was the relief Charles had been waiting for. He longed to get away from the artificiality of the home front. Baring senior, thinking it would cheer his son, had taken him to London to stay in the Piccadilly Hotel and to see three shows. But the cheerful atmosphere in the Piccadilly created by the de Groot orchestra had only made Charles's melancholia deeper. The futility of war and women, and the sheer hopelessness of the human species, had entered his soul. He was a ship without a rudder in a raging storm.

When his parents saw him off at Southampton they realised they had lost a son and the sadness of it brought Sarah and George closer than they had ever been before.

The second time Charles Baring set foot in France was totally different from the first. The amateurish excitement of a boy's adventure had been replaced by the steely, calculating resolve of a job to be done. The war was crazy. There was no doubt in his mind about that. The human sacrifice it entailed was diabolical: the nations which sent their men to die in this way were as outdated as medieval kingdoms. The type of society which the state aimed to protect by the war was class-ridden, antiquated and wholly unjust to the millions who were being slaughtered. Charles knew his life had no purpose unless all that could be changed but he had made up his mind that — first things first — the militaristic Hun, as the worst of evils, had to be defeated before any reform could be attempted.

Charles was sent to join the British Second Army of General Sir Herbert Plumer engaged, under Haig's command, in the Flanders offensive. The officer commanding his Brigade quickly saw in Lieutenant Baring qualities of leadership which were desperately needed by war-weary troops. The French army had mutinied and it was needing all of Petain's discipline and threats of summary execution to bring them back into line. If the morale of the British collapsed then the Boche could soon walk over the allies. Officers with Baring's determination and guts were desperately needed to shore up the ranks and to stop the French disease from spreading and the Colonel welcomed him back with enthusiasm.

The third battle of Ypres had resulted in a small British advance. Charles was put in charge of a key unit, one of several which would spearhead the attack on the Belgian seaports which had to be taken to eliminate the German U-boat threat to shipping. The Americans had just joined the war, but nobody expected their contribution with raw troops to be of any use for at least a year. It was up to the British to break the Hun and the main attack would be on the Belgian sector.

The mud of Flanders was worse than anything Charles had experienced on the Somme. The weather had been atrocious throughout the summer and as the Belgian drainage canals were broken there was nowhere for the water to drain away on the clay soil. The shells, vehicles and horses churned the mud up into a morass which stretched as far as the eye could see. It seeped everywhere through Charles's puttees and caked his uniform. Even the rations had a muddy taste. Despite the terrible conditions of the terrain Haig ordered the offensive to continue; the objective was the Passchendaele Ridge on which the Germans had a small strategic advantage. The British casualty figures mounted day by day, the weather worsened and the Germans used mustard gas for the first time, which added to the hazards as it settled in a deadly film on the ponds and puddles on the crater-filled countryside.

One day early in November Charles's unit was positioned in a mud-filled trench on the front line waiting for an order to advance on the Ridge which the Germans held in force. That morning four men including the Sergeant had been killed by a machine gun strafing from enemy aircraft; the Germans had established air superiority and the situation seemed completely hopeless, while the German artillery was also well entrenched. Charles called his platoon to give them a pep talk. By this time, after more hardening months on the battlefield, he was totally obsessed by the need to destroy the Hun; in the thick of defeat and defeatism he would try to inspire the men under his command as no other officer could. As he was addressing them the sentry was suddenly shot dead, falling backwards in their midst, and the leader of a

German patrol appeared on the parapet carrying a bomb which he dropped into the trench mud before disappearing quickly.

'They'll shoot you if you run. It's a trick,' shouted Charles. 'Stay in the trench, keep your heads down.' As the men cowered, he turned to the bomb, now sinking into the sticky mud and with all his might pulled it up. Before any of the shocked platoon could help him he was over the top carrying it into no-man's-land where it could explode safely. After five yards with shots whizzing around him he dropped it and turned to run back to the safety of the trench. Just then the bomb exploded with an almighty roar and Lieutenant Baring was thrown unconscious into a shell crater.

In the trench a Corporal took command and when there was a lull crept out with two others to retrieve the officer's dead body. They were all convinced he was dead. No one could have survived that blast, but to their intense surprise he was still alive. He had just become one of the 300,000 British casualties in the four month battle for the capture of the Passchendaele Ridge.

It was a long time before Charles regained consciousness, and when he did, he could not remember what had happened. His head was still buzzing days later in the base hospital as doctors worked to remove pieces of shrapnel scattered throughout his body. By a miracle no vital organs had been hit.

This time he was taken to a specialist hospital in Sussex where the staff had experience with shell-shock cases and where the emphasis was on mental health as well as on physical recuperation. The rantings and ravings of Lieutenant Baring, awake as well as asleep, gave the Brigadier-Surgeon in charge cause for concern. For the sake of the family, as much as the patient, all visitors were banned. Christmas 1917 was a lonely one for Charles; he was allowed only to receive messages and gifts but he was incapable of recognising who they were from.

Early in 1918 Lieutenant Baring, patient number 121 in the Royal Alexandra Hospital in Horsham, began to respond to the care of the V.A.D. nurses. Every day they talked quietly to him, trying to calm his screams, sudden yells and long disjointed ramblings about things they could not understand. His brain was gradually learning to cope with enormous pressures. At last the conscious mind asserted itself. The angry and deep unconscious was exhausting its protests against the horrors the psyche had suffered. Within the mind of an innocent teenager the forces of reason and good had fought against unreason and evil. Rationality, of a sort, was emerging. The doctors, delighted with patient Baring's speedy recovery, wished the other officers could find their senses as quickly. Many of them would be incurably insane, sentenced to exist in a twilight world where no one could ever reach them.

By the end of January Charles was transferred to the rehabilitation ward away from the noise of the anguished and the demented. He began to read papers and books again. His parents were allowed to visit him and found their son subdued and coherent though he refused to talk about his experiences. They imagined the shock of remembering would be too much for him but his thoughts and memories were crystal clear and controlled. He kept them in a reserved compartment of his brain as they were too potent and powerful to be shared.

Three months after Passchendaele, on his twentieth birthday, Charles had a party in his ward which his parents and sisters attended. As they were cutting a cake made by Sarah with scarce sultanas, the Colonel commanding Charles's battalion walked in with his face wreathed in smiles.

'Back in Blighty for a spot of leave,' he said on seeing the Lieutenant's surprised look. 'I had to visit you.'

'Thank you,' said Charles curbing the question about deaths in the battalion which had immediately sprung to his mind.

'And I've got some good news for you,' the Colonel said jovially, 'and as the Medical Superindentent tells me this is your birthday, my timing is impeccable isn't it?'

'What's the good news Colonel?' asked Baring senior.

'Your son's been awarded the Military Cross for exceptional bravery in the face of the enemy and for saving the lives of his platoon. The Regiment is enormously proud of him.'

'Wonderful,' said Sarah, hugging Charles with tears of joy.

Emma and Edith jumped and clapped and their father said firmly 'Well done Charles; we're mighty proud of you too.'

Sitting upright in his wheelchair, Charles said nothing but nodded his head.

'What's more there's a promotion for you' added the Colonel. 'You'll be Captain Baring when you get your discharge from this place and I'm glad to hear that will be soon.'

Charles nodded again, showing the least emotion of any in the group. To him personal honour and achievement were no longer of any significence except as tools in the task to which he had been secretly dedicating himself. There was no point in allowing feelings to intrude on his motivation.

Sarah as a mother could sense the deep change in her son. 'Aren't you pleased Charles? Aren't you proud you have achieved so much, so young?'

'Yes Mother,' he said to placate her, 'of course,' and turning to the Colonel asked, 'What were the battalion losses at Passchendaele?'

'Enormous, the worst we've known, Baring, I'm afraid. Three-quarters of the battalion were wiped out and I've had to replace them with raw eighteen year old conscripts.' His heartiness was subdued by the subject. 'Now that the Russians have pulled out of the war, the Huns are transferring their armies from the East to the Western front and we'll need all we've got to break them. At least the Americans are beginning to arrive in some numbers.' The

Colonel broke off, realising he was discussing military matters in front of civilians, and said more heartily 'We need you back soon, Captain. Officers of your calibre are worth their weight in gold to me.' He paid the new Captain the compliment of a comradely salute which Charles with his arms wrapped in a blanket could clearly not return, shook hands with the family, turned smartly on his heels and left.

In the days that followed, Captain Charles Baring began to mix with his fellow officers in the rehabilitation ward. Most had been shell-shocked or brain injured but their capacities were gradually returning. He played card games and chess and invented a new word game which a few of them enjoyed. As far as conversation was concerned they were a disappointing lot. Their repertoire consisted of silly reminiscences, crude jokes or boastings about the girls they had seduced. Charles was disgusted not so much by their animalistic instincts — every man was entitled to those — but by their total inability to grasp more than the shallowest understanding of what was going on in the world. The war, in three and a half years, had torn Europe asunder, millions of lives were being sacrificed and the old order was obviously finished, but all this officer class could do was talk in banalities. The disappointing experience of finding his brother officers so dismally dull reinforced Charles's determination to keep his intellectual integrity intact, immune from their soporific influence.

There was one exception to the general dullness in the rehabilitation ward, Arthur Haycraft, four years older than Charles, who had seen his first action in the debacle of Gallipoli. After that retreat he had been transferred to Egypt. Charles heard accounts of life in Cairo, a city overcrowded with Mullahs, pimps and prostitutes. Lieutenant Haycraft's military career ended when he was severely injured in the head by a Turkish bullet during General Allenby's attack on Gaza, but fortunately was returned on a hospital ship to a Britain he had not seen for three years. Haycraft's experiences had chastened him. He described the British Middle East strategy to Charles as a shambles, thousands of men squandered in an abortive attempt to secure the Dardanelles, followed by huge losses in the attack on Turkish-held Palestine.

Arthur Haycraft, a tall red-headed man with strong noble features, an engineer in civilian life, came from Manchester. Charles found his down-to-earth Northern manner refreshing and welcomed his accounts of the war he had experienced.

'I'd had no idea that our losses were so bad at Gallipoli' Charles confessed one day when they were alone in the sunroom.

'Believe me it was horrifying. Our boys and the Aussies fought like tigers but there was nothing they could do to break the Turk's grip. The place was impregnable. Whoever ordered that attack should have been impeached.'

'It was Churchill, wasn't it?' said Charles.

'Yes but Lloyd-George was also behind it. The politicians in this country are a total washout. If the British people knew half the mistakes they've made, they'd get rid of them in a jiffy. Hardly anybody in the old country knows what's been going on out there.'

'It's censorship. It's a powerful weapon,' said Charles. 'The people are not allowed to know. This is supposed to be a democracy but that's a joke; in reality the leaders once there can do what they like as the public are bamboozled with false information. Patriotism is the trick they use to persuade the British to be led on by the nose. It's the biggest confidence trick since Napoleon gave the French illusions about ruling Russia.'

Haycraft had never met an officer with Baring's outspokenness and understanding of history. The two quickly established confidence and Charles's new-found ability to communicate his thoughts was like a spring released from an underground lake.

'What you've described in the Middle East is a picnic

compared to the war in France,' he said with suppressed anger. 'Our men are being thrown into battles for a few miles of terrain without any regard for lives. The Generals have gone insane and the politicians are as bad.'

'Don't the public know what's happening?' It's much nearer than the Dardanelles after all.'

'The public know!' repeated Charles ironically. 'The public aren't allowed to know. They're just the miserable losers in all this shambles. They're losing husbands, fathers and sons but they're never told the truth. Instead the papers are full of stories of gallantry larded with optimistic jingoism. If anyone tries to tell the truth they're locked up under the Official Secrets Act.'

Together Charles and Arthur covered many subjects. The Northerner, although he had never studied history or politics, had an acute appreciation of the problems of government. He had experienced depressing poverty in the pre-war years and had been drawn to socialism. When Charles preached the good sense of Marxism he found Haycraft a willing and sympathetic listener.

'I want to help change society when this lot's over,' he confided.

'As a Labour man?' asked Haycraft.

'No. I don't think the Labour Party is ideologically strong enough. At the moment it's simply a mouthpiece of the trade unions and although they pay lip service to socialism they would be satisfied with simply a bigger slice of the cake. They're not in politics for the fundamental change I believe in.'

'How would you do it then?'

'Get into the centre of the British Establishment by appearing to support its aims and then destroy it from within.'

'That's a tall order.'

'It's the only way that makes sense. The world needs a revolution from which a Communist society based on justice can be developed. H.G. Wells has the right idea. He believes the new society can only work if it's a dictatorship run by an élite. If I can get to the centre I can use its power to achieve that sort of Communism.'

'In fact to use their own methods to defeat them,' said Haycraft, attracted to the idea.

'Yes, exactly. They use the tricks of patriotism. They control the press, the schools and the churches. With all that, they manage to enslave the people and to maintain their class system and their privileges. By infiltrating that power structure I can help turn it to achieve the opposite aims. They can repulse a full frontal attack only too easily but my way they can never defeat.'

'What about Russia? They've had a revolution, can't the same be achieved in Britain? asked Haycraft.

'Russia is a special case,' said Charles, 'there had to be a total collapse of Tsarism, and the divine rule myth, plus the Court scandals, before the proletariat would move. We're unlikely to ever get the same conditions here.'

'Don't tell anyone your plans.' said Haycraft. 'But do it.'

BOOK TWO

Vecheka's Trojan Horse

CHAPTER 14

When the *City of Marseilles* slipped moorings at Newcastle dock and began steaming down the Tyne only the two Generals on board knew their destination. The captain of the ship had sealed orders. On that mid-June morning in 1918 there were no farewell waves at the quayside; only the embarkation officer from the War Office and a few dockers were there to see the vessel leave.

The troops, leaning over the railings on the crowded decks, saw the swirling mists over the estuary disappear with the rising sun which hit the spires and rooftops of Gateshead and the King Edward VII bridge and turned the murky waters of the river into a scintillating sparkle of light. The industrial towns of Hebburn and Jarrow, with the gaunt Pelaw factories of the CWS, appeared on the starboard with North Shields on the port side. Ahead lay Tynemouth, the open sea and uncertainty. The soldiers, already war weary from years on the battlefields of France, watched England slip away and wondered if they would ever see the old country again. Most had been seriously injured and were now categorised in a low physical grade. In normal circumstances they would have seen out the war in a home posting but the times were far from normal. The war had gone badly for the Allies and the German High Command was boasting of winning. The Bolshevik signing of the Brest-Litovsk surrender had taken Russia out of the conflict and a million German troops in the East had been transferred to the Western Front. Thus strengthened, they had retaken all the hard-won territory on the Somme and were advancing on a Paris reeling from a shelling which Kaiser Wilhelm had personally supervised.

Except for the two Generals, the officers and men on board the *City of Marseilles* did not know how serious the situation had become. Censorship had stopped the full impact of the disasters getting through. The rumours and the casualty lists, which could not be suppressed, had given them some idea and added to the sense of foreboding they felt. They could not tell their relatives where they were going as they did not know themselves; they had been allowed only to leave a G.P.O. box number as an address and hope against hope they would be alive to receive the family letters if they were ever sent.

When the ship reached the open sea two destroyers took up the escort. The small convoy steamed at full speed towards the expanse of the North Sea and before long the coast of Northumberland was barely visible behind.

Two officers on the second deck watched the land disappear. One of them was smoking State Express cigarettes with a nervous mannerism indicating apprehension.

'Do you have any idea where this old tub is taking us?' he asked his companion.

'The orders are dead secret I understand. Only General Maynard is in the know,' replied the other.

'Can't understand what they could want to do with a scratch mob like this. Did you see those troops on the train coming up from London? Half of them aren't fit for active service.'

'I agree. They've been rounded up from the hospitals for this mission. What's for sure is that we're not going to France otherwise embarkation would have been Folkestone or one of the south coast ports.'

That's one thing to be thankful for, I suppose. France is a running sore. We are well out of that mess. Casualties were seventy-five percent in my regiment, the East Lancs.'

'Mine too.'

'Your's was the Essex wasn't it?'

'Yes.'

Both officers had the three pips of newly fledged Captains and had met only that morning.

'By the way my name's Harvey, Henry Harvey but my friends call me Harry,' said the first.

'Charles Baring,' said the other, 'but please, I don't like to be called Charlie.'

'Alright,' said Harvey, 'just as well to know. We're going to be together for a long time wherever it is we're going.' He paused as though collecting courage and said with a tremor, 'Do you think we're part of a landing on the North German coast — a sort of suicide force to take the heat off our chaps defending Paris?'

'Anything's possible. The War Council are desperate enough to do that I suppose.'

'I was thinking all night about it and can't think of another explanation unless we're going to occupy Denmark,' said Captain Harvey.

'General Maynard's called a briefing for officers so we'll learn soon enough,' said Captain Baring who wanted to keep his own counsel.

'I was wounded on the Somme,' said Harvey lugubriously. 'I never thought I'd be fit enough for another lot. They seem to be running out of officers.' He was in his mid-thirties but looked at least ten years older. In contrast Charles Baring looked very young. 'I hope Maynard's got some good news for us. I don't fancy taking the motley crew we've got below into battle. It would be certain curtains for us all.' He threw his butt into the heaving sea below.

The *City of Marseilles* zig-zagged across the North Sea towards the north east with the destroyers constantly on the look out for U-boats, the boom of the occasional depth charges warning that they were either lurking around or passing through on their way to the shipping lanes of the North Atlantic.

It became clear to anyone on board who had the slightest sense of geography that the ship was not heading for

Germany or Denmark. It was skirting the Norwegian fjords
and heading further north away, it seemed, from the war. The
curiosity about the destination grew more intense as the
voyage became more difficult. The lascar stokers, along with
many others, were struck down with Spanish influenza and
without energetic stoking of the coal the ship was in danger of
lagging. Some ratings were winched across from the
destroyers to fill the breach but as their ships were oil fired
they were not much help. When the message was passed to
the Tommies below that a slowing up would make the ship
more vulnerable to a torpedo attack, volunteers came
forward in dozens to heave the coal into the boilers and a
crisis was averted.

On the third day out of Newcastle, Major General
Maynard called the officers to the mess room on C deck.
There was an expectant mood as he opened the conference
with a curt 'Good morning gentlemen. Our orders have been
top secret, direct from the War Cabinet. You've all been
specially selected to join missions of utmost importance to
the outcome of the war. Indeed these missions may decide its
very outcome.'

He looked intently at the attentive gathering and went on,
'We are heading for Murmansk, a port in North Russia,
where we already have a small detachment of marines sent in
earlier to safeguard the supplies we sent to the Russians when
they were still fighting the Germans. As you know the
Bolshevik traitors around that German agent Lenin have
taken over Russia. According to our intelligence sources the
Kaiser personally approved the plan for Lenin to travel in a
sealed train through Germany from his exile in Zurich so he
could destroy the Russian resistance. They have succeeded in
that. The job we've been given is to trump the Huns' ace card
by going in ourselves to destroy the illegal Bolshevik
government.'

The audience of officers broke into applause which the
General calmed by raising his arm. 'Gentlemen I admire

your enthusiasm. We do have a noble cause but I must warn you that our task is not an easy one. The troops we have been allocated are unfit for service in France and as you have seen, not the best physical specimens. Furthermore, because of the haste, there's been no way we could weed out the pro-leftists from the ranks. Make no mistake some of them might feel mutinous about fighting fellow socialists.'

Captain Baring, sitting in the second row, felt a tightening of his nerves. He had already guessed where they were going and this confirmation of the army's purpose was not to his liking. It was immoral to use British troops against a country which had lately been an ally and against whom no war had been declared. The Revolution had been the Russians' business and Britain had no legal or other right to get involved. Troops, whatever their physical condition, would be better used in fighting the Germans.

The General became emphatic. 'If there are any doubters among the men you command I want you to tell them the facts. It is best they understand. Fact number one: the Germans aim to take over Murmansk as a submarine base. If they succeed they get an ice free all-year port from which to destroy shipping in the North Atlantic. The consequences of that would be awful, completely undermining the American support for the war. Fact two: The Bolsheviks have no popular support. When we intervene their regime will collapse and a legitimate government can take over and resume the fight against the Germans on the eastern front.'

The officers were feeling more confident as the General spoke, the mystery replaced with a pride at being chosen for such a highly important mission. They listened carefully as General Maynard went on. 'I will be in command in Murmansk and my task will be to hold the port and the peninsular against German attack which we expect them to mount with Finnish support from Northern Finland. The Russians built a railway from Murmansk to Petrograd and we shall take over as much of that as possible to protect ourselves from Bolshevik attack. However many of you have been attached to an operation code-named Elope. I now turn to the supreme importance of that operation.'

Captain Baring sensed the even sharper attendance of the officers. He had read in his own orders of his attachment to Elope. Most of the others — including Captain Harvey — had also received them.

'Elope,' the General said, 'is the attack we are launching on the Bolsheviks in Archangel, the biggest city in North Russia. Some of you may know that Archangel was established as a trading base by an Englishman called Richard Chancellor in the sixteenth century. It has a lot of history behind it unlike Murmansk which was not even established until this war. There is even a story that our Alfred the Great went to Archangel in the ninth centry. So you see you are not the first Englishmen to visit Archangel. Elope is going in to defeat the Reds and establish a legitimate Russian regime which will cooperate with us in defending the Germans.

Having dropped the two escorting destroyers the *City of Marseilles* battled on alone against the rough seas of the Arctic. At the North Cape a thick fog obscured vision but it cleared in time for the lookouts to see the two escort ships meeting them from Murmansk. They turned out to be armed trawlers and were markedly different from the sleek destroyers. There was general relief that the rendezvous had been made safely and that they would soon reach the haven of a port.

Without the fog visibility at night was as clear as during the day with the sun still visible. This phenomena amazed the other ranks who knew nothing about where they were going and had been told nothing about the new enemy they were soon to engage.

On the fifth day the ship turned into the Kola Inlet and started the thirty mile journey down the estuary. The men looked without enthusiasm onto a vast land, uninhabited and uninhabitable. The banks of the shore were steep and covered with firs.

Charles Baring found himself standing beside a ragged, hirsute merchant marine officer who was leaning on the rails and looking into a barren distance. 'Been here before?' he asked.

'Many times,' replied the mariner, weather-beaten from thirty years at sea, and shrugged his shoulders as if there were few ports in the world he had not seen. 'This is the worst hole I've ever known. Murmansk has nothing except a few shacks. It was only built two years ago as a supply base.'

'So I heard,' said Captain Baring.

'Did you hear about that incredible railway to Petrograd. They say there's a German prisoner-of-war under every sleeper. The death toll was enormous. The Russkies needed that railway real bad.' The mariner shook his head in disbelief. 'Don't understand how that ramshackle affair can possibly work. They built it on tundra you know.'

'What's a tundra?'

'Frozen swamp. When it melts in summer it's a quagmire. Whole sections have been known to disappear in the bog. Give me a ship anytime. It's safer.'

The *City of Marseilles* rounded a bluff headland and Murmansk suddenly came into view. It was on the port side and consisted only of oddly-shaped and scattered log cabins, not a single stone or brick house to be seen.

The mariner went towards the bridge muttering, 'This place is terrible, anyone who chooses to live here is a lunatic.'

Charles looked towards the town and saw nothing to redeem it. There was no vegetation apart from the firs and the place was squalid beyond belief with piles of rubbish littering such streets as there were. The ships by the quayside, including *H.M.S. Glory*, the admiral's flagship which shone like a jewel against the bleak shore, provided the only contrast to a general impression of extreme neglect.

Baring discovered within a few days that the Chairman of the local Soviet, a Communist called Yurev, was co-operating with the British because he had not approved of the peace treaty signed by Trotsky at Brest-Litovsk. Trotsky, who had become the Commissar for War, was livid with rage about the British presence and telegrams from him poured in from Moscow ordering Yurev to eject the foreigners. Trotsky had tried reasoning with him, then ordered him to be expelled from the Party and, when captured, shot for treason.

General Maynard decided that the sooner the British presence was established further down the railway line the more secure Murmansk would become. He commandeered a small force of soldiers including Serbians who had come over to the Allies after the collapse of the Eastern front and, having requisitioned a train, set off towards the south. Captain Baring and two officers went with him. It was the most bizarre railway journey any of them had ever attempted. The problems of collecting enough cut timber as fuel for the engine were formidable as no supply organisation had been set up and the local workers were either indolent or sabotaged the operation because they were secret Communists. Then the engine driver refused to drive the train but a seventy year old retired pro-Tsarist man was pressed into service together with a corporal in the Hampshires who had driven an engine on the L.S.W.R. before the war. They had to drive slowly as the track was broken in places or had, as the mariner said, sunk into the melting bog. When they came across a dangerous patch the train stopped with a bump in the middle of nowhere and a gang of troops jumped out with shovels to shore up the bank and ensure that the narrow rails were in place.

They travelled three hundred miles to Kandalaksha and Kem and met a huge detachment of Red Army troops travelling north to take over Murmansk. General Maynard took his officers to meet the Bolshevik commander, a man called Spiridornoff who had been drinking heavily but was coherent enough to make his intentions clear through an interpreter. 'We are coming to take over Murmansk on the orders of Lenin and Trotsky,' he said.

'That is unnecessary' General Maynard replied. 'We can protect the port. You should use your men to fight the Germans.'

'We've signed a treaty with the Germans,' said Spiridornoff, who was determined to get to Murmansk to execute his orders. Maynard kept him in parley and taking advantage of the Commander's drunkenness sent orders for all the Lewis guns the British troops had to be set up on both sides of the carriages the Red troops occupied. When this manoeuvre was complete he gave Spiridornoff an ultimatum. 'Turn your engine round and take all your troops towards the south. If you don't obey I'll give the order to my gunners to blast all your men to death.' Spiridornoff whose force outnumbered the British by eight to one had no alternative and the first hostilities between Britain and Soviet Russia had resulted in a blooodless British victory.

Sir Eric Geddes, the First Lord of the Admiralty, had arrived in Murmansk, wanted to join the mission, but was persuaded to stay on a cruiser in the harbour. Captain Baring thought the Cabinet had been mad to send a senior Minister to such a delicate trouble spot. He wondered if perhaps the hotheads in Whitehall wanted such an excuse.

Baring was pleased there had so far been no casualties, but was angry about this fool-hardy intervention against the Soviets, and doubtful about the legality of the action. His concern was vastly increased when he attended a briefing on the Elope venture on *H.M.S. Glory.* The plan was to move on Archangel as soon as the thick ice on the White Sea had begun to break.

Baring was assigned to General Poole in command of the venture, which consisted of a trawler fleet with *H.M.S. Attentive, H.M.S. Salvator* and an aircraft carrier *H.M.S. Nairana* to support it. At the end of July, when the ice was relatively clear, the force set out from Murmansk with a total of one and a half thousand men. No declaration of war had been made against the Soviet Government which had in fact proclaimed its peaceful intentions to the world.

Off Archangel there was a barrage of fire from the Bolshevik batteries set up on Modyugski Island and seaplanes from the *Nairana* were ordered to silence them. British troops were landed on the island and Bolshevik resistance collapsed.

In Archangel itself it was expected that anti-Bolshevik elements would rebel when the fleet was on its way, and the plan succeeded as the Bolsheviks had been intimidated by the show of superior force. The British fleet sailed towards Archangel without more ado. They steamed into the estuary of the great Dwina River passing banks crowded with fir forests. The timber wealth of the region seemed immense. Then at the turn of the corner Baring suddenly saw the cupola and four spires of the cathedral brightly shining in the sun. As they came nearer he noticed the beautiful murals painted on the side of the cathedral and thought it must be the most northerly of man's expression of art. It had an Eastern flavour.

The invasion was achieved without any casualties among the attacking forces. It all seemed too easy and he had a worrying feeling that the policy makers in London would develop as false an idea of their capacity to conquer Russia as Napoleon before them.

Baring was even more amazed by the reception the British invaders received. As they disembarked at Cathedral quay people gathered to cheer; an immense crowd grew which swept Baring and the other officers towards the Government Buildings where speeches were made in their honour. The enthusiasm was infectious and even Baring, with all his misgivings, was moved.

On the following day an advance party of Americans arrived and, within a week a French contingent, giving the occupation force an appearance of Allied solidarity. But Baring knew they were there to maintain British control of the intervention and to ensure that the Americans and others obeyed British orders.

In the first heady days of success the British troops enjoyed
the excitement of establishing themselves in Archangel. The
great wooden houses of wealthy German traders, who had
fled at the beginning of the war leaving their treasures behind,
were requisitioned as officers' barracks and command offices.
The fashionable Troitsky Hotel became the Officers' Mess
and life seemed so secure that afternoon tea dances were
started so that officers could entertain the wives and
daughters of the Archangel middle class. Baring was secretly
disgusted by his fellow officers, so totally divorced from the
political realities of Russia. In Petrograd and Moscow the
Bolsheviks were firmly in control; they heard the news of the
execution of Tsar Nicholas at Ekaterinburg. The seething
mass of the Russian people, achieving power after
generations of Tsarist dictatorship, could not be contained by
a tiny force of a few thousand, physically sub-standard
troops, sitting on the Arctic top of Russia.

Baring did not dare discuss his feelings with any of his
colleagues, who were all convinced that the Reds — or 'Bolos'
— would soon be defeated by the White Russians and other
Tsarist elements. They also believed that the peasants, the
moujiks, would rise up against the Bolsheviks. They sat in the
comfortable armchairs of the Troitsky Hotel sipping
requisitioned vodka, which they had not yet learnt to gulp.
They swallowed propaganda better than vodka, believing
devoutly in the mission, but they were totally unaware of the
basic causes of the Russian Revolution and unmoved by the
suffering of the oppressed under the Tsar. Three days after
his arrival Baring met Captain Harvey in the bar of the
Troitsky Hotel. The red faced and overweight officer, bulging
in his tight uniform was no longer the frightened man he had
seen on the ship crossing the North Sea.

'Hello Baring,' he said jovially. 'Better than France, eh.
Not a decent enemy for 500 miles. I think the War Office sent
us here to have a rest cure.'

'Don't be so certain yet,' said Baring. 'I don't think the

Bolsheviks will give in so easily. They will send troops against us soon.'

'I hear the Czech troops have turned against the Reds and are heading here from Siberia to join up with us.'

'That's a lot of country to cross. The Bolsheviks will fight like hell to stop any link-up.'

'Don't believe it old man. They haven't got the guts or the leadership. All the officers have gone over to the White Russians who want to get things back as they were.'

'I don't think they will achieve that,' said Baring frustrated at having to keep his thoughts private.

Harvey prattled on. 'I hear that Jew Trotsky is their Commissar for War. What does he know about war? The idea is ludicrous, giving people ideas and ambitions above their station. The Red Army will sink as soon as it is engaged by the professionals.'

The vision of Captain Harvey, who was frightened by anything more deadly than a popping Champagne cork, regarding himself as a professional suddenly filled Baring with hilarity.

Baring felt out of place as an officer in an army trying to undo a cause he believed in. The memory of the carnage on the Somme and at Passchendaele came welling back with the force of an exploding bomb and with it a hatred of the generals and the politicians whose crass vain decisions had forced hundreds of thousands of young men to their deaths.

'Are you alright, old chap?' Captain Harvey was saying. 'You went very pale and your eyes were miles away. You must be tired. Let me get you a tot.'

Baring looked at the insipid, unthinking face of his fellow officer and felt a spasm of pity. Harry was a kind enough, simple-minded man. In his limited way he meant well but like most of his class was totally unaware of the forces of destiny shaping a new world.

'I'm alright,' said Baring. 'I was dreaming of something else.'

'Home sick, I'spect,' Harry smiled, 'it affects us all, don't worry old chap we'll get this little lot over and have you back soon. We've already set up a new government under Nikolai Tchaikovsky, it will be the rallying point for our victory. The Russians here are disgusted by the murder of the Tsar's children. That's the last straw for them. They won't put up with that Bolshevik butchery.'

Baring did not want to drawn into discussing atrocities and was loathe to jump to conclusions about the Tsar's death on the basis of rumours and propaganda.

'Is that fellow Tchaikovsky related to Peter Ilyich? he asked.

'Peter who?'

'The composer.'

'Oh him. I doubt it. He wouldn't be likely to be related to a musician.

CHAPTER 15

During the remainder of the brief Autumn of 1918 the allied army in North Russia used the long days to consolidate its position. Cross country links were established between Archangel and Murmansk and supplies were sent on river boats down the Dwina to establish a front against the Red Army. The threat of an approaching winter, when the sea lanes to Archangel as well as all the rivers would freeze, gave an urgency to the preparations for what promised to be a long and hard campaign. The false optimisms of those like Captain Harvey who had thought they would be out of Russia within weeks after a little 'tidying up' was replaced by the realisation that they were in Russia to stay. The Provisional Government depended on the British troops to hold it up as was soon demonstrated when a coup against President Tchaikovsky by ex-Tsarist officers had to be put down.

Captain Baring was given the job of liaison officer to the Central Gaol in Archangel. He did not relish it. The gaol was under the nominal jurisdiction of the Russian Public Prosecutor but was in an appalling mess. Five hundred prisoners were kept in cells designed for a hundred and the stench of their bodies and the decaying leather of their sheep shubas was overpowering. None of them ever washed, hardly any of the prisoners had appeared before any court, and as the prosecutor insisted on dealing with each case personally and with bureaucratic meticulousness, it would take months to bring the place under control. Baring's sympathies were with the prisoners, most of whom were inside as suspected

Bolsheviks. He intervened to get some of the obvious cases of injustice or ineptitude released, as the Russian prosecutor — like most bureaucrats — was easily malleable to pressure, which Captain Baring used as subtly as he could.

The Ambassadors of Britain, France, the United States and other countries had come up from Vologda to establish embassies in Archangel. This lent diplomatic respectability to the Tchaikovsky Government which was formally recognised, but everyone knew the British were the real bosses. The Russians were puppets on a string being pulled in far away Whitehall.

He was relieved to be transferred from the gaol and put in charge of a supplies corps, and glad to get away from Archangel, where the atmosphere was effete and unreal. The frail seventy year old ex-professor who was supposed to be President had become a sick joke like the rest of the ramshackle administration in the town. Things were made worse by the arrogant attitudes of the former officers of the Russian Imperial Army parading around the town in their baggy blue breeches with broad red stripes and jackets with extravagant gold-lace epaulettes. The Troitsky Prospekt with its long pavements of wooden planks became more like the stage of a musical comedy as more allied officers were sent in to add to the legality of the intervention. To Baring's jaundiced eye the Japanese colonel in a picturesque blue-braided jacket, trailing a long sword, the more prosaic French infantry colonel in sky-blue and the American captains in dull khaki kit added only colour to the scene. The Ambassadors might be impressed by this show of support but the ordinary Russians in the town were showing increasing signs of waning enthusiasm. The welcome given to the British troops on their first arrival in Archangel had turned out to be a flash in the pan: the Bolsheviks had not collapsed and most workers were becoming apprehensive as it became clear that the town was cut off from the rest of Russia by the Red Army, which was steadily moving up from the south.

Baring's expeditions took him eighty miles across country to Onega in the west and down the route of the Vologda railway to Oborzerstaya. Once out of Archangel there lay a vast expanse of forests, lakes and morasses and only an occasional tiny settlement of hunters. From his interpreter and guide, a small, old but tough, wiry Russian who had once lived in New York, Baring learnt that the aboriginal people in the area were known by their tribal names of Samoyedes and Zyryans and had little, if any, knowledge of what was happening in Archangel let alone Moscow.

'It's all the zame to zem,' the Russian would say scratching his huge nose whenever he needed to emphasise a point, 'their lives never change whether the Tsar or the Reds are in power. They have a hard enough time without worrying about politics.' And looking as if he polished a philosopher's stone he added, 'Politics is only for town people.'

Baring found the practical humour of his guide a refreshing contrast to the artificiality of command headquarters. They decided to travel light without accompanying forces, as this would make it easier to avoid ambushes from any marauding bands of Bolsheviks which might infiltrate the northern area. Until the frosts came and sleighs could be used over the frozen ground, ponies were the best means of transport and would give them the speediest way of avoiding trouble if any flared up. But they never met any Red Army scouts.

The days were still incredibly long although the hours of darkness lengthened as the weeks passed. The guide told Baring that the longest day in the summer was twenty-two hours but the shortest in the winter had only three hours of daylight. 'What do the people do then? Baring asked.

'Go to bed,' said the guide, adding, 'that's why most of the babies are born in late summer or at the beginning of the autumn.'

The mornings were foggy and the mists often persisted all day giving the giant firs a mystical quality. The quietness of the deep forests was something Baring had never before experienced and until he became adjusted it was painful to the ears. The steady plod of the patient ponies broke the sepulchral silence like a coughing in a cathedral. When the ponies were resting and tethered the quiet was absolute and deafening in its intensity. When an animal broke a twig in the distance it was like a sudden pistol shot piercing the all-embracing quiet.

During the short night-stops Baring rolled up in a sleeping bag by the trunk of a large fir. It was necessary to keep body heat in as the deceptively hot days gave way to some bitterly cold nights. At these times Baring felt snug and secure and at peace with the whole world. There seemed to be more sanity in those close contact with the earth in the solitude of Russian forests than in the company of his fellow men.

After one week-long trip he reported back to headquarters in Archangel to find a new man had arrived as Commander-in-Chief of the intervention forces. He was Edmond Ironside, at thirty-seven the youngest general in the British army and reported to be a direct descendant of an English king. He had a reputation as a courageous leader from his days as subaltern in the South Africa war against the Boers and in France. Large reinforcements of British, Canadian and American troops had also arrived and gave a great feeling of confidence to the Troitsky Mess. Baring found Captain Harvey full of bonhomie when he was accosted by him in the bar.

'Hello, old chap, things are warming up now,' he asserted bravely 'with Ironside we're going to make the big push south to link up with Kolchak coming in from Siberia and Denikin fighting up from the Crimea. We'll have the Bolshies caught in a grip.'

The further he was from a torpedo or a front line the better Captain Harvey could jest about the war.

Baring was, as usual exasperated, by Harvey's simplistic approach and decided for once to rile him with argument.

'When we arrived here, we were told the Russians would join our army in droves. They haven't. The few who came in did so merely for the rations and the issue of a warm uniform. We'd be fools to rely on their loyalty.'

'The Russians are a funk-ridden lot.' said Harvey, 'Look how they gave up against the Germans. Obviously we can't rely on them.'

'But they're joining the Red Army aren't they? Perhaps they believe in what they're fighting for.'

'The Bolshies are promising them riches when the war is over. They say all the big farms are to be divided up and given to the peasants. Of course there will be some idiots who will fall for their promises but the mass of the moujiks couldn't care less. If we show them strength they'll be on our side.'

'You mean to say we have to be here for their own good, even if they don't see it.'

'That's right,' said Harvey, 'it's the British mission to give peace and order to the world. It's better for our trade furthermore. We can't have the Bolshies giving a bad example to our own workers can we?'

'I suppose not,' said Baring to avoid being involved in rancorous discussion.

That night he left the Troitsky Hotel at eleven and walked in the half-light towards his billet a mile away. The trams, which ran during the day along the Prospekt and gave a touch of normality to the beleaguered town, had stopped an hour before. After five minutes he heard a shouting behind him. 'Charles, Charles.' It was Arthur Haycraft pounding the pavements towards him.

'Good heavens Arthur, what are you doing here?' said Baring with pleasure.

Came over with Ironside on the *Stephen* from Dundee, said Haycraft. 'It was quite a voyage criss-crossing the North Sea to miss those German subs.'

'What luck to meet you,' said Baring with feeling, 'this place is perilously short of intelligent company. Come back to my place for a Scotch, believe it or not I've got a bottle left. You'll have time enough to get used to the vodka.' They walked arm in arm like Pop members at Eton exchanging reminiscences and oblivious of the curious looks of the few Russians on the street.

'How are the operations?' asked Haycraft when they were sitting in Baring's room.

'There's been sporadic fighting with some Red Army units coming up the Dwina but they haven't made a concerted attack on us yet,' said Baring. 'We're holding our lines on the railway and on the rivers about a hundred miles south of Archangel. The forests and the bogs make it impossible to have anything like a front in between. The plan is to push down the railway towards Vologda and the Dwina to Kotlas to join up with Admiral Kolchak's White Army.'

'Are the Russians with us?'

'Truth is they're apathetic. I've had a canny Russian guide and he says politics is for the towns and he's right. In Archangel we've had four volunteers. Frankly I think most Russians on this side of the line are waiting to see who wins before they jump, those who understand there's a war on. I've met nomad tribesmen in the forest and lonely hunters who haven't a clue what's going on. Their lives are totally unaffected.'

Charles Baring soaked up the news of England, the improving situation in France where Foch had six weeks before being made a Marshal by Clemenceau and was at last turning the tide against the Germans. The friends parted at two in the morning by which time the sky was pitch-black apart from the stars sparkling in the crisp night.

There were increasing skirmishes on the Dwina front as the Red Army strengthened its troops for a winter campaign aimed at pushing the British and other occupation troops out of North Russia. For the time being the river was still navigable but within weeks it would be frozen and the gun boats would be laid up. Both sides were trying to gain the few vantage points on the Dwina and on its tributary the Vaga.

Baring was confirmed as supplies officer, a formidable task

as the tracks through the forests were becoming a morass of mud before the frosts froze them, and some of the pony stations had been raided by bandits. There was also the curse of illicit trading or *skolkuring*. Everything was available for barter and some British soldiers had been stealing supplies to exchange for local goods. The prize acquisitions were the furs caught by Russian trappers; three tots bought a fox fur and a bottle a blue fox. The men who acquired these trophies had no idea how they would get them back home but they seemed good bargains at the time. Baring had to deal severely with the men found filtching food or clothing supplies in an excess of *skolkuring*.

The Americans totalled about 4,500 men and had their own supply lines, but Baring coordinated his pony trains with theirs to ensure maximum security against maraudings. He came to like the Americans. They were a bluff, open lot of men from Wisconsin and Michigan and had none of the hard slick ways of men from the big cities. The relationships between officers and enlisted men were friendly to the point of informality, which disgusted the British officers in the Troitsky mess; they lamented the bad examples given to British rankers.

Baring found the officers hospitable when he visited their camps on the Emtsa front and hungry for information about the world outside. For months they had not even had a leave in Archangel and little news had filtered through. Most of them were amazed to be fighting against the Russians and the commander, a Captain Odgaard, a tall handsome man of Danish ancestry, was frank in his views when he and Baring were alone. 'Can't understand why we're here at all,' he lamented. 'The Russians are not our natural enemies. If they were left to their own devices they would take the Revolution in their stride. By this foolish intervention we are only building up the anger of the revolutionary leaders.'

'Wasn't Trotsky in New York? asked Baring.

'Yes he has a lot of friends in the American trade unions

and he likes America. We had our revolution too, don't forget that, and a lot of Russians were inspired by it. They are only trying to emulate us, it's a more difficult problem with the Tsar at home. George III was three thousand miles away from Boston which made it easier for us.'

'Do you think Washington will try to get a ceasefire?'

'They're probably working on it now. I'm sure we were only sent in to show solidarity with the Allies and as a bargaining counter. It's no part of American policy to get bogged down in the Russian snows. I expect as soon as the Germans are defeated we shall be pulled out.'

'The British have gone beyond the original idea of creating a second front against the Germans,' said Baring. 'I understand Ironside has arrived with orders that the war against the Bolsheviks must go on until they are crushed. Even if the Germans are defeated it doesn't make any difference. We still stay on here.'

'Well that's plum crazy,' said Odgaard with emphasis. 'Who the hell is behind that policy for Christsake?'

'Winston Churchill,' said Baring. 'As Secretary of State for War he's the strong man in our Cabinet, and passionately opposed to Bolshevism.'

'Well I tell you one thing for sure, our men won't stay here after the Germans are defeated. There'll be a mutiny,' said Odgaard.

Charles Baring returned to base deeply troubled. He felt a tremendous sympathy with the revolutionaries who wanted to apply the ideas of Karl Marx whose writings had impressed him so much. Baring remembered his tutor, Mr. Cordell, who had died too young to see this opportunity to create a new and just society. He recalled Mr. Cordell's advice to keep his thoughts secret. He would otherwise by now be a marked man, discharged in disgrace or possibly shot for treason. Baring had witnessed enough execution of mutineers in the Russian auxiliaries to know that the British command in any war can be brutal and Ironside was not a man to be trifled with.

Back in Archangel events were moving fast. It was mid-October and the German army on the Western front was collapsing. The French troops in Archangel were war-weary and homesick; they called a mass meeting and presented a demand to their officers. 'The war is over. Why are we fighting here? France has not declared war on Russia or Bolshevism?'

The British command were furious and insisted that the ringleaders be arrested: ninety men were shackled and put into dungeons; Baring never heard what happened to them but he suspected the worse.

Early in November he was on the Dwina front, organising supplies. There had been an unexpected thaw which enabled boats to get through as far as Topsa and Gorodok. At a bend of the river near Kotlas the British supply boat was suddenly attacked by two Red gunboats. Baring saw the three and six inch guns fire shelling them and as they had no armament to match this the ship was turned in a sharp arc, taking a blast of machine gun fire on the side. Three Russian auxiliaries were killed and the rest of the crew scurried for shelter. Baring crouched at the stern, looking through binoculars at the Red boats, saw an erect figure in a long grey overcoat and a high fur hat standing with his right hand resting on his chest in a Napoleonic gesture. He had a goatee beard and a pince-nez which seemed strangely out of place on this stretch of a remote Russian river. The supply boat was able to get up a full head of steam, and moved out of range of the attacking gunboats. Baring was relieved to escape but intrigued by the sight of the man in the greatcoat, whose bearing and appearance of authority gave him an electric foreboding.

CHAPTER 16

The news of the Armistice with Germany reached Archangel on the afternoon of the 11th November and soon after a message from George V, thanking all ranks in the Army for their fortitude. The troops were paraded to hear the tribute of thanks read by their officers and signals and messengers were sent south so the soldiers defending the outposts against the Bolshevists could also hear it. 'Germany, our most formidable enemy, who planned the war to gain supremacy of the world, full of pride in her armed strength and scorn for the small British Army of those days, has now been forced to acknowledge defeat. I rejoice in this achievement that the British forces now grown from small beginnings to the finest Army in our existence have borne so gallant and distinguished a past.'

The officers went to the Troitsky Hotel for a celebration, the soldiers to their barracks where special supplies of beer, rum and vodka were laid on with as much food as could be spared from the stores. The men had been through the worst of the war in France, had seen most of their friends killed, and now expected it would only be a matter of days before the orders came for their return to England.

In the Troitsky bar the atmosphere was carnival with toasts and impromptu songs of home as the freely-flowing liquor began to have its effect. Baring sat in a corner with Haycraft but only nursed a glass of beer, happy the war was over but far from sure that those who had led the country so disastrously would win the peace. He was also profoundly disturbed by the confirmation from Ironside that afternoon that the war against the Bolsheviks would continue. Haycraft was more cheerful: 'It won't be long before we're out of this,' he said.

'Don't be so sure,' said Baring. 'The King's speech sounded as if it had been written by Churchill. Did you note the reference to those who "fought in more distant fields: around the snows of Russia and Siberia." That's the clue, the British Army never fought the Germans in those places, why put it in the message unless Churchill sees the war against Bolshevism as the continuation of his holy mission. I tell you, Arthur, it is very sinister. The General told the conference he is expecting reinforcements now the German war is over, so as to finish the Red Army off quickly.'

Arthur Haycraft looked perplexed, torn between his anxiety to join in the jollifications, now getting more boisterous, and his wish to understand and commiserate with his friend. 'You musn't be so sensitive Charles,' he said 'It will be your undoing. Don't try to take all the world's problems on your shoulders.'

The noise of the ribaldry in the mess now practically overwhelmed them and Baring shouted at Haycraft, 'Let's get out of here, it's deafening.'

They collected their greatcoats and walked into the cold November night. The sky was completely overcast and black. The only light came from a few lanterns outside the big timber houses on the Prospekt and the occasional Russian pedestrian carrying flares. The sentries at the Troitsky entrance presented arms and both officers returned the salute.

'I bet American officers are celebrating with their men not apart from them' said Baring as they got out of earshot. 'It's a pity we cling to class divisions in our Army.'

'It's a way to maintain discipline I suppose,' said Haycraft.

Charles Baring walked on into the dark night without replying, his thoughts as dark as the forbidding Arctic sky.

'Charles, dear friend. You'll have to snap out of your

moods,' stated Haycraft, as their steps crunched on the frosty road.

'Do you remember in the trenches,' reflected Baring, 'how we used to look over no-man's-land and wonder what the troops on the other side were thinking?'

'Yes,' said Haycraft who hadn't been there but had had the same thoughts in the Dardanelles.

'Well I feel now as though I am in a no-man's-land between us and the Bolsheviks. This time I know what they're thinking and I'm torn in the middle. My mind and my emotion is with them but my traditional loyalty is stuck with the British side. I feel split.'

'Do you think you should put in for some leave?' said Haycraft with concern.

'Leave! On what grounds?' Baring shouted. 'Cowardice, treachery, nervous breakdown. Can you imagine how the General and the medics would interpret that application?'

'But you're clearly too wound-up to carry on. You'll have to do something to protect yourself,' said Haycraft.

'Yes I will,' said Baring, and he shook his friend's hand when they said goodnight. It was an unusual gesture for officers.

Early next day Ironside sent orders for Haycraft to take command of a unit being sent down the Dwina to strengthen the outpost on the River Vaga at a village called Shenkursk. After briefing, he rushed to see Baring before he embarked. He found him at command headquarters.

'I'm going to the front at Shenkursk. They say the Reds are attacking in strength. Ironside is determined to hold our lines there to be in a good position to launch an attack against Kotlas in the spring.'

'But that's 250 miles further on.'

'Ironside believes we can still link up with the Czechs and Kolchak who is advancing towards Kotlas from Omsk, and if we can do that Moscow would be in our grasp.'

Baring looked doubtful. 'I still think we have all totally

underestimated the Red Army. The prisoners we've captured have a high morale and they believe in their war of liberation. We're an enemy of foreign devils to them trying to bring back a Tsarist dictatorship without a Tsar. Its impossible to defeat that spirit.'

'Maybe you're right,' said Haycraft, 'time will tell. Meanwhile I'll be doing my best to save British lives', enough have been lost in this damn foolish war.'

'Save your own life Arthur,' said Baring, 'don't sacrifice it on an altar of capitalism. It's worth more than that.'

At the Troitsky mess that evening Baring sat down to have a solitary meal. Rations were running short and the menu was restricted to bully beef fritters or venison and dumplings. He chose the venison although it was invariably tough the way army cooks prepared it. Many of the officers who had previously enjoyed the afternoon tea dances with the local ladies and the night long drinking parties had left for the front with their platoons. The war of intervention they had all expected to win with the first waving of the Union Jack was proving a harsh battle.

Captain Harvey came in with his left arm in a sling and seeing Baring joined his table.

'What happened to you old chap?' asked Baring.

'Caught it in my elbow. Piece of shrapnel from a Red shell at Tulgas. The blighters are becoming more daring. I've lost over ten of my men.'

'It's not a piece of cake then as you expected?'

'We certainly need some reinforcements to finish this off. They should be sent now the war is over in Europe. Perhaps we'll get some A1 troops to replace the disabled lot we're loaded with. Must admit I was surprised by the ferocity of their attacks and the moujiks are going over to their side.'

'The peasants always know which way the wind is blowing,' said Baring.

'We'll show them a thing or two once Ironside gets to grips with it.'

'Let me cut up your venison,' said Baring, solicitiously, 'you can't manage with one hand.'

Over the next few days the atmosphere in Archangel changed noticeably. It was not only the freezing up of the post which gave the place a beleagured look but the obvious feelings of resentment shown by ordinary Russians. The welcoming smiles of three months before had been replaced by ugly stares which made it clear the British were unwanted guests. Baring sensed that they were acclimatizing themselves to the idea of a Bolshevik victory.

A number of events had made a laughing stock of the occupation forces. Every week there were executions of spies who had been captured in the town. By this time the coffins could not be buried as the ground was frozen solid and they were taken to the harbour where a hole was bored in the ice where the bodies could be dropped. As a working party of Russian auxiliaries was doing this one day two coffins suddenly sprang open and two bodies began racing towards the warehouses zig-zagging in case they were shot at. The officer in charge was so shocked that the two spies got clean away. After this coffins were taken without lids to check that none of the bodies were feigning death.

Another event of a totally different character had also undermined the British occupation. The currency in circulation had been a mixture of Tsarist, Kerensky and Bolshevik notes. It was decided to declare all of it valueless in favour of a new British backed rouble which could be redeemed in London after hostilities at the rate of forty to the pound. The Treasury in London masterminded the operation to convince any doubters of the British determination, as well as to solve an economic problem. The notes when they were supplied caused ructions with the Provisional Government as they had been printed from an old Imperial plate and showed crowns on the heads of the double-headed eagle. Every single note had to be rubber stamped to obliterate the crowns before the notes could be issued but the evidence of British bungling was soon in everyone's hands.

The conscription of young Russians into the auxiliary forces proved a disaster when a group of them mutineered and barricaded themselves in their barracks waving red flags from the windows. Lewis guns were brought up by Russian officers and the barracks shelled. The mutineers eventually surrendered and were sentenced to death, but Ironside commuted their sentences and then exchanged them with the Bolshevists for British prisoners of war. Baring met some of the returning prisoners before they were sent to England and was pleased to hear how well they had been treated by the Bolshevists.

'It was amazing, Sir,' said a nineteen year old corporal from Birmingham. 'We was expecting to be shot. Our officers had told us to expect no mercy from the Reds but they treated us like comrades. They even shared their rations with us and their rations weren't much to write home about.'

'Did you understand what they said?' asked Baring.

'Mostly it was sign language but when we were taken back to Kotlas we met one of their commissars, as I think they call them. Every battalion of the Red Army has this political commissar attached to them. He's the bloke what knows their policy and that.'

'I see,' said Baring. 'What did he say?'

'This chappie knew a lot of English. He'd been at University and seemed to know about England. He said we were all free men and that the Bolshevists were fighting just as much for us as for themselves. He said they wanted to liberate us from the evils of capitalism.'

'What did the men do?'

'They laughed. It seemed a big joke but two men from B company took it seriously and went over to the Bolshies. The rest of us refused and insisted on being treated as proper prisoners of war.'

In the Troitsky mess Baring found Captain Harvey still

nursing his damaged elbow but ever full of gossip. The returned prisoners-of-war were being kept isolated and were being sent in a sleigh convoy to Murmansk next day on the way back to England.

'Best thing that could happen,' he pronounced, 'those men have to be got out of here in double quick time. They're a bacillus designed by Bolsheviks to infect our troops and destroy their morale. If we'd let them loose in our ranks can you imagine what the effect would have been? Most of our chaps are fed up with being here now the German war is over and if they thought the Bolshies were nice people they'd refuse to fight.'

'They're lucky to be going home,' said Baring. It was a neutral enough comment.

Baring's misgivings were strenghtened by a conference called by General Ironside for senior officers. The meeting took place in the Commander-in-Chief's headquarters in the old Town Hall on Troitsy Prospekt. The council chamber, with its semi-circle of leather chairs, where once the local councillors sat in peaceful days, was crowded with Brigadiers, Colonels and Majors from the various British units plus a sprinkling of more junior officers who were there for specific reasons. The hubbub of noise subsided suddenly as General Ironside, a massive giant of a man swept in with three other generals.

'Sit down please, gentlemen,' he said firmly and the company settled in their seats resting their batons, notepads or elbows on the benches in front of them. A large framed photograph of George V looked down on the gathering from the wall behind the General's table. Baring noticed it was slightly smaller than the previous frame as the dirt marks clearly showed, which had very likely been that of Tsar Nicholas whose bearded appearance was almost identical to that of his cousin, the British king. No doubt many of the Russian workers would have thought the dead Tsar's likeness was still hanging on the wall.

General Ironside wasted no time in coming to the reason for the conference.

'We face now a difficult winter and three enemies in the Bolsheviks, the terrible cold and the weaknesses of our own morale.' From his towering six foot four inches he looked at the officers stirring a little uncomfortably in their seats and added, 'I regard the last as our biggest enemy by far. We can deal with the Bolsheviks and we can cope with the cold but the weakening of the morale is an insiduous business. It strikes deep and destroys a man's will to fight. Without will man is a useless fighting animal.' Baring glanced at the normally taciturn Colonels falling under Ironside's magnetic spell. The General had a rare, dominating personality and without raising his voice he managed to increase the emphasis of his remarks. 'The tide of the war in France turned at Mons against superior German odds because we had the will to win and they did not have the will.'

The officers had nearly all seen service in France and all knew that morale in those trenches, however bad the conditions, had been immeasurably better than today. 'There seems to be among the troops a very indistinct idea of what we are fighting for here in North Russia. This can be explained in a few words. We are up against Bolshevism which means anarchy pure and simple. Look at Russia at the present moment. The power is in the hands of a few men, mostly Jews, who have succeeded in bringing the country to such a state that order is non-existent. Bolshevism has taken over the uneducated masses to such an extent that Russia is disintegrated and helpless and therefore we have come here to help her get rid of the disease that is eating her up. We're not here to conquer Russia but we want to help her and see her a great power again. When order is restored we shall clear out, and only when we have attained our object and that is the restoration of Russia.'

Baring could not help thinking to himself that the anarchy of which Ironside complained was being made worse by the

British intervention. The Bolsheviks in Moscow and Petrograd could hardly enforce order in a vast country when three armies were advancing on them from the North, East and South. He had noted the gratuitous remark about Jews. Lenin was not a Jew and how could Ironside complain about Trotsky and other non-practising Jews, when a non-practising Jew had so recently been one of Britain's greatest Prime Ministers. He remembered the anti-semitism prevalent at Eton.

In the third week of November the weather deteriorated rapidly. For several days a storm raged which reduced visibility to a few feet and covered the town in a thick white blanket. Baring was grateful for the extra warm clothing which was issued and especially for the top boots which were two sizes bigger than his normal size so that he could wear thick felt soles and two pairs of thick woollen socks. A soldier in the Murmansk sector who had left his hut during the night to visit the latrine had foolishly failed to put on his boots. Frostbite affected a foot so badly that it had to be amputated but the discoloration continued to climb up his limb. Amputation followed amputation as the doctors vainly fought to save the man's life. Cold was indeed the second enemy in North Russia.

As it was no longer possible to ride ponies to the supply stations that his unit had set up, a sleigh was organised by the guide. There was nothing picturesque about it. The crude wooden structure was battered with wear and smelt of the last loads of passengers it had been carrying. The bottom of the sleigh was covered with coarse senna grass for warmth and Baring was shown how to lie snug full length with rugs and skins covering him from the arctic cold. In these conditions Baring found he could travel as far as three hundred miles in ten days and nights. Sometimes the sleighs were pulled by ponies but usually by reindeer hired out by Lapps in exchange for rum. Under the Lapp's control the reindeer were remarkably docile animals who responded to the commands by pulling on a single rope of hide attached to their antlers. At stopping points they were untethered and allowed to wander freely to look for moss. They never seemed to have any wish to escape their bondage and Baring marvelled at the almost psychic hold which the Lapps held over them. Whole herds were kept by the Lapps who used the venison as food, the hides as coats and the horns as knife handles.

In addition to the ponies and the reindeer the transport needs of the Army were supplemented by Siwash dogs brought in from Canada. These fierce dangerous animals could only be controlled by their Canadian trapper handlers and everyone else gave them a wide berth.

Baring's survey of the supply line took him to Ust Padenga a village on the River Vaga and as far as the intervention army had penetrated. The Americans were in position at this section of the front and were having a hard time holding the Red Army which regularly attacked the blockhouses which they had built. Baring found Captain Odgaard in a very depressed mood. His men's morale was at its lowest ebb. The war with Germany had been over for a fortnight and they could not understand why they had to fight on in Russia. The gentle farms of Wisconsin were better places to spend winter than the harsh forests of a snow covered country where everybody and everything was hostile.

'My troops get more alarmed about what's happening to them,' said Odgaard, 'every time they have mail from home. No one in America seems even to know we're here. In the papers all the praise is being poured on the victorious Pershing boys and we're forgotten completely.'

'It's as bad for the British troops,' said Baring.

'At least you can fly your Union Jack but we're forbidden to show the Old Glory at any time.'

Baring had no answer to this complaint about which the other nationalities under the overall British command had also complained.

'And the Red propaganda is beginning to get through to the minds of my men. They've even had an orator haranguing our lines with a megaphone. Can you believe that and have you seen the latest they've distributed on our side? They must have collaborators to bring these through.' He brought out an English language paper called *The Call* and handed it to his visitor. It was published in Moscow and was crudely but clearly printed like a village newsheet. Baring read the lurid prose with fascination. 'Do you realise that the principal reason the British American financiers have sent you to fight us is because we were sensible enough and courageous enough to repudiate the war debts of the bloody corrupt old Tsar?'

He glanced at Odgaard. 'Powerful stuff,' he said.

'Read on,' said Odgaard, 'it gets worse. I'll get you a hot rum toddy. You'll need it after you've read that vitriolic garbage.' He left Baring, now reading avidly.

'You soldiers are fighting on the side of the employers against us, the working people of Russia. All this talk about intervention to save Russia amounts to this that the capitalists of your countries are trying to take back from us what we won from their fellow capitalists in Russia. Can't you realize that this is the same war that you have been carrying on in England and America against the master class? You hold the rifles, you work the guns to shoot us with and you are playing the contemptible part of the scab. Comrade don't do it.' Baring read on. 'This is the beginning of a great world revolution which knows no national limitation. It will set the producers free. Join the Soviet Party. We are fighting your fight against the unprincipled capitalist class. Comrades you are playing the contemptible part of scab. For shame comrades! Kill your officers, then shoulder your rifles and come over to our lines which are your own.'

Odgaard came back with the toddy in a huge mug. Baring took it gratefully, despite the wood stove in the middle of the cabin the place was still bitterly cold and his body felt it. The months of tension, travelling and danger had worn down his resilience and the deep doubts he held about the war against the Bolsheviks seemed to sap the efforts he made to bring the body back to its former strength.

'That'll do you good,' said Odgaard. 'I'm beginning to prefer it to schnapps. What do you make of that Bolshevik claptrap?'

'It's in surprisingly good English,' said Baring.

'I'm ashamed,' said Odgaard, 'for it sounds as if it is written by an American communist. The jargon could easily be that of a militant garment worker in New york. We expelled a lot of leftists from the States and I suppose some of them have gone to Moscow.'

'Are there a lot of foreigners in Moscow then?' asked Baring.

'I believe so,' said Odgaard, 'veritable hothouse of them; exciting each other in agitation.'

CHAPTER 17

Baring had a fitful night on the floor of the American's cabin. Normally the bed of hides and skins would have been comfortable enough and the total exhaustion after a day's travelling enough to knock him out. The rum, too, was usually a powerful sedative and guaranteed to ensure a long lasting sleep. The noise of sporadic firing and the occasional thump of a Mills bomb in the distance was no problem to a graduate of the Western trenches.

Baring was disturbed more by his inner thoughts than by external distractions. The pressures on his conscience had been growing ever since the Ironside speech. He could not accept the British aims in Russia and his belief in socialism had been increased by his association with those who were trying to destroy the only socialist experiment to emerge from the horrors of a terrible war. He was serving in a military machine crushing common people who were trying to assert their human rights. The propaganda of the Bolsheviks might be crude and couched in the language of a trade union meeting but essentially it was true. The war interests of the allies were more concerned with protecting investments and trade than establishing a decent order of society.

By morning he had made up his mind. He could no longer ride two horses that were pulling his body and spirit apart. As a man of integrity he could no longer accept the idiocy of Ironside and the militarists and politicians in London or Washington, already responsible for so many deaths who now wanted more blood on their hands. First he had to see his friend Arthur Haycraft, the one man in a thousand miles who might understand his motivation. In case he did not survive there had to be one confidant who, one day, might be able to reveal his secret.

He said goodbye to Captain Ordgaard in a dazed way and set his sleigh north down the Vaga towards Shenkursk. As he left, the American troops were firing at a group of Red Army troops who had suddenly appeared on skis with white smocks to camouflage them against the snow. Baring did not know that Odgaard himself would soon be killed as the Bolshevik attacks intensified.

The day was dark, damp and bitterly cold; the mists hung over the firs cutting off all sounds. All Baring could hear was the padding of the reindeer on the frozen track and the swish of the sleigh on the snow as it swerved over the bumps of the occasional buried tree trunks. Apart from a guide and a Lapp driver he was cut off from all humanity. He felt he was in a tunnel travelling from the uncertainty and duplicity of a previous life towards an opening where his spirit could be at one with himself. As the sleigh surged forward he wrestled with the problem of how to get over to the other side. He had to do it with the greatest caution. His purpose would be entirely undermined if anyone suspected what he had done. Only Haycraft could know.

At Shenkursk he reported to the Colonel at the British command post and made some routine dispositions about supplies. He had to appear as normal as possible. When his duties were completed he went to find Haycraft who was with a forward unit on the outskirts of the town. He found him in a hastily built blockhouse looking out onto a vast clearing. They embraced with more fervour on Baring's part than usual.

'You look whacked out,' said Haycraft.

'I haven't slept well for days,' said Baring, 'and last night hardly a wink. I was up with the Americans at Ust Padenga.'

'How are they doing?' asked Haycraft.

'They're badly outnumbered and the Red Army will

overrun them soon. It's a hopeless battle and the Americans have no heart in it.'

'If they collapse we won't be able to hold Shenkursk for long,' said Haycraft. 'We'll have to withdraw to Kitsa. We're short of men here too. The locals have been conscripted but their loyalty is questionable. I would guess a quarter of the Russians in Shenkursk have defected to the Bolsheviks and most of the rest would like to do so but don't want to leave their families.'

Baring looked intensely at his friend and wondered how he could tell him. There was no other way than the plain unvarnished truth.

'I'm going over to the other side too,' he announced firmly.

'You are what?' said Haycraft in horror.

'I'm joining the Bolsheviks,' said Baring, 'I can no longer support this criminal war against a people whose ideals I support. It's as simple as that.'

'What about your loyalty to your country?' Haycraft asked in disbelief. He could hardly believe that a King's officer could calmly announce his traitorous intentions.

'My loyalty is to the people,' said Baring. 'I would go mad if I did not follow my conscience. It's been telling me for weeks what I should do, but it's only now I have summoned up the courage to do it. Before I go I wanted you — as my only friend — to know the truth. I may be killed of course. I recognise that. It's a risk I have to take. If I am killed you have my permission to tell my parents what I did and why I did it, that is if you get back yourself,' he added sombrely.

'You're crazy to take such a risk,' said Haycraft, 'why don't you apply for some leave so you can recover yourself? The strain of these last few years have taken a big toll. You are not your normal self.'

'I'm not crazy Arthur — not by a long chalk. What I'm doing is not on a sudden impulse. I believe in it passionately and if I don't go through with it I'll never have any respect for myself again.'

'If the British knew what you intended you would be court martialled in the field and shot,' said Haycraft, desperate to warn his friend off his mad venture, 'how would your parents feel about that? Their own son shot as a traitor!'

Baring looked at the Capain's earnest face, full of genuine caring and anguish. As an officer it was his duty to report Baring's intention to defect, but as a friend he wanted to shelter him.

'I might be a traitor to a militaristic, capitalistic clique,' said Baring in a burst of Bolshevik-sounding rhetoric, 'but I am loyal to human needs and human freedom. They have no frontiers and I see no reason why stupid nationalism should curb them any longer.'

Haycraft was in despair. He knew he would keep the secret and pray that his friend would survive this breakdown and re-emerge a sane man somewhere, sometime.

Early next morning Baring went to the supply post to establish an alibi for his next move. The next few hours would be critical and it was vital that no one should suspect a defection. He told the guide and the interpreter that they should make a reconnaissance to Shishova to establish the supply line to that part of the front to the west of Shenkursk and he informed the duty officer that he intended to go to Sergievskaya to check out the situation there. It was a bit unusual to make a journey alone but it was accepted without question that the shortage of personnel sometimes made it necessary. Sergievskaya was only ten miles away and the track was well defined. He wrapped himself in his warmest clothes and took a sleigh with the healthiest-looking pony and headed towards the East. Within minutes the village petered out as he passed the last farm buildings and clearings and entered the forest. Fortunately it was not too dense at this point and he could see the direction the track was taking. He had a map supplied by the War Office, but as this was based on a Tsarist government survey carried out in 1889 it was not particularly accurate. It did, however, show a track leading south off the main route about seven miles out of Shenkursk. He had to find this track for he might otherwise inadvertently reach the British positions in Sergievskaya.

As the pony plodded on Baring watched the watery sun breaking through the trees from the south indicating the direction he needed to take. He looked at his compass, compensated for magnetic north and compared it with the sun's position. It was good to have a cross-check: compasses had been known to go haywire in these northern latitudes.

At about the six miles point, which he calculated by estimating the pony's speed against his watch, he looked more carefully at the terrain on his right. Everything was covered by snow and it would be the easiest thing in the world to pass a little-used track; there were no signposts on these roads. People who came this remote way had to know exactly where they were going. After a bend he suddenly saw a small cutting through the trees on his right hand side. It was not wide enough for a clearing or a firebreak and it led to no obvious habitation. This was the track he was seeking. It was insignificant, covered in snow and he might easily have missed it completely.

He drove the sleigh another two hundred yards on the main track and then doubled back using the same sleigh path as neatly as possible. At the small track he turned south, went about a hundred yards and then tethered the pony to a fir. He trudged back to the main track and retracing his steps did his best with a shovel to cover the sleigh marks with fresh snow. As he looked back on his handiwork it did not look too good. It would be obvious to an experienced eye that someone had come this way as the snow was disturbed but he could only shrug his shoulders and hope for an early snowstorm which would soon cover everything again.

After another hour's journey he felt relieved he had chosen the right track for it continued to run south and then south east. The old map was not so bad after all. By this route he should avoid the British position and could only hope he did not run into an allied patrol. It was unlikely as there were no plans to strenghten this section of the front.

By midday he thought the pony deserved a rest and some fodder. He stopped in a clearing, lit a fire, melted some snow for the pony and heated some soup, a kind of borscht with bits of venison for himself. It was frozen solid and took a long time to defrost but was extremely nourishing and warming. The weather had turned for the worst. The sky was now completely overcast and snow was falling gently and silently. It was like being in a gigantic sound chamber because falling globules absorbed any sound. Baring knew that if he shouted even the echo would be muffled to nothing.

He took a swig of rum and started to cut off his pips and the other insignia on his uniform, throwing them deep into the firs where they sank into the anonymity of the forest. It would be foolhardy to travel into Bolshevik country dressed as an officer. A posse of Red scouts might take it into their heads to execute him on the spot as a class enemy. As an ordinary soldier he stood a much better chance of being accepted. He kept his documents. He would need those later to prove he was not a spy.

He started the sleigh and felt the pony pull gratefully, glad to be on the move again. There was no joy for man or beast hanging about in a North Russian forest in late November. The snow was falling steadily now, covering his fur hat and his ear caps and freezing that part of his cheeks, mouth and eyes still exposed. He wrapped a scarf around his mouth and nostrils. The snow was quickly melted by his breath and then froze into a thick band of ice on the wool like a carapace. He was grateful he was not in a blizzard as that would destroy visibility completely and make it impossible to go forward or back. Then he realised there was no going back with his insignia missing. He had shot the last bolt or nailed the last nail. There was indeed no going back. In physical and in spiritual terms he had crossed the great divide between slavish adherence and freedom of conscience.

The track came to a junction that did not seem to be marked on the map. The route to the left probably led to Sergievskaya and he could not take that. The other way would take him back to Ust Padenga and the American outpost. He chose the right path and hoped he would find another track leading towards the South. There was now no way of knowing where the sun was and he had to rely on his compass which might well be misleading. He took another swig of rum and set off again hoping he had chosen correctly. In this terrain it was perfectly easy for an inexperienced traveller to complete a full circle whilst convinced he was going in a straight line.

After another hour he found another southerly track and took it gratefully. There was still no sign of any habitation. Apart from the track itself there was no evidence that another human being had ever been in these parts. The ominous silence and isolation began to play on Baring's mind. There appeared to be a path between the firs and skirting the frozen lakes but as the thick blanket of snow obscured everything he could not be sure. As he looked back, the marks the sleigh had made were also covered and there was no guarantee he could retrace the track. It was becoming desperate; the light was failing fast as the sky became heavier with snow and the night began closing in on the short day. Baring took another rum tot to give himself courage as well as warmth and calculated the risks. The prospects were frightening. In an emergency he could attempt to build an igloo or even a primitive wooden shelter but no one could survive long in these conditions. In the summer he had been happy to sleep for nights under the firs but those times seemed an age away. He felt he had no alternative but to press on as far as the pony could take him in the hope of reaching shelter.

The weather worsened. The snow was blowing into his face and covering his eyes every few moments as he vainly tried to wipe it away. He would have given a fortune for a reliable Lapp who could see him calmly and safely through this blizzard. The wind was now so strong it was breaking lumps of snow off the firs. One of these fell on the sleigh drenching it like a miniature avalanche. He tried to clear the load but it was hopeless. The loyal pony was faltering too. Baring broke off the long icicles hanging from its nose and massaged the animal's nostrils as he had seen the moujiks do. It seemed grateful, looking at its benefactor with baleful eyes, and it accepted more fodder which Baring dug out from the bottom of the sleigh under the mountain of snow. The stamina of the beast was impressive and gave the traveller hope that he could carry on.

After another hour into the dark forbidding night with the weather showing no signs of abating the pony finally showed his panic by screaming like a frightened child. Baring had heard the anguished cry before, but this time it was poignant beyond belief. The creature knew his life was threatened by the elements and that the only human within miles was incapable of helping. Baring knew he could go on no longer. Somehow they had to shelter until the blizzard blew itself out. He persuaded the pony to bed down under a large fir on some senna grass which he extracted from the sleigh. He covered the animal with hides and it cowered down exhausted. Before long it would be covered with snow. Baring then turned to his own problem. He now wished he had spent more time listening to Sir Ernest Shackleton who had visited the Archangel command to advise on arctic conditions. What Shackleton had experienced in the Antarctic was immeasurably worse than these conditions and this recollection was a little encouraging. He decided to emulate the Lapps and build a tepee. Fortunately the biting wind had subsided; he could rig up some sticks from the sleigh into a tent pole and lash the longest hide he could find to the top. Then he threw other hides and skins around it forming a primitive structure, three feet high, about which he worked quickly piling mounds of snow to hold it firm. By a miracle it held and he dragged his knapsack into the tent and sank exhausted into the tiny space. He had to curl his body up like a foetus because his legs would stretch outside the tepee where they would freeze. At all costs he had to avoid frostbite which meant certain death.

He tried to move his toes inside the double layer of socks and the outsize boots to check they were still intact and gratefully found they were, then he rubbed his hands vigorously in their leather gloves to bring circulation to the fingers. They responded with a warm glow. In the tiny space available he could not attempt to light a fire as the Lapps did in their tepees so there was no question of having any food, but he wrapped his body around the flat loaf of black bread in the hope it would thaw sufficiently to eat in the morning, if he ever saw the morning. The rum was his only solace and he drank it greedily leaning on one arm to balance himself, feeling the burning spirit coursing through his blood and listening to the raging storm outside. Of such experiences the greatest poetry is written, he thought, as he slipped down on his side into a tight crouch with his knees touching his chest and his head touching his knees. He slept, exhausted and tipsy, and dreamt he was in the womb of Mother Russia.

When he awoke at dawn he was so stiff and cramped he could hardly uncurl. The storm had obviously stopped as all around him there was heavy, deathly and oppressive silence. When he tried to pull open the gap in the hides to look outside the snow came falling in. Clearly it had drifted almost to the top of the tepee. By opening the top he was able to clamber out, relieved that he had had the good sense to employ some ingenuity in building a structure which had saved him from being suffocated in his deep sleep by the snow. His first thought was for the pony. He found the shovel and then used it to clear a path to the place where he had left the animal. It was completely covered and he dug feverishly to release it. When he found the skins he quickly flung them aside, fearing the worst. The sight of the dead, frozen pony shook him with a spasm of horror at the nearness of death. The wicked frost could easily have killed him too. It had been loyal and trusting and did not deserve to die. Baring covered the corpse with the hides which were no use to him now; neither was the sleigh which lay buried somewhere in the snow.

Finding his knapsack he made a fire and broke off a lump of frozen soup to heat up some borscht. He would need all the nourishment he could get. The bread had thawed and he munched it slowly. The chances of survival were very dim as the nearest habitation was miles away and the tracks so deep in snow that walking would be difficult if not impossible. In any case he had no certainty of the direction he should take.

Staying put, he decided, would be the silliest thing to do, and going back almost as bad, as the main track to Sergievskaya was so far that it would take two days of walking to reach it. His only hope was to walk forward towards the South where there might be a respite from the awful and threatening isolation. Something had to be done about his boots which buried themselves in the soft snow and impeded progress. By digging strenuously he found the sleigh and broke off some of the pinewood slats which made up its sides. Using the rein rope he tied them together to form crude snow shoes about eighteen inches in diameter. These he tied to his leather boots which required an awkward balancing trick as he could not dare to take them off which would have given his dry feet a soaking in the snow. At last he stood up feeling as ungainly as a giant on stilts but the trick had worked and he found he could walk fairly easily on top of the snow rather than trudging through it several feet deep.

There was no time to lose; he gathered up his knapsack, the rum and what food he could carry and set off towards the South, walking gingerly on the mushy snow.

CHAPTER 18

Commissar Naumov looked at the pitiful figure lying on the floor of the hut. 'How long has he been here?' he demanded gutterally.

'Two days Comrade,' answered a Red Army soldier who wore no rank.

'He still looks half dead,' said the Commissar, 'any idea where came from?'

'No, he hasn't talked yet, just moanings in his feverish sleep but his documents show he is a British officer.'

'And you confirm he was on his own?'

'Yes Comrade. There was no sign of enemy activity within eighty versts of the place he was found.'

'Where was that?'

About a hundred and fifty versts north of here. He was lying unconscious. One of our patrols picked him up. They checked his track back into the forest for six versts but they found no signs of any other soldiers nor any means of transport and concluded he must have walked at least two hundred versts on the snow.'

'That's incredible in those conditions and without proper equipment. I would say its impossible. Perhaps he was dropped by parachute from one of their planes to infiltrate our lines. Clearly he must be a spy.'

'Yes Comrade,' the Red Army man said. He had no reason to argue with the political Commissar whose word in the battalion was law and even superceded that of the Commander. Trotsky had decreed that all operations of the people's army had to be countersigned by the local representatives of the Bolshevik party so as to maintain the political purity of the military campaign.

'Wake him up,' said Naumov peremptorily, 'for all we know he is feigning sickness and laughing at us.'

'His temperature and fever were genuine enough,' said the soldier.

'They carry tablets to induce that sort of thing,' said the Commissar. 'What you see is what they want you to see. The imperialists are cunning people. Wake him I say!'

The soldier lifted the sleeping man's head on to a makeshift pillow and threw some water on to his face. It dribbled through the stubble on his chin.

'Ah, he's coming round now,' said the Commissar, 'lift him up further.' As Baring's eyes slowly opened he had a dreamy vision of four rough looking men standing by his bed. They were not dressed in any recognisable uniforms but in a motley selection of German, Tsarist, French, Serbian and British cast-offs, culled over the years from the armies they had fought. Their only common feature was the red hammer and sickle insignia which the men wore on their lapels. Standing behind them was an altogether more impressive figure. He was wearing a smart long grey overcoat, which could have been tailor made. Its padded shoulders gave him a commanding presence and an Astrakhan hat emphasised his height.

Baring felt one of the soldiers put a cup to his lips and he sipped cautiously. It was a strong spirit of some description and it went straight to his brain jerking him into a further consciousness.

The tall man was speaking firmly. 'I believe you Englishman so I will talk you in English. I study your language at University before war. It is good, yes. Understand you?'

'Yes,' said Baring weakly, 'I understand.'

'You must explain me,' the interrogator went on, 'how many drop from plane and explain me where they are.'

'No men dropped from any plane,' said Baring.

'You liar,' said the tall man. 'You cannot get so many versts behind our lines without plane. You not walk that far.'

I had a sleigh. The pony died,' said Baring, 'and then I walked.'

'My scouts found no sleigh. You lie,' said the tall man.

'I'm not lying,' pleaded Baring, 'the sleigh is buried under the snow. I had to abandon it and then walk.'

'Abandon,' said the tall man, 'that means destroy?'

'No, no,' said Baring 'it means leave behind because it's no more use. I had to hack off the sides to make pads to walk on the snow. Look at my boots you'll see.'

'Bring the boots,' ordered the tall man.

The improvised snow pads were still tied to the boots and the evidence seemed to impress the interrogator. 'You come spy sleigh,' he said.

'No, not, *niet*,' said Baring emphasising the last word as he had heard Russians do. '*Niet.* I am no spy, *niet* spy, *niet* spy. I am *Tovarish.* I am with you.' And to settle it he groped into his greatcoat pocket and pulled out a tattered copy of *The Call.* 'Look, you ask the British soldiers to stop fighting and to join you. I am doing that.'

The tall man pulled up the propaganda newspaper and glanced at it with a curious expression as if trying to fathom a new and unexpected dimension.

'But you officer,' he said speaking slowly for effect, 'officer for King and country. King like Tsar. You swear oath for him.'

'I have renounced my King,' said Baring. 'I am communist. I believe in freedom for all peoples,' and as he spoke his voice gained in strength.

'You Bolshevik?'

'I am Communist.'

'Are you support Kerensky or Lenin?'

'Lenin,' said Baring relieved that his essential message was getting through and the frightening prospects of summary execution for spying were receding fast. 'I support Lenin. I oppose the imperialists.'

'*Tovarish,* welcome,' said the tall man calling for vodka for the six comrades to toast the revolution and the solidarity of the working class.

The tension over, Baring found he was ravenously hungry and he ate the stew of potatoes, turnips and other vegetables quickly, using a wooden ladle as the moujiks do. The tall man had removed his hat and sat by the bed. Baring could see he was only a young man in his early twenties. His hair was very short as if his head had been recently shaved. 'I from Petrograd,' he said, 'all workers Petrograd for Lenin. Great leader. We win with Vladimir Ilyich. Now all Russians follow him. Petrograd today, Russia tomorrow and then all Europe go Communist. Yes *Tovarish.*'

'I hope so,' said Baring. 'Communism will stop all wars between nations.'

'You fight war Germany?'

'Yes, in France,' said Baring with feeling, 'there were many deaths of young men. Wasted lives. They should not have died.'

'I no fight,' said the tall man, 'you say refuse, yes? I refuse to fight for Tsar and Okhrana put me in prison. I nearly died there. My comrades release me early last year. When Bolsheviks took power I join Army as Commissar. I Commissar Naumov,' he said proudly, 'Commissar Sergei Naumov.'

'My name is Baring, Charles Baring.'

'Charles Baring,' said Naumov relishing the difficulty of pronouncing the name. 'Commissar Charles Baring,' he repeated. 'You become English Commissar, yes. Have revolution in London, yes?'

'I hope so,' said Baring refreshed by the warming food and relaxed now the strain had passed. 'Where are we?'

'Kotlas,' said the Commissar, 'this Red Army area headquarters. From here we advance Archangel and push

White British into White Sea. Our Commissar for War here three weeks ago tell us Red Army is winning war on three fronts. Against Tsarist Admiral Kolchak in Siberia, against that Tsarist General Deniken in Crimea and against that British General Ironside. Trotsky say we win against all enemies.'

'Trotsky was here?' said Baring, recalling the impressive figure on the Dwina gunboat.

'Trotsky here, Trotsky there, Trotsky go everywhere,' said Naumov proudly, 'he is great leader like Lenin. Special train go everywhere.'

As Baring's strength returned he was able to venture out onto the streets of the small town. There was no attempt to restrict his movements except that usually one of Naumov's assistants accompanied him. 'To protect you against trouble,' the Commissar had said.

The headquarters were in an old Tsarist school for the children of the Kotlas merchants — it had been an important trading centre — and there were still books in the cupboards including some in English which Baring borrowed gleefully. One useful find was an English phrase book from which he tried to improve his knowledge of Russian although the difficult Cyrillic script nearly defeated him. He was already able to master a few words and greeted the soldiers with a cheery '*dobra outré*' in the mornings and '*horosho*' as acknowledgement when they asked him to do something. He was greeted as *Tovarish* and shown great friendliness. It was clear Commissar Naumov had decided he was *horosho* and the word had been spread around the headquarters. The pair of Borzoi, which had been adopted as the battalion's mascots, became friendly after some initial hostility and Naumov joked, 'If Borzoi Bolsheviks like you, your stink is *horosho.* They say Mensheviks smell different because bourgeois wash underwear.'

The food was rough but adequate and was shared equally in an old staff room where a wood burning stove kept the atmosphere gloriously hot. At night a balalaika was brought out to accompany soldiers who took turns singing sad songs, but gradually the mood became more boisterous as tots of vodka began to have their affect. At the end of the night they stood arm in arm in a semicircle around the room and sang the *Internationale*.

The streets and squares of Kotlas were filling up with more troops which had been brought up from the south. As an army they were the strangest mixture of types imaginable — squat, dark and swarthy moujiks from the countryside, workers from the towns and a variety of Germans, Poles and Czechs who had opted for the Bolshevik camp. Naumov confirmed that the big offensive against Ironside would soon be launched, Trotsky had proclaimed the importance of a clear victory in the north to discourage the Americans from supporting the British in the war.

On the third day after his interrogation Commissar Naumov came to Baring in some excitement. 'My telegrams to Moscow about you. The Party has now sent reply.' Waving a piece of paper '*dobra*,' he said '*dobra* good news we go Petrograd. Party want you there.'

Next morning they set off in a troika on the long journey. By changing horses en route they made good progress to Veliki Ustyug and Totma and arrived in Vologda at the end of the next day. Thanks to Naumov's authority as political Commissar they were able to get seats on a military train going to the former capital.

After their arrival, and safely installed in the Hotel Astoria, Sergei Naumov explained to his new comrade that the Party was planning new initiatives in an attempt to win the propaganda war against intervention. It was essential to win the minds of the intellectuals in the west and the hearts of the working class. With such powerful allies in France, Britain and America, it would be impossible for the allies to support the Whites and the Tsarsists. In Petrograd, meetings with foreign visitors were being organised to explain the Bolshevik viewpoint that they were friends with all people and only opposed to imperialism and reactionary governments.

That afternoon they went to see Karl Radek who had come from Moscow to organise such a meeting. As they walked along the Nevsky Prospekt Baring marvelled at the calmness of the scene. People were going about their daily tasks and there was nothing of the ferment he had half-expected to see; a few troops were on the streets and guarding important buildings but it was obvious they had the support of the people. There was no terrorizing by armed revolutionaries as the revolution belonged to the ordinary people. They were already suffering privation for they looked pinched, hungry and cold. There were very few vehicles to be seen. The carts were mostly being pushed by old men. It struck him that there were no dogs and he wondered if they had been eaten as the food shortage had worsened.

When they reached the vast square in front of the Winter Palace Naumov said proudly, 'I was here that day. It was glorious. My friends got me from prison. A hundred of us escaped. All politicals were being starved to death for what we believed in. The revolution saved my life.' As they went into the big building facing the Winter Palace the Commissar flourished a pass and the sentries, who were in smarter uniforms than any Baring had yet seen, came to attention smartly. Naumov acknowledged them with a nod and marched down a bleak corridor.

Radek's office was reached up a flight of stairs on which a dozen bedraggled men were sitting. 'Waiting for meetings,' Naumov said, 'always meetings. Petrograd is same as I remember.'

'Who are these people?' Baring asked.

'Workers' representatives. They come from local Soviets to ask for food. After revolution workers expect food but for months things have got worse. The food is in the country but the peasants will not part with it unless they get goods in exchange. They won't take roubles. Roubles buy nothing.'

'Are people starving?'

'Yes. We can only save them if we break the Kulaks. Once this war is over we shall do that. With bread the revolution will succeed.'

They were shown into Radek's office. It was tiny and littered with papers. Radek stood to greet Baring with a firm handshake. He was a slightly built man with chiselled features, a huge head, protruding ears and a large mouth with yellow, tobacco-stained teeth. He was wearing a dark serge uniform buttoned up to the collar, a leather holster with a revolver and leather boots. He peered at Baring through small round metal-rimmed spectacles as if to sum him up and motioned him to sit on a rickety chair.

'*Parlez Francais?*' he asked.

'*Un petit peu,*' said Baring.

Radek turned to Naumov and said in Russian, 'Pity I was hoping to get some practice.' He then called for an interpreter who arrived after a few minutes. At Radek's invitation they lit up cigarettes. They had cardboard stems which were like long holders. The ritual of lighting them helped to break the atmosphere which at first seemed rather tense.

The interpreter was a woman of about thirty with long light brown hair tied in a bun and a fine, nobly, attractive face which was completely without make up.

She sat on Radek's right as he outlined the situation and translated every few sentences in clear precise English. Now and then she put her hand on Radek's arm to restrain him so she could keep up with the flow.

Radek explained that the Party was pleased to welcome any soldiers from the capitalist countries who wanted to serve the Bolshevik cause but as it was unusual if not unique for an officer to come across he had to be absolutely certain the officer was genuine. He would therefore produce a dossier in which Baring's life history would be recorded and which would explain why a Captain in King George's army could sacrifice his privileges and desert his class in favour of the proletariat. Radek said, 'We can understand an ordinary British soldier joining us for our revolution is as much his revolution against his rulers. Many have come over already. They are free to walk our streets as any Soviet citizen. You are the first officer to volunteer to come over and naturally we want to know why.'

Baring wanted to speak but Radek restrained him. 'Wait, I want to hear you speak later and Comrade Cherepova will translate every word faithfully. She will also keep a written account so it can go to Moscow. They are very interested in you there.' Radek went on to describe the strategy of the Bolsheviks towards the foreign world. All the workers parties from whatever country, even those who were engaged in the war of intervention, were being invited to send representatives to meetings. 'We have one next week, on December 19th, here in Petrograd. It is our plan to have you at that meeting where you can speak about your conversion to communism and convince those people that we don't want to fight their armies. We want to be their friends. I believe that the fact we can accept you — a Captain with a Military Cross — as our comrade will prove to all those foreign comrades that we mean what we say. Do I make myself clear?' he stretched out his arms towards Baring inviting him to respond.

'Yes,' said Baring, 'I understand and I will do what you ask. I believe that only through a workers revolution in England can the injustices of the exploitive system be removed. It is true I come from what is regarded as our upper class but that has not prevented me from feeling as passionately about socialism as any worker. I've read Karl Marx and I know that only his interpretation of history can make sense of the economic system. At present the common people are destroyed by a system that crushes them in the interests of the ruling class.'

They worked long into the night preparing a file on Baring's background, with meticulous details about his life at Eton and his family connections being recorded. Radek appeared to be fascinated by his story and especially by the influence of William Morris and H.G. Wells on the young officer. He said he would invite Wells to visit Moscow. 'The socialist intellectuals must see our struggle at first hand. We fight our battles with ideals as much as guns and need allies to help spread them,' he explained.

Radek explained his own conversion to Marxism as a schoolboy in his native Poland and told how he was expelled from school for subversive activities at the age of sixteen. 'My story might have been different if they had let us students think, but after that experience I became a militant. At the Krakow University I studied law but spent most of my time organising the workers. Then I met a man who inspired me with revolutionary fervour. You must meet him when you go to Moscow,' he added enthusiastically. 'He's the head of our Extraordinary Commission. Yes, Felix Edmundovich Dzerzhinsky has one of the key jobs in making our revolution succeed.'

Radek described how early in the war he went to Switzerland to escape persecution and met Lenin. 'I must tell you about the Zimmerwald Conference,' he laughed 'just to convince you of our small beginnings. Our left group had no resources but we decided to issue a pamphlet. Vladimir Ilyich contributed twenty francs, a German comrade another twenty francs and I borrowed ten francs on behalf of the Polish comrades. The future Communist International therefore had fifty francs at its disposal to conquer the world. But we needed another forty-six francs to print the pamphlets and borrowed it from a mineral salts manufacturer who employed Zinoviev, another comrade. He was repaid out of the proceeds but we're still grateful to the mineral salts which helped launch the revolution.'

Radek related how he left Switzerland with Lenin and crossed Germany in a train to reach Russia, then still at war with Germany. 'It was a lie that we were German agents. A dirty imperialist lie. The legend of a sealed train is equally without foundation. The train was not sealed at all — we merely pledged ourselves not to leave the coach.'

By midnight they were exhausted talking, but exhilarated by their rapport. Some weak potato soup and tea without the precious lemon had been their only refreshment, but Baring did not seem to notice his hunger. After meeting this amazing Radek he felt he had at last joined the stream of purposeful history. Here was a man who had lost his father at the age of four and had been brought up by his widowed mother on a pittance and yet by his own efforts had been able to join the small circle of Communist leaders in Moscow who were reshaping the world. The fact that he was not a Russian and could not even speak proper Russian convinced Baring that the revolution was truly international.

As for the coming meeting Radek proposed that Captain Baring M.C. should be kitted up in a full British officer's uniform from which he would symbolically remove the insignia in front of the assembled gathering as he explained why he rejected imperialism and had chosen to become a comrade.

Baring felt totally committed and saw no reason to disagree. It would be dramatic but his action might help to convince others.

'It should be great theatre. I'm sorry I won't be there to see it,' said Radek, 'But I've to go to Germany to help form a German Communist Party. Now the war is over they are ripe for revolution too.'

CHAPTER 19

After two days Commissar Naumov had to leave Petrograd to return to his unit at Kotlas. Comrade Cherepova, the interpreter, was allocated to remain with Comrade Baring as his guide and mentor. She had already given him a concise account of the revolution in one of the briefing sessions but now there was an opportunity to show him the sights where history had been made. After the incredible excitement of being in the furnace of the revolution, Baring was beginning to relax and enjoy himself.

They took a train for a rouble each to half way up the Nevsky Prospekt and began walking towards the bend in the Neva on the outskirts of Petrograd. Cherepova was talking cheerfully when a broken down pony pulling a cab came into sight. 'Look,' she said hailing it, 'an *izvostchik*, what luck we're in. I'd thought they had all gone.' They climbed in and she explained that pre-war St. Petersburg had been crowded with horse-drawn cabs but they had all but disappeared as fodder ran out and desperately starving proprietors ate their animals.

'I'm taking you to the Smolny Institute,' she said, 'it was a school for daughters of the aristocracy in Tsarist days but became the seat of the Petrograd Soviet. It was from there the October Revolution was launched against the Mensheviks and their bourgeois collaborators. It became the first headquarters of the Soviet Government before they moved to Moscow.'

Through some much neglected gardens they approached an impressive building with a portico of eight ionic columns.

It was topped by five domes which shone white on the bright sunlight. In front of the entrance stood an enormous statue of Karl Marx, thick and heavy on a pedestal, and holding behind him an enormous top hat.

'Let me see if I can take you to Lenin's room,' said Cherepova. 'They sometimes allow visitors and if I explain you're a British comrade they'll probably let us in.' At the doorway there was the usual collection of deputations. They were impoverished and gaunt after months of hunger. 'There's not much we can do to get them food,' said Cherepova, 'until the countryside is reorganised.' Her pass got them safely into the building and down a corridor they pushed into a crowded office. Harassed officials were trying to cope with a motley line of visitors but Cherepova found one of her friends and pulled her out. 'Comrade Krylova meet Comrade Baring from England,' she said introducing a stunningly beautiful woman of about forty. 'She was one of Lenin's secretaries when he was here,' she added.

Krylova collected a key and took them upstairs to Lenin's room. 'We're keeping it as he left it,' she said. 'One day it will be a shrine.' She unlocked the door of a modest office. 'This is where he worked and slept,' she said. 'This was the home of the revolution.' She was excited to hear that Baring came from England. 'Vladimir Ilyich is very friendly with the English, despite the war they're now fighting against us,' she confided, 'he told me his research was done in the British Museum in London.'

The room was extremely untidy with the the small desk littered with notebooks, pens, sheets of paper, copies of *Pravda* and other newspapers and a score of books in German and English. As the two women exchanged gossip Baring picked up books which included, surprisingly, copies of *White Fang* and *War of the Classes* by Jack London. Then he looked at another cluster of volumes on the floor, intrigued that a revolutionary leader planning an armed insurrection and then heading a fragile regime with a war on five fronts, could have found time for so many books. It reminded him of Radek's statement that ideas were as powerful as guns. At the side of the room there was a horse hair settee and it too had books stacked around its head.

'How did Comrade Lenin manage to read so much?' he asked Kyrlova.

'His head is the most fantastic machine I've ever encountered,' she replied, 'he was able to absorb thoughts from these books, correlate them to our conditions here in Russia and then pour out a constant stream of documents and pamphlets as guidance to the Party. He is a brilliant theoretician as well as administrator. His energy is phenomenal. I have known him to work non-stop for three days without more than an hour or so's snatched sleep on that settee. His meals were brought to him here so he had no social interruptions but he always insisted on having the same rations as everyone else.'

Krylova took Cherepova and Baring to the kitchens of the Smolny Institute where they sampled a soup of vegetables with shreds of horse flesh followed by some kasha. It was simple fare and made Baring think of the disappearing izvostchik horses, but it was appetizing after the bleak diet of thin gruel and black bread at the Astoria.

When they left Cherepova said cheerfully, 'Hope you liked the meal. We have to get food where we can now. The Smolny is always a good place to go if you've got a pass. I'll have to get you one. You'll never go hungry at the Smolny. By the way, did you see that man with all the hair and the smooth face on the next table to us?'

'Yes,' he replied.

'That was Comrade Gregori Zinoviev. He is one of the revolutionary leaders. He's speaking at the meeting next week.'

'Do all the leaders eat in the same dining room?' asked Baring.

'Yes, everyone shares the same rations. The revolution

abolished class distinction and we're not bringing it back.'

'They all look so young to be leaders,' said Baring, thinking of the fifty and sixty year olds he had seen in the Westminster Parliament. 'Radek is only just over thirty isn't he?'

'All the Bolsheviks are young. The older socialists tended to go with Kerensky and the Mensheviks,' said Cherepova. 'I think Zinoviev is thirty-seven and Trotsky is thirty-eight. Lenin is the oldest one, he's forty-eight.'

As they walked along the embankment of the frozen Neva Baring asked about her own life.

'My husband was murdered by the Okhrana,' she said bitterly, 'he was a socialist but not a revolutionary. He wanted reforms of the Duma so the elections would reflect what the people wanted. Cherepov believed we could get progress in this country by democracy. Those Tsarist monsters arrested him and put him into the cells of the Peter and Paul fortress where Alexander Ulyanov — he was Lenin's elder brother — and Maxim Gorky were imprisoned before him. My Cherepov never survived. I became a Bolshevik after that.' Her deep brown eyes nearly brimmed with tears. 'I honour his memory as a martyr by serving the revolution in every way I can.'

Cherepova led Baring past the Smolny convent along a road towards Petrograd explaining that she'd lost her husband a year after their marriage when she was still only twenty. They had no children, which she regretted, but she had no intention of remarrying. 'This has been a revolution for women too,' she said. 'We are now the equals of men. We don't need the servitude and bondage of marriage to survive. We can do that by our own efforts. Your suffragettes in England should learn that only Communism can give them real freedom.'

'How do you know about our suffragettes?' asked Baring.

Before the war I read many English newspapers. I worked as interpreter in our biggest exporting house and they used to get the *Morning Post* by subscription. I had to report to our directors on the operations of the British stock exchange, because some of them had shares in Britain. They didn't know I was a member of a secret Bolshevik group preparing to overthrow their corrupt business.'

'Where are they now?'

'Fled or dead,' said Cherepova. Baring asked no further questions.

At the Tauride Palace, a magnificent building standing in the corner of a glorious garden surrounding ornamental lakes, Cherepova described the violent scenes which had taken place eighteen months earlier. 'That was the time the Kronstadt sailors led vast crowds here to protest to the Mensheviks about the continuation of the war against Germany. The people wanted no more war. I was in that crowd,' she went on 'the atmosphere was electric. We Bolsheviks could easily have seized power with that crowd behind us but Lenin wanted no violence. They were going to lynch Chernov the Minister of Agriculture, but Trotsky came out of the building to plead for Chernov's life. I thought they were going to lynch Trotsky too but he converted them with his bravery and oratory, calling on red Kronstadt to be loyal. It was that demonstration which led to the Bolshevik revolution three months later. The people demanded it. There could be no cooperation with the bourgeoisie after Lenin and Trotsky had seen the power of the people.'

Along the southern bank of the Neva they walked back to the centre of Petrograd. The wind was blowing cold from the frozen river and there were few others about. Cherepova pointed across the river to the mass of the Peter and Paul fortress which towered into the leaden sky like an ugly reminder of the terror endemic in Russian history. They kept their silence which was more expressive than anything either of them could say.

When they parted Cherepova said, 'Next time I'll take you to the Winter Palace and the Hermitage to see some of the treasures we've saved from the Imperial family. And we shall also go across the river to see the *Domik Petra Velikova*.'

'What's that?' asked Baring.

'The original cottage of the city that was built in 1703 so that Peter the Great — our greatest Tsar — could live here and direct the building of St. Petersburg which he conceived and planned as one of the most beautiful cities in Europe.'

'The Tsars weren't all bad then,' said Baring.

'In their time they had an historical function. Russia was very primitive then and had to have a window on the west. Peter the Great was as important in our history as Elizabeth was in yours. The Romanovs were unworthy successors to Peter. They destroyed any hope that the monarchy could survive by clinging to their belief in their divine right to rule. Didn't you execute an English King for believing that?'

'Charles I,' said Charles. 'The Parliamentarians took over under Cromwell and abolished the monarchy.'

'Then why are your Parliamentary leaders now so critical of us. We're only following your example,' said Cherepova. 'When we have more time, please tell me more about your leaders. From what I've read they seem so — what you say,' she searched for a word, 'looking two ways, saying one thing and meaning another.'

'You mean hypocritical,' said Baring.

'Yes, why are they so hypocritical?'

'I'll tell you tomorrow,' said Baring, looking forward to another day with this lively lady.

Between sightseeing and political discussions Baring tried to get from Cherepova more news of the war of intervention and the situation of the British troops in North Russia. He knew that Commissar Naumov had returned to Kotlas to be with his Company when they launched the big offensive against Ironside. As the Russians were better adjusted to winter conditions it would be the best time to defeat the invaders. Baring was apprehensive as he did not want his old colleagues to die. Cherepova assured him that his appearance at the meeting for foreign socialists would be fully reported in

The Call and that thousands of copies would be distributed to the British troops with his photograph. 'This is your chance,' she said 'to say what you feel about the foolish war and it will reach them. Someone's got to make them see sense.'

On one of their visits to the Smolny Institute he was introduced to Bill Shatov, a big, bluff American who had been in the thick of the revolution. Baring was surprised to discover that he was an anarchist who had found himself in Petrograd fighting shoulder to shoulder with Communists. 'It's easy,' he replied, beaming over his sugarless tea in the Smolny canteen, 'I came here because after the Tsar was overthrown, Russia became a beacon to the world — this revolution can succeed, then we can have one in America to destroy the selfish, rampant capitalism which has given most of our wealth to a hundred powerful families.'

'But I thought anarchists were against all government,' said Baring.

'Sure we're against government, we want the people to have the freedom to govern themselves. Communism for us is a step towards true anarchism. Remember what Engels wrote, once Communism is achieved the State will wither away. That's what we want: the State to wither away. It will come.'

Shatov had misgivings about the Bolsheviks's shift to the right but thought it inevitable with the allied interference and the blockade. Once that was over the true objects of the revolution could be reached. Because of his disagreements with the Petrograd Soviet which he never hesitated to express, Shatov was being sent to Siberia to be Minister of Railways in a buffer government which the Soviets would establish when the Whites were pushed back. Baring thought the situation as bizarre as any he had ever read about; foreigners — even Americans with the broad accents of the Bronx — and Poles who could hardly speak Russian were rising to positions of influence. He resolved to include a reference to this in his address to the visiting socialists as confirmation of his belief in the internationalism of the Bolshevik revolution.

The night before the meeting on the 19th December he was summoned to the Foreign Affairs Commissariat to be given some unexpected news. Fortunately Cherepova was there to translate and she was able to soften the blow. Radek's assistant was forthright. Baring had only seen him as a lowly official who said nothing when his superiors were around but now he seemed to have found a new personality. 'The instructions from Moscow are definite. You are not to address the meeting tomorrow.'

'Why not?' he asked politely, 'don't they trust me yet?'

'Not that at all Comrade. Felix Dzerzhinsky has seen your file and has talked to Trotsky about you. They have plans for you which are very confidential at the moment. We are not allowed to discuss them. All I am allowed to say is that you can go to the meeting but only as an observer and your presence is not to be revealed to the participants. On that the instructions from Moscow are categorical.'

'Can't you give me any idea why there's this change of plan?' Baring asked.

'No Comrade. In this revolution we have our appropriate roles. Your's will be made known to you in Moscow, as I have said. And Comrade Cherepova is being allocated to you on a permanent assignment,' he said, as if it was a mark of honour to have one's personal interpreter. 'She will go with you to Moscow next month.'

Next day they went to the international meeting. It was presided over by Maxim Gorky. Zinoviev gave the opening address and said, 'We have among us today guests who are neither Marxists nor Communists but all of us here are agreed on one point, in our hatred of the bourgeoisie, in our hatred of a class guilty of the death of millions of men in the interests of a small group.' There was vigorous applause, in which Baring participated at the back of the theatre. He was now dressed in the anonymous buttoned-up tunic of a

Bolshevik official and none of the delegates around him could suspect he had been a British officer.

Baring followed the proceedings with fascination. Reinstein, a white haired seventy year old, was the delegate from America, Fineberg from Great Britain and Sadoul from France. There were delegates from Serbia and Bulgaria and Turkish, Chinese, Hindu, Persian and Korean representatives. Baring listened intently as Maxim Gorky introduced 'the delegate from Scotland'; he was a Scottish soldier who had been captured on the Archangel front and who declared in the broadest Glaswegian accent his support for the Bolsheviks. English and American soldiers followed his example. They didn't need me, thought Baring, the propaganda effect of having these ordinary soldiers speaking was every bit as good as anything I could do. He wanted to go forward and greet his compatriots but Cherepova restrained him. 'Take care,' she said, 'keep the secret; you have greater things to do.'

The foreign delegates were not housed in the Astoria which was otherwise known as the First House of the Soviets and reserved for the senior members of the Bolshevik Party. Baring was impressed that he had been given such superior accommodation although he had not as yet done anything to help the regime. He was beginning to feel frustrated but Cherepova, who was with him constantly, advised patience. 'Believe me, Comrade, the Central Committee in Moscow must have something extremely important for you. Let us enjoy our easy days, there can't be many of them when we get to the capital. They will expect us to work there.'

There was no official celebration over Christmas but Baring was aware that despite the privation there were attempts by the common people to capture a holiday atmosphere between Christmas and the New Year. He saw groups of people singing carols and there were decorations in some houses. One day he persuaded Cherepova to come with him to St. Isaacs Cathedral, which was surprisingly crowded with people of all ages. The beauty of the place took his breath away. The entrance had huge columns like photographs he had seen in the Pantheon in Rome and the golden dome looked higher than St. Paul's. Cherepova was scornful of the worshippers. 'We will make this place into a museum,' she said, 'there is no place in Communist society for religious idolatry.'

On New Year's Eve Cherepova suddenly said 'Come with me to my room. We'll have a celebration to welcome 1919. My friend who shares it with me has gone to stay with her family forty versts from here. We'll have it to ourselves.'

The room was in a large house near the Fontanka River. When they were out of sight of the Astoria, Cherepova impulsively took Baring's arm and held it tightly. He thought this an unusually bourgeois gesture but accepted it willingly. His experiences in Bolshevik Russia had been exhilarating and stimulating but in his quieter moments he felt extremely sad that he could not communicate with his family and friends back in England, all of whom would be thinking he was killed. It grieved him that in order to achieve some good it was necessary to sadden those he loved most. He had reflected on the cruelty of the human dilemma and relieved that Cherepova, the widow who had appeared so hard in her emotions, was beginning to relax toward him. Baring had been starved for too long of soft human kindness.

In the jet black night, only lightened by the occasional flare burning outside a house as a sign of celebration, they crossed the narrow frozen Moyka, passed the darkened Mariya Palace, crossed the frozen canal and turned by the Vorontsov Palace. 'Soon be there,' Cherepova said still clinging to Baring in a way which would have made the few people scurrying by naturally think they were a married couple. She had not neglected her role as a guide which prompted Baring to comment 'In this city there seem to be palaces on every other corner.'

'Yes,' replied Cherepova. 'This city was built for a Tsar and for two hundred years its life revolved around the needs of the Imperial family and the aristocracy — hence all the palaces. Now they will all be converted to the people's use.'

They reached a street of magnificent houses separated from the road by strips of garden covered in snow. The entrances were reached by glass covered ways supported by delicately designed ironwork. As they approached Baring noticed that many of the glass panels had been broken but the overall effect was beautiful. 'What lovely houses,' he said as Cherepova indicated their entrance. 'They were once. The wealthy merchants lived in this area and these houses were miniature palaces vying with each other in magificence. This one was owned by a German timber exporter but he disappeared at the beginning of the war. After the revolution these places were all taken over by the Petrograd Soviet to house the homeless workers.'

'Were you homeless?'

'Yes. Cherepov's house was confiscated after his murder because of his alleged debts. Those debts, mostly trumped up, were the result of fines imposed by the State but it gave them the excuse to throw me out of my home. Since then I've lived in any place I could get.'

The front door was open on its hinges as the lock had not been repaired. The large entrance hall was bleak, a wire was swinging where a chandelier had once hung, one of the walls was daubed with slogans, the plaster was showing in places and the bannisters had been removed.

'Forgive the mess,' said Cherepova. 'When the mobs broke in they took everything that could be moved. Their anger was that intense.'

'Why did they break up the stairway?' asked Baring who could not understand mindless destruction.

'They wanted the firewood. They were cold.'

Holding hands and feeling their way up the stairs gingerly to avoid the broken steps they reached the second floor after passing rooms where noises indicated families were living.

'Here we are,' said Cherepova, 'this is my castle.' She put a key into a padlock and removed a chain holding the door firm.

After tallow candles had been lit, Baring could see that Cherepova had furnished the huge room with flair. The two large, low divans in the corners were covered by finely worked tapestries, the brightly polished hardwood floor was scattered with rugs and felt-covered cushions and on a magnificent red rosewood sideboard stood a silver samovar. It appeared to be brooding as if out of place, as if it had known better times. On three of the walls were oil paintings in large gilt frames but the fourth wall had been covered between the large windows with the contrast of revolutionary posters and a sombre photograph of Lenin. The room's decoration seemed to symbolize the dichotomy in the Russian character. The regard to the ancient cultures and customs and the striving towards the new challenging future.

'It's cold, I'll get the fire going,' said Cherepova putting tapers to the already laid logs in a marble fireplace.

'You've made this very comfortable,' said Baring.

'I was lucky. My friends helped me to collect some odds and ends of furniture and to keep a few of the treasures of this house. Look,' she said, 'I've even got my own kitchen and bathroom.' In an adjoining room was a decorated porcelain bath, a lavatory and a bidet; beyond a washroom converted into a kitchen by the addition of a stove.

'I've been here ten months now,' said Cherepova. 'I'm hoping soon we shall get the electric light connected again.'

The meal she prepared exceeded all Baring's expectations. Where and how she had acquired the ingredients was a mystery and he did not dare to ask. The first course of fish soused in vinegar with black bread was followed by delicious Pyelmeni, dumpling full of meat, and the meal was rounded off with *staken kiselya*, a kind of jelly made of cranberry juice. During the meal Cherepova talked of her parents who had left Petrograd during the war to return to their native village near the Latvian border. 'They thought it would be safer there but the Whites now occupy the area and if they found out I was a Bolshevik activist I can't think what they would do to them.'

'When did you last hear of them?'

'Over eighteen months ago.'

Over tea Baring looked warmly at Cherepova and said, 'Here I am enjoying your marvellous food which is the best I've had for months and I don't even know your Christian name.'

Cherepova laughed. 'There you go again. It will take you a long time to learn Comrade. We Bolsheviks don't have Christian names; we're atheists not Christians.'

'Oh well — you know what I mean,' said Baring, 'What's your atheist name then?'

Cherepova now threw back her long brown hair, for she had unclipped the bun when they had arrived, and laughed again.

'You mustn't take offence Charles — you see I know your name — but I have to guide you so you don't make a mistake with other comrades who may not be so forgiving. My names are Nina Semyonovna and from now onwards when we're alone you call me Nina.'

'It's beautiful and simple,' he said, his feelings for her expressed as much by his eyes as by his words.

When all the crockery had been cleared away Cherepova took Baring's hand and led him to one of the divans making him lie flat on his back. He felt like a child being put to bed by his mother but did as he was directed. The room had been warmed by the log fire and the comfort of the good food added to his feelings of well being. He had not needed wine to feel intoxicated; the mellow atmosphere had relaxed tensions and soothed a mind tired after the struggles with his conscience over the months and the years. Cherepova's gentle hands had a hypnotic effect on him as she unbuttoned his tunic and carefully removed it. There was no haste in her movements which were methodical and deliberate. When he wanted to speak she motioned him to be quiet by placing a forefinger on her lips.

She knelt on a cushion on the floor, rested her left elbow on the divan and brought her right hand over his forehead as if to calm him. Gradually she let her fingers stroke his hair and brush his ears. He made no move to restrain her as the progression of her caress was almost imperceptible.

After minutes, which might have been hours, she unbuttoned his shirt and lifted it off his body letting the fingers of both hands run over his chest and down to his belly. He stirred as if to make an artificial protest but she held his shoulders and coaxed him to remain still. As Baring had taken off his long boots soon after their arrival, Cherepova was able to ease his trousers down his legs and off in a heap on the floor before he was prepared to be aware of what was happening to him. The protest seemed to be pointless as his arousal was evident and he was powerless to resist her touch. She stroked him slowly and softly until his involuntary writhings became too pronounced when with a squeeze and a quick caress she suddenly left him prone on the divan. Her own clothes, which had become incongruous, were dropped by deft, quick movements until she stood naked in the flickering light of the fire and the candles. Her breasts were large, rounded and firm and limbs, though strong and muscular, were sensuous.

Cherepova bent over Baring, kissed his lips for the first time and let her breasts rest on his chest. He raised his arms to hold her to him but she disentangled them with a firm grip and put them back by his side. Then she ran her hands down his body feeling every crevice until she was stroking the sides of his thighs. The evidence of his passion was now incontrovertible but she held him again as she kissed his now quivering mouth. Within what seemed a fleeting second she had mounted him and he had entered her as naturally as if they had been mates all their lives, but unlike experienced lovers the explosion happened in a flash as he came and came in a throbbing thrusting which left him exhausted.

CHAPTER 20

In the morning, as a weak sun tried to break through the thin curtains, Cherepova brought him tea. Baring sat up with a start. 'What time is it?' he exclaimed, surprised to find himself in a strange bed.

'Nine o'clock; you slept solidly for ten hours.'

'Good heavens,' he said as memory of the night before came welling back. 'I was knocked out, wasn't I?'

'You were darling, you were like a boy, composed and peaceful after a long fractious illness.'

'I feel different now.' He supped the weak tea. 'Pain and stress I never knew I had has disappeared. Amazing! I never realised I was so taut. Isn't it amazing,' he reflected in disbelief, 'how one never feels the real mental pain until it's gone and then one wonders how one ever coped with it.'

'I guessed that you were wrapped up in tensions,' she said, 'but I never thought it was so bad. You must have built that up over years. It was like wrinkled elastic which unravels suddenly.'

'You're a miracle worker,' he confessed shyly, unable to think of other words to express his gratitude.

'Were you a virgin?'

'Yes,' he said quickly, too surprised by her frank question to be evasive.

'I thought so. You needed to release yourself badly.'

'It's not how I expected it to happen,' he admitted.

'What do you mean?'

'Well,' he hesitated finding frankness, despite her example, difficult to grasp. 'I always thought the man had to take the initiatives.'

'That's an antiquated idea,' she scoffed, 'it goes with the subservience of women and the idea that they are only chattels or playthings for the all-powerful male. In our new society we're changing that. Women are equal now.'

'Do you take any man when you feel like it?' Jealousy forced his reluctant question.

'Only when I love them,' she replied, 'and that's very rare indeed. In the ten years since Cherepov I've only had two men.'

'Where are they now?'

'Both are dead. Aleksey Ivanovitch was killed by the Germans — I would have married him; Nikolay Ilych died on the streets in the great October revolution, shot in the back.'

'I am sorry,' he muttered.

'We all make our sacrifices,' she said, 'but at least you know I do not give my favours freely. It's fifteen months since I had a man and there have been plenty of opportunities.'

'I am sure,' he said with feeling. 'You are a beautiful woman and any man would like to have you. I'm afraid,' he added as an afterthought 'I wasn't much use to you last night.'

'It was your first,' she said understandably. 'It takes time to learn.'

'Will you have patience with me?' he asked, conscious of his pathetic inexperience.

'Of course,' she said, 'patience is the essence of love and I can wait for my young Englishman.'

'I'm not too young for you then?'

'Ten years is nothing. Cherepov was ten years older than me but that made no difference. Why should it to us?' she asked. The raking over of their relationship threatened to become maudlin but fortunately they had to leave for the Smolny Institute where they had an appointment at midday with Zinoviev. They found him in a buoyant mood.

'Comrade Baring,' he said, 'clearance has come through for your trip to Moscow. You are going to the Kremlin to collect your instructions there and Comrade Cherepova is to accompany you as interpreter. You will leave tomorrow. Here are your train passes. Good luck Comrade.'

In the Smolny canteen they spooned the meagre soup, both thinking it would be their last meal there, happy that the Party had chosen to send them to Moscow together.

'What a bit of luck, Nina,' he said, '1919 is going to be a vintage year if it continues like this.'

'I've never been to Moscow,' she said.

'Why do you think they're sending you and not finding me another interpreter? Surely they don't know we're in love?'

'The Party is not that efficient or interested,' she replied. 'I'll be frank with you Charles. They asked me to keep an eye on you. They had to be sure of your reliability. You can't blame them for that.'

'Have you been submitting reports on me then?'

'Of course,' she said, 'it's the usual form for interpreters. I even did it before the war for my private firm when the foreign buyers came.'

'Will you tell them of our new relationship, Nina?'

'I'll have to. It's my duty to the Party. Anyway if they were to find out without me informing them they'd never believe me again and we would be separated.'

'I suppose it's best,' he said doubtfully.

'Believe me it is,' she said with a renewed earnestness in her voice, 'you have been chosen for some very important work and you can't expect the Party to trust you without knowing the basket they are putting their eggs into.'

Charles laughed. 'You didn't mean it like that did you Nina?' and when she looked perplexed he explained '"basket" is slang in our language for bastard.'

She laughed and shrugged her shoulders.

'I'm glad to be able to correct you for once,' he jested. 'Do you have any idea what they have in store for me?'

'No but it is a top secret for senior comrades only to know and I've had instructions that you are not to mix with the foreign visitors here. That's one reason we're leaving

Petrograd, the place is busy with them.'

Next day at Nikolai Station they found reserved seats in an old third class wagon. It was divided in the middle by a door and there were open coupés and side seats which became plank beds when necessary. Charles and Nina were able to stretch out and sleep for part of the night. At every station there was a great commotion as passengers streamed out to the taps to collect drinking water for their tea-making rituals. There was a general friendliness and Charles wished his Russian had been good enough to enter into the family atmosphere.

At Moscow there was a crowd milling around the station. They wore greatcoats, fur hats and boots of all descriptions and Baring thought the Moscovite looked a little smarter than his Petrograd compatriot but no one could be seen who was wearing anything remotely new.

They were at a loss to know where to go when he spied a board being held up at the end of the platform reading *English bring report here.* 'That must be us,' he called to Nina over the hubbub and they went to the little man who was trying to attract attention to his sign.

'Good,' he said in halting English. 'I am from the Commissariat for Foreign Affairs. Are you Comrade Bring?'

'Baring, actually there's an "a" in it,' said Baring.

'Good, Commissar Chicherin asked me to take you to the Hotel. It's difficult in Moscow to get rooms but we reserved a room for you at the National and one for Comrade Cherepova, of course. He looked at Nina admiringly. 'Come I have a sledge waiting.'

There were dozens of sledges touting for business and Baring was shocked at this evidence of private enterprise. 'They're asking a hundred roubles for a short journey,' whispered Nina, 'that's extortion and should be stopped.'

On the way they saw trams running, crowded with passengers hanging on to the platforms, the pavements were full of people trudging through the snow and Baring, surprised by this extraordinary bustle, asked 'What is everybody doing?'

'They are going to work or to barter for food,' said Nina. 'Moskva attracts all Russia now. Petrograd created the revolution but Moskva took over.' Baring noticed that most of the shops had been closed but others had improvised signs over them and he asked Nina what they meant. 'They've been nationalized,' she said, 'the names are the 5th Boot Store of the Moskva Soviet and the 3rd Clothing Store of the Moskva Soviet. All the goods are rationed to prevent speculation.'

At the National they were allocated two separate rooms on separate floors and as they parted Charles chided Nina, 'Your report on our new relationship doesn't seem to have reached Moscow yet. Perhaps I should put one in myself and ask for a double room.'

'I shall have to watch you, I see,' said Nina, 'you are talking like a liberated man not the — how you say — reticent Englishman.'

Baring found his room bleak with heavy furniture and dark brown paint but it was clean and there were sheets on the bed and two blankets.

Their appointment with Chicherin was not until two o'clock in the morning and the two visitors spent an hour arranging their food rations. The hotel gave them a card each with the days of the week printed along the edge giving the right to buy one dinner daily consisting of soup and a second course of potatoes and a scrap of meat or fish and costing between five and seven roubles. In the kitchens they found some of the hotel guests cooking their own rations in the belief it gave them a better bargain. Boiling water was always available to make tea.

Once the domestic arrangements were completed they walked on the Moscow streets like a couple of tourists. The Kremlin stood across the wide square with its twenty or more golden-top-onion shaped cupolas glinting in the afternoon sun and surrounded by a forbidding wall. 'Lenin is there,' said Nina, 'turning a revolution into a nation. Millions depend on him.'

'Why do you think he emerged as leader and not Trotsky who was the Chairman of the Petrograd Soviet where it all started.'

'His intellectual clarity and consistency. Trotsky is brilliant and an outstanding Commissar for War but he was a Menshevik once and these things are not forgotten in a hurry. Lenin is head and shoulders above all the Commissars. We're lucky he's still so young and can give us another twenty years of leadership. Finding a successor to Vladimir Ilyich would not be easy.'

They passed the Kremlin walls and St. Basil's Cathedral and walked towards the Moskva River. Charles noticed a number of army-looking men in leather suits with guns in their belts. They were not in the usual gear with an assortment of army clothing. 'Who are those men?' he asked.

'Vecheka,' said Nina, 'the men of the *Vserossiskaya Chrezvychainaya Kommissiya po Borbe s kontrarevolyutsiyey i Sabotazhem*, the All Russian Extraordinary Commission for the Struggle against Counter-Revolution Sabotage. Vechecka are its Russian initials. Most people call it the Cheka and it's doing a wonderful job destroying the opposition to the revolution. It's run by Comrade Dzerzhinsky who is Radek's Polish friend. He's a dedicated man and completely uncorruptible, they say.'

'But those men look vicious,' said Charles.

'They are vicious; they have to be. The enemies of the revolution have to be liquidated,' said Nina, 'there is no other way.'

After supper in the dining room of the National they had a few hours sleep before braving the cold night air for the short walk to the Metropole where thy were to see the Commissar for Foreign Affairs. It was the coldest Charles had known since his night in the forest near Shenkursk and even their breath seemed to freeze as they hurried through the now deserted streets. 'Why does Chicherin work such peculiar hours?' he asked.

'He's known as the night owl, he prefers the quiet of night and I suppose it reduces the number of deputations he has to receive.'

At the Metropole, part of which was still used as an hotel, they showed their *propusk* at the back door and were shown up a narrow stairway to the Commissar's office. He greeted them warmly, and offered tea with the coveted lemon which Charles had not tasted since Archangel. Baring was struck by his old worn look and his white, sickly complexion as if he were broken by fatique.

'Welcome to Moscow,' said the Commissar speaking in English with a faint accent. 'I have been looking forward to meeting you,' he said to Baring, 'and of course Comrade Cherepova whose work for the Petrograd Soviet is renowned.' The Commissar had the manners of an aristocrat and the charm of a diplomat.

'We are very glad to be here,' said Baring.

'I've read your file with the utmost interest,' said Chicherin. 'You do not know it, Comrade Baring, but we have a great deal in common. You see my family had a big estate but I had to turn my back on that when I realised the cruelty of the class system. I was influenced by a liberal grandfather, just like you and my reading turned me into a Communist. Tell me did you ever read Nietzsche?'

'No I didn't study the German philosophers,' said Baring.

'Nietzsche has great lessons for us,' he said with a spark in his tired eyes, 'and through our communism we can develop the concept of the superman as Nietzsche envisaged him and turn it to serve the needs of the people.'

'That's how I feel,' said Baring, 'squalor, waste and war can be eliminated with inspired leadership once capitalist exploitation is destroyed.'

'Exactly,' said Chicherin, 'it can't be left to the common people alone and bourgeois ideas are suffocating. Communism is the inspiration but it must also provide the organisation and the hierarchy to make our ideas work in practice.'

'You speak excellent English?' said Baring.

'I spent a long time in London,' he replied, 'and I had the good fortune to be a guest of His Majesty.'

'You were?' said Baring in some surprise.

'That was in Brixton prison where your English friends kept me without trial until I was exchanged for Buchanan, the English ambassador in Moscow.'

'I see,' said Baring a bit non-plussed by the range of the Commissar's experiences.

'But I hold no resentment against the English,' Chicherin continued. 'I made some excellent friends there particularly, in the Independent Labour Party, but not among the aristocrats and their hangers-on. Those creatures are in the same mould as the Russian aristocrats I knew as a child but with a difference. They have greater cunning. They know how to cling to their privileges by making tiny concessions to the workers and telling them that they've made tremendous gains.'

'That's true,' said Baring thinking of the types he had known at Eton.

'My view is that direct revolution would not be easy to set up in England and I don't think democracy can work as minds can be manipulated by the powers who control the newspapers. To change British society will take a lot of aristocratic cunning. What do you think Comrade Baring?' he opened his hands as if to offer a rostrum.

'Britain is a tightly-knit country,' said Baring, 'it is possible for ideas to travel fast but authority can move just as quickly to counter them. I don't believe the trades unions will ever be revolutionary so the hope for real change will only come if communists can take over the power elements.'

'I think that myself, but I think it can only be done by infiltration. I'm bound to admit many of my comrades here in the Central Committee don't agree with me.'

'What do they think?' asked Baring.

'They imagine that the Bolshevik success will spread like a bushfire through Europe as the Proletariat get to hear about it. Radek's in Germany now setting the scene for a revolution there. They always quote Marx who thought the industrialised states would be the ones to go communist. They think for it to happen first in Russia was an historical accident. The reason it happened here was because the Petrograd workers grasped an opportunity out of chaos as Comrade Cherepova knows from her part in it.' Chicherin smiled at his other visitor.

'Do you think I can have a role to play?' Baring asked directly.

'Yes I do,' replied the Commissar. 'With your background you can get right into the English establishment and undermine it from within. It's the kind of attack the ruling classes in Britain would not expect and therefore it's the one most likely to succeed.'

Baring nodded his understanding of Chicherin's meaning rather than his agreement. The plan had attractions but Baring preferred to be frank rather than subversive about his views. A state of war was different. As an army officer he could never be allowed to entertain, let alone express, treacherous thoughts, but once the war was over he wanted to campaign openly to convince people of the sense and humanity of his convictions. He felt that the British liberal tradition could be influenced by communist ideas and that communists could achieve power though the merit of their arguments.

Chicherin could see doubt written all over his visitor's face and said, 'Comrade, I don't expect to convert you overnight. Anyway we must all move forward by agreement. No one person's views can be imposed on another. Vladimir Ilyich has to argue through everyone one of his proposals until he achieves a majority support so I must do the same.' He called for more tea and turned to Cherepova to exchange gossip about Petrograd personalities. As they talked in Russian it gave Baring a respite from the ideological assault and a chance to take in the scene in the room from which the foreign affairs of the Bolshevik Government were being conducted.

It was an ordinary hotel room with a bed on one side where the Commissar for Foreign Affairs could snatch a few hours sleep, mostly in the daytime from all accounts. The desk was covered with State papers, memoranda and foreign telegrams in neat piles. Along one wall were box files and Baring could see from his limited knowledge of the Cyrillic script that each concerned a country with whom Russia had diplomatic relations. They were few. Another shelf held the box files of the countries which were at war with Russia or were hostile. They were many.

On the wall behind the Commissar's head was a photograph of Lenin which Baring had seen many times. It seemed to be regulation issue.

Chicherin broke off from Russian and turned to Baring again.

'We can't expect to win world revolution in a straight line. It has to be approached by deviation and intrigue. Sometimes we must compromise. Do you think I enjoyed signing the Brest-Litovsk Treaty with the hated German military? I didn't but I accepted it as a necessary tactic in our struggle. It was Lenin's inspiration to sue for peace and it turned out to be correct, without it the Germans might have destroyed our Government before it could establish itself.

'I see that,' said Baring.

'The situation in England is more complex,' said Chicherin, 'there's not a revolutionary situation there yet but there could be in time if we work to undermine the ruling class and break the Colonial Empire which helps to keep them in power.' He paused a moment to let his words sink in and added, 'I want you to think about our discussion before we make a proposal to you, Comrade. Commissar Trotsky has been informed about you; he is at the southern front but he's back here next week for a Politbureau meeting and I will arrange for you to meet him. By then we might be able to come to a decision. How about some more tea? he added.

Cherepova and Baring left the Metropole at four in the morning. The Foreign Minister had talked with them for two hours. Baring knew that political leaders in Britain were stuffy and distant and the openness and apparent frankness of the Bolshevik Commissars in the midst of their struggle against internal chaos and foreign intervention, was the biggest surprise of all his Russian experience, including even his affair with Nina who clung to his arm even more firmly as they retraced their steps to the National.

CHAPTER 21

For a capital of a country struggling to survive, Moscow had a surprising air of normality. Baring could see that although food was extremely short the ration, available to all on coupons, was sufficient to avoid starvation. Nina told him about the speculators who sold bread at twenty roubles a funt as against twenty kopecks on ration, as well as other goods in short supply, proving that private enterprise dies hard even when the Vechecka was around.

Nina and Charles spent their days walking around the city looking in the museums that were still open and in the bookshops. The Commissariat had made them a generous allowance of roubles but despite their hunger they did not patronise the speculators, preferring to spend the money left over from the hotel bill on books or theatre tickets. Under Nina's tuition Charles was improving his Russian, although he had long since realised he did not have a natural gift for languages.

The range of entertainment available in Moscow amazed Baring as it nearly matched the choice he would have had in London. *A Christmas Carol* was at the Komissarzhevskaya theatre and *Cricket on the Hearth*, another Dickens, at the Moscow Art Theatre. Shakespeare's *Much Ado About Nothing* was at the Korsh sharing the programme on alternate nights with *Le Misanthrope* by Moliere and the *Coppelia* ballet was at the Opera House. The Russian playwrights were represented by Merezhkovsk, Lunacharsy, Gorky. Charles counted over a dozen theatres providing a wealth of culture which the people, although hungry, still flocked to see.

Nina and Charles went to the Great Theatre to see *Samson and Delilah* by Saint-Saens and managed to get seats in a box above the orchestra. From here they could see the audience as well as the performance. The place was packed and most people were in ordinary, everyday or working clothes if they had come straight from work. A few Tartar women wore shawls. As the theatre was without heating it was cold and everyone left their overcoats on. Members of the orchestra wore a hotch-potch of regimental tunics, inherited from army service, and various jackets. Only the conductor wore a frock coat and he looked like a survivor from a past age suspended between orchestra and people.

That night they walked back through the snow, music ringing in their ears and overwhelmed by the passionate feelings aroused in the audience. It seemed to Baring that the revolution had not only opened the opportunity for economic reforms and the end to expoitation but it had found the key to the human spirit, which was riding free again. Nina felt it too and sharing it they fell into bed to make love in a way which satisfied them both fully, physically and spiritually.

By the morning Charles Baring's mind was made up. Uncertainty was set aside. He felt within him a demanding imperative. It told him that whatever his misgivings might have been there was now no alternative. He had to serve this cause and no other. It absorbed his emotion in a way which nothing else in his life had done or could ever do. It was a fulfillment of all his tentative longings which he had never really been able to fathom. Here in Moscow he understood it all. In the cold crystal air of a revolutionary city, shouting defiance at the old order, he could breath deeply and feel a sense of purpose in his being. That purpose had eluded him because he had been forced to conform to Eton, the army and membership of a class with which he could not feel any identification.

On Tuesday word came to the National that Trotsky was ready to receive him. No mention was made of Nina

Semyonovna Cherepova who assumed she was included in the invitation, but in the afternoon a functionary of the Commissariat for War arrived in a large official car explaining, to her evident annoyance, that she would not be required at the interview. As he left the foyer she whispered to Baring, 'This is your chance; Trotsky is the most powerful man in Russia after Lenin. What he says is law.' He had no time to reply as the official was hurrying him into the car.

They swept off down the Krasnaya Ploschad scattering frozen snow which had been collected in mounds ready for removal. The official who spoke English with a hint of an American accent was anxious to prove that an interpreter was not necessary and said, 'Do you like Moscow Comrade?'

'Yes, it seems livelier than Petrograd,' Baring answered not knowing what was expected of him.

'There's a lot to see here. I hope you'll have the time. Look over there,' he added, playing the guide, 'that's the Lobnoye Mesto.'

Baring saw a high platform of white stone. 'Executions were carried out there in ancient times,' said the official 'and the Tsars used it for proclamations.' The car turned right into a gateway of the Kremlin and recognising the vehicle, the guards, all smartly dressed in long greatcoats and high felt hats, saluted and waved it on. 'This is the Spassky Gate. It dates back to the fifteenth century but the tower was added a century later by a Scottish architect. Are you Scotch?'

'No, I'm English' said Baring, too interested in the Kremlin to elaborate. They were going deeper into the fortress and approaching a long yellow building. 'The Arsenal,' said the guide, showing Baring into a building facing it.

At the door to the Senate the three guards carefully examined the passes the official produced from his greatcoat pocket and once fully satisfied allowed them in. The efficiency and order was in sharp contrast to the other government offices Baring had visited. Here there were no bedraggled deputations waiting in the corridors for hours in the hope of catching the sleeve of a Commissar. The change implied that the leadership had distanced themselves from the lax ways of the Smolny Institute and were donning the Tsarist mantle of an austere and secretive authority. They climbed some steps, the official bowed out and, without any more delay, Baring was ushered into the presence of the Commissar for War. Trotsky was alone at a huge desk covered with papers, rubber stamps, an inkstand and lots of pencils. A telephone was at his left side and behind on the wall was a huge map of Russia with pointers and marks showing the disposition of forces. The office was meticulously tidy and had an air of bureaucratic efficiency about it. The Commissar finished what he was writing and then stood up.

'So you are Baring,' he asked needlessly, 'sit down over there,' indicating a leather armchair. 'Let's look at you.'

Two fierce, dark blue eyes searched Baring's face through their pince nez for what seemed a full minute. Baring did his best to relax under the magnetic stare from a man who did not suffer fools either gladly or otherwise. 'So you're Baring,' he repeated. 'What do you have to say for yourself?'

'My hope is that I can serve the revolution,' Baring said simply.

'What can you, an aristocratic Englishman,' Trotsky said disparagingly, 'possibly do which other comrades won't do better?'

'Your Commissar comrades thought I might have a role in helping to destroy capitalism in Britain.'

Radek and Chicherin both speak highly of you but why should I believe them? They could be wrong. Radek's a Polish romantic and Chicherin is drawn to any professed revolutionary who comes from the Elite because they mirror him. You have to convince me yourself.'

Baring was determined not to be intimidated by this man in the tailored army tunic, buttoned to the neck. He looked at Trotsky calmly, taking in the pointed black beard, the flowing black hair and the glowering black countenance.

'You nearly killed me two months ago on the Dwina.'

'So you were up there,' said Trotsky thoughtfully.

'I decided I could no longer fight for the interventionists after that. My cause is with you.'

'How can you be a Bolshevik when you were born with a silver spoon in your mouth?'

Baring was surprised by Trotsky's attack and his easy use of colloquial English. The man had the tongue of a rapier.

'I was convinced by the socialist writers. Wealth should not be a barrier to understanding misery. What about Tolstoy?' he countered.

'True, true,' Trotsky pursed his lips. 'I remember reading *Oliver Twist* as a boy; it influenced me much but I could feel the suffering of the peasants. I lived with them. My parents home was a clay hut with clay floors and clay ceilings which leaked, but you,' he said disparagingly, 'you were brought up in a magnificent Hall with servants. The moulding in boyhood is what matters to a character and your's was soft.'

'My experinces in the war made up for them.'

'Tell me about them,' he said and Baring went on to describe how the horrors of the trenches had changed his outlook and how the war had finally converted him to realise that only a total change in society could improve human conditions.

As his story unfolded Trotsky became perceptively warmer in his attitude to his visitor. 'To be frank with you,' he confided, 'I am inately suspicious of the British. They are the most cunning people in Europe. The Germans are brutal but they don't wrap their cruelties in honeyed words like their hypocritical cousins. The Americans have their wide open country with expanding frontiers and can afford to be naive, but the British live in a cramped, decaying island and use guile to rule and exploit a vast Colonial Empire. I could never trust the British.'

'Do you really know any Englishmen?' asked Baring, 'there might be many exceptions to your rule.'

'I know the British,' said Trotsky with feeling, 'let me tell you a true story' and he went on as a fascinated Baring listened. 'When the Tsar abdicated I was in New York with my family. We were exiles but with the news of a new government in Petersburg we wanted to get back and to that end we obtained all the proper visas, including a Russian entry permit and a British transit visa. We sailed from New York on the *Christiana fjord* a neutral Norwegian ship. Of course we expected no trouble but in Nova Scotia the British naval police came on board and arrested me. Arrested me,' he shouted angrily, 'because of my political views. The cunning British were trying to stop the Bolsheviks getting back to Russia, interfering again in other countries' affairs. But I tell you I had the last laugh. They put me in a camp with eight hundred German prisoners from sunken submarines and I taught them about communism and how they should rise against the Kaiser. We had meetings all the time. The British commandant didn't like that and forbade me addressing the prisoners, but five hundred of them signed a protest at the ban. After three weeks the British had to release me and the Germans cheered me off with their camp band playing the *Internationale.*'

'No wonder you don't like Britain,' said Baring.

'The British need to be liberated from their class-ridden backwardness and their subservience to a corrupt élite. Then they'll find a true destiny but first we have to defeat them in this war for the survival of the Russian revolution. Your War Minister, Winston Churchill, is trying to strangle us at birth because he knows if Bolshevism succeeds here, it will spread to England.'

'That is what I hope,' said Baring.

'There's no point in achieving revolution in one country alone. It must roll on until it covers the world, but I don't think the revolution will succeed in Britain without some cunning work on our part. We have to match cunning with cunning.'

'What do you mean?'

'To defeat the English ruling class we have to infiltrate their power structure and destroy it from within. A direct assault will get nowhere and the pussy-footing socialists like your pacifist Lansbury will achieve little except minor reforms. We must put dedicated communists into the British establishment so secretly that no one will suspect; when the time is ripe they can make the moves which will help break the Colonial Empire and destroy Britain's strength.'

'Do you believe it is necessary for Britain to break up before it can be rebuilt on communist lines?'

'I do,' said Trotsky, 'the old order must go completely. Look at the situation here. Tsarism, the divine rule of Kings, has gone leaving a vacuum which we can fill with our new ideas. It's the only way. In Britain it will take longer to achieve the same result. We will have to be patient but we can do it. The British proletariat will be grateful to us.'

Trotsky cancelled other meetings and declined to take telephone calls as the two men talked for hours about political philosophies and the tactics of revolution. Baring was irrevocably drawn under the hypnotic influence of a man whose electrifying personality was so intense that Baring could feel it as a physical force. Trotsky for his part was impressed by his visitor's honesty and sense of purpose. Baring was an unusual Englishman with whom he could be frank. 'I feel,' he said, 'a destiny has fallen on me. I was born into a simple farmer's family as Lev Davidovich Bronstein and they called me Lyova.' His fierce blue eyes softened as he recalled his childhood. 'But there was something pulling me on to greater things. I took the name Trotsky from one of my warders in prison and it is as Trotsky that I have this mission to change the world. Just over a year ago, on my thirty-eighth birthday, I led the Bolshevik revolution in Petrograd, by my forty-eighth I want to see a Communist Germany and by my fifty-eighth, Britain and America well and truly in the Communist-fold. Before I die I want the whole world to be

Communist. Will you help me to succeed in that Baring?' he asked.

'I will,' Baring replied.

'Then I have a big role for you, the biggest role,' Trotsky said in excitement as he stood up from the desk and paced the room munching a piece of black bread which had been brought in with soup on a tray. 'I want you to be our trojan horse,' he exclaimed.

Baring looked doubtful.

'You are aware of the story of Troy?' Trotsky asked, 'the huge wooden horse as a gift which is full of soldiers who emerge to conquer the enemy?'

'Yes,' said Baring.

'You will be our trojan horse in England. You will go back a secret Bolshevik and I mean *secret*, no one except a handful of trusted comrades here in Moscow will know. You will climb into the top echelons of the British hierarchy and you will guide the policy of Britain towards its own destruction.'

'Do you think that is really possible?' asked Baring.

'Of course it is because they won't suspect you. We will match our cunning against their cunning,' he repeated, 'and we will win because our Bolshevik cunning can be more cunning than their's.'

Baring was flattered but expressed doubts. Trotsky swept them aside. 'You have everything in your favour, the right family background, the right education, the right connections and with a little help from us there is no reason why you shouldn't rise to the very top.'

A secretary burst into the room and spoke in rapid Russian to the Commissar. He looked dismayed for a brief moment but, recovering his poise, said to his visitor, 'I'm sorry we'll have to break off now. Vladimir Ilyich wants me. Will you come here tomorrow at nine; there is a great deal we have to decide. Meanwhile I ask you to reveal nothing, talk to no one. What we have discussed is the highest State secret.'

When Charles Baring returned to the National he found

Nina waiting expectantly. 'Do you know how long you've been?' she said. 'Hours and hours. Tell me, what did Trotsky say?'

'I'm not allowed to discuss it,' said Charles.

'Oh,' she pouted, 'a woman comrade is not to be trusted I suppose. Anyway, I've already guessed what they have in mind for you from what Chicherin said. Anyway, Krylova is coming from Petrograd to work for Lenin and I'll get the news from her.' Charles said nothing.

'You can tell me,' she begged, seeing his vulnerability.

'I can't, I can't,' he replied. 'Trotsky ordered me not to, but I'm seeing him again tomorrow and I'll ask if you can be one person who knows.'

'I hope he agrees,' she said, then changed the subject 'but do you know what time it is? We're too late for the dining room. I've collected our rations and we'll cook our own supper and then we'll go to bed and I'll show you how to release all those tensions which have been building up in your lovely body,' she squeezed him passionately.

The official with the American accent again took Baring to the Senate Building in the Kremlin, promptly at nine o'clock. This time he was almost obsequious in his attitude. The status of this young Englishman had been confirmed by the length of time he had already spent with the Commissar.

Trotsky, punctilious and courteous in his manner, inquired how Baring had slept and invited him to have tea. Then before the visitor could relax he turned his eyes on him with a steady stare and said slowly 'How do I know you are trustworthy? How do I know you are not a British agent planted in our ranks to find our secrets?'

Baring went on to reply but Trotsky stopped him with an angry wave of his right hand. 'I've had trouble enough with British spies. There was one here called Sidney Reilly — we found out his real name was Rosenblum — who had a plan to murder me and Lenin. He paid the Lettish guards to do it but they were loyal and told us. He was aiming to destroy the

Bolshevik revolution and set up a military dictatorship.
Another spy was Bruce Lockhart, the British Consul. He was
involved in allied plots and gave false papers to Kerensky to
escape north to Archangel with a group of returning
Serbians. We had to put Lockhart in the Lubyanka to stop his
mischief and then swop him for Litvinov who the British had
arrested in retaliation. Tell me,' he looked directly at Baring
who was by now apprehensive and showed it, 'how do I know
you are not another Reilly, another Lockhart?'

'You can only take my word for it. I can give you no proof of
loyalty. It's impossible to do that, but I can assure you that I
am absolutely trustworthy and I will always remain loyal to
the communist cause.'

'Will you accept our instructions without question?'

Baring hesitated and Trotsky added, 'We will consult you
when we can, but when an issue arises which might be a
matter of life or death for the revolution, there may not be
time for that.'

'If the instructions are clearly conveyed and can be
understood, of course I shall obey,' replied Baring.

'Then I accept your word,' said Trotsky, 'there is no room in
our struggle for the faint hearted or the half-hearted. There is
only one commitment we can accept and that is total;
anything less than that would mean accepting a rotten apple
in the barrel. I warn you that if it ever becomes clear that you
are a British agent I shall not hesitate to have you liquidated.'

'Without a trial?' said Baring in a shocked voice.

'It would be a summary trial as I've conducted with traitors
at the front — even political Commissars have had to be
executed if they show treachery or cowardice. You will be
presented with the evidence and if you can't refute it you will
die. It's as simple as that. So you make your decision now. If
you want to walk out of this, you will go unharmed and you
will be treated as a prisoner of war, but if you decide to be with
us in our struggle for world revolution you will accept my
conditions and authority without question.'

'I accept,' said Baring.

'Then I welcome you as a comrade, Comrade Baring. Henceforth you will be under my direct command but for the sake of your training arrangements are being made for you to be attached to Vecheka. When we went through the files of the Okhrana, we discovered that a network of Tsarist agents had been at work in England, there were even two in Buckingham Palace. That network is being replaced. Dzerzhinsky has been building up a special section to deal with our secret foreign work using the best skills of the old Okhrana. You will learn all there is to learn about secret methods of communication and about the other techniques of espionage in case you have to use them. Frankly, I don't see you as an ordinary agent but it's important you have the skills; you might have to escape from a tight corner one day.'

Baring indicated his understanding as calmly as he could but in the pit of his stomach he felt a spasm of tension which tightened his muscles, drained the blood from his head and made him feel faint.

Trotsky went on, apparently oblivious to Baring's reactions. 'Naturally we have to produce a cover plan to prepare you for your return to England. I've already given instructions that the records of our unit at Kotlas will show you as being captured and that you were slightly injured whilst trying to escape. For the record this took place on the road from Shenkursk to Sergievskaya. The British Army at Archangel has already been informed of your capture and your family will soon know you are safe. Whilst you are in Russia and before you are returned to England as a repatriated prisoner you will have complete freedom, but your documents will show you as a Swedish comrade from Stockholm. Vecheka will work out the details of your cover but I want you to understand how vital it is that you do not reveal your true identity to anyone especially the inquisitive English journalists who are coming to Moscow. A lot of Swedes speak good English and the fact that you do won't surprise anyone, but don't try talking to Scandinavians, they will find you out in no time.'

Baring's tension was pacified by the suggested ruse which appealed to his sense of adventure. He felt bold enought to ask, 'Can I tell Comrade Cherepova about the plan?'

'That's the woman from Petrograd you're sleeping with isn't it?' asked Trotsky.

'Yes,' said Baring.

'I remember her,' said Trotsky, 'she's a reliable comrade. Yes you can and we'll arrange a special Vecheka briefing for her.'

'What about my return to England?'

'All in good time, Comrade. There is much for you to do here. I want you to understand what the revolution really means by attending some of our international meetings — as an observer only — and also by seeing our workers fight the patriotic war against the capitalist interventionists. You will come in my train on my staff for that. It's far too early to be thinking of repatriation but when it comes we will put you into prison with British officers who are prisoners of war so you can establish your *bona fides* with them. When the war is over you will go back with them to England. Then your real task will begin.'

Trotsky stood up from his desk and gave his visitor a firm hand shake and as Baring left the Commissar for War turned quietly to his map and battle plans.

CHAPTER 22

Two days later the Vecheka came to the National to collect Charles and Nina. By this time she had received her own intensive briefing on the mission her Englishman had been chosen to undertake. She had also been given the loyalty or death oath which emphasised the need for security. Their induction into the world's youngest secret service gave their relationship a new poignancy. The elation they felt at sharing a purpose was subdued by the realisation of the awesomeness of it. Each, without exchanging a word, sensed the other's controlled trepidation. What they had done was irrevocable. Any of those decisions which a man or a woman might take in the course of a lifetime have emotions of excitement, of joy and of foreboding associated with them, but the commitment which they had undertaken was so great the emotions it provoked were as intense as the approaches to hell.

It was worse for Charles as he had made the conscious decision to renounce his country in favour of a creed which had to be ruthless to succeed. The end justified any means and this included the elimination of acolytes foolish enough to renounce the faith.

On the journey in the Vecheka sledges to the outskirts of Moscow, Nina and Charles sat holding hands under the hides which protected them against the bitterly cold January day. They said nothing but let the streets swish by them as the unusually well-fed horses kept up a steady trot.

They were taken to Tatarova, where a bend in the frozen Moskva river surrounds a beautiful copse of larch, pine and silver birch in which the dachas had been taken over by the

Vecheka as a training centre. As they approached they saw a massive stockade with machine gun replacements protecting it.

'Don't worry; we're not being imprisoned,' Nina broke her silence. 'The stockade is to protect the camp against unauthorised visitors.'

At the entrance, manned by leather-suited armed men, their passes were carefully examined and the sledges were waved on to take them immediately to a magnificent single story dacha on a bank overlooking the river.

'This is our's,' said Nina.

'All of it?' asked Charles in amazement.

'They tell me so,' she replied, 'the Party leadership obviously regard you as one of the elite.'

'I thought all comrades had equal treatment and equal privileges. Why should we have extra?'

'Equal means different things to different people,' she replied. 'You keep your pony in an outshed and a thoroughbred in a stable. They have the equal treatment they each deserve and need. You are one of the thoroughbreds and have to be treated accordingly.'

When their two small bundles of belongings had been unpacked they stood and warmed themselves in front of a huge log fire which had been lit in anticipation of their arrival. Charles said, 'It appears Communism has already established its own system of privileges.'

'I'm a bit surprised. I didn't realise it would be so grand,' said Nina, 'but I can understand the reasons for it. You have an historic role on behalf of the revolution. It would be ludicrous to handicap you by making you live in conditions some others have to suffer. They don't have so much to give as you. Tell me Charles, would you be willing to accept the most degrading conditions of squalor and hunger that exist in this country today? I could show you some which would make your stomach turn in disgust and horror. Does your sense of equality mean that you have to be equal with those? Don't be ridiculous; you can't throw your life away like that; you could die before you'd achieved one verst of progress for Communism.'

The contrast was greater than anything even she had expected. They soon discovered the dacha had two bedrooms with freshly laundered linen, a book-lined study, a kitchen with a larder of scarce food, a dining room and a maid who brought them tea and the promise of home-cooked meals. Each room had a wood-burning stove giving the place a cosy warmth which neither had known for years.

After a lunch of omelettes, rye bread and soft goats cheese, they stretched on the rugs in front of the open fire and made love. It was enjoyable and efficient, but mechanical. The lustful, abandoned, excitement which Baring had felt earlier had been replaced by the sybaritism of the sated. The crossing of the line from the exposed and uncertain life of the ordinary citizen to the protected and comfortable privilege of the Vecheka stockade had altered both their outlooks and their personal relationship. They had taken the first steps from being revolutionaries to becoming functionaries.

The regime within the stockade was strict. The leather suited men were housed in barracks and the servants in other quarters. The central offices — a series of log cabins hastily constructed unlike the original dachas which had once belonged to the rich Moscow merchants — provided small conference and class rooms where Charles Baring went every morning for training. Under the tutelage of former Okhrana officers, educated men with exquisite manners which disguised their hard core of brutality and callousness, he learned about espionage techniques. He mastered the arts of recognising codes and deciphering them and of maintaining surveillance on unsuspecting victims. It was explained that although he might not need to use these methods in a positive way, it was necessary for him to know them to avoid being trapped. He studied the ways a skilful agent can kill — by poison in food or injection by handshake, by strangulation using the silk scarf, suddenly and quietly, and by the traditional daggers or guns. Every situation has its appropriate method he was told and it was important to be prepared for all eventualities.

After a month during which neither Nina or Charles had left the stockade, he was given a disorientation session. It was designed to strengthen his resistance to the stress of the double existence he would have to lead in England. The interrogators spared nothing; for five days and nights they bombarded the hapless trainee with questions and outrageous statements. The sessions were continuous. After a few minutes fitful sleep he would be woken and again the treatment would be repeated over and over until he longed for respite. To pass the tests the victim had to adhere to a pre-arranged story whilst the examiner strove to divert him from it by every conceivable means of mental torture. The temptations to waver were immense as the needs of the body for rest overcame the spititual resolve to survive and Charles was near breaking point when the time came for him to return to the dacha.

Nina welcomed him like a mother comforting a son who had had a breakdown. She washed and fussed him and sang him to sleep with gentle peasant songs and when he awoke fed him soft meals with a spoon. He had lost much weight from his already lean body and looked gaunt and skeletal. Nina worked on his spirit as well as his body. 'They tell me you did very well,' she said proudly, 'they never expected an English aristocrat to have the psychological strength to withstand their bombardment. They were determined to break you to prove a point. They admire your steadfastness.'

'What exactly are they trying to achieve by that hideous torture?' asked Charles who had been completely shaken by the experience and the unexpectedness of it.

'They want to know if you are able to retain your integrity as a Bolshevik when you are exposed to the pressures of capitalist society: in other words are you a "words only" comrade or do you have the strength to be totally dedicated.'

'They did some diabolical things,' Charles shuddered, remembering them. 'They brought in a fellow who had been my chess companion. I must have played a dozen games with him. He was a delightful man. At that stage they were playing the part of British officials pressing me to reveal the secret of my Bolshevik connections. I was exhausted for what had gone on for hours and hours before. I'd lost all idea of time. They said that they would kill the man if I didn't tell the truth. I refused of course, that was understood as part of the exercise, and then they proceeded to kill that man by a series of injections stopping each time to ask me to relent and so save his life. I allowed him to die Nina. I allowed him to die, just to prove I had the strength or the obstinacy to keep my secret.'

'Oh you poor boy,' she said comforting his head on her chest.

'If I knew it had been you they'd brought in I would have cracked,' he admitted, 'and then what would have happened? It doesn't bear thinking.'

'I know, I know,' she shook with emotion, 'if you fail their tests they don't let you leave the stockade. If you fail you can't be trusted and as you're no further use to them there's only one thing they can do.'

'Good God,' said Charles involuntarily invoking a Christian symbolism, 'what barbarity have they sunk to?'

'There's nothing new in it,' she said, 'they were the Tsar's men who did it, they were serving the government of today in the same way as they did Nicholas. They would say they were only doing their job.'

'It's horrific,' said Charles 'I hope this barbarism will cease once the revolution has found its stability. I suppose it's the constant threat from internal sabotage and external aggression that creates the need for these measures. Perhaps if we can hasten world revolution and achieve a world communism then the roles of the spies and inquisitors will wither away.'

'I expect it's only temporary,' Nina soothed him, 'old habits die hard and the state has been traditionally brutal in Russia. True communism will change all that in time.'

'I've just remembered,' said Charles, 'I had my twenty-first birthday when I was in that hell hole. In England they would say I was at last an adult, entitled to the key to the door.'

As the first stage of the course was complete, Nina and Charles were able to visit Moscow again to sample the theatres. This time they had no trouble in getting the best seats as their Vecheka passes gained them priority in everything. They saw Shakespeare's *Romeo and Juliet* with Charles improving his knowledge of Russian by following the play from an English text he had found in the dacha library. They also went to the ballet and the music of Delibes enchanted him; the infectious enjoyment of the crowded theatre made them happy that human joys were still alive. The Vecheka stockade seemed another life away. Charles was confident enough to joke that Dr. Coppelius, the puppet maker, had simply anticipated Dzerzhinsky who had succeeded through the Vecheka in creating human puppets on a scale Coppelius would have greatly envied. Nina did not laugh, she cautioned him. 'Your English sense of humour will be your undoing. Russians are a romantic and emotional people but they take things very seriously. Jokes like that would not be understood. Felix Edmundovich would take that as a direct insult and if you repeated that in the hearing of the Vecheka people it would certainly be reported to him. You would make an enemy and, believe me, he's a dangerous man to cross.'

By coincidence next day a message came through that the head of the Vecheka would be pleased to receive Baring at his office in Moscow and that Comrade Cherepova was to accompany him.

They were taken to the headquarters of the Vecheka at number 2, Bolshaia Lubyanka, a grey stone building which had been the offices of the All Russian Insurance Company before the revolution. The security at the entrance was greater than at the Kremlin. 'Political prisoners are kept in the Lubyanka prison here,' whispered Nina as they climbed the bare stairs. 'Some of them are dangerous counter-revolutionaries and security has to be strict.'

On the third floor they were ushered into a big, ornate, carpeted room which had a light, airy atmosphere thanks to the high windows and the potted palms which were scattered around. A tall thin man came towards them and Baring was struck immediately by his ascetic and fanatical look. He had a high forehead, watery and limpid eyes with drooping eyelids, a long bony nose, a small moustache, and a goatee beard. Although he was only about forty years old and dressed in a military uniform of high boots, riding breeches and a field jacket, he had the manner of an eccentric grand vizier and addressed the visitors in disjointed sentences whilst looking over their heads into the distance.

'Comrade Dzerzhinsky says he welcomes us to his centre and he hopes all is well with the comrade from England,' said Nina as the head of Vecheka invited them to sit at a long polished table. Bowls of fruit, jugs of water and glasses were arranged down its centre and there were three places set with notebooks and pencils.

'I am very impressed with Comrade Baring's progress at the course,' said Dzerzhinsky, 'it is not an easy one but you will appreciate it is necessary to be tough to be kind. We have to weed out the weakest plants for only the strong ones will grow in a hostile environment.'

'Yes I understand that,' said Baring.

'In your case you have not had the advantage of prison experience and it is important to find a substitute for the stresses and tests that entails. I was incarcerated by the Okhrana many times and sent to Siberia. Every time I escaped I was rearrested because of more revolutionary activity and each time it added to my backbone of resolve. It is by far the best education for a revolutionary.'

'My education was in the trenches on the Western front against Germany,' said Baring. 'To a thinking person that experience is enough to make a revolutionary.'

'I saw that in your file,' said Dzerzhinksy. 'It obviously had a big influence on you.'

'One of the reasons I became a Communist is because I believe it will help to stop war,' said Baring.

'You are correct,' Dzerzhinsky said, peering across the table. 'Only Communism can eliminate the capitalist greed which is the cause of war. The common people will revolt against war if we give them the inspiration. The German sailors at Riga brought the war against England to an end by their revolt but now the British are supporting the bourgeoisie in destroying Communism in Germany. Our friend Karl Radek has been arrested.'

'That's terrible,' said Baring remembering the intense Pole he had met in Petrograd.

'The bourgeois German government fears the Communism he was preaching, but it will succeed in the end. We shall make sure of that.' He slammed the table. 'Radek is my old friend from Poland, he is a great revolutionary and we shall make sure his sacrifice is not in vain. You will join me in some tea, will you?' he added with a faint smile softening his austere face.

The servants brought in a delicate silver samovar, which they placed on a stand on the table near the Commissar's right hand, and a plate of sliced lemons — a rare sight in Moscow which was cut off from the traditional source of supply of citrus in the Crimea.

'The American government of President Wilson has been playing games with us by first suggesting a peace conference at Prinkipo and then dropping the proposal when the White Russians objected to sitting at the conference table with us. It was a trick from beginning to end. The allies don't want peace, they simply want to crush Bolshevism as they know if it survives in Russia it will spread to their countries just as surely as night follows day. Now, Comrade Baring,' he said in a curt way, 'let's get to work,' as if the social exchanges had taken up enough time.

Dzerzhinsky explained that the Vecheka, the All-Russian Extraordinary Commission for the struggle against Counter-Revolution and Sabotage, had been established with the primary role of combatting the anti-Bolshevik elements still remaining in Russia. As Commissar for Internal Affairs he had control of all the police and internal security organisations for that purpose. Then he described the Vecheka's external role which came about because the revolution could not succeed in one country alone and had to expand until it covered the whole world. Direct action by the Bolshevik Government would not be realistic as the enemy was too strong in military terms and would be able to drum up enough nationalistic fervour in their proletarian masses to persuade them to die for a system that oppresses them. The way to destroy capitalism, explained Dzerzhinsky, was to find its internal weaknesses and then to exploit them. Taking an apple from the bowl of fruit in front of him he illustrated his point. 'Here is a perfect fruit. A strong skin but notice here a small blemish. Through that the microbe enters and within days reduces the apple inside that skin to useless pulp. The apple then might still look robust but pick it up and it disintegrates.' The task of the external Vecheka was to get the microbes into the right apple of capitalism to destroy it from within.

'You have been chosen for the most important task in England.' Dzerzhinsky had eventually reached Baring's proposed role and became more intimate in his manner. 'Henceforth you are an officer of Vecheka. I am appointing you from this day but, of course, this is a secret appointment and will be known only to Radek, Trotsky, Chicherin and Vladimir Ilyich who must be informed of an appointment of this importance. Apart from the few Vecheka officers who will liaise with you, and Comrade Cherepova here, they will be the only ones to know. You will therefore be able to operate in confidence. When the war of intervention is over you will go back to England as a returned prisoner of war. You will express your vehement opposition to the Bolshevik system so you can curry favour with your aristocratic friends. That will get you into the apple because sycophancy is one of the blemishes of capitalism. Once you have established yourself as an enemy of Bolshevism you will be highly regarded in England and you will get preferment.'

'What exactly will I be expected to do when I'm in a position of responsibility?' asked Baring.

'In your remaining time in Russia you will be coached by some of the best experts on the economic and social problems of capitalism. We have a few of those in the universities. You will be able to make those problems much worse and probably insoluable by the actions you can take from inside the English establishment. Separately and apart from your work we shall be arranging for the English working class to revolt through their trades unions by using strikes. The colonial workers will also struggle for independence against the English Empire. There will thus be several simultaneous attacks on the capitalist structure. We will destroy it like this.' He crushed the apple in the palm of his hand.

He lent over the table and gripped Baring's arm. 'We have great confidence in you,' he said with feeling. 'We trust you and want you to feel a deep identification with our struggle. Our mutual cause is a noble one and so that you can understand it fully, arrangements have been made for you to attend some of our meetings. As an observer of course. Your secret has to be kept even from our most senior foreign comrades.'

At the beginning of March comrades Baring and Cherepova received tickets for the meeting of the Third International, the first meeting of the most important international communist forum. It was held in the Kremlin in the old Courts of Justice which had been built in the reign of

Catherine. Two smart Red Army soldiers guarded the doors as officials checked the visitors' papers and Charles and Nina were shown to the back seats of a room which had a dais at the other end.

Baring felt he had stumbled into the theatre of history, for the theatrical atmosphere was predominant and history was certainly being made. All round the room were banners in red in various languages that proclaimed *Long Live the Third International.* There was a lively bustle as delegates took their seats and greeted their neighbours enthusiastically. There were many languages spoken. The whole world seemed to be represented and Baring marvelled that a country torn by war on five fronts and facing extinction could manage to organise such a display of international solidarity.

The three members of the Praesidium walked in by a side door and mounted the dais taking their seats behind a long red covered table. Baring recognised the small figure of Lenin who sat in the middle.

'Who are the other two?' he whispered.

'A German and Swiss' said Nina. 'In the International the Russians, although the biggest, are only a minority of the delegates.'

Four or five of the front row seats had little writing desks and Nina pointed out Trotsky, Zinoviev and Chicherin, all of whom Charles recognised, and Litvinov. — 'He was in London as the Bolshevik Ambassador but had to leave when the British started fighting us,' said Nina — and Bukharin, a striking looking man of about thirty about whom Nina whispered 'after Vladimir Ilyich he is our greatest intellectual and theoretician.'

The speeches, in several languages but mostly in German as the most generally understood language, were difficult to follow as neither Charles nor Nina could speak it. Lenin spoke fluently and persuasively in several languages switching from one to the other with great ease as Trotsky, sitting below him in a leather coat, military breeches and a fur hat with the Red Army insignia, made notes. The British delegate, Fineberg, and the American Reinstein made stirring speeches in English. Baring remembered them from the Petrograd meeting in December and realised they must have spent the intervening months in Russia with little or no contacts with their parties back home. When a delegate from Korea was speaking in some oriental tongue, listened to by delegates politely without comprehension, Nina touched Charles's arm and whispered, 'That man two rows across is an English journalist. You'll have to be careful you don't bump into him. He is very inquisitive.' Charles saw a young man with a balding head and a large brown walrus moustache writing feverishly on his lap.

'Is he a Communist?'

'No, but sympathetic to the revolution. His reports in the *London Daily News* have been helpful to us. They say he put the revolution in a good light because he fell in love with Trotsky's secretary, a nice girl called Eugenia I used to know in Petrograd.'

'What's he doing at this secret meeting if he's not a Communist?'

'Arthur Ransome is able to get anywhere by making friends with the leaders but some say he's a spy for the British Foreign Office and won't trust him.'

At the end of the fifth day the conference ended with the singing of the *Internationale* and the taking of photographs. A stir was created when a photographer kept insisting that Trotsky return to the rostrum for a suitable pose. He resisted until someone shouted out, 'It's not the dictatorship of the proletariat, it's the dictatorship of the photographer' and amid the general laughter Trotsky did as he was requested.

That night Baring and Cherepova joined the crowds for a huge meeting in the Great Theatre where a public announcement was to be made. The excitement was intense as Kamenev, the thirty-five year old chairman of the Moscow Soviet, opened with a statement that the Third International had been founded and the whole audience rose and sang the *Internationale* as one man. It was a moving occasion and Baring, touched by the emotion of it, felt the way was now open for Communism to sweep the world with its appeal. The capitalist countries would be helped to disintegrate and collapse from their own internal complications and then the Third International would take over as a world government.

Lenin rose to speak and the applause from the workers in the audience boomed in crescendo after crescendo. There was no doubt about his popularity with the crowds in that theatre. Other speakers followed him and when Charles eventually left he was both exhilarated and exhausted by the passionate purpose which had been generated.

CHAPTER 23

Captain Charles Baring, who had now been granted the equivalent rank in the Red Army, continued his intensive training at the Tatarova stockade of the Vecheka. He also kept in close touch with the progress of the war by attending conferences in the war room where the maps and charts showed the seriousness of the situation. The public of Moscow were not aware of the dangers the Bolshevik Government faced as *Pravda* was not allowed to print the full story to avoid panic. Officers of the Vecheka however were kept fully informed.

In the East the White Russian forces under Kolchak had advanced on a broad front towards Volga but a determined defence by Trotsky held them at bay. In the South the White Russian General Denikin was moving into the Ukraine and taking it without resistance. Morale had slumped as he advanced on Tsaritsyn and Kharkov and moved nearer towards the capital.

One morning Baring received a command from the Commissariat of War to join Trotsky who was returning to the southern front. With the newly promoted Lieutenant Cherepova he rushed to the Kursk railway terminal on the other side of Moscow and found the Commissar's armoured train waiting in a siding. The Commissar was still delayed at the Kremlin in a meeting of the Politbureau and there was much speculation about its outcome. There were rumours that a serious disagreement had emerged in the leadership and that the Commissar for Nationalities, a Georgian who was born Joseph Dzhugashvili and called himself Stalin, was criticising the conduct of the war with the aim of undermining Trotsky's position. Trotsky's aides had fanatical devotion to him and bitterly resented these scurrilous attacks by his opponents in the Politbureau. The group on the train were fulsome in their praise as they waited for the Commissar. 'His courage, his leadership are second only to Lenin's,' they said. 'We've seen with our very eyes at front after front how, when the enemy has broken through, Commissar Trotsky gets down from the train and personally leads the Red Units into battle. When their energy flags he calls the troops to a meeting and inspires them with his oratory to carry on. It's phenomenal, comrade, what that man can do with words.'

When Trotsky arrived, smartly dressed in a greatcoat over the same uniform Baring had seen him wearing at the Kremlin meeting, the troops let out a cheer which he responded to by holding his right fist clenched high above his head.

The train had already picked up steam and had left the siding, pulling coaches crowded with Moscow workers, newly recruited as reserves for the hard-pressed units at the front. Baring was in the command wagon as Trotsky threw off his greatcoat in a gesture of exasperation and said for all to hear, 'It's bad enough to fight seven armies who are squeezing us into an ever smaller centre, without having to defend one's back against one's so-called friends. I need all the support I can get but Moscow is full of amateur strategists who've never used a gun except against a passive victim. They make me sick. Comrades we must push back Denikin's attack so I can return to Moscow and get the authority of Vladimir Ilyich to fight the war in my way. I can't stand this constant carping from the sidelines. Will you help me?' He asked looking drawn and tired.

'We shall Comrade Trotsky,' shouted a voice and others took up the call. 'We're with you Comrade Trotsky,' said another and the officers came forward to grip the

Commissar's hand and pledge their loyalty to him.

Later Baring was called into Trotsky's private compartment as the train trundled south through the night. 'I've got a present for you.' said the Commissar. 'This has been my own revolver and in many actions it saved my life. I want you to keep it as a mark of my esteem. You have courage in coming over to our ranks and giving us support at this time of our lowest hour. More courage than some of those hangers-on in Moscow I can say,' he said with anguish, handing Baring a highly polished Nagant.

'Thank you,' said Baring who was touched by the Commissar's generosity. 'I shall treasure this.'

'I heard what you went through at Tatarova,' Trotsky said, 'and now I know you are one of us. It's easy to be a Communist when you have nothing else to cling to or when you are a Russian and drawn into it but to make the decision you made to renounce your whole background in the interests of the cause is courage indeed. I salute you Comrade Captain. Anything I can do to help you I will. Meanwhile,' he turned to the maps on the table, 'let me tell you about our immediate problem.'

Baring looked at the map of Russia showing the position of the enemy. The Bolsheviks were surrounded on all sides with Moscow as the middle.

'We have this circumference of five thousand miles to defend and armies are coming at us from all directions. Although I've got half a million men in the Red Army they are not trained or sufficiently armed to hold back this onslaught. In various places on this circumference the Whites can find our weak points and strike deep into our territory. We can force them back but only by withdrawing troops from another place which makes our weakness felt there.'

Trotsky explained how with his train he had been able to move from one front to another as the war situation demanded, bringing fresh troops to staunch the huge losses the enemies were inflicting on the Red Army. 'We've everything we need on this train,' he said proudly. 'It has a printing press so we can give news and heart to our men on the front lines, we have a library — including,' he added with a laugh 'some very good novels, we have a radio and telegraph station to keep in touch with our other units, and we have an ammunition store. Do you know what is the most popular part of our train?'

'What?' asked Baring dutifully.

'The Bathhouse. The weary troops are overjoyed to see us with reinforcements and supplies but most of all because they can have a bath and get rid of their lice.'

'Makes sense,' said Baring who recalled his own longings for the simplest of the creature comforts when in the trenches.

As the train pulled through the night Trotsky became more relaxed and relieved to be away from the wrangling in Moscow and in the familiar surroundings of his travelling home. 'There is good news,' he said, 'from Bavaria and Hungary. Both countries have declared Soviet Republics. We're trying to link up with them but the Ukrainians are fighting with the Whites and we can't get through. There's good news too from Odessa. The French soldiers there read our propaganda and they have mutinied. The Clemenceau Government in Paris has had to withdraw all French troops. If only the British would do the same we could win this war in a couple of months. Your compatriots have a lot to answer for, but one day they will reap the whirlwind for the evil they are doing here.'

After a night and a full day travelling to the south and east the train reached the river Volga and the Commissar and his supplies were transferred to a flotilla of gunboats to sail down the river to Tsaritsyn. Baring and Cherepova walked the small deck of the leading boat as it chugged southwards. The spring sun was shining brightly and the countryside on both sides looked deceptively peaceful although it had only recently been the scene of bitter fighting between the Red Army and Kolchak.

'Do you think this war will ever finish?' asked Nina. 'It seems to ebb and flow all over Mother Russia. It's nearly two years since the revolution and that was after a bloody war of three years. I really wonder whether the Russian people can take much more of this blood-letting.'

'With leaders like Trotsky we're bound to win and the hotter the furnace the tougher the steel. The victors who come out of this will be strong enough to withstand anything.'

'I hope so,' said Nina, 'but I fear what it is all doing to the soul of Russia.'

The gunboats kept up a steady rate of knots and after some hours stopped at a village quayside to pick up fresh water and food. The peasants came to stare at the sight of soldiers in uniforms with their Red Army badges, not knowing whether this visit in the crazy see-saw war would be followed by a wave of Whites bent on revenge against collaborators. Baring had seen several villages which had been burnt out by avenging armies on the rampage.

Trotsky came onto the top deck resplendent in his long greatcoat and high fur cap. He waved to the peasants but either they did not recognise him or simply took fright because they all ran off into the fields.

Later that day and further down the Volga, Baring was in Trotsky's cabin when they heard the noise of aircraft approaching and shouts from the lookouts.

'It's an attack,' said Trotsky.

'Whose aircraft?' asked Baring surprised to hear of any in that remote area.

'British,' said Trotsky as the anti-aircraft began to open fire.

Baring rushed to the deck in time to see three Sopwith Camels overhead and the clutch of bombs falling. He ducked as a twenty-pounder exploded on the starboard sending shrapnel and bits of the boat's superstructure flying in all directions. He caught a jagged bit in his left arm which began to bleed profusely. A Red sailor saw his injury and crept to his side tearing off a piece of his shirt to use as a bandage and quickly improvised a tourniquet with a stick of the loose timber. Baring felt his arm go limp but the blood rushed back to his head preventing him from fainting.

The Camels were circling again and dropping more bombs when six other aircraft suddenly appeared. 'They're ours' said the sailor in Russian with gestures Baring could easily understand. The Camels turned to escape the attack with the Red planes in pursuit.

Lieutenant Cherepova who had been below deck came to Baring's side 'We'll have to get you on a bunk and clean up that arm before you get toxaemia. That was a close run. Your English friends are getting daring.'

Trotsky came to see him. 'You're our only casualty,' he said. 'I wonder what those English pilots would think if they knew their only hit was a British officer.'

'Are you sure they were British?' asked Baring.

'Certainly. The Royal Air Force have their number forty-seven squadron at Ekaterinodar. We know about it from intelligence reports. It is commanded by a Canadian called Lieutenant-Colonel Raymond Collishaw.'

'Actually I think it's called the Royal Flying Corps,' said Baring.

'You're out of date Comrade, the British have re-named it the Royal Air Force and all its active units are being deployed against us. In future years they'll be able to boast that the history of the R.A.F. was launched on the blood of Red workers fighting for their country and socialism.'

'What were those aircraft who chased them off?'

'Spads and Nieupots. We inherited them from the Imperial Air Force and from the Germans. Actually the pilots are German who came over to our side. We haven't had time to train Bolshevik pilots.'

The gunboat although damaged was river worthy and able to complete the journey to Tsaritsyn where Baring was taken to a military hospital to have his injury checked. Next day he was discharged with his arm in a sling as he joined Trotsky at Red Army headquarters.

A regional conference of Political Commissars and army commanders was taking place. Lieutenant Cherepova joined Baring to act as interpreter.

Trotsky held the fifty or sixty regional army leaders spellbound with his oratory which flowed like a cascade of scintillating water from a fountain. With Nina's occasional help Charles could follow some of the more familiar phrases. 'Comrades we must turn back the wicked Imperialists who are using all their military might in an attempt to destroy our people's revolution. They fight for money; we fight for human freedoms.'

The state of the front was analysed. White General Wrangel's forces had been forced back to the Tchervlennia river but were regrouping for an attack on Tsaritsyn and British aircraft had created havoc by strafing Red Army positions. The British air supremacy had to be countered if the town was to be held.

'It's vital for us to hold Tsaritsyn,' declared Trotsky. 'We're only just holding a corridor north of the Caspian between Deniken's and Wrangel's forces in the south and Kolchak's and the Cossacks in the east. If they are able to link up it would be a severe blow to our defence strategy. Of course this town is a misnomer, once the war is over we shall re-name it in the Soviet style with a name of which its gallant defenders will be proud.'

The conference broke into a round of applause which died out as the crunching sound of bombs was heard. The conference broke up in confusion with shouts of 'take shelter comrades' and 'save Trotsky!' as the Commissar for War was hustled into a corner.

Baring and Cherepova scattered with the rest just as the building was struck. They found themselves in a courtyard with masonry and bricks flying around their heads. By a miracle they were not hit. Baring heard the drone of the returning aircraft and saw two de Havilland 9s making another low level bomb drop. He clutched at Cherepova with his good arm and dragged her to a wall where they cowered for shelter as the bomb scored a direct hit.

When they dared to get up they saw pieces of bodies and corpses lying about the place and wounded men groaning. Cherepova went to comfort some but there was not much she could do.

A Spad and a Fokker triplane came across the horizon to intercept the DH9s but were immediately attacked by Sopwith Camels. The Spad crashed in flames and the Fokker fled. The R.A.F. planes had the skies to themselves and completed the bombing of other targets.

Looking at the scene of destruction, smelling the unmistakable stench of burning flesh, Baring was torn between horror at the deaths of his fellow Red Army officers and an odd sense of residual pride that the Britishers had done it against all odds. The pilots above were his contemporaries who had probably served with him on the Western front and might even be O.Es. He sensed a spasm of guilt that he could admire their action when his loyalty had been pledged to the Bolsheviks and resolved to cast out the remnants of bourgeois nationalism which still coloured his outlook. He knew that a true international Communist could never allow any thought to cloud the sharply defined issues of revolution against imperialism and justice against exploitation.

His reflections were broken by Cherepova, 'You looked shocked, are you alright?'

'Yes I'm alright,' he replied.

'They must have killed Trotsky,' she said in alarm. 'The place he was in has been completely destroyed. It's just a mass of rubble. He couldn't survive that.'

It was not until two hours later they heard that the Commissar for War had survived by sheltering in a cellar and then moving out to a disused well before the second attack.

There was a smell of despair in the air; Trotsky soon left for another front and no one was able to inspire confidence in the defenders. News filtered through of a disaster to the north. A relieving column of Red troops led by General Budyonny was caught in a ravine by a British aircraft attack. Five Sopwith Camels had dived on them from the skies and strafed them with automatic fire again and again. The slaughter was frightful and at least eight hundred men were killed. The rest retreated into the steppe in disorder. The news had a catastrophic impact on morale in Tsaritsyn which collapsed completely as the expected attack by the Whites took place.

Back in Moscow, Baring found conditions had worsened. The weather was better and the people did not have to contend with the biting cold but food was extremely short and even the meagre rations could not be honoured in the State shops. Many people were obviously near starvation. As a Red Army Captain attached to the Vecheka, Baring was allocated accommodation in a guest house on the Mala Hortonoyskaya and Cherepova moved in with him. The food was better here although nothing like that at the Tatorova stockade, but Baring willingly made the sacrifice in not returning to that place of mental torture.

The most disturbing aspect of life in Moscow was the artificial air of normality. The theatres were still full and the parks had their quota of strollers enjoying the summer sunshine. People although hungry seemed to be oblivious to the threat posed by the truth of the situation although it was full of calls for revolutionary sacrifice against the imperialists and interventionists.

Several times Baring and Cherepova went to the Vecheka headquarters at the Lubyanka, with its Chinese looking guards at the entrances, to advise the section dealing with foreign affairs about Great Britain and America. Baring was impressed by the amount of intelligence already accumulated. There were loose-leaf volumes full of the biographies of leading personalities in all the political parties and the trades unions. He was amazed that, during such a critical war effort, that time could have been devoted to such a task. The brains behind the operation were as usual former Okhrana officials who had joined the Vecheka, putting their expertise at its disposal.

Baring was also asked to check through the files of the captured British troops in case he could see clues indicating a potential recruit for the espionage services. He found the name of Haycraft; the Lieutenant, an engineer, had been captured on the Dwina front in July. Before he fully had time to take in the news that his friend Arthur was being held on the outskirts of Moscow the secretary brought a letter. It was addressed to 'Captain C. Baring, M.C.' and had been sent through Red Cross channels to a prisoner in Russian custody. It had an English stamp and was postmarked *Saxmundham.* Baring recognised his mother's handwriting and tore at the envelope eagerly. The letter was closely written and bore the marks of at least two censors. It was dated 24th May, 1919, and had taken three months to arrive. It read:

My dear boy, we all send our fondest love to you in these terrible times and pray for your safe return to England. The first report said you were dead and you can imagine our relief when the official telegram came saying you were alive and a prisoner.

Now I have some terrible news. Be brave. Your dear Father was killed last month in a motor accident. It happened late one night when he was returning from London. He'd been for a school reunion and wanted to get back to the Hall to be with me. Since your disappearance he tried to spend as much time with me as possible otherwise he would have stayed in London at his Club. The best intentions lead to disaster and your dear Father was fated to go in this way. The motor was totally crushed when it hit a tree somewhere between Colchester and Ipswich. I never went to see it, of course, I was too distressed. Fortunately no one else was killed or injured which is a blessing.

Your Father was a very fine man who loved you and I hope you will always remember him with love and kindness.

The funeral was held at Saxmundham church (where we were married) and was a most moving occasion. The church was packed with people from the Estate, the village and miles around and some even came up from London. It was so sad you could not be there but Edith and Emma put flowers on the grave for you.

They are well and send their love as does grandfather Tallen who is hail and hearty although getting on now, but then a doctor can take care of himself, can't he!

Your Uncle John has been very helpful organising things on the Estate although he cannot spend much time because of his political work. We are all longing for the day when you can come home and take over the reins. Be brave. Your dear Father was proud of you.

I do not know if this letter will reach you but the War Office promised they would do their best.

My kisses come from my heart. God bless you.

Your loving Mother

For a moment Baring sat transfixed staring at the words in an uncomprehending way; the tears came to his eyes but he controlled them.

CHAPTER 24

The Vecheka would not listen to Baring's request to return home and when after three days he eventually saw Dzerzhinsky the Chairman was adamant. 'You are suffering an emotional spasm, Comrade. You can do no material good by returning to England but you could do a lot of harm. Although difficult it would not be impossible to get you out of Russia, but if we did, how do you explain your imprisonment and your premature release. Our whole cover plan for you would be exposed and harm not only you but the cause we both serve.'

'When are the prisoners being released?' asked Baring.

'Not until the war is over. There have been a few exchanged at the fronts but the general release must await the end of hostilities. The allies have to stop beating us into the ground if they want their men returned.'

Baring then raised the question of Haycraft.

'I've seen the name of a British officer in the prisoner lists and I think he could be recruited.'

'Our people will attend to him,' said Dzerzhinsky.

'I thought I should talk to him.'

'And reveal your commitment to Bolshevism?' Dzerzhinsky asked sternly.

'I know him well and I'm sure he can be trusted.'

'If you are sure, Comrade, but you have to be as sure as I am of Vladimir Ilyich. There is no margin for error. If you are wrong you know what the consequences for this man would be. You would have revealed your secret to him and that's the heaviest responsibility he can carry in his lifetime.'

Baring, who was desperate to have some human contact with a fellow Englishman, swallowed any faint doubts and said categorically, 'I have every confidence in him.'

'Then have him brought here. Do your best to enrole him — obviously he would be very useful if you succeed but if you fail we will have to take care of the problem.'

When they were well away from the Vecheka Chairman's room, Nina Cherepova took Charles Baring's hand as if to console him. Later in the privacy of their room she said, 'I am sorry you can't go to be with your Mother but these are the dreadful years. There is so much suffering in Russia you can't expect the powers here to be sympathetic. Dzerzhinsky is a most human person with a lot of emotion and kindness in him but he's had to develop a hard, cruel streak to do the job he does. He won't relent. If you'd been able to see Vladimir Ilyich it might have been another story; he can perform miracles.'

'Do you think I'll ever get to see him?'

'I'll talk to Krylova; she's arrived from Petrograd to join his secretariat and she'll arrange it if she can,' said Nina. 'But on that British officer friend of yours. Do you think you did the right thing? He's in enormous danger if you fail to recruit him.'

'I'm certain to succeed,' said Charles irritably, knowing he had been caught out in what was at best a gamble and at worst a lamentable error of judgement.

After a week they brought Lieutenant Haycraft to the Lubyanka under close guard. Baring persuaded the Vecheka to dispense with the usual depersonalisation techniques until he had had a chance to talk to his friend. He knew that an all-out onslaught on Arthur's personality would get the interrogators nowhere. The Lieutenant could be as obstinate as a mule unless some kind of carrot were dangled.

As Baring in his Red Army Captain's uniform sat at a desk in the external affairs office he wondered how Arthur

Haycraft, the frank friend of the hospital days many years ago, would respond to the new relationship. Then he thought with a sudden start that it was nothing like years before, it was only about eighteen months. A mere one and a half years and his life had changed so much as to be unrecognisable. The seeds of his conversion to Bolshevism had always been there but the gulf between imagination and reality was as wide as the North Sea and had been every bit as rough. Would Arthur Haycraft understand and could he possibly relate? Whatever might be Haycraft's personal wishes Baring determined that he would, by any means, convince his friend as the alternative was too horrible to contemplate.

The guards showed in a dishevelled British officer in a torn and dirty uniform. Haycraft looked thinner and much older than Baring remembered him and he had not shaved for three days. At first the Lieutenant looked around in a confused state unable to understand why the guards had left him alone in the palatial office with an unprotected Red Army officer and then Baring said, 'Hello Arthur, it's been a long time.'

'Good God,' said Haycraft, 'it's you! What on earth are you doing here in that get up?'

I'm a Red Army officer now and this is my office.'

'Heavens galore.'

'Sit down Arthur I'll get you some tea and it'll have lemon too. I don't 'spect you've seen that for a long time.'

Baring went to the door and called out for the servant to bring the samovar.

'My you're well set up here,' said Haycraft, 'is this what you get for selling out to the enemy?'

'You know it's not as simple as that, Arthur. I told you I was coming over. That was after the Armistice with Germany when we both thought all fighting would finish. Well it didn't, did it. Here we are eight months after and the interventionists are still trying to smother a revolution which is no concern of their's.'

'We're pulling out of North Russia though,' said Haycraft,

'the proposed evacuation was announced just before I was captured.'

'I know about that but it's not before time. Do you know why the Cabinet decided to pull out?'

'You tell me,' said Haycraft resentfully.

Because of the mutiny of the Russian you'd conscripted into Dyer's Battalion, and the agitation against the war in Britain was too much for the imperialists to handle. In other words the ordinary people decided the outcome. Ordinary Russians and ordinary Britons. The day of the arrogant imperialist politician and war lord is over. A pity this couldn't have happened five years ago in 1914. It would have stopped the senseless slaughter of millions.'

The tea came in and Haycraft sipped his gingerly, reluctant to acknowledge any gratitude and still bristling from the rigours of his imprisonment. Baring could see the tension in his friend and decided to play his fish with a long line.

'Were you in some nasty operations before your capture?'

'It became much worse after you left us,' said Haycraft. 'The Bolos attacked in January on the Dwina and the Vaga fronts and at Ust Padenga against the Americans. Remember Otto Odgaard, he was killed.'

'Poor Odgaard, he always thought the war was crazy,' said Baring.

'The Americans lost over two hundred and fifty, killed in one way or another before they withdrew. That was a very high number for their small force.'

'Not as big a proportion as the carnage on the Western Front but a senseless waste all the same,' said Baring.

'You were right,' said Haycraft. 'It was the mutiny which finally decided Ironside to pull out. Did you know the mutineers killed five British officers?'

'Who were they?' interrupted Baring and nodded his head in sorrow as he recalled some of the men named.

'A hundred men deserted,' continued Haycraft, 'we knew

then that the Russian conscripts had no stomach for the fight. I felt we were on a hiding to nowhere but I didn't want to be captured like you did. I only wanted to go home like the rest. They will be sailing off this month if they keep to the original plan.'

'Are they taking the White Russians with them? asked Baring.

'All who want to go, but the White General Miller is staying on to hold Archangel in the hope of a White victory elsewhere in Russia.'

'There's no chance of that,' said Baring emphatically, 'every day that passes gives greater vigour to the revolutionaries. The people can't be crushed. Look Arthur.' He became more intimate in his tone. 'I've attended meetings in the Kremlin and I've seen these chaps fighting in the field. They have the sort of will that can't be defeated.'

'I've always thought we were damned stupid to get involved in this war,' admitted Haycraft.

'That's right,' said Baring seeing his advantage, 'but it goes on. The British are now using their aircraft and tanks in South Russia putting everything into the attack on our positions there.' Unconsciously he had slipped into the habit of calling the British 'they' and the Bolsheviks 'us'. Haycraft noticed but did not comment. 'The war could go on for years yet and you could be in prison all that time. There's no sign of a general agreement for the exchange of prisoners.'

'I'll just have to grin and bear it won't I,' said Haycraft a little more relaxed.

'You don't have to. I'm authorised to offer you a job.'

'Join the Bolsheviks,' Haycraft laughed, 'not on your nellie.'

'Don't be ridiculous, Arthur. You're a qualified engineer and your skills are going to waste. I'm not asking you to join the Red Army, I'm giving you the chance of working as a civilian in Moscow helping to re-establish their factories. You'll have decent accommodation; the food situation is rough but better grub than you get in prison and you'll have your freedom to move around although you shouldn't leave Moscow.'

Haycraft looked as if he could be interested.

For the rest of the day and over *blinies* which Haycraft ate hungrily and at last appreciatively they talked about the scene in Moscow and Petrograd, how Haycraft would get organised and how and when the war was finally over both of them could be put back into the returning prisoner stream without anyone on the British side being any the wiser. Baring deliberately did not develop the subject of Haycraft's future cooperation with the Bolshevik Government after his return to Britain, except to hint that as a sign of gratitude Haycraft might do some favours for them. This he accepted in a cheerful uncomprehending way.

Baring called in Nina Cherepova to introduce her to Haycraft and went to report progress to the supervising Vecheka officer that the catch had been made. His recommendation was accepted without question and Haycraft was released immediately.

Early in October Trotsky sent an invitation to Baring to visit him in his rooms in the Kremlin. This was the first time Charles had seen the family accommodation appropriated by the leaders of the revolution and he was excited by the prospect. It was in a building previously occupied by Tsarist officials and did not quite have the Grand Ducal splendour of the other apartments which were being turned into a museum.

Trotsky greeted him as an old friend. 'Come in Baring; it's good to see you again.' He called to his wife in colloquial Russian and turned to say politely, 'Meet Natalia' and in English, so his visitor could understand what he said to his wife, 'This is the Englishman I told you about. His friendship is my living proof that I don't hate all the English although their government is trying to crush all I believe in.'

Baring shook hands with a diminutive snub-nosed woman

who was rather pretty despite her pixie-like appearance. Trotsky added, 'You might as well meet the whole family. This is Bronstein my father; he won't understand a word you say but he'll sum you up all the same.'

Baring met the well-built, tall man in his mid-seventies with a white beard and was struck immediately by the deep-set blue eyes which his son had obviously inherited.

Trotsky went on, 'My father had to leave our family home at Yanovka to seek safety in Odessa and he walked the whole distance on foot. What an achievement for an old man. He was stopped by different groups of partisans and threatened by them all. The Bolsheviks thought he was a rich Kulak and the anti-Bolsheviks who knew his identity abused him as my father. It's safer for him here with me until things settle down, though he wants to get back to the land soon.'

After they had talked for an hour Natalia brought some supper to the dining table. It was a simple meal of potato and mixed vegetable soup and black bread but it was served with great ceremony on plates decorated with the double-headed eagle.

'Usually when I'm in Moscow we eat with Vladimir Ilyich and Krupskaya who live just across the corridor, but they are away just now,' Trotsky said. 'Of course most of my time is spent on the command train; the troops at the front like to see me. Their situation is desperate and it's vital the leadership should be seen to be with them at this fateful time.'

'The military position is still bad, I presume,' said Baring.

'It could hardly be worse,' Trotsky said solemnly. 'Deniken has taken Kharkov, Kiev and now Orel and is threatening to break through to Tula which is the last big town before Moscow. Tudenich has reached the very edge of Petrograd and the city of the revolution could be lost to the Whites.'

'Are you confident you can push them back?' asked Baring concerned to detect a hint of desperation in the Commissar's voice.

'No I am not. My Red army is starving and half are without

boots or decent clothing. They have to fight the Kulaks as well as the Whites but we are marshalling all our resources and as we are compressed in a small area we can spring back against their extended lines, but there's no guarantee of victory. It is very very difficult.' Trotsky hesitated as though slightly uncertain whether his frankness was leading in the right direction. 'I have been playing with the idea of sending you to the West as our peace emissary. The impact of your appeal might be enough to persuade informed opinion in Britain and America to stop their governments supporting the Whites. We were prepared to go to Prinkipo and agree to another peace conference.'

'Would that mean you would have to accept the dismemberment of Russia?'

'It would; but it would be a price we'd have to pay to save at least part of the revolution. The Soviet republic in Hungary of Bela Kun has been overthrown and we'll have to accept a buffer state in Siberia. Compromise has been made the order of the day.'

'I would be willing to perform any role if it will help you to survive this onslaught.'

'I hope it won't be necessary,' said Trotsky. 'From our point of view it would be better to stick to the original plan and keep your secret so that in the long term you can help us in Britain. The decision can be delayed but only by a week or so. The decision might be made for us in Petrograd. If we can hold the city then there is a chance we can force back the enemy on other points but if we lose the city of the revolution, our whole morale could collapse and the Whites could soon be in Moscow.'

'It's a frightening thought,' said Baring

'I won't give up Petrograd,' said Trotsky firmly. 'Some Politbureau members are pressing Vladimir Ilyich to abandon the city and gather all our available forces for the defence of Moscow, but I won't have that. Tomorrow I go to Petrograd to organise its defence. Will you come with me? If

we lose we'll smuggle you out to England through Finland
and you can take our case to the forum of the world. If we win
then you must stay on in Russia because we will then be on
the road to victory.'

Next day Baring and Cherepova joined the Commissar's
train on the sidings by the Byelorussia station. As they were
driven in a little Ford car along the Tverskaya Ulitsa they
held hands, both sensing the tremendous electricity in the air.
Although the streets looked normal enough there was a sense
of foreboding everywhere in the dour expressions of the
pedestrians. Even the few horses pulling *izvostchiks* looked
more miserable than usual.

On the train Baring and Cherepova joined Trotsky in his
command coach. They found the Commissar for War in a fit
of feverish activity. He was dictating to his secretaries,
drafting proclamations and lecturing all and sundry on the
dangers of the situation.

Nina told Charles, 'No one has ever seen him so worked up.
He is like a human dynamo sending bursts of energy in all
directions. Yesterday the Politbureau authorised him to draw
reinforcements from the White Sea and the Polish front and
they are disbanding the government departments in Moscow
to send more personnel to save Petrograd. Everybody is being
called to arms.'

'Lenin wanted to abandon Petrograd but Trotsky wouldn't
let him. By an irony of fate the city of the revolution has
become the fulcrum for its survival,' Charles said.

'What is fulcrum?' she asked.

'It's the place you put the lever on when you're trying to lift
something or move a great weight. It's the point of the
greatest pressure; by using the lever on it you can increase
your power by a huge factor.'

As the train neared the threatened city Trotsky asked
Baring to join him in his compartment. 'I've written a reply to
Winston Churchill,' he said. 'His boasting about the anti-
Soviet crusade of fourteen nations and our imminent fall is

premature. Even if Yudenitch does succeed in entering Petrograd I've issued a battle plan to fight the invaders in every street, on every square, from every window and from every cellar. After two or three days of that they would become demoralised. But I hope these desperate measures won't be necessary for they would destroy the beauty of a great city.'

When they reached Petrograd the news was extremely serious. The White Army had taken Krasnoe Selo, where the Tsar once had a palace a few versts to the south, and Yudenitch mounted scouts were already in the outer suburbs. Zinoviev, the chairman of the local Soviet, had all but given up and a sick mood of defeatism permeated everywhere. Trotsky took command and called an immediate meeting of the Soviet.

Through the now deserted streets Baring and Cherepova retraced their steps to the Tauride Palace, the meeting place of the old Imperial Duma and the scene of so many historic events. They had last been there as sightseers ten months before. In the back row of the theatre Nina translated Trotsky's address: 'In these dark, cold, hungry, anxious, bad autumn days Petrograd presents to us again the grand picture of rallying self-confidence, enthusiasm and heroism.' Charles thought how untrue a reflection all this oratory was. Trotsky was converting his vivid imagination into reality and forcing the reluctant defenders to adopt his own optimism. He listened fascinated as the Commissar continued: 'The city which has suffered so much, which has burned with so strong an inward flame and has braved so many dangers, the city which has never spared itself, which has inflicted on itself so much devastation, this beautiful Red Petrograd remains what it has been — the torch of revolution.'

The delegates of the Soviet rose to Trotsky, cheered him to the echo and sang the Internationale with a fervour they had rarely felt before.

With Lieutenant Cherepova by his side Baring threw

himself into the campaign by helping to organise supplies, training boys and women in the use of guns and getting factories to turn out improvised armoured vehicles.

He was with Trotsky on the outskirts of the city as the invaders approached and saw with horror that British tanks were being used in the advance as they had been at Tsaritsyn. Panic spread like wildfire amongst the defenders and streams of them were fleeing. To Baring's amazement the Commissar for War requisitioned a horse and jumping on its back called 'Follow Me,' then rode into the retreating mob, waving them back into the fight. Baring saw the surprised looks of the men as the Commissar for War rode towards the enemy with his orderly running behind brandishing a revolver and calling, 'Courage boys, Comrade Trotsky is leading you.' The Red Regiment turned to fight and the Yudenitch advance was stemmed.

Back in the city which he had saved, an exhausted Trotsky summoned Baring and said, 'This is our darkest time but although we are fighting English tanks and English supplied troops, I want the people of Petrograd to understand the real England is not their enemy. I only wish I could tell them how you — an English officer — have fought in their defence, but your secret must be kept. I've done the next best thing and written a proclamation.' He handed it to Baring who read, 'But even today when we are engaged in a bitter fight with Yudenitch the hireling of the English, I demand you never forget that there are two Englands. Besides the England of profits, of violence, of bribery and bloodthirstiness there is an England of labour, of spiritual power, of high ideals of international solidarity. It is the base and dishonest England of the stock exchange monopolists that is fighting us. The England of labour and the people is with us.'

'I hope one day the whole world can read that,' Baring said with feeling.

After a week of bitter fighting the defence of Petrograd was secured and with the enemy in retreat, the military train with

Baring and Cherepova on board returned to Moscow. The news came from Siberia that Kolchak was utterly defeated and on the second anniversary of the revolution Trotsky was proclaimed the father of victory and awarded the Order of the Red Banner. Baring considered that no honour had ever been better deserved.

CHAPTER 25

The modest party that Charles and Nina held in their apartment to see in the New Year of 1920 was the happiest occasion either of them had known for years. Arthur Haycraft brought his new girlfriend, an eighteen year old Natasha, and Krylova brought her current man friend, a handsome forty-five year old Colonel in the Red Army who had been placed in charge of the outer Kremlin guard.

Everyone contributed to the feast: Charles his Vecheka rations and Nina some bottles of vodka which the Vecheka had requisitioned from speculators; the Colonel brought a box of food from the Kremlin kitchens and Natasha the best prize of all: three plump *tsyplyonkas* — chickens which she had smuggled into Moscow in a sack from her peasant father's hut thirty versts south of Moscow.

There were toasts to the three couples, toasts to the revolution, toasts to Lenin and Trotsky, toasts to Peter Kropotkin, to whom the Colonel was distantly related, toasts to the victorious Red Army and toasts to the victory of the working class all over the world. Eventually when the vodka ran out they all slept in various stages of stupor until the stove burnt out and the cold morning air chilled them awake.

A month later Haycraft called on Baring and it was obvious that the normally happy engineer from Manchester looked depressed.

'The war might have taken a turn for the better with the White armies in retreat, but I don't think you realise Charles how bad the situation is in Moscow. I've been allocated to four factories where gradually we're getting the machinery into working order by cannibalising useless equipment for spares. The workers, the women and a few men who can be spared from the front, are prepared to work, but they are starving and literally collapsing at the benches. It's so bad that much of the production is being stolen so that workers can barter it for food from the peasants.'

Charles nodded. 'I know it's bad. The chaos caused by war won't be overcome in weeks. It'll take years to sort this lot out.'

'If they survive that long,' said Arthur.

'Trotsky's transferring his energy to solving these problems now the military threat is passing. The leadership are calling their policy War Communism and are prepared to use all measures to win the peace, including mobilisation.'

'The people won't take any more compulsion,' said Arthur. 'I went to visit Natasha's family.'

'But you're not supposed to leave Moscow,' interrupted Charles angrily.

'I took the risk. I had my reasons.'

'You're a fool. If you didn't have me to protect you they could throw you back into prison or worse. What were your special reasons?'

'I'm marrying Natasha and she wanted me to meet her folks first.'

'You can't do that, Arthur,' Charles shouted in alarm, thinking of the consequences.

'Why not pray! I thought Russia had become a country where men and women were free from the old restrictions.'

'You're in a totally different position from an ordinary Russian. Have you thought what you're letting Natasha in for? You don't have any guarantee she'd be allowed to go to England or do you intend to try to stay in Russia?'

'Oh no,' said Arthur, 'I'm taking her back even if I have to hide her in my kit bag.'

'Be reasonable. You're supposed to be a prisoner of war in

custody. How can you possibly produce a wife and ask for her to be repatriated as well?'

'Perhaps she can follow me home. I don't want to stay in Russia a day longer than necessary. Surely this government can do something. They're supposed to be all powerful.'

'It's highly unlikely. You should call this stupid marriage off. You'll both live to regret it. You've been thrown together from diametrically opposed backgrounds: she's a Russian peasant and you're an English engineer. Back in Manchester or wherever you'll want to slip back safely into the comfortable circles of the English middle class. They won't mix. She doesn't even speak English and your Russian is barely enough for you to tell her you love her.'

'We can communicate,' said Arthur.

'It's all very well at the beginning when you're happy bed-mates but what happens when that sexual attraction wears off. You've got to have something more substantial than sex to make a marriage last. You'll have to give her up when you leave Russia, Arthur. See sense now and don't lead the poor girl up the garden path.'

'I'm not changing my mind. It's gone too far. I've got to get Natasha out of the mess Russia is becoming. I couldn't leave her here. I was going to say how bad it is for her family and all the peasants in the country. The roubles they get for the requisitioned produce is worthless and there's nothing they can do to improve their land. They can't get seed, farm equipment or animals. Their horses have been requisitioned and most of the rest taken for food by the gangs of foraging workers who come out from Moscow. Natasha's parents are desperate but the reports that the richer peasants are being slaughtered by thugs worry them more. They're not rich but they fear they might be next. There is complete lawlessness in the countryside.'

'I can understand why you want to get Natasha out but it won't last for ever and you have to think of your own long term future.'

'Don't argue with me, Charles. I've made up my mind; I'm marrying her next week and I wanted you to be my best man.'

Arthur Haycraft had his way and married Natasha Chaikana in a simple ceremony at a Moscow People's Office with only two witnesses: Charles Baring, who signed the book as witness with the name of Erik Andersen, and an excited and happy Nina who brought flowers and advice for the bride, thirteen years her junior. They opened a rare bottle of wine to celebrate and for the day Charles shelved the worries he still harboured about his friend's rash action.

Later that night Charles who could not sleep, turned to cuddle a sleeping Nina. She surprised him by whispering, 'I know what's worrying my Englishman but you're not to worry. You should sleep.'

'What is it then?'

'You think you owe a duty to marry me.' As Charles began to answer, she slapped him playfully under the thick covers and said firmly, 'Don't interrupt me. It's an old Russian custom for the woman to have the first rights in the bed and that includes talking. You'll have to hear me out. You must never think of marrying me however much I may want you to and I do very very much, believe me. But marrying me would put the whole plan for your work in England in jeopardy. You can't afford to take that risk and nor can Trotsky, Dzerzhinsky and your other sponsors.'

'I know,' said Charles, 'it's been worrying me for days that when the time comes I won't want to leave you. However hard conditions are here, I've had the happiest days of my life with you.'

'There's nothing we can do about it. Go to sleep, there's more work to do in the morning. The revolution won't wait because we've fallen in love.'

Once the military threat was stemmed, Baring's training had been resumed in earnest. As a graduated captain he was free to move in and out of Vecheka installations at will and he greatly valued the trust shown in him. One day Krylova told

Nina that Lenin had agreed to meet Comrade Baring of the Red Army and the Vecheka. She brought the news home excitedly. 'This is a big honour for you: Krylova arranged it but Vladimir Ilyich would not see you unless he knew how loyal you are to Bolshevism.'

Baring took an official car to the Kremlin and passed through the Spassky Gate and the inner courtyards. In his smart Red Army uniform with short cropped hair he was indistinguishable from the other Army officers in the city and the guards showed him much respect, especially when they saw his Vecheka pass. At the Senate building he was shown to the fourth floor where the Chairman of the Politbureau had his office. As he passed through the corridors he was struck by the greater sense of orderliness in the offices. The government had obviously gained in stability as the dangers of the White attack had receded but this was not translated into the streets outside.

Krylova met him at the door of the secretaries office and said 'You'll have to come through here to Vladimir Ilyich's, there is no other way in.' They passed through a large square room where those working were almost exclusively women. Lenin who had been warned of his arrival came to the intervening door to welcome him. Baring saw a squat, rather plump man with a short thick neck, broad shoulders and a high intellectual forehead which was accentuated by the bald head. He had a small moustache and a short trimmed beard but what he noticed most about him were his steely hypnotic eyes, with their oriental slant, which displayed a boundless self-confidence. In his presence Baring could appreciate the force of dynamism which had propelled a country through revolution and a devastating war and which was determined to win against all external odds. The leader's personality was electrifying in its impact.

'Come in and sit down,' Lenin said, '*ezverete mayo plakhoye praeznashenyé* and as Baring looked somewhat perplexed 'that means "forgive any poor pronunciation." My spoken English is not so good as I spent my time in London reading at the British Museum writing.'

Baring sat on a deep leather chair alongside the long table covered in red cloth used for small meetings that Lenin also used as his desk. It stood at right angles to Lenin's smaller desk which was cluttered with candle holders, a paper rack, a desk lamp and a bronze model of what appeared to be a bear pensively holding a human skull. On two sides of the room were bookcases full of volumes and the other walls were covered with maps and charts. There was a pile of papers on the desk but otherwise the room was tidy and orderly, unlike the office the leader had occupied at the Smolny in Petrograd.

'So you are our Englishman,' said Lenin as he settled his broad bottom into his cane hardbacked chair. 'Lev Davidovich calls you our "trojan horse". He was always a fine one with descriptive epithets.'

Baring did not know what to reply and remained silent.

'I've heard of your courage at the front,' Lenin added more encouragingly, 'those were tense days; it seemed the interventionists would get Petrograd and even Moscow. I was prepared to fight on from the Urals if necessary.'

'It's a relief the tide has turned,' said Baring. 'Now there's a chance for the revolution to show what it can achieve and spread its message.'

'The workers in England helped us by their agitation against Churchill and intervention,' said Lenin. 'I've no doubt that even if we had collapsed the revolution would still come in England and other industrial countries. Our survival makes it uncertain.'

'Is the war nearly over?'

'All the signs are that that will soon be the case. We're having trouble with the Poles but Litvinov has been in Copenhagen to sign an agreement with an English Member of Parliament called O'Grady who has the authority of the London Government. That will allow us to swop prisoners in North Russia. There's also talk of the Empire wanting trade talks with us. That's a good sign. Once we get down to trade, political recognition will follow. The capitalists have given *de facto* recognition to the Menshevik governments in Georgia, Azerbaijan and Armenia but we won't allow them to last. The allies had their chance to secure some states for their White Russian friends when they called the Prinkipo conference but the Whites would not soil their fingers by shaking hands with us. That's their loss. We will take over the whole Imperial lands of Russia apart from Finland and the three Baltic states which we've had to give up. Not one more inch of territory will we concede.'

'Will the agreement in Copenhagen between Litvinov and O'Grady cover the return of the other prisoners held in Moscow and Petrograd?' asked Baring.

'Ah,' said Lenin, wagging a finger from a cultured hand, 'you are concerned about your own return to England I see. It's not time for that yet. There is no general return of prisoners until we get peace and it would be a mistake to return our "trojan horse" too early.'

Baring must have looked disconsolate as Lenin added quickly, 'You will be back there soon enough, Comrade Baring. I know how eager you are to get on with your work for Bolshevism in England. Tell me do you know anything of the Labour Movement in England? I saw no reference to this in your file.'

'No,' said Baring, 'no contact except through the books of Bernard Shaw, William Morris, H.G. Wells and so on.'

'Shaw is a good man fallen among Fabians,' said Lenin. 'Wells is an excellent thinker and he wants to visit us here which is a good sign. The English writer I enjoyed best was Jack London, but he was an American wasn't he? Tragedy about his suicide.'

'Suicide?' Baring said in surprise.

'Yes he killed himself three years ago. A pity he didn't live to see our success. It would have inspired his writing and we need good writers to spread our ideas. Have you read Sidney Webb?'

'No.'

'Avoid him. He has more industry than brains. However, Comrade, we shouldn't get caught in a literary discussion should we — however interesting — we should talk about your coming mission. It is quite clear in your mind?' Lenin leant over the desk with an intimate sweep of his left hand as if asking his visitor to speak openly.

'I am to keep my Communist sympathies secret so I can gradually climb up the ladder of the British Establishment. Then I wait for guidance from Moscow about the actions you want me to take.'

'Yes, yes,' said Lenin, 'stealth at all time so they don't suspect you. I believe the contradictions of capitalism are enough to secure its own destruction but the ruling clique will do its best to avoid the inevitable. Ramsey MacDonald for instance will cooperate with the capitalists to stop a revolution. The voice of the working class in the West is blunted because of these collaborators. That's why we have to use our own methods to push capitalism towards its collapse.'

'I shall be proud to be part of the struggle,' said Baring.

'It will not be an easy task. At times you will feel isolated and desperately lonely, but when you do, remember those of us who had to spend months and years in the wastes of Siberia before we could win our aims. You will be in your mental Siberia. Make sure your spirit is strong enough to resist the seduction of the physical pleasures of England. Enjoy them by all means — you'll have to be seen to be doing that to be credible as the English ruling class doesn't understand or like ascetics — but never let those delights divert you from your chosen path.'

'How do you think we will eventually achieve Communism in Britain?'

'We have a saying that a man may have typhoid while still on his legs. Twenty, maybe thirty years ago, I had abortive typhoid and was going about with it, had it some days before it knocked me over. Well England and France and Italy have caught the disease already. England may seem to you to be untouched, but the microbe is already there.'

'But the labour disturbances in England might well be an abortive revolution as your typhoid was abortive,' said Baring.

'Yes that is possible. It is perhaps an educative period in which the English workmen will come to realise their political needs and turn from liberalism to socialism. Socialism is certainly weak in England. Your socialist movements, your socialist parties!' Lenin said with evident despair. 'When I was in England, I zealously attended everything I could and and for a country with so large an industrial population they were pitiable, pitiable,' he repeated the word slowly to emphasise his feeling, 'a handful at a street corner, a meeting in a drawing room, a school classroom, pitiable. But you must remember one great difference between Russia of 1905 and England of today. Our first Soviet in Russia was made during the revolution. Your shop stewards' committees have been in existence long before. They are without programme, without direction but the opposition they will meet will force a programme upon them.'

The visitor spent longer with Lenin than he had expected; throughout the talk they had no interruptions except for the ritual of the samovar tea, served in glasses with sugar, and a tray of sliced lemon. Baring left the meeting in an elated state which bordered on an hypnotically induced daze. One phrase stuck in his mind. 'I believe I will end in paralysis,' Lenin had said and told the Englishman to remember that the cause is greater than any man.

In July Baring had an invitation to attend the Second Congress of the Communist International and this time he decided to take Arthur Haycraft as part of his continuing education in the Communist cause. Haycraft had performed valuable services in the Moscow factories and his marriage to

Natasha had proved to be a remarkably stabilising influence. No steps however had yet been taken to make clear what his role would be on his return to England. Baring decided that attending the Congress would generate enthusiasm in Haycraft which would make it easier to recruit him for his future espionage role.

Baring went to see Karl Radek, who had returned from imprisonment in Germany to become the secretary of the Comintern. His offices were in the building of the former German Embassy, a magnificent house standing in its own grounds.

'Glad to see you after all this time,' said Radek. 'You notice I have used my time in German prisons to learn English.' He spoke it atrociously but it was understandable. 'It is justice I come to this former Embassy of my German oppressors isn't it? This is the very room where Ambassador Mirbach was assassinated by the Social Revolutionaries two years ago. The S.R.s opposed our peace treaty with the Kaiser and wanted the killing to break the treaty. They would have started the war again on the Eastern Front. History would have been different if they had succeeded, because the Germans would have crushed Russia before we'd had any strength.

'The way of the revolutionary often has to be devious,' he added, 'and you will have to remember that. We made peace with Germany and had Mirbach here while the Great War was still going on. That compromise was necessary but we didn't like it.'

Baring collected three observer tickets for Cherepova, Haycraft and himself and left the former German Embassy. For once he felt he had enough of the constant philosophising of intellectuals; his brain was becoming addled with the reiteration of Marxist and Leninist slogans and he longed for the uncluttered conversations of friends, unencumbered with the baggage of theoretical socialism. He walked back to his apartment through the streets of Moscow bathed in summer sunshine and breathed freely in the unpolluted atmosphere.

He saw old women carrying bundles, children playing hopscotch and reflected that whatever political leaders might say and do in their cloisters the lives of ordinary people go on their simple way.

On 16th July, 1920, all the delegates of the Communist International went to Petrograd, where the Congress was to open in solemn session as a tribute to the city of the revolution. Charles travelled with Arthur Haycraft and Nina Cherepova, who was returning to her home town with the first prospect of seeing her parents in three years. The mood of the travellers was totally different from that of Trotsky's military train on the same route nine months earlier, when no one could have been sure of the outcome of the war. Now there was little doubt that the Whites were discredited and defeated. There was still fighting on distant fronts in Siberia, in the north and the south and with the state of Poland, which had been created by the Versailles Treaty a year before, but the allies had all but withdrawn their support for the intervention. The Bolsheviks were winning against all odds. The meeting in Petrograd would be a celebration and shared with those foreign comrades who had supported the cause in their own countries.

Baring was caught up in the spirit of the occasion and Haycraft too could feel it. He finally said, 'If only this tremendous enthusiasm, could be reproduced in Britain, the old country could be transformed. If only we can do the same without all the sacrifice, death and misery.

'I agree,' said Baring, 'that's exactly what I shall be working for.'

The delegates who came from as far afield as Korea, India and America, congregated at the Smolny Institute and walked to the Tauride Palace to take their seats in the Great Theatre where the old Imperial Duma had met. Baring took his seat in the back row with Cherepova and Haycraft. They were dressed in typical Russian light summer clothing and the foreign delegates could not have guessed that the two men were English. They talked quietly to avoid drawing attention to themselves.

In the evening Cherepova went to her parents and Baring and Haycraft to the Great Square of the Winter Palace where the delegates and the Petrograd crowds were to be entertained to a tableau. They sat on reserved platforms and, over thousands of heads, watched a succession of scenes illustrating the march of socialism. Across the colonnade a massive red banner appeared with the words from the Communist Manifesto *Workers of the World Unite! You have nothing to lose but your chains.* It was lit up by projectors from ships anchored in the Neva. This was followed by a scene of the Paris Commune with songs and dances of the Carmagnole and the opening of the 1914 war with the leaders of the Second International — the hated social democrats — shown as grovelling before their governments and capitalism whilst Liebknecht, the German Communist, picked up the red flag they had dropped and cried 'Down with war.'

The two Englishmen watched in fascination as cars loaded with armed workers drove from several parts of the square and knocked down a makeshift Imperial Palace of the Tsar. A figure representing Kerensky made a brief appearance followed by the projectors lighting up two huge portraits of Lenin and Trotsky which looked down benignly on the packed square as the sounds of thousands of voices singing the *Internationale* brought the proceedings to an end.

Next day the whole Congress returned to Moscow to continue its meetings in the Great Theatre of the Kremlin and Lenin took the major role in the debates, arguing with the delegates who were opposed to the formation of Communist parties in their countries and answering point by point. Against Jack Tanner, the British delegate who put the case for syndicalism, he countered that workers' control was not enough. The party had to provide the apparatus for victory and for state organisation. There were disagreements as to whether Communists in England should join the Labour

Party. Lenin argued strongly that they should, but the British delegation were opposed to the idea and put up a woman speaker to argue their case. She was announced as Sylvia Pankhurst and she spoke so feverishly she nearly fell off the narrow rostrum.

'Is that the Pankhurst who leads the Suffragette Movement?' asked Haycraft.

'She's one of the daughters,' said Baring, 'and a very militant one from all accounts.'

The Congress ended with an hour-long address by Trotsky made entirely without notes and with great fluency. He finished with the strong call 'Working men and women! On this earth there is only one banner which is worth fighting and dying for. It is the banner of the Communist International.'

After the strains of the *Internationale* had died away, Baring took Haycraft to his apartment where Cherepova prepared tea. All three were too exhilarated to think of sleeping for they felt that they had just participated in one of the greatest events of human history.

Baring told Haycraft, 'When you get back to England you'll be able to help this cause in a very valuable way.'

'I'd like to help, but I'm no politician or agitator,' he said.

'You don't have to be. The Soviets will only be able to survive in a hostile world if they have a modern economy and a modern industry. The war might be nearly over but the capitalists will still want to crush Communism by other means. It's vital that Soviet industry is kept up to date. You can pass back to Russia the details of the processes and techniques which made capitalist industry successful.'

'That's industrial spying and I don't want to be a spy,' protested Haycraft.

'The capitalists have stolen the ideas from inventors and workers who are hardly paid more than a pittance; you'll only be stealing them back for a workers' government.'

'That's one way to look at it, I suppose.'

'Look Arthur, I know that if you agree to cooperate in this, the authorities here in Moscow will do everything possible for Natasha to join you after your return. You'll have their promise on that.'

'That's good,' said Haycraft, 'she's expecting our baby and I couldn't leave her for long now.'

'Goodness Arthur, you do make things complicated; how many months is she pregnant?'

'Two,' said Arthur Haycraft smiling faintly.

'Seven months to go. There's no guarantee you'll be back in England in that time.'

'That's terrible, I wanted the baby to be born British.'

'You're living in a fantasy world, Arthur. Officially you're a prisoner of war and you can't be returned until Russia and Britain sign a peace treaty and there's no real sign of that yet.'

'But the British have withdrawn support from the Whites.'

'It will still be a long time before they recognise a Communist state. Anyway when you go back it will be as a returning prisoner. Natasha will have to follow you somehow. The government has promised to give all their help once you agree to be an agent.'

'I suppose I'll have to agree.'

'It would be the best way. It's not espionage in the usual sense; they simply want access to Western know-how so they can help Russian industry to catch up. You're a wise man Arthur if you go along with it. The Russians will show their appreciation in other ways.'

'I'll do it then.'

'Good we'll arrange for you to have the full briefings. The Vecheka will take care of that.'

CHAPTER 26

After the conclusion of the Congress Baring was told of a tour being made by several of the delegates to the Caucasus and he expressed a wish to join them. They were to see the area newly liberated from the Whites and it would be a journey of danger and adventure. Baring, who had finished his Vecheka courses, felt he had the time to make the trip before the prisoners were returned. His hopes were dashed when he went to the Lubyanka headquarters to see his new controller. The new chief of his section was a veteran Bolshevik called Mikhail Abramovich Trilisser, a bullet-headed strong man, who informed Baring that a formal establishment of the foreign department known as *Inostrannyi Otdel* would be completed before the end of the year. In the meantime all senior foreign agents would be under his direct control and there could be no question of any tourist trips. According to Trilisser it would be necessary to put Baring into the prisoners' stream within a month to prepare for his repatriation. The Vecheka chief seemed to relish the prospect as if resenting the soft life the Englishman had apparently enjoyed.

When Charles discussed the prospects later with Nina he found her distraught. 'I've been informed of my return next week to Petrograd. My assignment with you is over. We are being separated,' cried Nina.

'We both knew it would have to come to an end sometime,' Charles tried to comfort her.

'I know, I know, but now it's come I don't want to face up to it. It's too terrible. Charles why don't we get married and then

I could follow you to England just like Natasha is following Arthur?'

Charles took both Nina's hands and sat looking at her beautiful eyes brimming with tears. His Bolshevik girl who had been so strong was dissolving into a natural woman with all the normal emotions and weaknesses. The experience pulled at unknown and untested strings in his heart and made him speechless.

'Can't we get married?' Nina begged him again, sensing his vulnerability. 'We live in a free country now where we should do as we feel. I could help you with your work in England when we are there together.'

'Nina,' he said at last, 'Nina darling. I love you and I always shall. I would dearly like you as my wife but we have to face realities. My job in England will be a very delicate one. I shall be an undercover agent waiting for a chance to do something really important for the achievement of world revolution. It would be impossible for me to succeed with a Russian wife. The powers over there would guess I had a secret I was trying to keep. Also you would be open to big dangers.'

Now Nina was crying. He kissed her quivering lips, her cheeks, her forehead and her swimming eyes and tasted the bitterness of her tears. He caressed her long hair, drawing it away from her damp cheeks. He let his left hand run over her taut body and felt her tensions relax as his feelings of love and desire communicated themselves to her. She tried to speak but he placed a finger over her lips to stay silent, reversing the roles of the Petrograd experience many months before.

Gently and deftly he removed her clothing, piece by piece, alternating his movements with caresses and kisses to her lips, her shoulders and her breasts. She took it supinely as if she had surrendered her Bolshevik pride to superior forces.

When she was naked he kissed her stomach and let his fingers travel between her thighs opening them without assistance so that he could explore the crevices. She groaned and turned to hold him but he grasped her arm firmly and insisted by signs that she should stay inert. As her white body stretched in suspended animation waiting for his next desperately needed touch he threw off his own clothes into a disorderly heap. Then he kneeled over the woman and rested his penis between her breasts, squeezing them with his hands so they in turn could massage the growing evidence of his passion. Staying in this position he released his hands to stroke her hair which was spreading out over the cushion and on on to the floor in an abandon which typified the surrendered attitudes of the rest of her body.

He touched her head reverently, stroked her eyebrows and with the lightest forefinger moved around her dark eyes to smooth away the residue of tears. She looked at him with a deep longing and he could see from the desperation in her expression that she could wait no longer. With his knees supporting him he eased his body slowly over her's until he was ready and poised to complete the conquest of the woman who had once mastered him.

That night they made love again and again until, when he was capable no longer, he fell into the subterranean dreamless sleep that follows exhaustion and total satisfaction. When he awoke it was already ten o'clock and a bright sun was shining through the open windows revealing the disorder of an apartment where their passion had spilled over as never before. Baring sat up suddenly. He felt a new consciousness of manliness, a sensation which made him want to shout, and he leapt out of the divan bed to find Nina. She was not there. She had left him and taken all her things. There was not even a note to say 'goodbye'.

As soon as he was dressed in his Red Army Capain's uniform Baring hurried to the Lubyanka. As usual he was admitted on showing his pass and once in the building he ran through the long corridors towards the foreign affairs section where Lieutenant Cherepova might be. As he rushed by the offices their methodical desk-bound workers gave him surprised looks. In the Lubyanka it was rare to show emotion, excitement or haste. Breathless, he searched the section where he could find her but the officials looked at him coldly and blandly. 'Comrade Cherepova returned to Petrograd early this morning,' they said and as he turned to leave they ordered 'You are not to follow her, Comrade, she's returned to her other duties.'

Trilisser heard the commotion and came out of his office, cursing in Russian. Baring tried to explain that he wanted to go to the station to see Cherepova before she left but Trilisser would not hear of it. 'The decision has been made, Comrade. You can't overturn it. Comrade Cherepova's mission is over. She requested an early return to Petrograd and it has been granted. Come into my office,' he ordered peremptorily.

With an interpreter present to convey the chief's message without any doubt, Baring listened as Trilisser spoke.

'Comrade Captain, you have a great deal to learn. Your bourgeois attitude to your relationship with the woman Cherepova is all too obvious. In my view it was a mistake for her to come here from Petrograd and it would not have happened if I had been in charge. You could have found an interpreter in Moscow just as easily. I don't believe that any of our agents should pander to emotions which clog up their thinking processes.'

When Baring tried to explain his feelings Trilisser shouted at him, 'Don't bring your English ways here. Your attitudes are warped by your naive sexual needs. You'll have to cure that if you're to be of any use to us. For your own good your movements are now to be restricted until I can get further instructions from Comrade Dzerzhinsky.'

For the rest of the day Baring was kept in a locked office and when they came for him they brought his torn and dirty British army uniform and told him his fate. He was to be transferred to a prison where his fellow British officers were kept and he would wait there until the British Government signed the treaty and all prisoners could be returned to England.

Baring begged to be allowed to return to his apartment and to say his farewells. 'Not necessary, Comrade, everything you had is here and as you can take nothing else with you any delay is pointless. It's better for your cover not to go around Moscow saying "goodbyes" to all your contacts. Better you just disappear.'

That night a humbled and by now dishevelled Baring was taken to the Andronikov Monastery. At the entrance by the Svyatyye Vorota his Vecheka escorts handed him to a group of swarthy Red Army guards who pushed him into a nearby building. His spirits sank as he realised they had no idea of his status as a Red Army Captain and would deal with him as they would with any other hated English officer. Inside a swaggering Lieutenant confirmed his fears when he was forced to stand to attention before a small table as he was interrogated for his name which a clerk wrote laboriously in phonetical Russian in a large school exercise book which constituted the prison's register.

'Trying to escape,' said the Lieutenant in poor but adequate English.

'No, no,' said Baring.

'That's what the report says. The Cheka does not lie. You are lucky they didn't kill you as a spy.'

'I wasn't trying to escape,' said Baring.

The Lieutenant stood facing the prisoner; without warning he brought the back of his hand across Baring's face in a vicious swipe. 'Don't lie you filthy Englishman,' he shouted as Baring lost his balance. 'You will be punished. Two weeks solitary. Escape again and you will be shot.'

On the Lieutenant's order the guards seized Baring and dragged him into the courtyard giving him punches on his chest and stomach as he went. He was taken into a large stone building and down some steps to a dank cellar where the sergeant used his keys to open a large iron gate. He understood their curses in Russian which were not pleasant. As they flung him to the hard floor he had a feeling of relief that at least they would now leave him alone. His hopes were short lived as they were not done yet. They kicked him in the shins as he cowered on the cold stone floor holding his arms to protect his head. As the kicking stopped they spat on him. Then he heard coarse laughter and tensed his body to withstand more blows. Instead he felt a warm stream of sticky liquid falling on his head in a steady flow. 'My God, they're pissing on me,' he thought and he crawled into a corner but the stream followed until the guard had relieved himself fully on the sodden figure. Then the guards left, slamming the iron gate and padlocking it, guffawing to themselves.

Baring found some straw in the corner of the cell and sank into it in abject exhaustion. As sleep fought to take over he remembered with horror he had done nothing about Arthur and Natasha. Concern about his friend's dilemma worried him more than his own pitiful state. A fitful sleep only partially erased the memories, interrupted as it was by the most horrifying dreams. He woke hearing his own screams as vicious guards chased him with heavy sticks but the cell was empty, as silent as it was stinking, his calls for help still locked in his subconscious as unable to escape as he was. Once he felt a tugging at his leg and woke to find a large rat chewing at his trouser. It ran off but he saw its luminous eyes watching in the dark, waiting for him to fall asleep again which his physical and spiritual exhaustion would force him to do against his better judgement.

In the cold light of morning he got a better view of the condition of his cell. It was worse than anything he had imagined. It was about ten feet by six and so high he could not touch the ceiling or the tiny barred window just below it. The sun was low and its rays caught the top of the walls. They were made of stone blocks and looked as if they had been built to be completely escape-proof hundreds of years before. The floor of the cell was filthy beyond description with the unswept droppings of rats and men. In one corner was a bucket half filled with the urine and excrement of some previous inmate.

Baring felt the scab of coagulated blood on his chin where the guards had struck him and checked his bruised shins, shoulders, arms and legs. He ached still from the beatings and kickings but it seemed miraculously, that nothing had been broken. As he was ruminating at this relief a slovenly guard came to the gateway and shoved a dirty enamel mug through the bars and a chunk of rye bread and left without saying a word. The mug was three-quarters full with a tepid liquid which had the stale taste of reheated slops. Baring guessed it was meant to be tea and the vision of a silver samovar, a clean glass and a slice of lemon came into his mind with the taunting reminder that such delights were another life away. He had to accept he was no longer Captain Baring, alias Erik Andersen, of the Red Army, a valued member of the Vecheka. He had reverted to being Captain Baring M.C., an Englishman fallen amongst Russians who naturally hated the English for their invasion and who saw no reason to show mercy to a miserable class enemy.

For the next weeks Baring was isolated in a world of his own. The guards brought bread in the morning and a soup of fish heads or potatoes in the evening but they never talked even when he tried his little vocabulary of Russian words. There seemed to be no one in his part of the prison although he sometimes heard shouting in the distance and stamping or shuffling in the courtyard above his tiny window. Every four or five days they opened the gate to remove the latrine bucket, now overful, but carelessly allowed to slop on the floor adding to the filth and the stench. In the cellar there was hardly any flow of fresh air and the atmosphere hung like a stale sewer until Baring felt it permeating his clothes, his unwashed body and into his spirit. He wondered how much more he could take of this dark side of Bolshevism.

Eventually after an eternity of long empty days and frightening nights, which came and went unmarked and uncounted, the gate was opened by the sergeant. Baring was allowed to stagger on his weakened legs up the stairs where the air was clean and where he was put, without any accompanying violence, into a large room. As the door clanged shut behind him the relief overcame him, his legs gave way and he collapsed in a heap on the floor.

As he came round he heard a Scot saying, 'Pairr doog, he sure looks doone in' and someone pressed a mug of cool water to his lips which he drank gratefully. 'Are you alright now, old chap?' said another voice and he opened his eyes to see five British officers looking at him solicitously.

'We'd better clean you up,' said an officer still showing two pips, 'not to put too fine a gloss on it, you stink to high heaven.' They took off the filthy remnants of his uniform and brought buckets of water and a bar of yellow soap. He let them cleanse him. They then brought hot tea which tasted like tea and revived his spirits.

'You poor fellow,' said a Captain, 'what on earth did you do to deserve that treatment? They nearly killed you down there in that hell hole. We heard about you from one of the friendly guards. Those Bolos wanted to do you in and I think it's only because we knew about you that they finally let you out.'

'They said I tried to escape.'

'I heard they accused you of spying. Anyway you've arrived; we can take care of you now; welcome to the club.'

There were seven British officers in the room, a classroom of a converted seminary. They told how they had been transferred from the prison at the Ivanoffsky Monastery when it became overcrowded. 'We arrived here on September the third,' he heard one of them say as if in a dream. September seemed incongruous. What had happened to August? Surely it had been July when the foreign communists were at the Communist International. The memory of it loomed like a long-forgotten play. Surely it was July when Nina left for Petrograd? Her warmth and comforting love belonged to another life.

'What date is it?' he asked.

September the twenty-ninth,' one of them said, adding,

'nineteen-twenty,' as he saw the look of incomprehension on Baring's face.

'Good God,' he groaned, 'I was in that place for two months. It doesn't seem possible.'

Over the days they gradually nursed him back to health, feeding him small portions he could digest from the few Red Cross parcels which the Red guards allowed them to receive.

One of the officers, who introduced himself as Captain Vining, said he had been captured by the Bolos nine months before at Antevkoolskaya in Siberia. He had been attached to the British forces liaising with Admiral Kolchak. 'Came in through Vladivistock in May nineteen nineteen,' he said, 'arrived in Omsk a month later. We thought we had the Bolos on the run and then the attack collapsed. All the guts went out of the campaign,' he added sadly, 'country is in a terrible state. It took them six months to bring me to Moscow and I saw some deaths in that time I can tell you. Typhus is rampant all over. I had to check every day I did not have the *teiff* in my clothing. Once you get it there's not much hope.'

'What's the *teiff*?'

'The typhus louse. It doesn't live in wood, only clothes. It lays its eggs in the creases. Cleanliness is essential to stop it spreading and one must never shake hands as that spreads it rapidly. Fortunately we don't have it here and there's every chance we'll survive to get back to Blighty.'

Baring talked of his experiences on the Archangel front when his strength returned and slowly he began to feel more like a British officer than a broken tool of the Vecheka.

Vining who read Russian fluently had managed to procure old copies of *Pravda* and regaled the others with the news. The American Communist John Reed had died of typhus after returning from a visit to the Caucasus. 'He was in the Petrograd revolution,' Vining said, 'what an experience. He became a delegate to their Communist International — that propagandist outfit — and they sent him on the grand tour to the south. He got his reward alright. It says here they buried him by the walls of the Kremlin. I suppose by doing that the Bolos hope to curry favour with the reds in America.'

H.G. Wells is in Moscow,' Vining read from another issue.

'Bet he won't come here to see us,' said another.

'But it can't be bad for us can it,' said a Lieutenant, 'if those famous people are coming from London. It must mean relations are improving between Russia and Britain and soon we can go home.'

The premonitions were correct and on the 20th October the officers were told they were returning to England. One morning they were taken to the railway and crowded into a cattle truck for a thirty-six hour journey which took them to Petrograd. At the stops water was brought but no food and they were not allowed to leave the truck which, despite their best efforts, became fetid. But going home, they were happy and after all their ordeals could cope with any adversity. Baring recalled with irony his other train journeys to Petrograd in Trotsky's train.

In Petrograd the harsh treatment they were receiving suddenly changed. They were taken to a camp for foreigners and told they were free men, free to wander the city until their coming journey to Finland. It was an amazing contrast to what had gone before.

A Lieutenant was scathing, 'They're only trying to butter us up so we'll speak well of the regime when we get back. I'm not falling for any Bolo trick.' They were shown over the Winter Palace and treated to a lecture on the revolution, and given tickets to the Mariansk theatre to hear Chaliapin sing. The officers, despite their misgivings, could not help mellowing a little to their captors who seemed to be trying to make amends.

One night Baring broke off from the group to retrace the steps he had taken with Nina Cherepova from the Astoria Hotel over the Moyka river and the canal passing the palaces to the streets by the Fontanka river. He could not find the house with the broken door, with the room where a wonderful woman had made wonderful love to a young Englishman. The memory seemed too far away to be real however hard he tried to grasp it. It belonged to another life.

On the 30th October the group of British officers joined other returning prisoners on the journey to the Finnish frontier and were handed over by the Red Army to the Finnish border guards. In Terijori they were kept in quarantine for fourteen days to check for lice. It was a glorious moment to be out of Bolshevik Russia and in the free independent Finland of General Mannerheim.

On the seventeenth day of November 1920 the Britishers were piped aboard *H.M.S. Delhi* at Helsingfors and given a welcome fit for heroes by the Royal Navy officers and ratings. It was the last lap of the journey back to England and almost two years to the day since Captain Charles Baring M.C. had crossed the line between Shenhurst and Kotlas. As His Majesty's ship steamed towards the land of his birth Captain Baring of the Vecheka could not forget that the crossing from one loyalty to another had given him a new country and a new cause. The crossing was irrevocable.

BOOK THREE

An Ambition Achieved

CHAPTER 27

Britain at the end of nineteen-twenty, trying to forget a war two years finished, enjoyed a spree as its economy expanded on a wave of inflation and people learned to dance to bright new jazz rhythms brought in from New Orleans. Hardly anyone noticed the returning prisoners of war from Russia, the last survivors of the Great War to end all wars. They were dispersed without fuss or ceremony to their homes, kitted with new civilian clothes and the War Office was grateful to be rid of the remaining embarrassments of an anti-Bolshevik policy that had failed.

Charles Baring was pleased that he could get away without the trouble of lengthy interrogations. The Colonel who took notes for the Emmott Commission was only interested in atrocity stories and not concerned about the unexplained months of the Captain's Russian experiences.

The happy reunion at the Hall was subdued by the unmentioned but vividly noticed absence of Charles's father. For the returning soldier the memories of an irascible, domineering, reckless and wanton man were overwhelmed by feelings born of blood ties and love reciprocated. His mother bravely chattered about the good harvest on the estate and the problems of paying wages which had increased to ten shillings a week since the Armistice and Emma and Edith hovered for the attention they felt they deserved as the grown up sisters of the distinguished brother who had last seen them as little girls.

Christmas, when it came, with the rituals of the exchange of presents around a huge tree and the games in which grandfather Tallen joined with his customary verve, was nothing like the pre-war jollifications Charles could recall. He did his best to participate and relax as he had in the old days but he could not throw off the sense of unreality in his existence. His body was comfortably and safely at the Hall with the family where he belonged but his thoughts and his spirit were a thousand miles away.

Sarah was very concerned about her son's attitudes although she cautiously said nothing to him. In private and to her own father she was brutally honest.

'Daddy, I don't know what torture he suffered over there, and he won't talk about it, but whatever it was has changed his personality completely.'

'You're right Sarah,' said Dr. Tallen, 'I noticed it immediately. He has a glazed look as though the shock was so great he can't shake it off.'

'Is his health alright?'

'He's fine. Only needs to put on a bit of weight and he'll be back to his old physical shape. There are several deep scars on his back which show where he was beaten but apart from that there's no damage to his body. I wish I could say the same about his mind. I'd advise him to see a specialist but I expect it's only a temporary problem and we don't want to worry him with experts who can give their patients more phobias than we ever knew existed. Once he gets some new activity to absorb his energies I expect he'll snap out of it.'

Father and daughter agreed on a strategy. Sir John Baring, who had kept his seat as M.P. in the 1918 election, would be told about his nephew's condition and asked to make suggestions. It was agreed that no one — not even the girls — should mention any misgivings. It would be kinder and in the long run more sensible to act as if everything were perfectly normal.

During the recess over the New Year, Sir John came to stay at the Hall and when the subject of the conversation was safely out of earshot Sarah Baring explained the worries they all had about Charles. 'He's restless and uncertain and acts as if nothing in the world interests him. He won't talk about his awful time in Russia or about the war and when I ask him about his plans for the future his eyes mist over in a dreamy way and he says and does nothing except look mournful. He won't even read his precious books.'

'I expect he's still suffering delayed shock from all those ordeals, and he must find it difficult to come to terms with his father's death. A funeral is important to mourners; to be able to weep with others releases one's grief with a shared pool of sadness. He has to carry that suppressed sorrow as well as all the memories of a terrible war. No wonder the poor chap is distressed.'

'But how can it get better?'

'Time is a great healer and so is work. I will find some useful activity. Have you any idea what he wants to do?'

'He won't talk about it.'

'I'll try to get him to unbend. I'll do all I can, Sarah. As George is no longer with us I'll willingly be his surrogate father. That's if you don't object.'

'I'd welcome it,' said Sarah with relief.

Sir John Baring stayed at the Hall for ten days, cancelling all his political engagements to be with his nephew. Gradually he steered their conversations towards the prospects for the future. After a desultory discussion about the relative merits of Oxford or Cambridge Sir John volunteered, 'I could easily get you into Kings. It would be nearer to home for you but if you prefer Oxford just say the word and I'll sort out a College there for Michaelmas.'

'I've no ambition to go to university,' said Charles, 'the undergraduates would be much too young and foolish for me.'

'I see the point. They'd have no experiences to match your's.' said Sir John, 'perhaps you would prefer to run the estate. I know your late father was very keen you should do that. It could do with a firmer hand on the plough.'

'I love the country but I couldn't bury myself in it.'

'I can understand that. I feel the same way myself.' Fishing for ideas he went on, 'There's plenty of activity in the colonies and with my contacts in the Office I could practically guarantee a posting anywhere you chose to go. How about East Africa? It's an exciting area, especially now we've taken over Tanganyika from the Hun. That country alone is bigger than France and Germany combined and as District Commissioner you could be running an area bigger than the whole of East Anglia. If I were a young man I'd love to have a shot at it.'

'It would be boring to be cut off from London.'

'You prefer to be at the centre of things then?'

'Oh yes,' replied Charles in the dreamy way which disguises thoughts. Sir John who could sense that the ship was nearly into port pressed his advantage:

'To be at the centre of events is the definition of politics. The webs we weave in business, colonial government or any of the arts and sciences are all held together by political threads. The successful politician is holding the lever at the centre and he can often decide the way events are shaped.'

'He's at the fulcrum,' said Charles remembering Petrograd and Nina.

'Yes, that's right,' Sir John exclaimed, confident the ship was nearly home, 'if you hanker after an absorbing interest in life there's nothing like a political career. It has all the ingredients: excitement, glamour and, for those who become Ministers, an opportunity to perform great services for the nation. Nothing would please me more if you went into politics. Is that what you want?

'I want power,' said Charles deliberately, in a cold and dispassionate voice, and his uncle mentally shuddered at the impact of the ship as it found its berth.

As Sir John left the Hall to return to Westminster, Sarah congratulated him on his success in breaking through her son's sullenness. 'The change is quite noticeable. You've given him a new lease of life. He's taken up his books and riding again. How ever did you do it?'

'I think I've found his hidden ambition; now he's recognised and admitted it he can freely let it shape his future actions. Before it was acknowledged, it acted as a mental block rather than a stimulus.'

'What does he want?' Sarah asked anxious to understand the son who had become a stranger.

'To be a leader of men and to shape human destiny. It is a very noble ambition and we should do everything to encourage him.'

The next month, February, the estate was covered in a thick expanse of snow reminiscent of the wastes of North Russia. Charles made a sledge so Emma and Edith could enjoy the swish of riding on frozen tracks. He told them enough about his adventures on sledges to make them desperate to hear more but he never told them about the pony which died.

A letter arrived from Sir John inviting him to the Carlton Club for lunch and suggesting he spent a week in London as 'you might learn something to your advantage' he had added cryptically.

Charles took the train for Liverpool Street, exchanging the crisp snow of East Anglia for the slush of London caused by the hundreds of motors invading the streets where horse drawn vehicles resented an intrusion they could not prevent. He took a room at the Ritz, taking advantage of the prosperity with which his father's inheritance had endowed him. In any case his game plan for the future, beginning to crystalise, included the need to keep up appearances, to put the best image forward, to show he was a man of substance and worthy of confidence. He had a jaunty and confident stride as he strode down St. James's Street to the Carlton Club, the hive of Tory political machinations. The doorman, forewarned of the young Baring's arrival, escorted Charles to the writing room where the baronet was attending to correspondence.

'Ah there you are Charles, you've arrived early. Make yourself comfortable over there with the *Times* and I'll be with you in a moment. I can't leave these constituents waiting for their letters. Not with politics in such a turmoil.'

As he held the *Times* open at the Parliamentary report page Charles's eyes scanned the corner of the lofty room, savouring the sense of political power which passed through it. He thought he recognised a few of the men making their way to the dining room.

They ordered the *table d'hôte* which Charles noticed cost ten shillings each, of soup, roast lamb from the trolley and choice of puddings or cheese. Sir John chose a bottle of Chateau Lynch-Bages 1916.

'Some excellent claret was produced in the war years,' he said as he put the tasting glass on the table. 'It was lucky the Hun didn't get to Bordeaux. Could have made as much a mess of it as they did of Champagne. Actually this is not one of the first growths. It was only classified as a fifth in fifty-five but has improved since then. Recovered very nicely from the phylloxera.'

Charles sipped the wine which had been carefully poured by the steward to half-fill his glass.

'It's good, isn't it' said Sir John. 'Did you know the Lynch is for an Irishman who was Mayor of Bordeaux?'

'No,' mumbled Charles.

'They'd do better tending their vineyards than making political trouble for us. Lloyd-George gave in to terrorism and now we're reaping the consequences. De Valera and Collins won't be satisfied until they get full independence. They should be put down with more force.'

'Black and tans?' asked Charles.

'Don't believe the propaganda against our British troops. Remember what the I.R.A. did last November — you might have missed it as you were on your way back from Russia and had other things to think about — the I.R.A. took fourteen British officers from their beds and shot them dead in front of their families. These are the terrorists we are up against. We should show them terrorism doesn't work but Lloyd-George thinks otherwise. Trouble is he doesn't have any moral authority left.'

'Why is that?' asked Charles.

'His open immorality. It's becoming embarrassing to everyone who supports the Coalition. Parnell was forced to give up his leadership of the Irish because of his sexual peccadiloes, but now we have the British Prime Minister doing much worse.'

'In what way?' inquired Charles, interested.

'With his young secretary Frances Stevenson. He packed his wife off to Wales and spent Christmas with the girl alone at No. 10. Can you imagine the effrontery of it. And to cap it all he got the organist at Westminster Cathedral to come in to play the piano after their Christmas lunch *à deux*. The P.M. has totally forgotten that Christmas is a family occasion. Mistresses are acceptable only if used discreetly. What Lloyd-George is doing is an insult to the nation's standards.'

'It does seem brash,' mused Charles.

'Brash and foolhardy. The Tory party in the House is going to break the Coalition; we're just waiting for the right time. When it comes there will a General Election and that could be your opportunity to get a seat.'

'Do you think I could get one so soon and so young?'

'Why not? Tom Mosley won Harrow when he was only twenty-two. You're twenty-three next week aren't you?'

'Yes.'

'A dozen famous men were elected younger than you are now. Fox at nineteen, Pitt, twenty-one, Gladstone, twenty-two, and Palmerston, twenty-three, all beat you to it. It may be another two years before we can force an election. You'll be twenty-five then, time enough to be in the House. I think you should prepare for it.' Sir John turned to acknowledge a fellow Club member and said to him, 'See you in the smoking room after questions, F.E.' as the tall imposing figure walked off.

'That was Lord Birkenhead. He'd be a powerful support for you,' Sir John pushed his plate to one side and held his glass in two hands with his elbows on the table as if contemplating the oracle in the translucent claret. 'These days it's becoming less easy to get a seat by paying the constituency association. The party workers are demanding more of a say in selection. At Harrow some of the rejected candidates are up in arms because Mosley was selected instead of them but they can't do anything about it.'

'Do delegates select by democratic vote?'

'Yes, it's come to that in most constituencies. They say Lieutenant Mosley's military background in the Royal Flying Corps helped.'

They went to the smoking room to have their coffees served by deferential waiters in tails. Sir John sank into a deep leather armchair and stretched out. 'Tell me,' he said, 'what do you make of Britain after all your years away?'

Charles drank from the small cup carefully, placing it back on the marble table in front of them before measuring his words. 'I think the sacrifice of eight hundred and fifty thousand of our young men killed in the trenches deserves better. The post war boom was still on last year when I got back but already it's petering out. Something has to be done about unemployment. Those thousands being laid off by the decline in the coal, textile and shipbuilding industries have to be found other work. Unemployment could be up to two million in months unless action is taken.'

'I agree with you Charles. This Coalition has lost its direction and only we Conservatives can provide the remedy. Laissez faire liberalism will be the ruination of this country. We need to use our strength at home to stop the insidious spread of trade unionism. If you believe in positive Conservatism you can help us in the House. We need more young Members like Tom Mosley.'

'What do I do to get a constituency?'

'There's a lot of luck in it but as in most other cases you have to help luck by being in the right place at the right time. I have an idea for you to think about. If you're willing to be a party agent I can talk to the Party and get you allotted to a constituency where you can do useful work and make contacts for your own career.'

'Yes I'd like that,' said Charles, anxious to get into practical action.

They walked down through the Duke of York steps and into St. James's Park towards Parliament with Sir John silently congratulating himself on a most successful lunch. His nephew had opened up in a way his mother had never thought possible. There was now every chance that he could be steered into a safe Conservative seat and prevented from sinking into the post-war depression which had afflicted so many discharged officers of his generation. The excitement and challenge of war was difficult to match in peacetime.

As uncle and nephew passed by the back of Downing Street and the India office, the baronet put his hand on Charles's shoulder and said, 'Your late father would be proud if you joined us in Parliament. He was always jealous of me — we never really hit it off as brothers — and his own son having a political career would have helped us both to get to know each other better.'

In the next few days Charles visited the Conservative Party headquarters at Palace Chambers and was sent to Woolwich East to help in the by-election where Ramsey MacDonald was standing as the Labour candidate, trying to regain a seat to replace the one he had lost in 1918. The coalition candidate was a Captain Gee who had won the Victoria Cross for bravery in the war and Charles immediately saw the potential for building up support by a campaign on the pacifist issue. MacDonald had been vociferously opposed to the war in which Gee had been honoured as a hero. The contrast could not have been greater.

The campaign paid dividends and despite the unpopularity of the Government, Gee was elected.

When Charles saw Sir John on the day after the poll he found him ecstatic. 'Keeping the Labour leader out of Parliament is a great achievement. MacDonald will have to be a carpet bagger yet again.'

Charles shrugged his shoulders as though his contribution to the victory had beem minimal and Sir John sensing his modesty said 'Everyone says you played an important part in the campaign and that will certainly stand you in good stead. The Labour Party is seen as a bigger threat to us now the Liberals are hopelessly divided. MacDonald with his silver tongue is gathering support and we've got to keep him under control. At the last election the Labour Party scored two and a third million votes, nearly as many as both wings of the Liberals. Their alliance with the trades unions is going to be the most important factor in British politics. If they succeed it will undermine the economy of this country more than any war could do.'

'How is that?' asked Charles.

'They're against the Empire which secures our markets and they're for nationalisation which will ruin efficiency. They're engaged in a campaign now about the coal mines which is based on lies and deceit. They want miners' wages to go up but the industry just can't afford it. Do you know that of the thirty-three and three pence a ton that coal costs at the pithead no less than twenty-four and three pence goes to miners' wages and only two and a penny for owners' profits. There's no fat in the industry for the miners to take any more.'

'I can see that.'

'Trouble is the Labour Party is not facing up to the facts. It's giving the working classes false expectations. It's the politics of envy they're engaged in and we're going to have to work hard to withstand them. Funny,' said Sir John, pensively, 'the soundest intellectuals who bolster up the

Labour Party mostly depend on inherited wealth, but they soon lose it as a result of their foolishness. Look at Sir Thomas Beecham, that Fabian conductor fellow, he went bankrupt for over a hundred thousand.'

'They're a rum lot those socialists,' said Charles.

'The Conservatives are this country's only hope,' said Sir John vehemently, 'the Socialists are inept and the Liberals are corrupt. I hear Lloyd-George is selling knighthoods for ten thousand and peerages for thirty thousand. Under this Prime Minister we're sinking lower and lower. He'll have to go. Our party will have to pull out of the Coalition.'

Charles Baring had learned much from the political gossip in London and returned to the Hall much stronger in body and spirit. His mother was delighted to see the change in him and found him willing to talk about his plans. 'I'm standing for Parliament,' he declared.

'That's wonderful,' said Sarah Baring, 'what constituency?'

'That takes time to arrange. I'm hoping to find a good one where I'll have to pay only five hundred a year but I'm willing to go up to a thousand if necessary.'

'I thought you were paid for being a Member of Parliament.'

'Yes, there's a pittance of a salary. I'm talking about the amount I'll have to pay the constituency association to buy the seat.'

'Do you still buy seats? Didn't that go out with the rotten boroughs?'

'Even the Liberals do it. Only the Socialists get away without paying, but then the seats are bought by the trades unions or the cooperative societies.'

'It all sounds very corrupt to me.'

'It is Mother. Business is corrupt. Politics is corrupt. One simply has to live with the facts if one is to get on.'

'You sound more like your father every day,' said Sarah Baring.

Charles's cultivation of the officials at Conservative Party headquarters continued throughout the year. He had particular sucess with Douglas Rhodes, one of the research assistants to the party Chairman, Sir George Younger. Rhodes had missed any service during the war because of ill health and had been able to complete a course at Oxford graduating with a first class degree in modern languages. His father was Sir Lewis Rhodes a prominent industrialist in the Midlands who had arranged through Austen Chamberlain for his second son to be taken on by the party. Douglas Rhodes, a year younger than Baring had no political ambitions for himself, admitting he preferred the back room role. During the Woolwich by-election, where they had first met, he confided in Baring that his only wish was 'to help build up the Conservative and Union Party until it was an impregnable force which could never lose an election.' Baring could see the great potential for his own career in having a friend at Court and persuaded Rhodes to visit the Hall during the summer holidays.

Rhodes, who had grown up in a big house in Edgbaston and had spent little time in the country, enjoyed the wide open spaces of East Anglia with their long vistas. 'These skies inspired Turner, now you can understand why,' said Baring.

'I've never seen England so beautiful. In Birmingham I was locked too long in those dark satanic mills of Blake.'

'I'll teach you to ride and it'll give a new dimension to your life.'

Douglas Rhodes was tall with gingerish hair, spectacles for his myopic eyes and a weak, asthmatic chest. He looked more likely to ride a book than a horse but Charles produced the meekest pony and persuaded him to mount it. His friend managed to stay in the saddle but at the end of the afternoon complained of a sore bottom and a strain in his chest. Charles gave up the attempt to teach riding and settled on walks which his guest could manage without ill effects.

Charles talked of his experiences in Russian prisons and the need to destroy Bolshevism. Douglas, whose outlook was shaped by books and his father's wealth rather than direct experience, agreed enthusiastically. 'Winston was right when he tried to strangle the ambitions of those Jewish adventurers. Lloyd-George was so wrong to stop him. Winston you know has all the best characteristics of the Marlboroughs and that American influence from his mother gives him a world vision the little Welsh man sadly lacks. It's his natural political home. The Liberals are finished and can do nothing for him.'

'Do you think Winston could be Prime Minister one day?' asked Charles.

'Only if he joins our party,' said Douglas.

On his next visit to London Baring stayed with Rhodes at the flat his industrialist father had bought for him in St. James's. It was situated at the back of the Ritz Hotel and had a good view of Green Park through wide windows. Charles was struck by the ultra modern furnishings which were unlike anything he had previously seen. In the huge lounge a glass topped table stood low on a plain but deep carpeted floor. The armchairs were similarly low and three large cushions added to the emphasis on soft comfort. The walls, painted matt-white, highlighted three paintings executed in striking colours but, not at first glance, representing any recognisable shapes. Douglas proudly identified them as by Piet Mondrian. He explained he had been to Holland with his father and bought them there. In the corner stood a grand piano — a Steinway — also white.

'Goodness Douglas,' Baring exclaimed, 'what a dashing room.'

'I made it as unlike my parents' place as possible. Edgbaston is a mess; stupid cloth covers on the mantelpiece, crowded with dozens of ornaments, aspidistras in pots and awful high rosewood furniture dominating the rooms. In that house people were made to feel as if they were intruding. The place belonged to the clutter. The atmosphere was awful. It stopped one from relaxing and even from thinking. The house was only suitable for the silly tittle-tattle which masqueraded as conversation. I found it all quite suffocating. That's why I had to escape down here.'

'Does your father approve?'

'No he thinks I'm a philistine 'cause I don't like his Rembrandt and his other gloomy Flemish masterpieces. I like modern art. We're in the nineteen-twenties now. A new age for new art and away with all the fustiness of the past, I say.'

Charles was conscious that style at the Hall had barely changed in twenty years and that his friend must have thought disparagingly of it, but Rhodes read his thoughts and added solicitously, 'Don't think I want every house to be the same as this. Your Suffolk Hall has a grandeur about it which needn't be altered. It's the depressing oldness of the Victorian style I want to replace. After all it's twenty years since the old lady died, we can't go on for ever perpetuating her period.'

'That's true,' said Charles slumping into a seat and stretching out his legs. He found the posture extremely, almost guiltily comfortable as if he were in bed. 'Say, how do you get up from these chairs?'

'You see the reason for the design now, don't you,' said Rhodes 'my chairs are for resting on, not getting up from.' He went to the piano and played a Beethoven bagatelle so delicately it enchanted Baring, increasingly surprised by the impact of his friend's hidden personality.

Rhodes showed off his bedroom with a sunken bed and on the wall a large bevelled mirror, plain except for a jet black band on two sides and flush fitted wardrobes, matt-white as was the rest of the apartment. It was clinical in its simplicity. Only the study with its open bookshelves to the high ceilings and a large leather topped desk with a silver inkstand and pens showed any concession to tradition.

'You see Charles,' emphasised Rhodes, 'I believe homes should be for people.'

'I know what you are,' said Baring tauntingly.

'Tell me then. They say you can read a man by his books or

his wife. You can read me by my apartment.'

'Indeed I can. You are a modern monk. The Capuchin or Benedictine finds his soul by simplicity and you do the same.'

'My self denial I can assure you dear Charles is not of the same order.'

'I'm glad to hear it.'

To prove his point Rhodes mixed gin and vermouth cocktails in a shaker and served them from an ice bucket. He picked up a Turkish cigarette from an onyx box, put it in a long holder and lit it with a silver lighter.

'Have you never smoked Charles?' he enquired languidly.

'Tried it once but it didn't suit me. The fellows in that Russian prison thought I was mad. They could not have kept their nerve without nicotine. Do you think it's wise for you to smoke with your asthma trouble?'

'I consulted the best doctors. They tell me it should have no ill effect whatsoever, especially as I smoke through a holder. Men have been smoking since Raleigh and it hasn't done us any harm yet. The doctors say smoking cools my nerves and does me good. Asthma, they say is a nervous complaint. I expect it was brought on by my domineering father.'

'Could be,' said Baring, 'we have everything to thank our parents for.'

The two friends had dinner at the Ritz and went on to a nightclub in Bond Street where they danced with pretty hostesses to a white American band from New York playing jazz in the negro style. Douglas Rhodes became tipsy on his cocktails and wanted to take his dancing partner back to his flat. But it was against the club rules to take a girl home. 'Get the girl's address if you're that keen on her,' suggested Baring, 'and we'll send a cab for her another night.'

'Why not tonight?'

'Because you're too far gone. You'll be asleep as soon as your head hits the pillow and a lovely girl would have been wasted.'

CHAPTER 28

Baring found the Rhodes' company stimulating in some ways and enervating in others. The man had style, there was no denying that, was a constant source of amusing stories and political gossip but the unreality of the life he was playing annoyed Baring's streak of puritanism. The suffering of the unemployed made no impression on him. Nor did the distress of wage earners whose incomes had been forced down by tough employers anxious to reduce costs in a competitive world. Baring could not help feeling sorry for the miners in South Wales who had lost forty per cent and the fitters whose weekly wages had been reduced to £2.17s.6d. compared to the £4.9s.6d. of two years before. He could not see how a man could maintain a family and suffer a drop in pay of a third. It seemed brutal and callous and was a terrible indictment of the system which demanded sacrifices from men who had just fought, and won, a war for freedom. It did not make sense in economic or moral terms and Baring's socialist instincts made it difficult for him to hold back his true feelings.

Douglas Rhodes regarded the plight of his fellow men with benign indifference. 'If they don't like the wages they should change their jobs,' was his comment and when it was pointed out there were no jobs available he retorted, 'there's always work for the men who are prepared to look for it' and 'there's the unemployment insurance to keep them going.' He did not seem to care that the benefit was only 15 shillings a week and that was only for a maximum 22 week period. After that a man's only recourse was to the Guardians. For Rhodes it was inevitable that the economy should ebb and flow and that some unfortunates should have to suffer when it ebbed. For him the role of the Party was vital as it kept power in the hands of the intelligent and the privileged during periods of unrest. The democratic franchise which had been made even more ludicrous by giving votes to women had to be manipulated to ensure the Party never lost the reins for too long.

At all times Charles Baring humoured his friend by appearing to discuss the issues while concealing his innermost thoughts. From his strategic standpoint there were two broad objectives: one was to secure his own advancement within the Conservative Party and this meant going along with the prevailing wisdom, and two was to encourage by every subtle means the clash between the classes in Britain to bring the prospect of revolution nearer. When the workers were relatively prosperous, enjoying the crumbs of capitalism as they fell from the overfull tables of the rich, there would be no prospect of them rising against the system that oppressed them. Baring was appalled by the vain hypocrisy of Rhodes who took his father's money in spite of his deep contempt for him and theorised about creating a new culture and a new civilisation whilst remaining totally dependent upon the old. Baring told himself that he was morally superior, not recognising that his own reliance on inherited wealth and his arrogance in thinking he had a right to subvert society were perhaps even more despicable. The two friends made a sinister combination which became even worse as they became closer and began working out the intrigues which could further the causes they thought they believed in.

On the 16th October, 1922, Douglas Rhodes told Baring of the moves being made to break the Coalition. 'It's about time that goat Lloyd-George was put out to grass and we've got to plan to do it,' he announced proudly. 'I've been working on it for a week now and all is set to go.'

'What are you doing?'

'Austen Chamberlain is my father's great pal so I've been able to get to know him very well. He wants the Coalition to continue and thinks our members in Parliament will support him. I've told him they would and I drafted a speech for him defending the Coalition which he made in Birmingham last Friday. It was the thirteenth, quite a coincidence don't you think? If my plan works out it will be his last speech as leader.'

'You got Chamberlain to read a speech when you knew it was a load of rubbish and would destroy his own leadership? asked Baring incredulously.

'I did. Brilliant move don't you think? I included a defence of Lloyd-George's policy on the Greek and Turk quarrel knowing that our M.P.'s are dead set against that madness which could draw us into another war.'

'The Chanak incident?'

'That's right. Anyway Austen fell for it hook, line and sinker and as a result opinion in the party is moving strongly against him. He doesn't know it yet because we are not telling him. The Chief Whip is out of touch and he thinks that if he calls a meeting he'll get support to carry on the Coalition. He's so wrong. He can't see further than the end of his nose through his silly old monocle.'

'Who have you got lined up to take over from Chamberlain if your plan succeeds?'

'That's the rub. Our real man is Stanley Baldwin. He's a man of steel from Bridgenorth. His type is the bed rock of the party: sane, sensible and practical people, anti-Lloyd-George and anti-corrupt Liberalism. The party won't wear him yet so we're getting Bonar Law lined up as the compromise. He won't last long because of his ill health and then Baldwin can take over.'

'Brilliant if it works,' said Charles.

'It will work. Chamberlain is calling a meeting of all M.Ps for next Thursday. There's a by-election at Newport on the day before and he thinks the Coalition candidate will win. We know different. We've been pushing support for Clarry the independent Conservative. The result will come through just as the Carlton Club meeting takes place and it will knock the Chamberlain camp sideways.'

Douglas Rhodes asked Baring to canvass support from his uncle and from Captain Gee, the Woolwich East victor, and promised to get him a place to observe the famous meeting.

On Thursday Charles slipped into the side seats reserved for office staff and whispered to Rhodes, 'Is it going well?'

'Working like a charm. The Newport result has just come in. A smashing victory for Clarry. It will cook Austen's goose.'

Members of Parliament were crowding in. Some were in morning dress having left their long black overcoats and silk top hats in the cloakrooms; others were in the new style of waistcoated lounge suits. There was a hubbub of conversation filling the hall as the Leader of the Party walked in accompanied by the Chief Whip. All stood and the sound of a hundred voices died away in the shuffling.

Rhodes explained quietly to Baring that a modest and unassuming M.P. called Pretyman had been fixed to propose the motion that the Conservative and Unionist Party fight the next election independently. 'That way the personal ambitions are played down,' he whispered. Baring listened intently as Austen Chamberlain rose to defend the Government's record, arguing for an anti-socialist front and praising Lloyd-George as the only man who could lead the country.

'That's good for us,' whispered Rhodes, 'our rebels hate the Welsh evil genius and that reference will make them angry.'

Bonar Law followed briefly, but the devastating reply came from the President of the Board of Trade, Stanley Baldwin, speaking impressively like the solid county squire he was. The vote when it came was decisive. One hundred and eighty-six were against continuing the Coalition and only eighty-seven were for it. 'We've won,' said Rhodes.

Lloyd-George went to Buckingham Palace that afternoon to tender his resignation as Prime Minister. On the following

Monday Andrew Bonar Law was elected Leader of the Party by Conservative Peers, M.Ps and candidates, meeting at the Hotel Cecil. Three days later Parliament was dissolved and a General Election was fixed to follow in three weeks. Events were moving faster than Baring had anticipated and he still had not found himself a constituency.

Douglas Rhodes did his best to get his friend adopted, even in a hopeless seat, but failed. They had left it too late. 'Next best thing is to get you on to Baldwin's political staff. He'll welcome your support in his constituency and you can help draft his speeches. You'll pick up his style in no time.'

Baring found himself at the hustings, arranging meetings in town and village halls and generally acting as assistant to the newly promoted Chancellor of the Exchequer. It was his first experience of a General Election and he enjoyed it enormously while grimly working at his purpose. He especially liked making impromptu speeches to fill gaps when the main speakers were delayed on the road. It reminded him of the word games he used to play with grandfather Tallen.

He was so busy with Baldwin that he was unable to visit his uncle's constituency, where Sir John had a four-cornered fight with the Labour Party, an Asquithian Liberal and a Lloyd-George Liberal. He was confident that the result would keep one Baring in the new House with a huge majority. What he needed was to ensure his own selection for a safe seat before the next time around. The excitement of political campaigning was getting into his blood and he was anxious to be in the action for its own sake. Politics was like alcohol in that it stimulated the nervous system, making it demand more until the addict could no longer live without the daily dose. The Chancellor coaxed his audiences from two dozen or more platforms in a week, standing with his feet astride, two thumbs stuck in the top pockets of his waistcoat and confidently, calmly spreading the Conservative message. Baring watched and listened in fascination at the art of the consummate politician making the enemy — Lloyd-George or the Labour Party or the abstainers — sound like traitors to the solid England of true Tory values. It was evident the electors would not be voting for policies as they were ill thought out and would be scrapped overnight. Instead they were asked to endorse a mood not a movement; to vote for safety-first rather than dangerous experiment. At the grassroots of British democracy Baring studied the nature of the plant, learning the secrets of propagation, cultivation and the harvesting of political support.

The election resulted in a massive Conservative phalanx of three hundred and forty-four members elected and as Sir John Baring and Stanley Baldwin were among them, Charles was well pleased. It was a terrific result for all those who had campaigned against the Lloyd-George Coalition: the Liberal coalitionists were left with a rump of fifty-three and the Asquithian Liberals only sixty-two seats. The Labour Party emerged with one hundred and forty-two seats and became the real Parliamentary Opposition to the Conservatives for the first time. Winston Churchill, standing as a Liberal, was defeated in Dundee, and the victors were delighted with the prospect that he would be forced back into Conservative ranks and prised away from his association with Lloyd-George.

At the celebration parties, Champagne flowed through the night. There was a lot to celebrate. The Tories were back in their rightful governing position, the Liberals had been broken, and Labour was small enough to be kept under control. Great Britain would be great again.

Douglas Rhodes took Baring to a nightclub for their private celebration. This time they had a couple of girls to go with them. Dorothy Bagley and Helen Page, both just twenty, were helpers at the party headquarters. Their fathers were both stalwart Conservatives in the home counties who paid for their daughters to support the cause until suitable marriages could be arranged. They were both pretty girls whose understanding of politics was limited to knowing who stood where and who among the up-and-coming slept where, which was vastly more important and more interesting to them. They had ambitions to marry into power so they could preside over famous dinner parties where Cabinets were made and broken. Pre-war fathers would have demanded chaperones for their daughters or at least have made an attempt to do so. The modern attitudes of the post war era had made such customs seem antiquated. Women had enjoyed freedom during the war and were not going back to relinquish it so easily and votes for women at thirty appeared to confirm their equality to men in the eyes of the law. Dorothy and Helen reflected the new independence of their sex, as they wanted no petty restrictions on the way they ran their lives, but unconsciously they accepted all the old inferiorities as their simple aim was to catch a man and to ride on his shoulders rather than carve out a career for themselves. Douglas and Charles could take full advantage of the girls' aspirations without making any concessions to them whatsoever. Women's liberation from the shackles of the past was no threat to the masculine dominance; it simply made it easier to persuade respectable girls to lose their innocence.

Sometime after midnight Douglas took Dorothy back to his St. James's apartment while Charles slipped Helen through the back door of the Ritz, ensuring the compliance of the Commissionaire by palming him a couple of florins. Helen was the prettiest of the two girls. She had bobbed brown hair, bright red lips and a lily white neck graced with a long string of pearls, which looked genuine and were. Once in Charles's suite she threw off her cloak, took off her cloche hat, loosened her hair, smoothed down her frilly black evening dress which just reached her knees and straightened the back seam of her silk stockings.

'That was heavenly Charles,' she sighed, 'I haven't danced so much in weeks. It's such a relief to have that election out of the way. These elections do take up a frightful amount of time, don't they?'

'They are important. How else do people have their say?'

'But why three weeks of it?' she pouted her lips. 'I should have thought most people knew what they wanted. A week's campaign should be enough.'

'The electors like see the leaders. They couldn't get around the country in a week.'

'I suppose you simply loved it with Stanley Baldwin. He's such a steadfast man. One simply knows he can be trusted. Such a difference to Lloyd-George who looks so shifty. I'm suspicious of Welshmen anyway. That silly sing-song way of speaking they have always put me off.' She took a cigarette from a case and fitted it carefully into a long ebony black holder. Charles lit a match, held it for her and said 'How about another drink?'

'No dahling,' she replied, 'not for me. I've had enough already.'

'I've got some Bollinger on ice.'

'That's different. How could I refuse you.'

Charles lifted the bottle out of the ice bucket and gently eased the cork out of the top. It fell out with a plop and he poured the sparkling liquid into two stem glasses standing on a silver tray.

'Do you have political ambitions, Charles?' she asked.

'You know I have. I was upset I couldn't fight this time. I'm not a bit like Douglas. He's content to pull the levers. I want to be on the stage. It's the difference between playwright and actor though I want to be the playwright as well. I want to write my own scripts; not spout someone else's.' Charles spoke in the short, disjointed sentences of slight inebriation.

'This *is* exciting,' said Helen gushing, as she sipped the champagne. 'To know that you are to be a leader of men with your own ideas. That *is* the most exciting adventure of all.'

'There's no guarantee of success.'

'Oh yes, you'll be successful, with your friendship with Baldwin they'll be no trouble.'

'I still have to get a constituency and Baldwin doesn't hand them out on a platter.'

'He will if you ask him nicely,' she purred into her drink.

'It's not so easy for a party leader nowadays. The constituency associations like to make their own choices. It is something called democracy.'

'I know,' she said, 'my Daddy's the constituency Chairman. I've heard him discussing it with Mummy lots of times.'

Charles, swift to seize on the point said, 'I thought your father was a builder.'

'He is. His houses stretch for miles around, gobbling up the beautiful countryside. Mummy says he's spoiling the environment, but he says the people need somewhere to live and he's providing an essential service.' She prattled on, her tongue loosened by cocktails and wine. 'He buys land from farmers for next to nothing and builds houses on it for five hundred pounds each. He sells hundreds and hundreds of them. Think of all that lovely money, money, money.'

'But what about his party work?' demanded Charles.

'He became Chairman of the party so he wouldn't get opposition from the council for his lovely developments. Wasn't Daddy clever? He knows how to get his way.'

'Which constituency is it?'

'West Middlesex.'

'We held that one didn't we?'

'Oh yes. It's been a safe Tory seat for years but Daddy says it was radical in the eighteenth century when John Wilkes was the member.'

'That was before he built those houses.'

'It's getting safer for us all the time. People who own their own houses vote for safety. You should know that, Charles, you're the politician.' She purred at him sweetly, 'Our present member isn't standing next time; he's so old he had to promise to retire. Daddy insisted.'

Charles was quick to see the advantage, his intoxication all but dissipated by the the prospects.

'Has the constituency chosen his replacement?'

'Oh no. Only Daddy knows he's going.'

'Does your father want to stand in his place?'

'Heavens no. Daddy's not *that* interested in politics.'

'So I could be considered then?'

Helen looked at him thoughtfully, held out her glass and said, 'Yes you can, but only if you're a good boy and fill up my glass before all those bubbles disappear.'

'You'll deserve a jeroboam of Champagne if you can get me that constituency,' said Charles happier than he had felt all evening.

'Daddy will do anything for his little girl,' she gurgled and Charles, in gratitude, gathered her in his arms and carried her pliant, unresisting body towards the open door of the bedroom.

Within a fortnight Helen had introduced Charles to her parents. He found Thomas Oliver Page a bluff, robust, red-faced, fifty year old, who looked every inch of what he was: a self-made, self-opinionated businessman who had made money too easily and thought he was entitled to buy power and honour with the proceeds. His wife, a small mousey woman, confirmed that he had married very young when his emotions were stronger than his discernment or his discretion. Henrietta had sad lines on her face showing that no one had bothered to read the interests of this Page for the past thirty years. She had been trained into timidity, overruled and overawed by decades of married life and suffering the five minor Pages which had resulted from the union.

Helen was the youngest and the apple of her father's eye. Anything she wanted could be hers including the warmest welcome to her newest boyfriend. The tall, handsome, aristocratic ex-captain war hero appealed to Thomas Page, who saw him as a man who had been born with the distinctions which had eluded him. In entertaining Charles Baring the property developer felt he could gain glory by association. The prospects of a rich son-in-law with a

Military Cross were very tempting and the trade-in of a candidacy for the safe Conservative seat of West Middlesex was but a small price to pay.

Dinner at the newly built mansion of the Page's at Ealing was an embarrassing affair for Charles. It was a substantial feast of roast beef, Yorkshire pudding, roast potatoes and rhubarb tart served throughout with a semi-sweet white wine which cloyed uncomfortably to his palate. He had no wish to be matrimonially entangled with the scatty, spoilt daughter of a callow, small-minded Home Counties Tory and the hints the host dropped as soon as the soup was served were almost too crude to be ignored. Charles survived by turning the conversation to political issues, flattering T.O. Page by asking his views, and he skilfully managed to avoid any whisper of a commitment to the persistent Helen.

When the ladies had left them with the Port, Charles gratefully accepted a cigar — his only concession to smoking. 'Don't you agree that the sooner Stanley Baldwin takes over from Law the better it will be for the Party?' he asked passing the silver cigar-cutter back to his host.

'Indeed I do, Stanley's a businessman who understands what his country needs in this modern age. We need men with practical experience running Whitehall, not a bunch of old-fashioned mountebanks.'

They lit up the huge Coronas, Page had a better taste in cigars than he had in wines or wives, and Charles seized the lull to open up the main subject.

'I hear from Helen that there'll be a vacancy here in West Middlsex?'

'Yes, our man is too old to fight another election. He's over seventy now. Younger men should have a chance. Men like you with youth and vigour and the experience of war should be representing us. Have you thought of standing, Charles? You'd make a good member.'

'My uncle, Sir John Baring, who's been in the House for nearly twenty years thinks I should join him. I've had a number of interesting approaches from constituency associations but I'm anxious to get a seat with a strong base.'

'Our's is well organised, better even than Harrow, our nearest rivals. Since they elected Tom Mosley we've been looking for a candidate who could match him. I think you have it, Charles. You've got a strong character, a brave war record like him and a Baronet in the family. If we can field you next time we'll more than hold our own against Harrow.'

'I would be honoured to be asked,' said Charles as modestly as he could muster.

'That's settled then,' said Thomas Page as if he had just concluded the sale of a desirable property, 'lets have the ladies back in and tell Helen what we've got in store for you. I'll fix the association. We'll have to have a selection conference. That's the form nowadays. There's a matter of an annual five hundred for the association's funds but I'll take care of that for you, Charles. You keep your money for your other political expenses. I can see you going a long way,' he chirped, thinking of the reflected glory to come.

CHAPTER 29

Stanley Baldwin, the iron maker from Bewdley, took over from an ailing Bonar Law as leader of the Conservative Party and went to the Palace to kiss hands on becoming Prime Minister. Among those who went to Number Ten to celebrate were three aides of the new P.M. including a jubliant Charles Baring. At last he could feel his hand on the pulse of Britain if not yet on the lever. Baldwin was a solid figure who inspired confidence in those who wanted stability, but he was without imagination, and Baring had discovered he could be easily manipulated if one used the right combination of practical argument and unflowery flattery.

When he was shown into the hallway of Number Ten and escorted down the long corridor by the tail-coated attendant, Charles Baring knew he had arrived in a place destined to be his one day. He had premonitions of times ahead when he would be able to exercise power unalloyed by the necessities of manipulation or compromise. Climbing the stairs at the back of the building he passed the photographs of past Prime Ministers ending with Bonar Law at the top. He wondered how long it would take before he was there as the final incumbent of an office which would be abolished as no longer needed in a soviet republic.

At the entrance to the lounge Baldwin greeted him warmly, 'Lucy,' he said turning to the small lady by his side, 'you know Charles Baring don't you?' He's given me valiant service. I hear rumours he may be joining us as the new member for West Middlesex. I hope they're true.'

'Thank you Prime Minister, I look forward to supporting

you from the backbenches.'

Douglas Rhodes had also heard the rumours. 'Great stuff, Charles,' he said gripping his friend's arm with his left hand as the right balanced an overful glass of Champagne, 'you've turned over a new Page in your career, I'm glad to hear.'

Charles ignored the pun and replied, 'The prospects are not bad.'

'I hope that Helen hasn't been too clinging as a result, old chap. Bit much to have to pay that sort of price for a seat, isn't it?'

'I've never discussed marriage,' said Charles on the defensive.

'Make no bones about it. She's expecting it. So is her father, so I've heard.'

'I've done nothing to raise their hopes and I don't intend to.'

'But the spider's web is weaving old chap, you'll have to be careful you don't get caught.'

The adoption of Charles Baring as the prospective Conservative candidate for West Middlesex was achieved without hitch thanks to the ground work of the Chairman of the association. The new candidate courted the local Tory activists just as assiduously as he had the Pages and soon had himself entrenched. He needed an early election so he could dislodge the Member. Another four years delay would be too long and Baring turned his talents to devising an excuse for Baldwin to go to the country. He found it in the tariff issue and deliberately fed a pledge into a speech the Prime Minister was due to make at Plymouth on the twenty-fifth of October 1923.

Baring accompanied the P.M. to the meeting and had a thrill of anticipation as he heard him read the words he had written. 'This unemployment is the most crucial problem. I will fight it. I have come to the conclusion that the only way of fighting this subject is by protecting the home market.' Then Baldwin added a phrase of his own, 'I am not a clever man. I

know nothing of political tactics,' and then he returned to
Baring's text 'I feel the only honest and right thing I could do
is to submit my conclusion to the judgement of the
electorate.'

Baring was relieved. He had intrigued the Prime Minister
into virtually declaring that an election would be held. That
would give him the chance to get his own seat and to
consolidate his influence.

Douglas Rhodes was less than enthusiastic when he saw
his friend, 'What a crazy decision to have an election. It is
unnecessary. We have a big majority and could easily
introduce tariffs by stages. Why make such a big issue of it?'

'Stanley,' said Baring who had slipped into an easy
informality out of Baldwin's earshot, 'Stanley likes to be
known as an honest man. The tricks of politics are alien to
him.'

'More's the pity. I met Benito Mussolini at the Italian
Embassy last December. He's the kind of leader we need. All
this democracy rubbish doesn't add one fig to our efficiency
and it wastes energy. Once we have power we should hold it
as long as possible. Mussolini doesn't intend to give it up and
he's doing great things for Italy.'

'Making the trains run on time, I hear.'

'There's nothing wrong with making the trains run on
time.'

The election was held in a cold and bleak December.
Charles left Baldwin's team to devote two weeks to intensive
campaigning, making speeches in crowded school halls every
night. His most bitter attacks were on the pacifists and the
Bolsheviks who were waiting to take over Britain 'as they
have in the great country of Russia where instead of justice
and freedom only hunger reigns supreme. We have a noble
duty,' he declared in meeting after meeting hardly changing a
word of the effective peroration, 'a noble duty to defend our
King and country against those foreign ideas which are
creeping on to our shores through the Labour Party. Vote

Conservative, vote for stability and sense and vote against the evils of foreign ideology.'

The count, which was stated some hours after the poll was closed, became a tense affair as the voting papers built up into three equal piles. It was obvious the result could go any way. At one o'clock in the morning of 7 December 1923, after two recounts, the result was finally announced:

     Lees, Gordon Richard (Liberal) 8,642
     Baring, Charles Edward (Conservative) 8,630
     Lewis, William (Labour) 7,484

The scenes outside the Town Hall, despite the bitterly cold morning, were like a carnival with rival factions waving flares and banners and singing party songs. The socialists were in a big majority and gave ringing cheers for their candidate, the son of a miner from South Wales. The *Red Flag* prevailed over the Conservative workers trying to counter with *Land of Hope and Glory*. Strangely enough the successful Liberal had fewer supporters in the crowd than either of his two opponents.

Baring was bitterly disappointed but the Tories in the constituency had taken him to their heart and carried him shoulder high to the Conservative Club where they sang *For he's a jolly good fellow* and pledged to get him elected next time.

The General Election turned out to be Baldwin's disaster; although the Tories had won 258 seats, the Liberals with 158 and Labour with 191 had the majority in the House. The unthinkable happened as Ramsey MacDonald became Prime Minister. The illegitimate son of a poor Scottish girl had climbed to the pinnacle of power. The City and big business shuddered at the prospect. Baring returned to his work as the right hand assistant to Baldwin as leader of the Opposition. He was finding that by the strangest of alchemies there is nothing that succeeds like failure. Baldwin was now more dependent upon him, having been shattered by the result, and because of the narrow defeat in West Middlesex the

Tories there were now totally wedded to Baring as their standard bearer.

Baring now turned his energies to building his influence within the Conservative Party. He was able by virtue of his appointment as Baldwin's personal secretary to attend most of the important committee meetings although he had, as yet, no voice nor vote. By contriving to put his views into the Leader's letters and speeches he was able none the less to steer the Party in the direction he wanted it to go.

In January he was saddened to hear the news of Lenin's death and alarmed to read that instead of Trotsky taking over, the power in the first socialist state had been usurped by a triumvirate made up of Zinoviev, Kamenev and Stalin, the very man Trotsky had said he hated most. For the next few weeks Baring studied the papers trying to find clues why the brilliant leader of the Red Army had been passed over in favour of three less capable men. He could only find, hidden away in the back pages of *Le Monde* from Paris, the surprising news that Trotsky had gone to the Caucasus and had been absent from Lenin's funeral and the memorial meetings. There was no explanation, apart from a reference to a mild ailment, for this extraordinary lapse by the most astute of all the Bolshevik strategists.

In the three years since his return from Russia, Baring had not heard from his colleagues in the Vecheka which in the last year had been renamed the G.P.U. He scanned his mail carefully both at home and at the office in the hope of finding some hidden message but there was nothing. Once or twice at meetings he imagined that the person accosting him had come bringing the long-awaited signal of recognition from Dzerzhinsky, but they were only White Russian exiles trying to get political support for their anti-Bolshevik campaigns.

Baring disciplined himself to accept his isolated mission. The enthusiasm and energy he displayed for the Conservative cause helped him to work off the strain of not knowing whether Moscow needed him or had simply forgotten him. In his soul he knew he craved for some acknowledgement of his existence from the leaders of the first socialist state which would lead mankind towards the new era. The games of British politics were a sideshow compared to the success of the coming world revolution. Until that day came Captain Baring of the G.P.U., still proud of his Russian rank, would continue to hold himself in readiness.

Ironically the Labour Government of Ramsey MacDonald which Baring had resolutely opposed in his role as a Tory activist, made an early decision to recognise the Union of Soviet Socialist Republics and helped to open the link between the G.P.U. and its distant disciple.

When Charles Baring was adopted for West Middlesex he had bought himself a town house at Sussex Square, near Lancaster Gate, where he could do some entertaining. It was very convenient to Hyde Park and Kensington Gardens. It suited the new owner admirably as he preferred to walk whenever possible for the exercise as well as the chance to think.

One morning in April with Spring much in evidence in the Park's blooming daffodils, Baring walked around the Serpentine breathing in the crisp, invigorating air, calculating how an early election could be forced on MacDonald. He felt he needed to be in Parliament to get closer to the source of power. Unless he fought a by-election a general election would be his only ticket to the House. In theory the Labour Prime Minister could rule for another four years with Liberal support. The thought of waiting that long was very galling. Something had to be done to break the Labour/Liberal alliance.

As he walked he noticed a tall foreign looking man in an unusual sheepskin coat watching him from a few yards away. He supposed the fellow was someone who had seen him at one of his campaign meetings and was now plucking up courage to make his approach to ask a favour. Charles quickened his step but the stranger broke into a run to catch him up, and to his astonishment he thought he heard him say in breathless English, with a faint but distinctive accent, 'Cherepova sends greetings.'

'What did you say?' Charles asked, not believing his ears.

'Cherepova sends greetings, Comrade. She remembers you with warm feelings.'

Charles, suspicion aroused, feigned disinterest but his rapid pulse rate told another story. In truth he was exhilarated by hearing the name of the only woman he had ever loved, but his caution kept the inner excitement under control.

'I'm sorry I don't know what you're talking about.'

'Nina Semyonovna remembers you with great affection, Comrade. She asked me to bring you a message.'

'I'm sorry I don't know what you're talking about,' said Charles walking on as quickly as his leaden legs would carry him.

The man in the sheep-skin coat easily kept pace and so did the flow of greetings. When he said the name 'Felix Edmundovich' Charles slowed down to look directly into the eyes of the stranger. 'Yes Comrade, Felix Edmundovich particularly asked you to remember your connection with him; you spoke of your time in the Western trenches.'

'That's right,' said Charles, 'then you *are* genuine. You have to understand I have to be careful.'

'I approve of your caution, Comrade, the counter-revolutionary agents are everywhere. I have been watching you for five days and I am convinced that they are not aware of your connection with us.'

'Are you sure you weren't followed?' asked Charles.

'Of course, Comrade, it's the basic rule of our training.'

The two men sauntered into Kensington Gardens where they could sit in a more secluded area. Charles was hungry to have more news of Russia and fortunately had no pressing engagements at the office. Baldwin was away in Worcester.

'Where is Nina Cherepova?' he asked.

'She is well, living in Moscow and working as an interpreter for the Foreign Ministry,' replied the stranger. 'By the way,' he added as a diplomatic afterthought, 'she is married again.'

Charles felt an electric shock. 'Who to?' he demanded abruptly.

'One of the Ministry officials. A much older man. A mere functionary. A party member of course, but not a leader. We were surprised that Cherepova chose such a husband. We supposed she wanted stability after you left.'

The vivid memories of Nina's strange departure came welling back in Charles's mind but he did not bother to argue with the stranger. Seeing the Englishman's emotions, the Russian remained silent, letting the Spring sun in Kensington gradually dispense the far away mists of Petrograd.

'What's your name?' Charles said at last.

'Nicholai Yegorov, Colonel in the G.P.U.' said the Russian.

'How long have you been in England?'

'I came over with Radovsky, the Chargé last month. I am the first Secretary in the Embassy but the senior G.P.U. man in this country. If you meet the Ambassador, do not talk about me. He doesn't know your G.P.U. rank, Captain, so please don't attempt to identify yourself.'

'I *am* still a Captain?' Charles tested the Colonel. 'I thought when I was flung into that awful monastery prison that I had been stripped of all rank.'

'Not at all. That was all necessary to ensure your credentials with the British authorities. Felix Edmundovich is very impressed with the way you have found your way into the centre of the Capitalists' party. Very impressive. We have a saying in Russia "only the worm reaches the core" and you are an excellent worm.'

Charles realised it was not meant as an insult. From a Colonel in the G.P.U. it was a high compliment.

'I must say,' the Russian went on, 'I thought it a brilliant move to buy a house next door to Winston Churchill's. In that way, how you say,' he hesitated finding the words, 'you rub shoulders with respectability.'

'Your English is very idiomatic.'

'I studied it for two years using English prisoners as my tutors. They taught me much.'

'I bet,' said Charles who was reminded of a long forgotten friend. Talking of English prisoners do you know what happened to Arthur Haycraft? He was recruited after he married a Russian.'

'Haycraft? He is not on my list,' said Yegorov, 'but I will make inquiries. Now,' he said firmly, 'you must go. Tomorrow you leave an hour earlier and meet me at the Albert Memorial. Make sure you are not followed. Goodbye Comrade, until tomorrow, we have much to discuss.'

For the rest of the day Baring's mind was not on his work. The Opposition leader's office at Palace Chambers had become a mundane place compared to the electrifying excitement of the world stage which through Yegorov he could again glimpse. It was extremely satisfying to know for certain that his efforts had been appreciated in Moscow and that he still figured in the pattern of events which the leaders of the revolution were planning. He had been a ship at sea with a rudder but without a chart. Now with Yegorov's advice he could steer a direction.

Next morning he presented himself at the Albert Memorial trying to look as inconspicuous a tourist as possible. Within minutes Yegorov approached as from nowhere. 'Good morning. We will walk quickly towards the middle of the gardens.' As they strode off through the avenue of trees he added, 'I was followed early this morning and dropped my tail an hour ago. I feel sure they have not picked up the trail again but to be sure we shall go where no one can see us.'

Yegorov was more businesslike at this second meeting as he set out the G.P.U.'s political objectives in Britain.

'We have to ensure the collapse of the Ramsey MacDonald Government,' he said.

Charles could hardly believe his ears, 'But the Labour Government is pro-Soviet. It has just recognised the USSR and is starting trade treaty negotiations. Why should you want to lose such an ally.'

'You have a lot to learn, Comrade. Listen carefully. All you talk about are mere short term objectives. In the G.P.U. we are working for the Comintern's long term aims and they don't always correspond to what Russia needs in the short term. The MacDonald Government is like the Kerensky regime. It is Menshevik. While it prospers it gives the workers false hopes that their lives can be improved through the parliamentary system. What is needed in England is a sharp class confrontation so the best conditions exist for a revolution. MacDonald stands in the way of that and the longer he is in power the less likely it is that a revolution can take place.'

'I see,' said Charles.

'And furthermore,' went on the Russian, 'what we have gained already in recognition and what we gain in trade can't be taken away. If it is, the English workers will be even more angry,' he added.

'How do you think the MacDonald Governent can be brought down? They have a big enough majority with the Liberals,' asked Charles who now saw clearly that his personal interests in an early election were parallel with the G.P.U.'s plans.

'We're working on it at the present time. It seems the best way to push what you call a wedge between the Labour Party and the Liberals is to play on the supposed Bolshevik sympathies of Labour. It is their Achilles heel.'

'That's true,' said Charles.

'We are going to make the Treaty negotiations difficult for Labour. The Liberals won't like the terms we insist on. That will be a bone of contention. Is that the correct expression?'

'Yes,' said Charles.

'I like that one. The bone between the dogs of Labour and the dogs of Liberals. We will find another one too,' said the Colonel with relish. 'We are arranging for the Communist paper *Workers Weekly* to publish an article calling on British troops not to obey orders. The Government won't be able to ignore this treason, but when they act we are getting the left wing M.P.s to raise a storm of protest. That should frighten the Liberals more than anything.'

'It would indeed,' said Charles warming to the plot.

'We have the cooperation of the Communist Campbell, he is working directly under our orders and will print the article in June or July. It will almost certainly force an election.'

'What if the election produces a Labour victory. It's possible, isn't it, the whole plot could backfire? People might think MacDonald hasn't had enough chance and deserves longer. You might find that peace with Russia is popular with the electorate.'

'We have another plan lined up,' said Colonel Yegorov, now enjoying the dramatic unfolding of the master plan as if he were personally responsible.

'What's that?'

'It's a scheme to destroy Labour, ensure a huge Conservative majority in the House of Commons and eventually to undermine the White Russians who are still conspiring against us.'

'That's a tall order,' said Charles, whistling under his breath.

'What you mean?'

'A lot to do in one go.'

'It must work. It's a brilliant plan thought up by the head of the Comintern himself. It will be the biggest practical joke in history.'

'Is that Zinoviev?' asked Charles remembering the smooth faced man he had first seen in the dining room of the Smolny in Petrograd.

'Yes Comrade Gregori Zinoviev. He's now one of the triumvirate leading our country. A troika pulling the revolution in the direction it should go.'

Charles was dying to ask what had happened to Trotsky, but curbed his curiosity as the Russian continued, 'Zinoviev has devised an incredible plan and Stalin has approved it. All we need is your help with the Conservative Party and it will succeed.'

Charles Baring was proud to be included in a plan which had involved the Russian leaders. After years of isolation and neglect he was feeling a warm glow of appreciation after coming in from the cold.

The Colonel went on. 'We have infiltrated one of our men into a group of White Russians in exile in Berlin and they will be manipulated to forge a letter. To all intents and purposes it will appear genuine. We thought at one time we would produce the genuine article but then Comrade Zinoviev suggested it should be forged as it would then totally discredit the White Russians as well as achieving its original object.'

'What will the letter say?'

'It will be an order to the British Communist Party to organise the rising of workers in England. It will show the Labour Party and Government to be willing tools of us Bolsheviks.'

'The electorate won't like that.'

'Just so. That brings me to your part in this plan. We have an agent who now goes under the name of Sidney Reilly. He was in St. Peterburg in 1905 when he joined the Bolsheviks, who used him to get into the Rasputin camp. The mad monk was destroyed through Reilly's tricks. Then Reilly was introduced into British Intelligence and for years the British thought he was working solely for them. Actually he was doing our bidding. He helped to stop an attempt on Lenin's life in 1917. We had a Revolutionary Tribunal order him to be shot for his supposed part in the plot, so that the British would trust him even more. In fact he leaked the plot.'

'That was the man who was implicated with Lockhart?' asked Baring.

'Yes that's right.'

'Lenin told me he was a British spy.'

'Perhaps Vladimir Ilyich was never told he was one of our's or perhaps he was simply trying to improve Reilly's cover. I don't know, Comrade. I never discussed it with Comrade Lenin.' There was a slight peevishness in the Russian's voice at Baring's association with the dead leader. 'Anyway Reilly is now working for the British Foreign Office intelligence section. It is called MI One C, I believe. Reilly will bring the forgery to the Foreign Office shortly before the election whenever that takes place. He will choose a time when MacDonald is busy with electioneering. The Foreign Office will certainly endorse it as genuine. We will also arrange for you to get a copy and it will be for you to get the Conservative Party to publish it. If the Zinoviev letter is published just before polling day, it should ensure the defeat of the Labour Government.'

'Absolutely fantastic,' said Baring.

'It is rather good,' said Yegorov, looking pleased, 'I will contact you as the plan develops. Meanwhile keep up your good work Comrade.' He shook Baring's hand and quickly walked off across Kensington Gardens before he could be asked any more questions.

Charles sat nursing his admiration for the audacity of the scheme. For the moment his curiosity about Trotsky had been pushed to the back of his mind.

CHAPTER 30

Being in Opposition made Stanley Baldwin dependent upon his party advisers. As Prime Minister he had been surrounded by civil servants deluging him with memoranda and cossetting him at every turn. Without the support of these functionaries and bureaucrats the party leader was forced to rely on the unofficial team. This meant that Charles Baring, who had become one of Baldwin's secretaries, was able to exercise a big influence on his policies and tactics. Every weekday morning Baring walked through Hyde Park, skirting the eastern end of the Serpentine and crossing Rotten Row, always busy with exercised horses, to leave at Albert Gate. Then he crossed Knightsbridge to walk through Lowndes Square and Lyall Street to Eaton Square where Stanley Baldwin had his town house. The first part of the morning was taken up with answering correspondence and preparing speeches before the Opposition leader went to a luncheon or on to Parliament for Question Time at half past two.

In the morning before the pressures of the day had taken their toll, Baring found Baldwin at his most malleable. One subject on which they were agreed was the need to dislodge the MacDonald Government and Baring found it relatively easy to edge the leader towards a strategy for splitting the Liberals from their Labour allies. It would only be a question of time before the master plan could be put into operation.

Meanwhile Baring was able to observe the leader's skill in steering the party. Baldwin was a consummate politician and able to strike chords in his listeners' hearts with simple poetic

phrases. At the Annual Dinner of the Royal Society of St.
George held on the 6th May 1924, Baring noticed how
mesmerised the audience became with the words
>   The sounds of England,
>   the tinkle of the anvil in the country smithy
>   the corncrake on a dewy morning,
>   the sound of the scythe against the whetstone
>   and the sight of a plough team coming over the brow
>   of a hill
>   — the sight that has been seen in England, since
>   England was a land
>   and may be seen in England long after the Empire has
>   perished
>   and every works in England has ceased to function.
>   The wild anemones in the woods in April
>   the last load at night of hay being drawn down a lane
>   as the twilight comes on
>   and above all most subtle, most penetrating, most
>   moving, the smell of woodsmoke coming up in an
>   autumn evening.

Baring looked at the ranks of white ties and tails of men
who had done well out of England and who looked replete
after a meal which had cost more than most families spent on
food in a week. He felt a twinge of sentiment for an ancient
England, wondering how much the speaker had been
influenced by Baldwin's cousin Rudyard Kipling, but the
sentiment was overwhelmed by revulsion against the men
who lived so ostentatiously when millions of their fellow
countrymen were in poverty. Baring never questioned his
own hypocrisy in condemning others for enjoying what he
himself enjoyed. He felt his special role absolved him from
self criticism and this psychological trick of self protection
had become perfected after months of practice. Sitting among
the privileged, mixing with the rich and enjoying the side
trappings of power was to Baring a necessary part of his
mission. He would not acknowledge that he enjoyed them for

their own sake. His absorbing ambition to destroy the system could not be deflected as it had become the key part of his psyche but his body happily accepted any comforts that the system provided.

As he sat sipping the Port at the St. George's Day Dinner, Baring listened with secret disdain to the speeches of what he regarded as a decadent society, although applauding as vigorously as any of his fellow guests. His hypocrisy had become second nature.

The daily needs of intrigue and the routine tasks for his advancement up the political ladder provided enough activity to absorb his thoughts. There was never time for him to examine his beliefs or philosophies or his conscience. A strange alchemy of events in his past life had launched him on a course containing a momentum which overwhelmed and overruled his free will. Whatever Baring did was part of that momentum and like a religious fanatic dominated by dogma there was nothing he could do about it. He was slave to a cause, his integrity as a human being crushed and his ability to judge good from evil gone forever. Baring's mould was cast. He was twenty-six. The formative years had passed and what he had become could never be reshaped.

The other diners on that St. George's Day, in the euphoria of good food, fine wine and poetic speeches, rededicated themselves to the glory of England but Charles Baring thought only of its downfall.

Events in 1924 moved quickly in Baring's favour. The Communist paper *Workers Weekly* duly came out with its appeal for British troops to disobey orders with which they disagreed and the editor, J.R. Campbell, was arrested. When the left wing Labour M.P.s created a fuss about this the Labour Government relented and dropped the prosecution and this provoked the Liberals to withdraw their support. Ramsay MacDonald was forced into an election in an attempt to renew his shaky mandate. By October only ten months after his first try Baring was given his second chance to win

West Middlesex. This time he was determined to succeed.

Soon after the announcement of the coming election,
Baring was walking through Hyde Park on his way to see
Baldwin at Eaton Square. He became aware of a figure
stalking him. It was Yegorov. The Russian had discarded his
sheepskin for a neatly cut overcoat and over his now longer
hair he sported a smart trilby. He was barely recognisable as a
foreigner.

'Good morning, Comrade Captain,' said Yegorov.

'You surprised me,' said Baring, 'I wasn't expecting you,
especially dressed like that.'

'You like it? Now I'm like any other Englishman out for a
— what do you call it — a constitutional. This makes it easier
for me to merge into the background,' he laughed hoarsely as
if enjoying a private joke. 'Scotland Yard have started a
Special Branch to watch our people. We provide them with a
nice song and dance and lead them to contacts we're openly
too happy for them to waste their time on. You, Comrade
Captain, ah you, are in a different category. Rest assured,
Comrade, you we protect at all times.'

'Is that why you haven't contacted me for six months?'
asked Baring.

'That's right. The less contact the better. I'm the only one
in the Embassy here to know of your association with us, so
no one else will bother you. In our terminology I'm what is
called your controller. But obviously we don't want you to
take the wording quite that way.'

'Not to take it literally you mean?' said Baring.

'Not literally, yes. A controller is your contact man
bringing the instructions from the G.P.U. How you fulfil the
orders is for us both to decide. I don't want to dictate to you.'

Baring did not quite know how to respond to these smooth
assurances. He resented his unctuousness and suspected a
mailed fist behind the blandness, but someone had to bring
him the messages from Moscow.

'That's alright; I understand,' he answered, 'I'm a servant

of the revolution as you are, and we both have to do our duty.'

'Good,' said the Colonel. 'I have here a photograph of the letter forged in Berlin and carrying the signature of our Comrade Zinoviev. It's already been taken by our agent Sidney Reilly to the British Foreign Office and now you must use your contacts to ensure that the Conservative Party takes full advantage of it. A man called Donald im Thurn will also get a copy and you can use him to push the letter to certain newspapers.'

'That "im Thurn" that's a curious name. Is he foreign?'

'No he's as English as you are,' replied Yegorov, 'he was a British secret agent in the last war so his credentials are accepted.'

'Will he know our plan?'

'No. He is simply being used as a go-between. A dupe if you like. He wants money. He'll even ask your Conservatives for money and you'll be wise to pay him something.'

'He thinks the letter is genuine?'

'Oh yes,' Yegorov laughed, 'that's the big joke. Everyone is going to think it's the real thing, but our agent put the White Russian forgers up to it.'

As they walked around the garden and the deserted bandstand, they discussed the tactics to be used to secure the widest possible acceptance of the Zinoviev letter. Baring wanted to raise other matters with the elusive Russian. 'How is Nina Cherepova?' he demanded before the Colonel could stride off.

'She's not Cherepova, now Comrade but Akamarova. Have you forgotten? I told you she was a married lady; take my advice and forget all about her.'

'Can she not be a friend?'

'Personal friendship is corrupting, Comrade, and it could expose Nina Akamarova to extreme dangers.'

'What do you mean?' asked Baring.

'It's dangerous for anyone who knows of your role here in England. The G.P.U. could not allow any leak to happen.

You're too valuable to us for that. It is better for Nina Akamarova to forget about you and for you to forget about her. Let's hope she never mentions you to anyone.'

'Is she being watched?' Baring shuddered at the thought of Nina's danger.

'Of course,' Yegorov answered nonchalantly, 'and by the way, I checked up on your friend Arthur Haycraft in Manchester. He's being handled by our trade department and they're well pleased with the work he is doing for us.'

'Is his wife with him?'

'Yes, his wife was recruited into our service and she joined him last year with her son. She ensures his loyalty to the cause. I understand he was difficult at first.

'Will he be alright now?' asked Baring, hardly disguising his concern.

'Yes Comrade, he has his job to do. He's in a big engineering firm and passing us useful technical information. While he keeps up the flow he'll be safe enough.'

Baring cringed and the Russian admonished him. 'Stop your emotions getting the better of you Comrade. Haycraft will be in no danger if he behaves. However I would advise you not to contact him. As with Nina, it's important he doesn't talk about you.'

The cold wind blew over the lake and Baring felt his spine freeze but it was not the chill of the Autumn morning which shook him. The spider which had caught them might consume them all one day. The tremor in Baring's backbone was momentary, disappearing as quickly as it came. As Yegorov strode off towards Hyde Park Corner Baring remembered he had again forgotten to ask about Trotsky.

Baring retraced his steps towards Albert Gate and drew from his pocket the envelope Yegorov had given to him. He could sense the letter was dynamite. Here was the explosive which could blow all MacDonald's chances of re-election to smithereens and, as important, secure his own election in West Middlesex. He unfolded the paper, thinking that the written word is more powerful than the sword, and read the letter as he walked. It's impact was electrifying and Baring was impelled to stand still to give it his undivided attention. The document was a brilliant parody of Communist documents with a mixture of vituperation against class enemies and advice to British comrades on the action they should take. If Yegorov had not admitted it had been forged Baring knew he would have readily accepted its authenticity.

The letter said the Executive Committee of the Third International will place at the disposal of the British Communists information about British Imperialism in the Middle and Far East. Meanwhile, it went on 'strain every nerve for the ratification of the Treaty between the S.S.S.R. and England; it will assist in the revolutionising of the international and British Proletariat not less than a successful rising in any of the working districts of England.' Baring read on, sensing how the phrases would be torn from their context to magnify the impact, 'Armed warfare must be proceeded by a struggle against the inclination to compromise which is embedded among the majority of British workmen, against the ideas of evolution and the peaceful extermination of capitalism. Only then will it be possible to count upon the complete success of an armed insurrection.'

The letter called on comrades to take action to paralyse the British army and navy and to take steps to create the British Red Army. When Baring gingerly put the envelope back in his inner pocket and carefully buttoned down the flap he felt his heart pumping and was glad he still had a mile to walk to Baldwin's. It would give him time to cool down.

Before a fortnight had passed Baring had laid the ground carefully within the Conservative Party for the Zinoviev letter to have the widest impact. The *Times* was rejected as the vehicle for publication as it could well hold up release until after the election to check the letter's accuracy. The *Daily Mail*, with its reputation for buccaneering anti-Labour propaganda was chosen instead. The editor, Thomas Marlowe, cooperated magnificently and on Saturday 25 October, just four days before polling day, the *Daily Mail* plastered its front page with the headline 'Civil War Plot By Socialists' Masters' and the Zinoviev letter spread over four columns.

The impact on the Government was devasting. Ramsay MacDonald who was Foreign Secretary as well as Prime Minister was on the election tour when the news broke and he, predictably, dithered. The Foreign Office, prompted by the secret agent Sidney Reilly, seized the opportunity and released its own copy of the letter establishing to nearly everyone's satisfaction its total authenticity. Zinoviev, who had fulfilled his part of the plot by carefully staying on holiday out of Moscow on the date the letter was supposed to have been written, made a statement denying authorship. To most people this was another confirmation of the Bolsheviks' duplicity and, as expected, it cut no ice with public opinion in Britain. Buoyed up by its magnificent coup the Conservative Party sailed to a massive victory, gaining 412 out of 615 seats in Parliament.

Among these victors was Charles Baring, elected with a 7,000 majority at West Middlesex. In the celebration at number ten Downing Street, Stanley Baldwin singled him out for a special toast of congratulations. The Prime Minister knew just how much he owed to his astute secretary.

The day when Parliament reassembled became a Tory carnival as one hundred and seventy 'new boys', including a jubilant Baring, converged on the House to take their oaths along with the former Conservative members. The Conservative Party had achieved the unthinkable on a revised franchise of a total of M.P.s double that of all the other parties put together. There were now two Barings in the House as Sir John had been re-elected, and uncle was proud to show nephew the nooks and crannies of the Palace of Westminster.

They walked the long carpeted corridors behind the Speaker's chair to the corner where the Speaker has his library and his house and along to the Members Library with its serried stacks of reference books. 'Spend the minimum time in there, my lad,' cautioned Sir John, 'write your speeches at home, you'll have less interruption. When you're in the House spend your time in the Chamber being seen or better still in the Smoking Room along here where the real political bargaining is done.' They strolled to the next swing door and looked in on a tall gloomy room with deep leather armchairs and a bar in the corner. Members were reading newspapers or talking and sipping whiskies or drinking tea. It was four in the afternoon.

'Drinking at this time?' asked Charles.

'It's one of the perquisites of belonging to the country's best club. This is a Royal palace. The licencing laws can't apply here. When the house is sitting we can drink whenever we like.'

In the corner of the smoking room they could see the rotund figure of the new member for Epping holding a whisky in one hand and a large cigar in the other and haranguing his companions.

'Winston has a lot to celebrate,' said Sir John, 'he's back in Parliament and we're preparing to re-admit him to the Tory Party.'

'A wise move,' said Charles, 'it keeps him out of Lloyd-George's clutches.'

'S.B. has ensured his loyalty by making him Chancellor of the Exchequer,' said Sir John as they moved further along the corridor out of earshot of other members.

'Astounding,' said Charles who privately could not stomach Churchill.

'S.B. is as adroit as any in the business. With Winston in the Cabinet he can't stir up any mischief and he might even make a good Chancellor.'

'If he does to our economy what he did to our troops in the

Dardanelles he'll be a fine success,' Charles said sarcastically.

'Now, now Charles,' said his uncle taking his arm, 'you have to allow any man, even Churchill, a few mistakes in an illustrious career. Remember I advised you to get close to S.B., now you should do the same with Churchill. His stock is rising. I wouldn't be at all surprised if he didn't take over the premiership one day.'

'Instead of Chamberlain?'

'Neville could only be a stop gap. The country will need Churchill's quality of leadership when it's in a real crisis. In my opinion he's the only man strong enough to hold the line against Bolshevism.'

Charles Baring gave up his job as secretary to Baldwin, who was again as P.M. surrounded by a bevy of civil servants. In any case he knew his influence over Baldwin would be much diminished. His best tactic was to secure his position as a back bench member and cultivate new friends who could help hoist him higher. The situation in West Middlesex gave him no concern. Thomas Page, to whom he was now close enough to call by his nickname 'TOP', was delighted by his protegé's success. Although Page was disappointed by Helen's failure to entice Baring into matrimony he was compensated by his conviction that the new member would soon be in the Government and bring new credit to the constituency association as well as possibilities of profit to its Chairman.

CHAPTER 31

During the weekend after Parliament reassembled all the Barings had a reunion at the Hall. Grandfather Tallen came, proud as ever, to congratulate his grandson on his election to the Mother of Parliaments. Sir John came on one of his rare visits to astound everyone with the news that he had decided to marry. Sarah was agog; she had always believed her brother-in-law was a confirmed bachelor. Everyone was astonished to discover that the bride to be for the sixty year old baronet was a twenty-seven year old fashion designer, who had been a helper in his recent election campaign. 'It was love at first sight,' admitted Sir John, 'it will be a quiet wedding at her local church but of course you are all invited.'

Once he had unburdened himself of the news of the coming nuptials Sir John showed a new expansive side to his personality. He was becoming twenty years younger in his attitudes and for Charles his advice was becoming more like that of a brother than an elderly uncle.

'You should follow my example and get married,' he advised, 'wish I'd done it years ago. Would have helped my career a lot. I've often wondered why I was not given a ministry despite all my years in the House. I think it was because I was not able to do the political entertaining that goes hand in hand with political manouevres. Doesn't help to be a bachelor in politics.'

'Didn't harm Balfour did it?' said Charles.

'Exception that proves the rule. I doubt if we'll ever see a bachelor Prime Minister again in this country, especially now women have the vote. They will demand the respectable family image. My political ambitions have long since passed so I don't care what anyone says about me having a young wife. But in your case you should marry soon, marry wisely and it will do your career a power of good.'

'Maybe you're right.'

'Of course I'm right. I've been watching your progress Charles like a father. I know that Page girl in West Middlesex was trying to get you and you were wise to drop her. That type of lower middle class person with no breeding would not do you good at this stage. You need a wife from the aristocracy — more in your own class — who can lend lustre to your name and attract powerful friends to your dining table. Marriage for you is an investment in a career, for me it's the fling of an old man.'

Charles had already seen the advantages of the right marriage and hardly needed his uncle's advice. 'Actually I've got someone in mind.'

'Really,' said Sir John, 'who is it?'

'Not telling,' said Charles, 'you kept your engagement a secret for months and I'm entitled to do the same. Promise, not a word to my mother, she'd plague me with her curiosity.'

'Cave! cave!' said Sir John in uncustomary public school slang, 'the hunt is on, is it? Let me be the first to know when you have captured your quarry. I'll keep the secret. Parliamentary honour.'

On Sunday Emma brought her husband, an accountant from Great Yarmouth, to tea and showed off their new baby. Edith introduced her fiancé, a local farmer, to the assembled company and announced that they would be married in the New Year.

The weekend had been full of surprises for Charles who found the family a stabilizing force of great power, although he would have been the last to recognise or acknowledge it. He was arrogant enough to think that his convictions were alone strong enough to carry through turbulent seas. His Marxism had taught that emotions were irrelevant to the basic course of human events which were totally influenced by economic forces. In fact Charles Baring M.C., M.P. would not have coped with the strain of his curious double life unless the innocent family had been there to provide a bedrock of support and the fresh springs of unpolluted human love.

Charles found that his intellectual dilemmas could more easily be resolved when he was engaged in plenty of activity. At times of sloth the doubts in his mind would loom large. Had it been right to force the collapse of the first Labour government? Were the stories from Russia of widespread tyranny mere propaganda or based on truth? Could the revolution succeed without an economic and social collapse so great that the benefits were destroyed before they could be enjoyed? To escape from questions to which there were no clear answers Charles Baring fell back on an arrogance strong enough to propel him through feverish, hectic, work.

In the House of Commons he became one of the most assiduous back bench attenders and he joined a half dozen Parliamentary and party committees. He produced research papers, with Douglas Rhodes's assistance, on a few neglected subjects, occasionally made concise speeches which read well in the *Times* and he toured the country on party work.

He accepted his uncle's advice and spent long hours in the Smoking Room, sipping watered whisky, and exchanging the tittle tattle of generally useless political gossip which occasionally threw up a jewel he could use to full advantage. He made friends amongst his fellow Members by never taking an extreme line, never clashing with a bigot and appearing able and useful without displaying naked ambition. He had learnt that Members always resent a place seeker. Reluctance in the man of middling ability he found a more powerful lever than the pushing of the most brilliant. There were a score of well qualified Members who were ignored in the placings because their aspirations were too obvious and suspicion of motives had destroyed all attraction of their qualities. In the hothouse of Westminster, where exotic plants were exposed to the heat of an artificial environment, it was important to remain cool and calculating at all times. Charles Baring learnt the techniques quickly as he had realised the foundation of a successful Parliamentary career is established in the first few months. Enemies, made through foolish, hasty moves, last forever, but friends became a permanent investment paying interest in surprising ways.

One day in the corridor he was approached by a tall, handsome M.P. 'Remember we met at Eton, I'm Robert Eden though nowadays I prefer to be known as Anthony.'

'I remember we first met on the playing fields. When were you elected?'

'I came in at the Warwick and Leamington by-election last year.'

'Yes I remember now you beat the Countess of Warwick didn't you? Wasn't she once the mistress of King Edward?'

'Yes, she is a funny one, but then the Labour Party does have some very odd people in it.'

'So you had a year of opposition?' asked Baring with envy.

'It's a good introduction to the House, there are more chances to make attacking speeches. On the Government side we're regarded as lobby fodder. Our function is to vote, not speak. The Minister always resents it if a back bencher shows him up. Better to become a P.P.S. and get a toe hold in the Government.'

'What happened to your friend Tommy Dugdale?' he asked.

'He went on to Sandhurst, became a Captain, but now he wants a seat. The old school is certainly well represented here.'

'So I've noticed,' said Charles, 'the O.Es ties are much in evidence.'

Besides his Parliamentary work Baring cultivated his social contacts outside the House. As an eligible bachelor he received a dozen invitations to the coming-out parties which were becoming the custom. He contrived to attend most of them and meeting, as a result, some of the prettiest daughters of the aristocracy. One of the most beautiful was Lady Anne, the petite elder daughter of the Duke of Dorset. Her personality was effervescent rather than gushing, her beauty classical rather than modern, and she displayed a calm which set her well apart from her contemporaries, who tended to be hysterical or, at best, overexcitable. At their first meeting Charles decided he would marry her or at least try his damnedest to do so. Anne was just twenty-one. Although she had lived a protected life at finishing schools in Switzerland and on the family estates near Dorchester and in Scotland, she was remarkably well informed about current affairs. Her views, Charles found, were radical modern Tory. Anne believed that a Conservative government should take positive steps to provide employment and prevent the economy sinking. 'That's what governments are for,' she declared soundly, 'not for sitting around doing nothing.' She was also fabulously rich as several trusts had been settled on her both from her paternal and maternal grandparents. This was more a hindrance than an attraction as it meant the girl was likely to be plagued with fortune hunters which put her family on guard.

Baring arranged a party of ten to attend the first night of a Noel Coward play at the Royalty Theatre and invited Anne and her chaperone to join them. The play called *The Vortex* had the author, a young man two years junior to Charles, in a starring role and was reported to be a shocker. All Baring's guests felt a bit daring and defiant in going. In the event the play was received enthusiastically with the author and star called back for several curtain calls.

Afterwards at a Champagne reception at his home in Hyde Park Gate Baring made a special fuss of Lady Anne. In the *Daily Express* later that week the gossip columnist had their names linked. While his intimates wondered how the news could possibly have leaked, Baring thanked his friend, Douglas Rhodes, for telling the newspaper.

The only blemish on an otherwise successful manoeuvre was the initial reaction of the Duke himself who read that a veteran actor, Sir Gerald du Maurier, had denounced the Noel Coward play. 'The public are asking for filth. The younger generation are knocking at the door of the dustbin.' He wondered just who his daughter was seeing. When Baring's credentials, as an old Etonian Conservative M.P. with some family money and distinguished army service were produced, he relented and agreed to invite the suitor to a Christmas party at Dorchester.

Within four months an engagement was announced and in July the wedding took place at St. Margaret's, Westminster. It was one of the events of the year. The church was packed with relatives, Parliamentarians, party workers from West Middlesex and friends from far and wide. As the bridegroom walked down the aisle with his bride he saw Nicholai Yegorov in a pew dressed in a morning coat and holding a top hat to his chest. The Russian gave Baring a discreet nod but the groom was too astonished to respond. He seethed a little at this invasion of his privacy but his real concern was that it would obviously be impossible to separate his two lives. They were inextricably linked and only resolve could avoid them clashing. The supreme effort had to be made, especially on one's wedding day, but the prospect of a lifetime of this sort of strain was daunting. Marriage was important for him not only as another stepping stone to acceptance and advancement but as a support in the delicate tightrope he had chosen to walk.

Baring's thoughts of Yegorov were dispersed quickly at the reception at the Savoy, where vintage Champagne flowed like water and guests danced to a ten piece orchestra. The exhausted couple eventually left to spend their honeymoon on the Cote d'Azur. When they returned Lady Anne Baring set about redecorating the Sussex Square house so it could become one of the centres of political dining. Influential people soon noticed that the former secretary of the Prime

Minister was going to high places and they jostled to join the circle. Charles Baring was finding that success breeds success. As a back bench M.P. he found his capacity to guide events was much less than when he had been Baldwin's secretary, but he knew the basis of his future climb to office was being firmly established. He was finding new friends everywhere.

Anne was unwilling to take on a country house in East Anglia. 'Too distant and too cold,' she declared firmly. The newly married couple's visits to the Hall had been sucessful enough, but there could be no question of them settling there while Sarah Baring was still in residence. Charles had no thoughts of evicting his mother who still ran the estate — with the help of a manager — with aplomb.

Anne persuaded Charles to invest her dowry in a small estate of 120 acres four miles south of Amesbury in Wiltshire. The house was Georgian but had Palladian pillars at the entrance giving it a greater sense of grandeur than its sixteen rooms justified. Redecoration took two months and Mr. and Mrs. Charles Baring were 'at home' to friends before Christmas. They were well pleased with the acquisition. The house stood at the edge of a small forest and on the other side had an uninterrupted view of the rolling downs of Wiltshire. London was only two hours away by road or the London and South Western Railway, while Dorchester, seat of the Duke of Dorset, was even nearer.

Anne had two ambitions: to further her husband's career and to have a family. She devoted herself to both with enthusiasm. Hardly a week went by without the Baring's entertaining house guests. There was a constant stream of Government Ministers, M.Ps, editors of newspapers and leading journalists and foreign ambassadors. Anne was well pleased with her success as a political hostess: 'We can't rival Chatsworth yet, but we can certainly have a good try,' she said.

They found the cost of running the establishment at

Amesbury well within their budget as the permanent staff numbered only five, costing about £75 per year each. Other domestics were recruited for a shilling a day. The horses were more expensive than the servants.

Early in 1926 Anne told her husband she was pregnant. For Charles Baring it seemed that everything was going right in his life. Parliament had become an agreeable club where he could meet his political friends, make occasional speeches and his mark in Committees. Newspapers frequently asked him for articles and the newly fledged British Broadcasting Corporation sometimes asked him to do the book reviews. He was becoming known as a man-with-a-future and his acquisition of an aristocratic wife with a flair for entertaining propelled him into higher realms of acceptance. Now Anne was consolidating all his achievements by having a baby.

At twenty-eight Charles Baring had reached heights any other man would have envied and any other man would have settled down to enjoy a comfortable, interesting and well ordered life. But Baring was different to other men. He was obsessed with the need to undermine the very society which provided him with an easy and happy existence. It was not merely the sense of guilt that he had more than millions of other Englishmen, that he waxed rich while they slaved in mines and factories or barely survived on charity handouts. Guilt was only part of the story. In truth Baring nurtured a Nietzschean will for power. He saw in Marxist-Leninism the doctrine which could refashion the whole human race and create a world order based on sanity and regard for basic human needs.

All around him was waste, corruption and the pettiness of democracy. He enjoyed climbing up the political ladder, the perpetual intrigue and the rounds of entertaining which went with the jostling for advantage. At the same time he despised it as factuous nonsense as archaic as the charades at the courts of medieval monarchs. The way Soviet Russia tackled the immense problems of building a new society on the ashes of the old impressed him immensely. He believed that the leadership principle of Bolshevism could make an even better impact on Britain if the opportunity for it could be created.

Baring's greatest sadness was that he was cut off from all contact with socialist thinkers or activists. It was simply unthinkable that he could ever be seen in animated conversation with Shaw, Wells or the Webbs or go to a Fabian meeting. He could not even dare to invite the young socialist intellectuals, such as G.D.H. Cole, to stay at Amesbury. His range of contemporary friends had to be restricted to the Douglas Rhodeses, the Anthony Edens, the Randolph Churchills and the other sons of Tory Party worthies whose intellects had been warped by years of suckling at the fat breasts of capitalism, who could never understand how he felt even if he dared to tell them.

Charles Baring lived in a cocoon of comfort which his sensual appetites enjoyed but which his spirit abhorred. His only relief was secretly to read new books on Marx and Lenin and to relive in his mind his encounters with Trotsky, Lenin and Radek. It was small compensation and not enough to cool his brain. Anne often noticed his distress, especially at night when he broke into cold sweats and suffered fitful dreams.

One morning she summoned up courage to broach the subject: 'You were bad last night again, Charles; at times you were almost screaming.'

'It's nothing,' he replied at the breakfast table pulling the *Times* down with a gesture of annoyance. 'I suppose I've been over-working, that's all. I had two speeches and a talk on the B.B.C. last week. They all have to be prepared.'

In fact Baring had no difficulty in coping with his political work and Anne knew it.

'It's not that darling, here's something else troubling you. Who's Nina? You were calling her name last night.'

'Oh, she was a girl I met in Moscow years ago,' he replied carelessly and hastily.

Anne slowly spread some marmalade on her toast before replying.

'But how could you have known a girl when you were in prison all that time?' she said.

Baring flushed and was, unusually, lost for words.

'She must have meant a lot to you,' insisted Anne unwisely. 'You were calling for her desperately. Did you love her?'

'Of course not.' Baring threw his napkin on his uneaten breakfast and left the table before his wife could turn the unwelcome screw any further.

CHAPTER 32

As her pregnancy progressed Anne spent more time at Amesbury and during the Parliamentary week Charles stayed at Sussex Square to be nearer the House. He welcomed the chance to be alone at nights so his dreams could be unshared. Although he loved Anne for her beauty and gentleness and her assets as a hostess he knew he could never unburden his innermost thoughts to her. Given her background there could never be that degree of trust.

Baring had watched with fascination the way another M.P., Oswald Mosley, had married the daughter of Lord Curzon and having deserted the Tories for the Labour Party had converted his wife to socialism. Baring envied the man's brilliant handling of his switching of allegiances but that way could not be for him. Mosley was an extrovert who wanted to strut and proclaim his ideas to all and sundry; Baring had no respect for him. He felt Mosley had sacrificed the substance of power for the froth. He had no time for the way Mosley was trying to influence events. In the end Mosley would be shouting himself hoarse in the wind whilst the work Baring could do behind the scenes would be effective. It was easy for Mosley to exploit Lady Cynthia for his public posturing but Baring's situation was entirely different. It would be impossible to explain to Anne his secret role. She could never understand.

Inevitably the separation between Amesbury and Sussex Square became more pronounced. Anne suspected her husband of keeping a part of his life totally separate from her. His attempts to hide his *alter ego* aroused her finely tuned feminine intuition. She knew there was a mystery in her husband's background which still had an extraordinary influence on him. Her curiosity was greater than jealousy as she sensed there was more to it than a woman. Charles had a dark, sombre side to his nature which she could never penetrate however she exercised her wiles. They began to drift apart. On the surface everything was as before. Family and friends could suspect nothing as both husband and wife continued to perform the rituals of happily married life. Behind the facade they both knew the wall between them was impossible to break. A barrier of time or distance is infinitely easier to bridge than the gap of spiritual misunderstanding.

Charles found some solace in a squalid relationship with one of the servants at Sussex Square. She was a pretty little seventeen year old who had come to London from the North to find work as her father was unemployed and could not keep her. Within a month of her joining the Baring household as a downstairs maid her employer had taken her to bed and deflowered her virginity. Time after time he used her body callously. The sexual satisfaction he obtained was incidental to his need to release his tensions and vent a suppressed temper. By taking the young girl he unconsciously felt he was getting his own back on a wife who had become too independent and too unpliable. Eventually he grew tired and bored with the girl who was also making things difficult downstairs with the butler and the housekeeper who both knew what was going on. After four weeks Baring gave the girl £50 — more than a year's wages — and packed her back to Newcastle-upon-Tyne. Anne never found out and although she suspected her husband's infidelity she could never have believed he would use a paid servant.

Other events were happening and soon provided a new distraction for the Member for West Middlesex. The industrial situation had worsened and militants were gaining strength. The country seemed ripe for revolution when the coal owners, backed by the Government, tried to force a cut in miners wages. Baring was in a state of elation as the news unfolded. At the Trades Union Congress during the previous year a resolution had been passed calling for the workers to organise for the overthrow of capitalism pointing out 'Strong shop committees are indispensable weapons in the struggle to force the capitalists to relinquish their grip on industry.' The seconder of the resolution, a leading Communist called Harry Pollitt, had been arrested and sent to prison on a charge of conspiracy to mutiny. The stage seemed set for the dramatic confrontation which could bring the whole shaky capitalist structure to the ground.

Late in April 1926, on a clear, crisp morning with the sun reflected brightly in the Serpentine, Baring was walking over Hyde Park with a happy spring in his step. He was confident that his hopes and ambitions would soon be realised and that a workers' state with Russian support could soon be created. Out of the debacle of social and industrial collapse a new leadership would emerge. He would be an essential part of it as only he, with his stride reaching over the class chasm, could heal the wounds of conflict and create a new, sensible, British Communist order. The revolution would, if handled correctly, be bloodless and painless and would show the whole world what could be achieved when the downtrodden workers in an advanced society declared they would be slaves to capital no longer. The union of Soviet Britain with Soviet Russia would create an impregnable alliance and all the nations of Europe squeezed between them would be forced to join. The colonies would follow and within a few years half the globe would be Communist exercising such pressure on the remaining capitalist outposts of Japan and America that they would be bound to follow. It was a prospect which would eliminate war and hunger and for the first time in history allow intelligent human will to shape human destinies.

Baring also felt that the formation of Soviet Britain with him in its leadership would solve all his personal dilemmas overnight. He would, at last, be able to be an open and honest man in showing his true beliefs. For eight years he had lived with a clandestine role and it had worn away a part of his psychic organism. The inner gyro which kept him in balance between the operating and opposing forces of class selfishness and Communist idealism had worked well. Only Anne had ever suspected that he was not a totally well-integrated human being. But the strain was telling and one day, Baring feared, the gyro might falter and he could go berserk or have a mental breakdown. All that could be avoided once the revolution had liberated him from the dangerous games of deceit and duplicity.

As he walked, deep in his thoughts, be became conscious of a familiar figure at his side. It was Yegorov, smartly dressed as usual, carrying a cane.

'Good morning Comrade,' said the Russian, 'you seem to be miles away. Thinking of Moscow perhaps?'

Baring was both relieved and shocked to see the Russian after so long.

'It must be two years since we last met,' he managed to say.

'It's one year and six months apart from your wedding day,' the Colonel smiled. 'I must congratulate you both on your election and your choice of bride.'

'Why did you leave it so long?'

'I've left you alone, Comrade, because you have been doing so well. Don't think I haven't been monitoring your progress. I know everything, even about Tilly.' He allowed a smile to curl his lips as he mentioned the name of the discharged housemaid.

'Is it necessary to pry into my personal life?'

'Of course, Comrade, we must know. You are one of the most valuable possessions in the capitalist bloc. One day we might need to protect you against your own foolishness. Every man has his weaknesses. My job as your controller is to watch your's and ensure they do not destroy your effectiveness in our cause.'

'I can take care of myself.'

'With respect Comrade it doesn't matter what you think. The organisation is bigger than you or anyone in it. We serve it and in time it serves us. The days of amateurs are over.'

Baring wanted to make a comment but the Russian insisted on continuing. 'You do not seem to realise that in the years since the revolution the Bolsheviks have put our country on scientific Marxist lines. All our endeavours are properly coordinated. The place of the individual is diminished as we become more efficient. The old Vecheka you knew has also been transformed. It is now the *Obedinennoe Gosudarstvennoe Politicheskoe Upravlenie.*' The Russian words tripped off his tongue like music. 'In English that means the United State Political Administration and we call it O.G.P.U. for short. The O.G.P.U. is now part of the constitution of the U.S.S.R. It is the guardian of our Communist purity and is the vanguard of the campaign to achieve world revolution. Your rank as Captain in O.G.P.U. has been confirmed. Dzerzhinsky is well pleased with your achievements so far and you must not imperil your future usefulness by entertaining false bourgeois concepts of free will. Do I make myself clear, Comrade?'

Baring stretched out his now weary body on a bench and tried to clear his mind. 'Look I'm a Member of Parliament now. I have to operate on my own for years at a time. You have to trust me to use my own discretion.'

'You must never forget that you belong to us. In the last analysis our orders dictate your will. Any leeway you have is purely temporary and tactical.'

Baring grunted a reluctant acknowledgement as the Russian continued the lecture. 'We have now brought Britain to the brink of revolution. Our Communist agitators have performed their task well in fermenting unrest amongst the workers.'

'Harry Pollitt?' said Baring.

'Yes, Comrade, Pollitt is our principal tool but there are hundreds of others we are directing up and down the country.

They are beginning to get their hands on the real power in industry and soon they will strike.'

'Strike?' Baring asked, 'do you mean armed insurrection?'

'No, it is too early for that. The Army and Police are too loyal to the Government. Firstly the collapse of the economy has to be brought about by a General Strike. The miners' issue is the one we are choosing as the focal point of unrest with the slogan 'Not a penny off the pay, not a minute on the day.' Once the miners come out all the other organised workers will follow. The country will be paralysed.'

Baring listened intently.

'It is important that as the crisis worsens no concession is made to the strikers', the Colonel went on, 'and that's where you come in. Instructions from Moscow are that you must use your influence within the Tory Party and Parliament to persuade the Government to hold firm. The greater the confrontation the better the chances of the trades unions becoming the Soviets of the revolution as they were in Petrograd.'

'My influence is not all that great at this moment, as I'm no longer Baldwin's secretary,' said Baring faltingly.

'Do whatever you can,' emphasised the Russian. 'Baldwin must crush the trades unions so much that they become vicious like an ill-treated dog. The Foreign Division of O.G.P.U. is using all its resources to bolster the revolutionaries; we're providing the money and skills to tip the balance but we can't create a revolutionary situation. That can only come from the internal contradictions of the system itself. The opportunity this year is classic. There might not be another for ten years. It must be seized now.'

With that the Colonel was gone, strolling through the park like any other English gentleman on his morning constitutional. As Baring looked at the disappearing figure he was torn between joy at the prospect of his dreams being realised and despair that O.G.P.U. had relegated him to the part of cog in a relentless machine. When he reached the

House of Commons he was comforted by the atmosphere of club-like bonhomie in that private oasis isolated from the bleak desert of harsh realities outside.

The General Strike came, as the Colonel had predicted, at the beginning of May as organised workers in the coal, gas, electricity and railway industries together with dockers, printers and road transport workers refused to work. Buses, trains and vans were driven by volunteers to help keep essential supplies moving. Undergraduates deserted their studies to do their bit alongside titled ladies who had never done a day's work in their lives. Baldwin, under pressure from his backbenchers including Baring, declared no concession to anarchy. The Government bent every nerve to break the T.U.C. The Chancellor of the Exchequer, Winston Churchill, took over the *Morning Post* offices in the Strand and from the second day of the strike produced an official newspaper. Baring volunteered to join the team running the paper, *The British Gazette*, and for over a week he helped to churn out articles which gave the Government's view. Production difficulties were enormous as all the printers were on strike but the editorial staff, Baring amongst them, put on dungarees to keep the machines going.

Winston Churchill was impressed with the energy and enthusiasm of the young Member of Parliament for West Middlesex, wishing his own son could be as resourceful. As a result of the Government's firm stance the T.U.C. called off the strike after only nine days. The majority of trades unions leaders had no stomach for revolution. They knew that pushing the dispute could result in total chaos from which only the Communists would benefit. By their action the trades unions made a clear decision to accept the existing social system and to operate only within it and not against it. Baldwin had scored a great victory.

Baring went to the Savoy Hotel to join in the Champagne celebrations with the other leading strike breakers, but in his heart he was bitterly disappointed. The chance of breaking capitalism by one blow of organised labour had been lost and he knew the psychological impact of the defeat would be enormous. The mood of the workers would now be one of resigned acceptance to their position as sheep under the control of their economic masters. At best most of the trades unions leaders would be sheepdogs doing their owner's bidding. Baring's hopes of resolving his own personal dilemmas were also dashed. As he drank the Champagne and joined in the revelry he felt sick.

At the end of July he saw Yegorov and the Russian was in a flaming temper. 'The T.U.C. are worse than a bunch of Mensheviks,' he stormed in an emotional outburst which belied his previous scientific attitude to human affairs. 'We've given a quarter of a million pounds to the Miners' Federation, they are the only ones with any revolutionary guts. But it will get us nowhere. Baldwin will destroy them now the other unions have deserted the cause.'

'You wanted Baldwin to hold firm. I played my part as you advised,' said Baring.

'We never expected the unions to collapse so quickly. They've ruined the chances of revolution for a generation. There is now no alternative but to play the long-term stakes. We have to throttle British capitalism by eroding its strength over the next years, destroying the Empire and allowing Britain to decay. The British workers are lethargic. They will never rise in revolt unless they are really hungry. If that's what they want we'll work to that end.'

Baring was dismayed. 'Are you accepting defeat?' he asked.

'There is no alternative, Comrade. As an officer in the O.G.P.U. you are entitled to know the facts. Moscow has its own problems at home. Dzerzhinsky died of a heart attack last week. He collapsed at a meeting of the Central Committee after a speech denouncing the opposition within the party. There is a big crisis of leadership. New leaders have to consolidate their grip.' The Colonel looked pensive as if his inner doubts had to be suppressed before they revealed themselves. Then he went on. 'There are also pressing needs to build up the Soviet economy after years of turmoil. "Socialism in one country" is the slogan and Stalin won't allow dreams of world revolution to deflect him. We're entering a new era, Comrade Captain.' Yegorov appeared more relaxed now. 'The new era means we have to put Mother Russia first. Zinoviev is finished you know. The failure of the General Strike and the collapse of his strategy for revolution in Britain will mean he'll no longer be head of the Comintern. He's also thrown in his lot with that renegade Trotsky.'

'Trotsky?' said Baring perplexed. 'Trotsky a renegade, he was one of the leaders of the revolution and the head of the Red Army. How could he be a renegade?'

'Trotsky is a revisionist. Stalin is determined to edge him out of the Politbureau. I saw the writing on the wall last year when Trotsky was forced to give up as Commissar for War.'

'It's a bad day for world revolution if Trotsky leaves,' said Baring incautiously, 'he was the inspiration to many of us to take up the cause. Who is Stalin anyway?' he added petulantly.

'Be careful what you say Comrade. Such remarks might be alright in these London parks but in the Soviet Union they would be reported as treasonable. I've grown to like you, Comrade Captain, and admire what you are doing here in this rotten, decrepit England, so I won't put your comment in my report. Everything you do and say is on your file in Moscow. There is in Russia today a mood of reflection and a desire to examine credentials and assess people's reliability.'

'You mean a witchhunt,' said Baring, daringly.

'A witchhunt, what do you mean by that?'

'Rooting out those who don't accept the accepted doctrines of the day.'

'Yes I suppose you could call it that,' the Colonel mused.

'In England in the old days witches were burnt at the stake. What is happening to the so called renegades in Russia?'

'We wouldn't do anything so barbaric as burning. The comrades who can no longer lead the country because they have grown weak or foolish will be put out to grass like old horses. We only shoot traitors like that spy Reilly.'

'Reilly?'

'Yes, we found out he was acting as a prime agent for British intelligence all the time. We tricked him back to Russia last year and he was tried and shot. That's the way of all traitors. We can't afford to show mercy.'

'Didn't he do what you wanted in delivering the Zinoviev letter?'

'We had evidence he was plotting with Winston Churchill. Anyone who is in cohorts with Churchill is an enemy of the people.'

'I worked with Churchill during the General Strike. Is that held against me?' asked Baring.

'That's not the same. You are burrowing your way into the inner sanctum of the British establishment and you will have to do disagreeable things like associating with Churchill. That's alright. But if it were ever discovered you were plotting against us — as Reilly was — you would be tried and shot too.'

'I've always accepted that but I am no traitor. I can assure you,' Baring said.

'That's good to hear, Comrade,' said the Colonel and he turned to go as abruptly as on their previous encounters, leaving Baring with his anxieties and perplexed dreams.

In August Anne Baring gave birth to a son of seven pounds six ounces. He was a healthy, bawling boy who looked the image of his great grandfather Tallen. There were no complications at the birth, which took place at the Amesbury House and was attended by two doctors from Salisbury.

Charles was delighted and immediately put his son's name down for a place at Eton, recognising the extreme irony of his action in protecting the privilege of his kin whilst devoting his secret activity to destroying the class system which Eton represented. In fact Charles Baring found enormous pleasure in the spoils of the system he claimed to abhor and secretly wanted his son to grow up with all the advantages money and position could provide. The blood dictates a selfishness more powerful than any ideology. Baring's fantasy world of revolution and communist equality was real enough in that it controlled his intense life force. It provided the incentive for all his political machinations. Without the fantasy to inspire him Baring would have been nothing. He would have been devoid of ambition and content to live as a country squire in an East Anglian backwater.

The myth that had infiltrated itself into Baring's unconscious ruled his inner mind and his hidden spirit but the reality of every day, the reality of affluence and class, kept his body comfortable and provided the hedonistic trappings of a rich family environment. Only Anne had suspicions that all was not well with her husband but she would not dare to articulate them. Such disloyalty would have been anathema to her upbringing of an aristocracy which had always had its fair share of eccentrics who needed shielding from the uncomprehending lower classes. In any case she now had her son to whom she could devote her time and her love and in whom her own aspirations could be fulfilled.

CHAPTER 33

In the following March Baring made a speaking tour of the north of England for the Conservative Party. It was part of the Government's campaign to rally support from the middle of the road, law-abiding people who were fed up with industrial unrest. In fifteen towns from Birkenhead to Preston and across the Penines to Hull, Leeds and Bradford, he spoke to packed halls accompanied by the local M.P. or Conservative candidate. Although it was nine years since the end of the war he was billed as a war hero but the press also made much of his experiences in Russia as a prisoner and his reputation as an anti-Bolshevik. Through his association with Winston Churchill he had built up his image as a tough, uncompromising patriot.

The front seats at the meetings were usually packed with Conservative party members and supporters: shopkeepers and factory owners in their smart Sunday suits with their wives, wooed now for their votes, in long coats and unfashionably large hats. From these reserved seats the speakers could expect no trouble but the back of the halls were crowded with socialists and the unemployed who waited to howl down the representatives of the ruling élite. At several places the police had to be called to restore order. Baring's speech was virtually the same in each town. The country needed stability and firm leadership to enable it to recover from the ravages of the General Strike. The divisive activities of agitators have to be crushed. Working people wanted jobs, not dangerous tinkering with foreign Bolshevik ideas. They wanted the rights of property, which had been the cornerstone of Britain's prosperity, to be upheld. The coal mines, 'our greatest natural asset' would fail if taken over by the State.

Baring's onslaught on Ramsay MacDonald — 'that many-tongued romantic of uncertain origins' — always had the front rows roaring with approval and the back shouting in horrified disgust. Then he shook even the loudest opponent by attacking the tweedledum and tweedledee of corruption: Lloyd-George, the Welshman, for selling honours to the highest bidder and Ramsay MacDonald, the Scot, for taking bribes from his capitalist opponents. To the expected cries of protest he held up his arm and shouted, 'I have the evidence here and if you are quiet you'll hear it,' and the audience fell into an expectant silence as he spelt out the former Prime Minister's crimes in accepting a Daimler car and £30,000 in shares from the biscuit manufacturers, McVitie and Price, whose chairman had been given a knighthood by MacDonald in return. At each meeting he finished with a peroration 'There you have it. The Labour Party morality in a nutshell. They take the biscuit. What a Price to pay for a St. Vitie's dance' and to frenzied applause from the front of the hall 'No more corrupt celts for Prime Minister. England must back honest men from the backbone of England; Winston Churchill, the inventor of the tank that won us the war, and that man of iron, Stanley Baldwin who defeated the General Strike.'

At the last of the meetings in the Free Trade Hall in Manchester Baring's speech set the place in an uproar with over fifty hecklers having to be ejected. He felt tremendously fit. The excitement made the blood surge through his veins giving him a sense of physical, as well as mental, superiority. To Baring the content of his speeches was irrelevant, what mattered was that they should be dramatic enough to enable him to dominate and control his audience. He had contrived to include favourable references to Churchill knowing they would be reported back and put Baring in good favour with the Chancellor of the Exchequer. As he left the Free Trade Hall platform he felt his tour had been an unqualified success and the congratulations from Party officials confirmed that.

His euphoria was broken when a thick set man in his mid-thirties came up behind him and grabbed his arm. The stewards were about to eject him when he shouted to Baring, 'I'm your old friend Arthur Haycraft,' and to the disbelieving stewards, 'We were in Archangel together.' Baring recognised the former Lieutenant, despite his extra weight, and signalled the officials to let him free. He felt mixed emotions at meeting Haycraft but could hardly send him away. No one could predict what the man would do. It was too dangerous.

'I must talk to you,' Haycraft said when he was able to speak to Baring. There was no time for niceties in the milling crowd.

'Come to my hotel. Suite twenty-nine in the Midland. Say eleven o'clock,' said Baring before being carried off to a reception for party dignatories and financial backers.

On the way to the hotel Baring regretted his haste in making the appointment. Haycraft would only be an embarrassmant to him. The man knew too much from the past. But Baring's curiosity proved to be stronger than his discretion. In the quiet of the hotel suite and with a beer in his hand, Arthur Haycraft was amiable enough, but he had the haunted look of a frightened animal in his eyes. They exchanged news in an awkward and disjointed way. Haycraft explained that after five years Natasha had eventually joined him with a son called Ivan, who was now six, who did not know him as father. They had married again in an English ceremony because the problems of admitting the Moscow wedding were too great. Baring said he had a son called George, after the boy's grandfather, and was it not wonderful that they had both survived their experiences without harm. These exchanges, which went on for some time, had a false air about them, as neither man was being frank until Haycraft with his third beer suddenly said to him:

'Look Charles, I'm in desperate trouble. You must help me.' Haycraft looked as weak as a broken reed. His personality was a mere shadow of its former self.

'What is it, money?' asked Baring.

'Much worse than that. Much worse than that. I hardly know where to start.'

'Come out with it Arthur,' said Baring, who knew what to expect.

'Well it's like this,' said Haycraft diffidently for he was still awe inspired with Baring's rank and obvious status with the powerful men of Manchester, 'the Russians have caught me in a vice. I'm being squeezed dry. They won't leave me alone. I'm terrified of being found out.'

'What are you doing for them?' Baring asked, nervous now.

'I've been spying. Stealing the technical secrets at Vickers where I work. The Russians contacted me years ago and insisted I did it.' He looked crestfallen. 'It was the only way I could get Natasha to join me. It wasn't much at first, just the odd blue-print but then they stepped up their demands and I found myself taking whole piles of documents. They had me running scared.'

'Do you take money?'

'Yes I did. They're blackmailing me on that now. They have photographs of me and threaten to turn them over to the police if I don't cooperate.'

'You were unwise to take money,' said Baring who had never known financial need.

'I know that now, but Natasha was for it and we needed sixty-five pounds for the deposit on a house and extra money when the boy was ill.'

'What does Natasha say about it now?'

'She says I've no alternative but to do what my controller says.'

'Your controller?'

'He's a chap called Dmitri Kozlov. He's with Arcos the Soviet trade delegation in London. He comes up to see me every month and I'm terrified every time he's due. He's always asking for more, more, more. There's no end to it, Charles. As I said they're squeezing me dry, and to cap it all 'cause important files are missing at Vickers, there's an enquiry going on. I'm dead scared they'll pin it on me. What do I do?' he asked pathetically.

'There's nothing I can do to help you,' said Baring distancing himself from the problem, 'but I'd advise you to change your job when you can. Let things cool down.'

'That's what Kozlov wants me to do. They want me to go to one of the defence establishments. I think I shall be up to my neck even more if I do.'

'You've no alternative,' said Baring who now knew only too well how great the dangers were.

'Can't you help me. You must have influence. You must be working for them too,' Haycraft blurted out in anger at his impossible predicament.

Baring found the situation distasteful. Haycraft, a man without commitment, had allowed himself to be a shuttle-cock. Baring had forgotten how grateful he had once been to Haycraft for his friendship and attempts at understanding, at the time of his own personal sacrifice. Any residual loyalties from that experience had been long since lost in the welter of Baring's greedy rise to power and influence.

'Of course I'm not working for them, as you put it. You might as well say they're working for me,' he answered haughtily. 'We all believe in the same cause.'

'So you don't believe all that claptrap you were saying tonight. It didn't ring true to me,' said Haycraft.

'The Tory faithful expect it from a Tory M.P. It's all part of the game,' replied Baring.

'Bully for you. Is there no honesty in politics?'

'No, it's a filthy business. Democracy is the dirtiest trick ever perpetrated on the British people. That's why we have to dispense with it as soon as possible so we can get on with the task of running Britain efficiently. Democracy corrupts and it's wasteful at the same time. Its only use is as a safety valve, but it gives people false hopes and ideas beyond their station.' Baring regretted saying it as soon as the words were out of his mouth. He had not spoken so frankly for seven years. The presence of Arthur Haycraft — the confidant from the past — had acted as a catalyst releasing his pent up thoughts. He curbed himself from committing more indiscretions and attempted to gloss over Haycraft's problem.

'If you move from Vickers in a few months you'll be alright. Whatever you do keep your head. Do nothing which will make the investigators suspicious of you and if they question you never admit anything. I advise you to go home and destroy any evidence. Have a bonfire. Don't attempt to take any files back; they'll be watching for that.'

'I'll do what you say. Will you come and see Natasha tomorrow before you go back to London? She'd love to see you.'

'Good heavens, no,' Baring exploded indelicately, 'I couldn't do that.' Baring guessed that Natasha was an O.G.P.U. operative who would be reporting on her husband's activities and he went on to advise, 'I shouldn't tell Natasha you saw me if I were you. The fewer who know that the better.'

Haycraft looked dismayed as a little boy would if caught in some naughtiness. 'She knows,' he said, 'We left Ivan with a neighbour and she came to the meeting. After I met you I sent her home to send the boy to bed.'

'That's a pity. Tell her we talked about old times, not about your problem.'

'But she knows, Charles. We've talked about nothing else for days. I was sure you would be able to get the Russians off my back,' said Haycraft.

'Go home,' said Baring, exhausted by the enormity of a problem far greater than Haycraft realised. 'Go home,' he said like a judge uttering the capital sentence.

'That night Baring could hardly sleep. Thoughts of

Russia's crisis kept pounding in his head. He still could not accept Trotsky's expulsion from the Politbureau although it had happened months before. Lev Davidovich kept coming into his dreams arguing in his characteristic way and occasionally pushing his pince nez back on his nose as it threatened to fall. Then he had another vision of Trotsky in his Red Army greatcoat and little army hat with its red star, as clear as daylight addressing a crowd of soldiers from the back of his military train. He was denouncing Stalin — 'that evil Georgian', with his voice rising to a crescendo, 'Vladimir Ilyich denounced him and now we must all do Lenin's bidding and destroy Stalin before he destroys the revolution and all of us.'

The scene in his dreams switched to the Kremlin where a trial was taking place before the international delegates to the Comintern. He could see Sylvia Pankhurst and the British representatives as plainly as if they were in the same room. The Pankhurst woman was screaming as Stalin declared the death penalty on a disloyal comrade and Trotsky, also protesting, was dragged from the scene by thugs before he could even speak. 'Take the prisoner to the Lubyanka, to the execution chamber,' shouted Stalin in thick Russian with a Georgian accent. As he listened Baring had a fleeting thought of amazement at his memory of the language. He understood every word perfectly. And then to his horror he saw the condemned man. It was Arthur Haycraft who, strangely, was dressed in the smart uniform of a Lieutenant in the Royal Engineers. As Haycraft put up his arms in an appeal for mercy, Baring woke with a sudden start. The hotel room quickly came flooding back into his consciousness. Baring found he was bathed in sweat; the sheets were completely soaked; his head was heavy as if it had been hit with a sledgehammer but surprisingly it was cool. The fever was over.

Baring gave up attempts to sleep and caught the earliest train back to London where hectic activity could be a

distraction to his undisciplined thoughts. At Sussex Square
he found a hand-delivered invitation waiting on the hall table
where the butler always put the morning mail. it was from
Winston Churchill: 'Enjoyed reading your northern speeches.
Please call in as soon as you return. Winston.'

Baring went to Number 11 Downing Street. 'Glad you
came,' the Chancellor lisped, 'you can do some valuable
service in the cause we both hold dear. As you know I've been
pressing for the recognition of the Bolsheviks to be
withdrawn. It's a disgrace we allow agitators and spies to
operate here under diplomatic immunity.' Baring nodded
and the Chancellor went on. 'I've had evidence that they're
using the Arcos trade centre in Moorgate Street as a base for
spying. I am advising the Home Secretary to get the police in
there. If he does there will be an almighty row and I'd like you
to get our people in the House to speak out strongly for all our
relations with the Bolsheviks to be cut. The Foreign Office
want to keep in with the brigands but if you and the others
play your part we can beat them.'

Baring undertook to help and the two men talked for
another fifteen minutes about internal politics within the
Conservative Party. As the young M.P. left, Churchill gave
him a parting gift. 'You're doing well in the House, Baring.
When we get back after the election in two years time S.B.
should have a ministerial job for you; if not I'd like you to be
my P.P.S.'

Walking up Downing Street to Whitehall, Baring was in a
more cheerful mood. The efforts he had made for political
success were beginning to pay dividends. As one of
Churchill's legionnaires he could expect a bumpy ride but the
prospect of real power at the end of the journey.

On the 12th May, 1927, Scotland Yard raided the Arcos
trade centre and seized documents. Soviet protests fell on
deaf ears as Baring and other Churchill supporters had
established an atmosphere of distrust making it impossible
for Baldwin to make any concessions to Russia.

A few days after the raid Churchill took Baring by the arm in the library corridor and boomed, 'You did a good job my boy, come and join me in a whisky.' He ordered two whiskies from the attendant, assuming that was what Baring would be drinking. 'Damn good result, eh? Now we've got those Bolsheviks on the run; we'll withdraw recognition soon. We shouldn't give those evil men in the Kremlin a day's more support. Joseph Djugashvili is the most evil of them all. In Tsarist days in Tiflis and Baku he was a bandit known as Koba and was raiding banks to get money for the revolution. He was a dirty common criminal and even Trotsky denounced his activities. Now see what's happened, he's been able to get his own back by edging Trotsky out of the leadership. He calls himself "Stalin" because it means "man of steel" and gives a strong image.'

Churchill puffed energetically at his cigar. 'In fact he's the most shifty and untrustworthy man ever to become the leader of a great country. It must be our mission to destroy him, but first we must isolate the Bolsheviks and deny them the diplomatic respectability they want.'

Baring knew that Churchill as Chancellor of the Exchequer was miscast, as his knowledge of financial matters was minimal. His flair was in world affairs and, whatever his office, he contrived to exercise it. If Baring needed a powerful friend in the Cabinet to give him help in getting office, and he did, there was no other way than to act as a sounding-board and as a dogsbody to one and to flatter him by generally, but not slavishly, agreeing with his opinions. Baring had learnt that in politics it was not ability that counted, that sometimes it was a positive obstacle to progress, whereas knowing the right people and having the right sponsors was important. His uncle had advised him to stick to Churchill as a mentor. There were few better choices. Neville Chamberlain, the Minister of Health, was a narrow, dried-up bureaucrat without imagination and Sam Hoare was second rate.

These thoughts went through Baring's mind as he sipped

his whisky and water in the Smoking Room, giving a half-ear
to Churchill's rumblings. His reward as a patient listener was
to be asked to Chartwell to see the brick building. 'They
invited me to be a member of the trade union,' the Chancellor
said proudly, showing his card in the Building Trade
Workers' 'but the damned Executive decided I wasn't
eligible. They returned my cheque but I kept the certificate.'

That weekend Baring journeyed to Kent to see Churchill,
'meet Clemmie' who was charming as a hostess, and the five
year old Sarah. In the garden a tall bespectacled ginger and
crinkly-haired old man in his twenties came strolling over
nonchalantly as though he was accustomed to making
himself at home. Baring could discern a distinct likeness
between visitor and host and expected the young man to be
introduced as a relative.

'This is Brendan Bracken,' said Churchill, 'he's worked for
me in every election since the Abbey by-election; be in the
House himself soon with that experience.'

Baring shook hands with Bracken who was grinning like a
Cheshire cat, more as a defence against his defences being
invaded by a stranger than as a sign of friendship. 'You're
West Middlesex aren't you?' he said.

'Yes,' said Baring.

'You had some time in Russia I hear from Winston.'

'Yes, I was a prisoner of the Bolsheviks.'

The two younger men followed Churchill, dressed in his
shabby dungarees, to the wall where the Chancellor
demonstrated his bricklaying skills without inviting them to
try; after a tour of the gardens they returned to the oval table
for lunch where the conversation was divided equally
between political gossip and family chatter.

As Baring left Chartwell to drive back to London,
Churchill gripped his shoulder affectionately and said, 'If you
want to get on in democratic politics choose your enemies as
carefully as you choose your friends. It's better to be attacked
than ignored; opponents with the biggest mouths are the best

investment. Of course you need friends as well; no recluse ever won power and a select few who are loyal are better than a multitude.'

The Spring holiday traffic of motor cars and a few horse carriages caused congestion on the roads to London and Baring did not arrive at Sussex Square until late on that Sunday evening. He had no sooner taken off his overcoat than he heard a loud banging at the door. The butler was on weekend leave so he answered the summons himself. Yegorov was standing on the doorstep, anxiety reflected in his manner and with an unusually dishevelled appearance.

'Come in,' said Baring hesitantly, hoping no one along the road was watching.

Once in the hall Yegorov threw off his overcoat and began to relax a little.

'I knew your servants were away and I had to see you,' he explained.

'Wasn't it dangerous to come here?'

'We live in dangerous times, Comrade, risks are sometimes necessary.'

Baring took his unexpected visitor into the library. The Russian spread himself out on a settee and surveyed the scene appreciatively as Baring automatically fetched a drink from the cabinet. 'There have been urgent developments and I had no other time to contact you. All Soviet diplomats must leave tomorrow. The English Government has withdrawn diplomatic recognition.'

'I was expecting it after the Arcos raid. That was the warm up. Churchill's in a happy mood this weekend. He didn't tell me but I'm sure he knew his plot had succeeded.'

'He knew,' said the Colonel, 'Churchill runs the foreign policy of England. But I'm not here to discuss that. You must have your instructions for the years ahead. Ogpu has considered putting another controller in my place, but without diplomatic immunity it would have been difficult if not impossible. And the less people who know the better. So you'll be on your own now, comrade.'

Yegorov spent an hour explaining a simple code which Baring had to commit to memory, gave addresses in Zurich and Stockholm which Baring could use in emergencies and described a method of communication through the personal column of the *Times*. 'Always look on Tuesdays,' advised the Colonel, 'if we need you to make a contact the advertisement with the code word will appear on a Tuesday. The place of contact will be coded but the time will always be at nine in the morning on the following day. If you miss one day turn up on alternate days until contact is made.'

Baring was warned again never to commit anything to paper but it was unnecessary advice as his training at the Vecheka stockade was still vivid in his mind.

'You won't have to worry about Haycraft any more,' Yegorov added as an afterthought.

Baring shuddered involuntarily as the Colonel continued in his typically callous, matter of fact voice. 'Natasha, our agent, reported your ill advised meeting. Natasha's mission is finished in England. With her son she was taken to Hull and put on a ship sailing to Russia..'

'What happened to Arthur Haycraft?'

'He was killed by a run-away motor car in Manchester. A tragic accident,' said Yegorov, carefully removing the long holders of his cigarettes from the ashtray so that no evidence would be left of his visit for the servants to notice.

CHAPTER 34

In the General Election of May 1929 Baring retained West Middlesex and the Conservatives under Stanley Baldwin polled eight million six hundred thousand votes or thirty-eight percent of the total votes cast. The Labour Party had a percentage point less in total votes, but such are the quirks of democracy, emerged with twenty-seven seats more than the Conservatives and as the largest party in Parliament, Ramsay MacDonald was sent for by the King and asked to form a Government. He did so with the support of the Liberals who had scored over five million votes but with only fifty-nine seats were crushed as a leading Parliamentary party. With the collapse of the centre, politics in Britain had moved irrevocably towards the class confrontation for which Marxist revolutionaries had planned. It was a prospect Charles Baring M.P. welcomed, although his ego regretted he had for the time being lost the chance to get the ministerial office which his friendship with Churchill — and his work in the past with Baldwin — had promised.

The Labour Government proved to be a disaster as it was too weak to withstand the bitter winds of world economic depression and in two years the Labour Party split under the strain, with MacDonald leading a rump into a National Coalition with the Conservatives. He remained Prime Minister but the real power was Stanley Baldwin's.

For Baring the nineteen-thirties were a barren period of waiting and hoping. His political base in West Middlesex was firm; his popularity was so strong no one could hope to dislodge him. Page had been replaced as Chairman of the constituency association after a bribery scandal concerning town planning approvals which had netted him two million pounds. He kept the money but lost his influence. For him it was a fair bargain. Less happy for TOP was the disappearance of his daughter Helen. It was rumoured that she had gone to South America with a Colombian drug dealer. Unhappiness over her unrequited love for the local M.P. was widely believed to be the cause of her unnatural behaviour.

Grandfather Tallen died of old age having never seen the inside of a hospital except on his visits as a doctor. Sarah Baring, to everyone's surprise, married the Rev. Michael Caldicott, the vicar of Sudbury, who had lost his wife fourteen months before in a curious boating accident, and the vicar moved into the Hall. Edith and Emma each produced three more children giving Charles a total of seven nephews and nieces. The greatest surprise of all was the birth of a boy to Lady John Baring. Malicious tongues claimed the father could not be Sir John, but the old baronet kept a deaf ear to the gossip, if it ever reached him, and proudly presented his heir to all and sundry boasting that the succession was now secure.

Anne Baring lived most of the time in Amesbury when she was not visiting the Duke's, her father's, estates in Dorset. Her relations with her husband had become frigid since the death of a stillborn daughter two years after the birth of their son. Little George provided the main emotional contact between his parents. They had long since given up attempts to discuss politics except in the devious, calculating way of dinner parties, when they had guests who had to be entertained and manipulated. Anne still wanted her husband to succeed. That vicarious achievement could substitute for the disappointment of a marriage that provided no comfort or satisfaction in bed or anywhere else. The suspicion Anne felt about her husband had corroded everything of value between them. She had tried to build new bridges but Charles refused to take off his bland, self-satisfied face when she questioned him about his views and beliefs. Intuitively she knew he lied to her consistently. The squalid affairs with other women — usually servants or daughters of tradespeople — did not worry her as much as the dishonesty about his politics. Anne was intelligent and astute enough to know her husband was hypocritical about his political manoeuvres. That she could excuse; most successful politicians had the same traits. They were necessary. What upset her profoundly was the deep-set twist in Charles Baring's personality and psychology that she knew existed but which he steadfastly refused to acknowledge. She found it unfathomable, gave up plumbing the depths, and slipped into a practical relationship with Charles which was more like a business arrangement than that of a marriage of wife with her man.

Charles welcomed the new understanding which had grown out of the soil of despair. It suited him to keep Anne at arm's length away from his dilemma; he was terrified of sharing his secret with anyone. He loved Anne as George's mother, as a loyal partner and for the undoubted advantages her connections had given him in the political world but it went no further than that. He had no sexual interest in her, as carnal relations on a permanent basis would make demands on his doubled personality which he knew he could not deliver without cracking. He was like the Siamese twins: Chang was the Bolshevik and Eng, the English M.P., joined together in one body but with Eng's ambitions subordinated to Chang's dominant long-term aims.

Charles Baring never allowed himself to feel much dismay or distress at his situation. Some safety valve kept him on even keel and no one, apart from Anne, suspected any inner turmoil because he suppressed tensions as quickly as they appeared.

The greatest stress was felt when he tried to understand what was happening in the Soviet Russia he loved. His friend Trotsky had been expelled in disgrace to find refuge in

Turkey and he read frequent reports of executions of Stalin's political rivals. Baring allowed for the distortions of the Western Press but it was becoming painfully clear that the cult of the leader had replaced the ideals of the revolution. On the other hand he was impressed by the great leap forward of the Soviet economy, even if it had meant the dispossession of ten million peasants. He did not believe the stories that three million had perished in the change but felt pride that a nation which had fought for its survival against capitalist countries less than a decade and a half before was now able to deal with them on terms nearing equality. Stalin, he rationalised, might be a tyrant but he was a passing phenomenon as irrelevant to the long term success of Communism as Oliver Cromwell had been to the survival of the British monarchy.

Baring's new controller, who had arrived in London with the reopening of diplomatic relations, steadfastly refused to answer any questions on the Soviet scene. 'It's better for us both that we don't discuss such matters,' he cautioned. In their infrequent meetings there were few specific instructions for the foreign-based Captain of O.G.P.U. who, he was assured, was highly esteemed in Moscow. Vyacheslau Menzhinsky, the head of O.G.P.U., was content that Captain Baring should continue his secret role of burrowing away at the British establishment. Any premature action, Moscow felt, would jeopardise the chances of effectiveness in the future and might threaten Baring with exposure. It was out of the question, the controller explained, for Baring to undertake any espionage or the passing of secrets. There were spies to do that — 'more than enough' — and to use Baring in that way would be like putting 'the most precious ikon in Saint Basil's Cathedral in a village church' the controller said in a revealingly religious allusion.

After the death of Menzhinsky the O.G.P.U. was absorbed into the N.K.V.D. and Genrikh Yagoda became its head, but after two years he was arrested and shot as a foreign spy. His successor, Nikolai Yezhov, a dwarf of a man, was also shot on

Stalin's orders within another two years. Baring watched the reports of a succession of Moscow show trials with bewilderment especially as his controllers came and went with similar rapidity.

In pursuing his political career, Baring played a canny game. Unlike S.B.'s son Oliver or John Strachey he declined to be courted by Oswald Mosley who had set up a fascist party. The darling of the Harrow Conservatives who had gone on to become the hero of the Smethwick Labour Party was now demonstrating another eccentricity. Baring could understand why Mosley was attracted to the strong policies of Benito Mussolini or Adolf Hitler; the miserable slide of Britain into an industrial and cultural torpor was enough to make anyone despair of traditional political remedies. If Baring had not already committed himself to dictatorial Marxism he might well have found the call of dictatorial Fascism irresistible. Both doctrines depended on a mystical leadership to which the irrational individual was totally subordinated.

Baring avoided the temptations to declare himself for any doctrine. Instead he steered a pragmatic course in public by backing only those policies which could secure his own advancement. He supported Churchill's onslaught on Baldwin's plans to scuttle India and echoed Churchill's attack on Gandhi as a 'seditious Middle Temple lawyer, posing as a fakir, striding half-naked into the Viceregal Palace.' By doing so he alienated his old mentor Stanley Baldwin, but he calculated it was better to be linked with a rising star than a dying comet. But Baring did not anticipate Baldwin's dominance of the British political scene for most of the nineteen-thirties. They were the years of the doldrums for Britain as the country drifted towards a war for which it did not have the sense to prepare.

Adolph Hitler, the son of a brow-beaten half-Jewish mother, who hated Jews because of the syphilis caught from a Jewish prostitute in Vienna, became the Chancellor of a resurgent Germany. The right-wing of Britain flirted with him as he promised to be a bulwark against Communism. Only Churchill among the senior Tory politicians opposed Hitler with any vigour. Baring was glad he had linked himself openly with the Churchill camp, even though it meant sacrificing office under Baldwin and later under the bleak Neville Chamberlain, who took over as P.M. when he was nearly seventy. Baring could not help be envious when his Eton contemporary took office as Foreign Secretary at the age of only thirty-eight. As the years passed he began to wonder whether political office would elude him completely but political beds once made have to be slept in.

His Soviet controllers gave him little trouble; their advice to him was simply to hold firm to the advantages he was building up within the British political system. According to them the contradictions in capitalism would lead to war between Nazi Germany and the effete democracies. Early in 1939 they warned Baring that the Soviet Union would make a pact with Hitler to free them for an attack on the West. Moscow, he was told, was convinced that this war would so weaken capitalism it would make a Communist revolution inevitable and ensure the Soviet Union would take over the leadership of the world.

Baring was grateful he had been prepared for the shock of the Nazi-Soviet pact and the division of Poland between the unlikely allies. He welcomed it as presaging a fresh momentum in politics which had been dull for too long. At forty-one he felt middle-age drawing in; the political torpor had been debilitating and he longed for action.

His relations with Anne remained cool and controlled. She had taken lovers; he knew but never complained as her conduct gave him *carte blanche* for any affairs he needed. But sexual adventures were no substitute for the heady excitements of power and the satisfaction that comes from changing the course of human history.

On 3rd September, 1939, Britain's declaration of war on

Germany was for Baring like a shot of adrenalin. Something had happened with momentum enough to shake the foundations of the old system. Once he had hoped the revolution would be achieved without unnecessary bloodshed — memories of the Somme and Passchendaele were still vivid — but the failure of the working class to stir itself meant the nation needed a shock. War with Germany would provide that. The Soviet Union would maintain its strength and be ready to take over Europe after the debacle.

Baring tried to re-enlist in his old regiment but was refused on the grounds of age, as he had anticipated. He then used his talents in the House to campaign for Churchill to take over as Prime Minister from the pathetic figure of Chamberlain. When the Germans invaded Norway there was a censure debate and Baring persuaded many Tory backbenchers to vote against the Government, reducing Chamberlain's majority from over 200 to only 81. Resignation was forced on the ex-mayor of Birmingham and Churchill moved into Number 10 Downing Street.

Baring's reward for his steadfast support of Churchill over the lean years came in the new Ministerial appointments which also included Labour and Liberal nominees. Baring became Minister for Production and although not yet in the Cabinet was made a member of the Privy Council at the same time as Brendan Bracken who was not even a Minister.

The consequences of Baring becoming a Minister had an unexpected effect six thousand miles away in Mexico where Lev Davidovitch Trotsky, Baring's hero, was living in exile in a small villa. Despite his exposure to assassination he had been secure from attack, because Stalin had seen no point in incurring the opprobrium of killing him. Trotsky had launched a million words of invective against the dictator in Moscow but the wrath of the Georgian had not been aroused. Lavrenti Beria, who had become Stalin's trusted head of the N.K.V.D., had seen no point in wasting energies and resources on eliminating the Trotsky broken reed, but when a report came through from the N.K.V.D. man in Mexico City the policy was changed. Beria's spies within the Trotsky circle had reported that the renegade was about to release an astounding secret about a British Government Minister who was an agent for his arch enemy Stalin.

This revelation had to be suppressed at all costs. Orders went back to Mexico City and within a few days an assassination squad of twenty N.K.V.D. agents attacked the Trotsky villa with machine guns. The attack was botched and Trotsky escaped death.

In fact Trotsky never intended to reveal the secret of Baring, the Soviet trojan horse, as he was confident that once Stalin died or was killed by a jealous rival he would be called back to lead the U.S.S.R. But in an unguarded moment Trotsky had revealed to one of his assistants the fact of Baring's existence and joked that it was something the Americans would dearly like to know. The mistake was a signature to his own death warrant.

Three months after the failure of the machine gun squad an N.K.V.D. agent called Ramon Mercader, who had wormed his way into Trotsky's confidence, killed the leader of the Russian Revolution with an ice-pick.

When Baring heard the news he was deeply saddened but he had no idea that his own promotion to Ministerial rank had been the trigger leading to the elimination of his greatest idol.

CHAPTER 35

The Right Honourable Charles Baring, M.C., M.P., at the age of forty-seven was the epitome of the successful Tory politician. During the war he had held several Ministerial positions ending up in Churchill's Cabinet sitting alongside Attlee, Bevin, Sinclair and Eden at the long polished table in the backroom of Number 10. His work had received much praise, particularly in the Beaverbrook press where commentators had marked him as a future Prime Minister.

It was generally recognised that Sir Anthony Eden, the elegant Foreign Secretary, would succeed Churchill, but Baring was the next in line.

Hostilities were over and Germany lay prone with the grandeur of the thousand-year Reich as broken as yesterday's film set. Soviet and Allied troops crawled over Berlin and Vienna, and the Potsdam Conference of the 'Big Three', Stalin, Truman and Churchill, met to divide the responsibilities and spoils of victory. Baring, along with most political observers, confidently expected the Conservative Party to win the first general election for ten years with a huge majority on the strength of Churchill's popularity as the leader who had led the country to victory. For the Member of West Middlesex there could not have been a better development. He could expect even higher office in the peacetime government and could be in a strong position to influence the coming collapse of capitalism. It was vitally necessary to defeat the Labour Party as any worker participation in government would deflect the people's passion for revolutionary struggle. A sharp confrontation between Labour and Capital was, to Baring's mind, a necessary background to revolt.

Anne Baring shared a pride in her husband's prestige and success. She had long given up hope of understanding what motivated him and never bothered to ask as she preferred the relative peace that went with ignorance. They had separate rooms at Amesbury and at Sussex Gardens when she came to London to entertain at parties, and their lives were as separate as partners in a business which needed harmony to succeed.

The Baronetcy of Sir John, who had been killed by a doodlebug bomb at the end of the war, went to his son. Neither Anne nor Charles were over-concerned by the loss of the title which would otherwise have gone to them. Both knew that with the Tories continuing in power there were very good chances that, if he wanted it, Charles could have a knighthood in his own right and even a peerage at the right time. Anne, whose brother had become the Duke of Dorset when her father died, was anxious to achieve her own status within the aristocracy. It was as important as protecting the family land and investments against socialist encroachments.

The election held on 5th July, 1945, was an unmitigated disaster for the Barings and the Conservative Party. Electors voted for a change from the old order and Churchill, although revered as victor, was discarded as a remnant of the old one. The diffident figure of Major Clement Atlee emerged as the new Prime Minister at the head of the Labour Party, pledged to nationalisation and reform.

In West Middlesex Charles Baring was defeated by 1564 votes in a three-cornered contest. The winner, an aircraft worker and nominee of the Amalgamated Engineering Union, was as flabbergasted as anyone when the mayor declared the result. He had been expecting to come third and had merely put up a propaganda fight.

Anne and Charles left the Town Hall dismayed and distressed. Anne, her world of political parties and hopes of title shattered, and Charles, alarmed that a Labour victory

had put back his chances of revolution for years. The mainly
Labour crowds, wanting to cheer the new working-class
M.P., booed as they were driven away in a Daimler
limousine. They called out 'Down with Churchill! Down with
the rich!' and Anne sobbed in anger and fear. For the first
time in many years Charles showed his wife genuine
affection, nestling her head in his arms. Her vulnerability had
pierced his defences and melted his soul momentarily. For a
few moments he wondered if he had been right to pursue
strange ambitions which cut him off from the one woman
who still loved him.

Without a seat in Parliament Charles felt like an actor
without a stage. Overnight he was without Ministerial office
or constituency. The abrupt change left him feeling listless.
At the Amesbury estate he took his favourite horses for long
rides over the downs trying to blow away the cobwebs of war
and the disappointments of political defeat. The intense
physical activity made him feel sore and tired and failed to
disperse his malaise. After a month he thought he should go
abroad for a holiday but the prospect of coping with the
currency restrictions deterred him. He could not afford, in
the climate of austerity Britain, to be seen breaking the
regulations designed to protect the pound. He desperately
wanted to win back West Middlesex and bad publicity had to
be avoided like the plague. The constituency association were
loyal up to a point but young hopefuls were pushing
themselves forward to take over lost seats.

The doubt and chagrin was dissipated to some extent when
he was approached by two companies to join their boards as a
non-executive director. One was the aircraft company and
engineering concern Vickers, and the other a firm producing
machine tools in Coventry and Manchester. The companies
wanted the prestige name of a former Minister who might
also provide useful contacts with senior civil servants in
Whitehall where decisions were being made of great
importance to their profits. Baring did not question their

motives but accepted with alacrity. The money, only a pittance, was of no consequence; he wanted the jobs to give him an excuse to travel and to provide a stimulus in the vacuum which loss of office had created.

Before the end of the year he arranged to make a goodwill tour to the United States and Canada on behalf of the companies and made a booking by Stratocruiser.

On the morning before the flight he was riding on the Wiltshire downs when a man in the smart livery of the hunting set approached on a magnificent mare. The man was a stranger, but as he seemed anxious to talk, Baring pulled back.

'Hello there, good day for riding,' the stranger shouted.

'Yes it is. Haven't seen you in these parts; do you live locally?' said Baring.

'No, I'm on holiday, staying at the Bull in Amesbury. I hired this horse at the stables near there.'

'You seem well fixed up,' said Baring referring to the boots, breeches, well cut riding coat and riding cap which could hardly have been acquired on clothing coupons.

'I believe in doing things in style,' said the stranger smiling, 'it's expected in the N.K.V.D.'

Baring could not believe his ears and kept his face as impassive as possible. It would be foolhardy to lose his guard with a man who might be playing tricks. 'That's a fine horse you have there,' said Baring, 'I'm surprised you can handle her so well on first acquaintance.'

'It must be my Cossack blood,' said the stranger.

Baring looked closely at the horseman who was about thirty and looked every bit an upper class Englishman and whose accent was perfect. There was nothing Cossack about the man.

'You don't look a Cossack to me,' he said.

'Appearances are deceptive, Comrade. One of my grandfathers came from Zaporozhy, and was a hundred percent Cossack.'

'Are you Russian?' Baring asked disingenuously.

'Of course. You musn't be misled by my appearance. I lived in England as a child. My parents were exiles.'

The two riders led the horses to a gate and tied them up so they could happily munch grass.

Baring was wary but fascinated.

'Where is your home now?' he asked.

'Just south of Leningrad. It was destroyed by the Germans. Actually I spend most of my time in Moscow. I'm special assistant to Beria.'

Baring affected not to understand.

'Beria has sent me here specifically to meet you. He would like to do so himself but travel outside the U.S.S.R. would be impossible for a man with so many enemies.'

'When did you return to the Soviet Union?'

'In 1935. I was fifteen. My father had a crisis of conscience. The pull of Mother Russia was too great for him. If it had been left to me I would have stayed here, but once in my homeland I felt the blood ties too.'

'Is your father still alive?'

'Yes. He's the senior electrical engineer on the Dneiper plant. He learnt his skills over here.'

'He wasn't a White Russian then.'

'Never a hard liner. They would have killed him if he had been and probably me too. I was a Marxist by conviction and that helped to save him. I went to Moscow University and graduated to the N.K.V.D. and became Beria's assistant for foreign operations. That's why I'm here.'

Baring still did not acknowledge the stranger's role. He acted as if they were discussing an innocent upbringing in the Home Counties and an education at an Oxford college rather than a training as a top spy.

'You can drop your guard, Comrade,' advised the stranger, 'I know more about you than you do yourself. Your file at the Lubyanka is very thick. We have every detail about your life, career, your loves.' He grinned knowledgeably, 'and of course we know you are going to America tomorrow.'

'How is Nina?' asked Baring, impetuously.

'Nina is dead, Comrade,' the stranger looked hard at him. 'She died of starvation in the siege of Leningrad. I didn't know her but everything I've read about her is very impressive. She was a good Comrade.'

'She was,' said Baring wistfully. Nina had been out of his life so long he could not mourn her as could some recent friend. She was a poignant memory who could never die.

'She was only one of the many we lost during the great patriotic war,' said the stranger, 'there were twenty million lives we sacrificed in the cause of socialism. In the West there is no idea of the dimension of that suffering.'

'The Jews understand it,' said Baring.

'Yes, the Jews understand it,' nodded the stranger, 'their losses were even greater proportionately than our's. They must have their own land to compensate for those deaths. Why are you stopping the Jews going to Palestine?' he suddenly asked.

Baring was taken aback.

'I feel deeply about such things,' explained the stranger 'my mother is Jewish.'

'I think the Jews should have their national home,' said Baring. 'It's the latter-day Colonel Lawrences and the other Arabists in the Foreign Office who have sabotaged the Balfour declaration.'

'The Jews will fight for their rights and they would be right to do so,' said the stranger.

'You know so much about me, but I don't even know your name,' said Baring.

'It's Yuri Orlenko,' said the young man, 'Captain in the N.K.V.D. and I have to inform you that you have been promoted to a full Colonel within my section. I am therefore your subordinate. But as my orders are direct from Beria I don't think you will want to disagree with them, Colonel.'

Baring felt a surge of pride that his status in the N.K.V.D.

had been recognised, although for all intents and purposes it was entirely academic.

Orlenko took off his riding cap and revealed a magnificent head of black hair. It was obvious he was not a pure Englishman. He had a magnificent body, lithe and firm. His face had a slightly tanned look and the classic features of a Greek; dark, flashing eyes showed an acute perception and intelligence. Baring could not see the Jewish streak in the man.

'Are you with Maisky at the Embassy?'

'No, I have no connection with the Embassy. I am here on a British passport.'

'Forged?'

'In a way. Two months ago I took over the identity of a Welshman called Morgan Lewis who died during the war. It was easy. Remember I lived in Britain with my parents until I was fifteen. I spoke Russian at home but nothing but English outside. We lived in Wales for a time when my father had a job at the Swansea docks and I can even speak a little Welsh. To everyone in this country I am Morgan Lewis. There's no way my cover could be broken.'

'Did Lewis have any family?' asked Baring.

'As far as we could gather his people were all killed in an air raid. They were in the Eastern End of London.'

'East End,' Baring corrected.

'Thanks for the guidance, Colonel,' Orlenko said graciously. 'I made that silly mistake at the briefing.'

'How long are you staying in Britain?'

'As long as necessary, probably about two years.'

'And your mission?'

'Espionage,' said Orlenko, in a matter of fact voice, especially industrial espionage. We are a backward industrial country. We realised that during the war when most of our equipment was inferior to the enemy's. Stalin is determined to build Socialism on a strong economic base and that means developing modern factories. We intend to take all the know-how we can get from the West.'

'Why are you telling me all this, Captain?'

'Beria told me to, Colonel. He wants you to understand the new direction of Soviet policy. We are no longer seeking the immediate overthrow of capitalism. We have suffered too much in the war. This is the time for consolidation of Soviet strength, the healing of our wounds for the next great leap forward. Stalin is a cautious man. He wants no hasty action.'

'And there is Eastern Europe to amalgamate,' said Baring.

'Not exactly amalgamate. Not as part of the U.S.S.R.' said Orlenko. We are establishing friendly governments from Poland to Bulgaria and Albania. They will appear to be independent but will be subservient to Moscow. There are some difficulties in Yugoslavia, where Tito beat the Germans without the help of the Red Army and in Czechoslovakia where the Communists have to share power with Masaryk's social democrats but,' he added in a matter of fact way, 'we shall remove him in due course.'

'And Germany?' asked Baring.

'Germany is interesting. Potsdam couldn't make a clear decision on Germany. It remains, as you know, under military occupation. The Americans want to unite it under their aegis but we won't allow that. We're holding on to East Germany and will set up a separate Communist state there including Berlin.'

'The whole of Berlin?'

'Yes the whole of Berlin. It falls in our zone.'

Orlenko looked at his expensive Swiss watch. 'How much time do you have?'

'About half an hour.'

'Then we must get down to business, Colonel. There is an important task for you to perform.'

'Yes?' said Baring, intrigued.

'Stalin is anxious to build up the Soviet aircraft industry but we are short of skilled designers. Our techniques are way behind the West. We must put our people into the British factories where they can learn the modern methods of design.

We need you to introduce one of our men into Vickers.'

'That won't be easy,' Baring warned.

'If you go about it the correct way it will very easy, Colonel,' Orlenko said firmly, 'the man we've earmarked is in America awaiting your visit. We sent him from Moscow with all the proper papers. His cover is that of an Englishman, evacuated as a boy to the U.S.A. at the beginning of the war, who is anxious to return to Britain to a good job.'

'He's a designer?'

'He'll have the papers and references to show he worked in a plant in Baltimore. He will approach you for help and you will recommend him to join the Vickers design team.'

'How will I contact him?'

'He will contact you at nine in the morning a week today, he will be in the foyer of the Plaza hotel in New York holding the *Wall Street Journal* and the latest *Look* magazine open at page seven. His English name is Peter Nicholson. He only knows you're a Director of Vickers. He's not aware of your true status.'

'Why the games with *Look* magazine, won't that make him suspicious?'

'That's for another contact he's to make. You're not to notice but it's a double check for you.'

'How did you know I was staying at the Plaza?'

'We know all about you, Colonel. We have to protect you. I shouldn't tell you this, but Beria thinks you're our most promising property in the West.'

'Do you have others?' Baring asked.

'Hundreds,' said Orlenko carelessly. 'They're in the Foreign Office, Home Office, in Parliament of course, and in Fleet Street and the Army. There are scientists in the research establishments working for us and even a few placements in the higher ranks of the Church of England.'

'Do I know any?'

'Of course, but it's our policy never to allow lateral contact except in dire emergencies. The horizontal chain of command protects agents from exposure if someone defects. Very few people know about you, Colonel,' Orlenko added. 'Besides Stalin and Beria, maybe four of five others besides myself.'

'Nicholai Yegorov is one of them I suppose. How is he?'

'He was purged in 1937 along with his uncle the Marshall Yegorov who was guilty of a plot on Stalin's life. Yegorov was a counter-revolutionary and a spy.'

'I don't believe it,' said Baring.

'It's true Colonel. Believe me it's not wise to question the justice of the Soviet system. Harsh decisions have to be taken to protect the State.'

'I understand,' said Baring resignedly. He desperately wanted to know the fates of Radek, Zinoviev, Chicherin and the other Russian leaders he knew, but was too cautious to ask.

CHAPTER 36

The United States was in the midst of a post war euphoria and Baring found the atmosphere happy and relaxed after depressing austerity-bound, beleaguered Britain. He was surprised and a little ashamed that he liked Capitalist America so much. The hospitality was brash and the American habit of addressing him as 'Charles' on first meeting irritating, but the reception was warm and kind. What appealed to him most was the vibrant energy shown by Americans at all levels. People seemed to be enjoying their work and this contrasted with the grey, burdensome atmosphere of Britain. Baring could not equate the picture he saw with the Marxist concept of downtrodden workers being paid survival wages but he rationalised that the U.S.A. was not in a slump, that he could only see a small part of a huge country and that the war economy had boosted activity. He knew from his readings that only five hundred families owned most of the wealth of America and that a handful of men wielded all the economic power. He concluded that the transfer of their wealth and power to the State, representing the community as a whole, plus the retention of the vibrancy, would create the ideal Communist society.

Revolution arising out of class confrontation, however, was not a likely prospect. America was too open a society. The frontier mentality was still evident with everyone trying to make the most of their lives and acting dynamically rather than passively. What was certain was that America would be a hard nut to crack for communism. He wondered how far the Russians had realised this and were adopting a strategy of infiltration. However one looked at it, changes in the structure of the nation would take years.

Baring met Peter Nicholson, an eager young man anxious to show his credentials and proud of his bogus record, who would easily pass as an ordinary Englishman who had picked up traces of an American accent. Baring was impressed with the way Soviet intelligence trained its operatives and undertook to pass Nicholson's application to the Vickers design team. There was little doubt they would recruit him.

After a hectic, invigorating six weeks in America crossing the country by trains, luxurious in comparison to the dowdy British variety, and culminating in a visit to the dream city of Hollywood, the liveliest place he had ever known, Baring returned to a Britain where the cars were smaller, the buildings smaller and horizons were definitely more restricted. On the voyage from New York in the Queen Mary there had been plenty of time for reflection. Baring, approaching fifty, had realised his attitudes had altered, or as he preferred to understand it, matured. Driving through drab Southampton on his way to Amesbury confirmed his feelings. Britain exhibited all the signs of decay. Compared to America it was only half-alive. War had sapped its strength but there was more to it than that. There was a deadening of the spirit which could no longer dispel the mustiness from the past which permeated everything.

By the time he arrived at the estate he was in a very depressed mood and his greeting to Anne was curt and indifferent. She had given up expecting him to show warm emotions towards her but this effront after a long absence was more than she could bear. She retreated to her bedroom suite for the rest of the day to sob and sew and to listen to the B.B.C.'s Home Service.

Baring never ventured to his wife's rooms and she never intruded on his solitude in the library. It was his citadel; there he felt protected from the dilemmas of the times although he knew in his heart he would soon have to work out a strategy.

Whilst the war was on there was the demanding imperative of defeating the Nazi enemy but that discipline was no longer available. His previously held view about revolution following industrial chaos was also no longer tenable. There could be no revolution whilst the Labour Government under Attlee was giving the workers a new deal. There was no parallel with the Kerensky situation in 1917. The Attlee Government was entrenched for five years and would probably be elected for another five. There could be a long wait for political office and what could he do in the meantime? Baring was perplexed.

His convictions about changing the structure of society within a few years and substituting a benevolent dictatorship of wise men who could impose the concepts of equality had evaporated. In their place was a dirty residue, a mishmash of disjointed ideas which did not add up to a coherent philosophy. He hankered after an authoritative system and despised the dullness and inefficiency of democracy. The Soviet system still offered the best solution but it was no longer as clear-cut or as idealistic as he had known it years before.

To alleviate his indecision and boredom he took a book from the packed shelves of little-read books. It was Churchill's *My Early Life.* He flipped the pages until his eye caught some passage attacking the idea of granting votes to all and sundry. Churchill looked back with nostalgia to the days before universal suffrage when 'we had a real political democracy, led by the hierarchy of statesmen and not a fluid mass distracted by newspapers.' Baring read on, fascinated by Churchill's thoughts which so clearly corresponded with his own. He caught a telling phrase about the dangerous 'liquefaction of the British political system' and suddenly realised that Churchill himself would have made an excellent Communist leader: strong, benevolent, wise and having no truck with the excesses of democracy and thinking this he fell asleep in the deep armchair.

Out of Parliament and without influence Baring found his circle of friends and contacts had dwindled. Leading political figures hardly ever accepted invitations to dinner and Sussex Sqaure became a mortuary where ghosts and memories were the only company for the ex-Minister and the ex-Member for West Middlesex. Baring saw little point in extending his hospitality to the second-raters or to the butterfly-set who skipped from one host to another, guzzling free hospitality without giving anything in return. He found no compensations in his occasional visits to the companies which had made him a name-only director. The full-time managers regarded him as a useless ornament whose advice, if proffered, was politely listened to but quickly ignored. The real power in the companies was in the hands of the Chairman and the Managing Director and the boards were little better than rubber-stamps for their decisions. Baring used the companies as mercilessly as they milked the advantage of his waning name. It was not a fruitful relationship.

During the last months of 1945 Baring became more listless and depressed. He felt old and rejected. His life had run out of steam and other men had more than filled the roles he would have performed if the electors of West Middlesex had not rejected him so cruelly. Men like Richard (Rab) Butler, who had married Courtauld money and made a name as a reforming Minister of Education, were crowding the front ranks of the Tory party. In November, Harold Macmillan, a leading publisher who had married the daughter of the Duke of Devonshire, returned to Parliament in a by-election at Bromley and soon made it obvious he was still of front-bench calibre. Baring realised there was little hope for his political career unless he too could secure a seat through a by-election and get back to the centre of the action. Getting one was another story. Churchill, as Leader of the Opposition, could contrive to create vacancies by nominating Members in safe constituencies to the House of Lords but in the post-war climate there was no guarantee that associations would adopt the nominee from party headquarters. The wave of populism which had swept the Labour Party to power had infected the party of privilege. Ordinary party members of constituencies were demanding their own say and many had their own ambitions to sit on the green benches.

By the end of the nineteen-forties Baring felt his chances of ever again reaching Ministerial office had ebbed to the lowest point. The receding tide of adventure had left a thick mud of his accumulated thoughts. There was nothing to hide or to stir the sticky mess. The great dreams of his youth, the hopes that a revolutionary change could be engineered, were, as poppies picked on the Flanders' fields, dead before their beauty could be appreciated. Dreams and ambitions which once smelt so sweet were like decaying refuse left on the mud bank by the streams which had found somewhere else to flow.

It made matters worse when Lady Anne's health deteriorated. Her inability to understand her husband or even communicate with him built up terrible frustrations causing a succession of illnesses. The doctors in Amesbury and at the Infirmary in Salisbury recognised the symptoms of asthma and prescribed pills and sprays of varying ineffectiveness. A specialist in Harley Street did no better, although his fees were five times greater, and her condition worsened month by month. Eventually she was taken to St. Bartholomew's Hospital where isolation and treatment under a tent provided some alleviation, but whenever Charles visited her a relapse followed. Her brother, the Duke of Dorset, who understood more of the problem than the medical profession could see, insisted she went to his estate at Dorchester and he stopped Charles visiting her. Lady Anne's health improved but, left to his own devices and by now a very lonely man, Charles's despair grew until the heaviness of the depression was unbearable.

Respite came from time to time in the person of Morgan Lewis, the egregious Welshman who was better known in

Moscow as Yuri Orlenko. He visited Amesbury every other month and occasionally met Baring at Sussex Square. The relationship Baring had with this controller was freer than he had known with any of the earlier representatives of the Soviet secret service.

As he was not part of the diplomatic mission Orlenko was certain he was never under surveillance. His cover was totally successful. Morgan Lewis had established a wide basis of acceptance within English society by buying himself a house in Blackheath in south London and joining the local organisations — including the Conservative Party — and by setting up a company exporting British tools and equipment. His long stay in Britain from infancy to teenage gave him fluency and ease in English which no Russian, however well trained in the N.K.V.D. schools, could ever achieve.

Orlenko enjoyed the best of both worlds. He basked in the confidence of the Communist leaders in his patriotism but he did not have to pay the price by suffering the privations of post-war Communism.

Orlenko, alias Lewis, noticed Baring's disturbed state, his unhappiness and frustration, and the Russian was clever enough to use these weaknesses to gain a greater hold over him. Technically Baring was Orlenko's superior within the Ministry for State Security — the M.G.B. — in which they were both serving officers, but the Russian, as a fervent nationalist, regarded any foreigner as inferior. Baring's obvious incapacity to cope with the frustrations brought on by the lull in his political ambitions gave Orlenko an enhanced sense of superiority. Over the months and the years of their association he gradually consolidated his grip over the vulnerable Englishman.

Baring was vulnerable to Orlenko's influence as the Russian was the only person in England to know about the Baring dual personality. Orlenko, although a much younger man, became the ex-Cabinet Minister's virtual Father Confessor.

One evening after a quiet dinner at Sussex Square the two men adjourned to the library. The surroundings were as elegant as they had ever been in Lady Anne's days of superb entertaining. The servants had ensured that standards had not fallen. The rosewood furniture sparkled from the frequent polishing with Johnson's, and the antique brandy glasses glinted in the light from the smokeless fuel fire in the grate. The butler served the Hine and cigars, snipped with the silver cutters, and withdrew deferentially. Nothing secret or of any consequence was discussed before the Cognac to avoid any danger that the servants would pick up something suspicious about the frequent visitor. As far as they were concerned he was a Mr. Lewis who was important in the export trade and a valued helping hand to the master in his business activities.

Orlenko settled on the long settee and put his head on the high cushion, taking long puffs at his cigar from the half-reclining position.

'Colonel,' he said after a long silence, 'there's a great deal to be said for this way of life. I doubt if it's matched in the Kremlin.'

'It's comfortable enough,' grunted Baring, 'but it doesn't give the satisfaction Stalin, Molotov and Beria must feel in running the socialist sixth of the world. Sometimes I think I could die from boredom.'

'Your chance will come, Colonel. It's only a matter of a few years before the Soviet policy of building internally is translated into external expansion. The threats from the capitalist states will only be eliminated when they are eliminated. Stalin knows that. When the policy changes the countries opposing the U.S.S.R. will collapse like cardboard houses built without foundations. Britain will be among the first. I can assure you, Colonel, that your role will be vital. Beria has told me that he expects to appoint you to be the first President of the Combined English, Welsh and Scottish Soviets.'

Baring put his cigar in a large onyx ashtray, meaning to light it again later, and sat crouched with his hands tensed between his knees. He said, 'I hope it can come soon. This waiting is a great strain.'

'Look what we did in Czechoslovakia. The country was ripe for picking as the Communists were in the government and Masaryk could easily be overthrown. It will take longer here as the Communist Party is a washout and can never win elections or claim a place in government. The best strategy is to work through the confrontation of Capital and Labour to achieve the collapse of the British economy. We're getting Communists into positions in the Labour Party and the Trade Unions and from there they will be able to persuade the lazy British worker to demand more for doing less. They will say nothing about higher output being the precondition for higher pay. They will spread the falsehood that money is in unlimited supply and that strikes, go-slows and those other lovely idiosyncrasies of the British industrial scene can make life better for the workers.'

'That's a recipe for industrial collapse,' said Baring.

'Exactly,' replied Orlenko with a grin, 'in the Soviet Union or one of our satellites anyone suggesting they should get more money for less work would be shot as a traitor. Here in Britain our Communists within the Labour movement will be honoured for preaching just that line.'

'The leaders of the National Union of Mineworkers have been calling for more coal to help the national effort. What do you think of that?' asked Baring.

'They are the old-fashioned leaders still thinking in patriotic terms. Our people in the embassy are financing some of the militants to get into the miners' regional committees to fight against that policy. If other trades unions followed the N.U.M. example the Attlee Government would succeed and we'd never achieve the collapse of the economy. All our work would have been wasted. The patriotic leaders have to be exposed as the handmaidens of capitalism.'

'Even with the coal mines already under state ownership?' asked Baring who was slowing, sinking into an alcoholic stupor after his third brandy.

'The nationalisation of the mines has to be dismissed as merely state capitalism,' Orlenko said with fervour. 'If the workers once accepted it as a step towards socialism through democratic means our task of creating a revolution would become impossible.'

'What about the colonies they are bolstering up Britain.'

'Yes, the colonies are being raped by the Imperial power. They provide cheap raw materials and a tied market for British goods. Without them the British economy would be fifty per cent weaker. The tin and rubber from Malaya sold to America provides the dollars for British luxury imports from the United States. That's all the trick of the Sterling area. We're training agitators to change all that. They will fight for freedom and destroy the Empire,' Orlenko sneered. 'The loss of India is but the first step. It was the brightest jewel in the British crown. Now its impossible for Nehru to hold it together; it will go Communist just as our ally China has.'

'And Africa?' asked Baring.

'Gold Coast, Nigeria, Sudan, Kenya, Rhodesia,' Orlenko rattled off the names, 'must all be wrenched from Britain. Within ten years from now they'll all be independent and under our influence. We've set up a special University in Moscow to train their leaders; we don't want them learning silly ideas about bourgeois government from Laski at the L.S.E.'

The two men, sprawled on the settees with the abandon of the most effete fops of the Regency, were not aware of the words/action contrast their conduct implied. 'I think,' said Orlenko, 'that this mighty, arrogant country can be brought to its knees within a decade.'

'A long time to wait,' complained Baring, 'I'll be sixty by then.'

'If you Conservatives win the next election you can help

speed up the collapse. If you give in to wage demands you'll break British industry and if you give away the colonies you'll break British Imperialism faster than we can. Then Britain will be ripe for revolution before you're sixty and we can make you our Commissar for the Soviets while you're still young enough to be effective.'

Orlenko stood unsteadily to toast Baring's success, but as he tilted the brandy glass to allow liquid to flow into his gullet he lost balance and fell backwards letting the glass smash against the bookshelves.

Although shaken he still managed to say, 'There's good luck for you, Colonel; toasts are only effective if the glass is sacrificed.'

The glow of hope, induced by liquor and brave talk, had diluted Baring's blood and his mental depression. With some effort he raised his heavy body and picked up the antique glass to down the Hine more expertly than his guest.

'To the revolution,' he shouted, as he smashed the glass into the dying embers of the fire.

CHAPTER 37

Like a dried-out alcoholic grasping a bottle of whisky after severe withdrawal symptoms, Baring welcomed the general election of 1950 with excessive enthusiasm. The electors of West Middlesex had never known an onslaught like it. Baring canvassed personally in every street of the huge, now wholly urbanised, constituency and would have visited every house if the campaign could have lasted longer than three weeks. In sixty schoolroom and town hall meetings, at the rate of three an evening, he attacked the Attlee Government for failing to develop Britain and for imposing bureaucratic controls. 'Set the people free' was his call which had the small shopkeepers and commuting businessmen howling their support.

He accepted a few invitations to speak in neighbouring constituencies for appearances sake but refused all attempts to persuade him to go further afield. During the five long years he was out of the House he had been ignored by erstwhile colleagues who had left him to rot whilst they enjoyed their Parliamentary games. Bitter feelings of rejection had curdled into a sour spirit of selfish resolve.

Lady Anne attended her husband's formal adoption meeting and graced a few of his platforms. His new energy and purpose was infectious and she found it easier to cope with her own psychosomatic illness in the midst of the exciting activity especially when it pointed to a recall to the centre of the political and social stage. She knew that if Churchill became Prime Minister again Charles would certainly get a Ministry and it would be like old times. They would have a common interest again.

Anne Baring had long given up trying to fathom her partner's strange nature which was too deep to explore, like the depths of the ocean. She now accepted that splashing on the surface of her husband's life was all she would ever be allowed to do.

Woman's intuition warned her that Morgan Lewis, one of the business associates who turned up to help in the campaign, was far closer to Charles than ever she could be. She toyed with the idea that Charles's problem was repressed homosexuality and that his relationship with the young Welshman released some of the tension. She rejected this theory on discovering that his heterosexual affairs were as active as ever. It seemed odd to her that Lewis had managed to worm his way into Charles's confidence. Asking Charles about the man only produced bland, unhelpful replies.

After two recounts the Returning Officer declared Baring elected with a majority of 51. He politely proposed a vote of thanks to the mayor and the officials and thanked his own supporters. The defeated Labour M.P. politely seconded and was followed by the Liberal candidate. The Communist, who came bottom of the poll and lost his deposit with only 190 votes, cast convention out of the window and launched into a vicious attack on the Press and the B.B.C. as well as his opponents. It was unsportsmanlike but no one stopped him. Yuri Orlenko, attending the count as a teller, caught Baring's eye and winked.

Baring returned to the Middlesex Conservative Club for a celebration accompanied by Lady Anne. She found herself talking with Morgan Lewis and asked, 'Did you enjoy the campaign?'

'It was great fun, especially with such a close result. I come from South Wales where the majorities are in their thousands.'

'I thought everyone was Labour there.'

'Most, but not everyone. My family were always Tories. They had no time for the firebrands like Nye Bevan and Jim Griffiths.'

At the Club the steward's wireless gave the results as they arrived at the B.B.C. and these were passed quickly from ear to ear. At the end of the long day they called on the victor of West Middlesex to have the last word. Charles Baring, M.P., was hoisted onto the stage and the noise subsided.

'Friends,' he said, 'we have won a great victory here tonight. We have turned back the socialist tide. All over the country people have been giving their verdict on the Labour government which has given India to the barbarians and destroyed initiative at home. With my dear wife's support,' he paused to smile at Anne by his side and to give time for the crowd to applaud, 'I have been proud to be your standard bearer. I am proud of the work you have done for our victory. We must pray that Winston Churchill has the majority he needs to throw Attlee and his bag and baggage out of Number 10. So far the results are good but all will depend on the declarations being made tomorrow. Let us give three cheers for a Tory victory and no more socialism.'

In the hubbub Yuri Orlenko took Baring's arm and squeezed it in congratulation. 'Good show,' he said insidiously, 'you made that speech as if you really meant it. I'm very impressed.'

'The play-acting becomes easier the more you do it,' said Baring in a burst of candour.

Next day it became clear that the Conservatives had not won their victory and Attlee carried on with a tiny majority and a team of dispirited Ministers. Churchill, as Opposition Leader, gave Baring a front bench appointment with a wide ranging brief covering industry and commerce and the shadow Minister threw himself into Parliamentary activity. In some ways it was better than government as the game could be played with a certain amount of irresponsibility. He enjoyed using devious tactics to delay Bills and to expose Ministerial incompetence although he appreciated the enormous burdens his opponents had to carry. But democratic politics, he had learnt, were not about understanding or rationality. It was a cruel brash business where every possible advantage was seized to harry and embarrass one's opponents. Baring was determined to be ruthless. The memory of five wasted years was a goad on his back pressing him into ever more frenetic attacks on the Labour Party. The backbench Tories loved him for it and within a few months Baring found he had a coterie of Parliamentary admirers made up of genuine supporters as well as opportunistic place seekers. He did not discourage them as it would be good for his standing with Churchill to show he had as much support in the House as Rab Butler or Harold Macmillan.

Yuri Orlenko spent most of his time in Britain monitoring the work of Colonel Charles Baring, but occasionally went abroad on business, travelling on his Morgan Lewis passport. His export business with Eastern Europe provided a ready excuse for journeys to Leipzig, Prague and Warsaw. Once in Eastern Europe he contacted the M.V.D. resident and obtained the documents to switch to his Russian identity. Then he could reach Moscow quickly to consult Beria. The Kremlin were pleased with his work and secretly awarded him the Order of the Red Banner.

As one of their most trusted agents there was no intention to withdraw him from his mission in England. The British Secret Intelligence noticed that Morgan Lewis was making frequent trips to Eastern Europe and ran a security check over him. They found that his Welsh background was impeccable and his export business viable. There was nothing in his political background to suggest left-wing sympathies and Lewis's active membership of the Blackheath Conservative association confirmed him as reliable person.

He was asked to lunch at the Savoy Grill one day by a shadowy character who claimed to know about certain export prospects. Over coffee hints were dropped which Lewis did not discourage. He was than taken to an office near St. James's Park station and invited to become an undercover agent for MI6. Lewis demurred at first, protesting that he was merely a businessman without any interest in international politics and fearful that his work would suffer. After appeals to his patriotism and a guarantee that there was no real risk, he was eventually recruited as a courier and a low level spy.

Orlenko welcomed the appointment as it confirmed the impregnability of his British cover. It would also give him an insight into MI6 methods and some valuable details of the British intelligence network in Eastern Europe. Moscow was delighted. When, in the following year, the Conservatives won the General Election that Attlee had called prematurely, Baring was a natural choice for an inner Cabinet appointment. His standing in the party was high and he had proved himself in Parliamentary performance. Churchill also had an affectionate regard for the man who had helped him in the General Strike and had stood by him during the lean political years. Baring's investment had paid off; he again found himself surrounded by the trappings of power and able to influence events directly. It was intoxicating and invigorating. Gone completely were the depressions of the late nineteen-forties and gone were the withdrawal symptoms plaguing him during nightmares and waking hours. The flurry of Ministerial meetings, Parliamentary debates, Conferences and overseas deputations kept the momentum of activity moving at such a rate that he had no time to worry.

Yuri Orlenko was able to keep in close touch with the Minister. It helped that the Morgan Lewis export business with Eastern Europe prospered. His agency pulled off a number of valuable deals and a dozen major British companies appointed Lewis as their agent. It was remarkable how Lewis succeeded where others had failed and export managers concluded that somehow he had discovered a way of bribing the officials of the State purchasing commissions. It was generally believed that Lewis had become a multimillionaire and his purchase of a huge mansion in Berkshire lent currency to the story. The *Daily Herald* and the *Daily Mail* printed articles about the poor Welsh boy who had made good, and played up his contribution to winning exports for British industry. The British Institute of Management invited him to address its conferences and Heinemann commissioned a book to be ghosted for Lewis entitled *Exporting is Fun.*

When Charles Baring took over the Board of Trade in Churchill's first reshuffle, one of his first acts was to appoint an advisory committee on exports with Morgan Lewis as its first chairman. As a result Minister and advisor were able to have official meetings whenever they felt like them. Baring often visited the Lewis mansion and when Lewis married a pretty Swedish au pair girl, Mr. and Mrs. Charles Baring were among the many guests at the Lutheran church in Uppsala. No one found it strange that a close friendship had grown up between one of Churchill's most dynamic Ministers and the successful businessman who epitomised the type of initiative the Tory Party advocated.

Stalin's death in March 1953 caused a turmoil in the Kremlin and after three months Yuri Orlenko was recalled to Moscow along with other overseas agents. He covered his tracks with the British intelligence Service, ostensibly by going on a long holiday with his new Swedish wife to visit her relatives. When he reported to Dzerzhinsky Square he found Beria in a very dejected state. After a giving a brief report on Britain in which Beria showed little interest, Orlenko was surprised to hear him utter, 'The revisionists have seized power and Malenkov is their tool. I shall have to use the power of our Ministry of State Security to reverse this and restore Stalinist authority without Stalin. The State will disintegrate if it does not have firm leadership. My duty is obvious. I shall have to take over.'

'Are you sure you can succeed?' asked Orlenko.

Have I ever failed?' said Beria, 'he who controls the secret police controls Russia. I know everything my opponents are planning, my agents are everywhere and I can pre-empt them. Needless to say,' he added with a smile, 'my trusted aides like you can expect promotion.'

For three days Orlenko struggled with his conscience and the assessment of his own self-interest before making his decision. Stalin was dead and people wanted a change. Beria was one of the most hated men in the world. It was unlikely he would survive, and even if he did, Orlenko had no wish to transfer his life from the comfortable secure world of the millionaire Morgan Lewis to the tension-ridden and dangerous existence of an official in the Soviet Union. The attractions of power were heady but the sacrifice was too great.

Next weekend Orlenko drove to the country and used his Ministry State Security pass to get through the guards at Nikita Khrushchev's dacha. He chose to visit the second most powerful man rather than the new leader as Malenkov was surrounded by Beria's men and had a reputation for being indecisive. If any hint of his treachery got back to Beria, Orlenko knew his life would not last longer than a candle in a snowstorm. Khrushchev was in the garden of the dacha picking flowers and when Orlenko was identified by his escorts the Politbureau member dismissed them curtly and turned to his visitor with curiosity.

'Why do you come to see me on my holiday, Comrade? Is there no peace for the leaders in this country. I was told you hold a top category pass and only for that reason did I agree to see you. State your business. I hope it's interesting and important because I might be angry.' He laughed heartily showing his gold teeth.

Orlenko started diffidently. 'I know how valuable your time is Comrade leader and would not have come except the matter concerns the security of the nation and the integrity of the Revolution.'

'You sound like a farmyard cock at dawn. I have no time for

pretty little speeches,' said Khrushchev putting his arms akimbo.

'Beria is planning to take over the State by an armed insurrection next week. You, Malenkov and other Politbureau members are to be arrested as anti-Stalinists and counter-revolutionaries.' Before Orlenko could continue, Khrushchev exploded in rage.

'May that evil genius be drowned in pig shit,' he shouted, that son of a Georgian whore won't succeed. I'll get him first. Come with me,' he gestured to Orlenko, 'we're going to discuss this further in the privacy of my study.'

'I wouldn't advise that, Comrade leader,' said Orlenko holding his ground. Beria has your dacha bugged with new listening devices. Tiny microphones which are undetectable except by the experts.'

'I know what they are, you fool, but how could Beria get them into my dacha?' Khrushchev bellowed.

'The State Security people have all Politbureau members under daily surveillance. It's supposed to be for your protection. In fact Beria uses it to maintain power.'

'The dirty cunning weasel. I suppose you'll be telling me the head of my guard is under Beria's orders.'

'He is. And the routine report will go back that I've visited you. It would be wise if you acted quickly, Comrade leader.'

'We're going to Moscow, Orlenko. We'll waste no more time in prattling.'

In his black limousine Khrushchev ordered the chauffeur to drive the thirty versts into the capital at breakneck speed. Before leaving he cut the telephone lines and ordered all the guards to remain together in the dacha under threat of liquidation if any of them left. 'There's a traitor in our midst,' he hollered, leaving the guards with their guns cocked waiting for one of their number to make a false move.

In the car Khrushchev took a swig of vodka from the cabinet and soon regained his composure. He asked Orlenko about his job within the Ministry. When the agent explained he whistled under his breath. 'So you are controlling a British Cabinet Minister,' he gasped. 'I know we have spies in the Foreign Office and in Buckingham Palace but a Conservative Minister! That is like telling me Rasputin was a Bolshevik!'

'Baring's been a Bolshevik for twenty-five years,' Orlenko said, longer than some of our Russian comrades. He knew Lenin and Trotsky. Trotsky had to be eliminated because he was threatening to tell the Americans about Baring.'

'So that's why Stalin did it,' Khrushchev mused. 'He never told us.'

The car reached the outskirts of Moscow and sped towards Red Square. Traffic on the warm Sunday in June was heavier than usual but quickly gave way when the limousine's siren sounded its approach. Muscovites knew the noise of a Politbureau's vehicle and always gave it a wide berth.

Khrushchev asked, 'What were Beria's orders to you?'

'To remain in Moscow and wait for the coup and then I would get a top position.'

'Beria's a moujik idiot. Your job's in England. You're the best man to control that English Minister. Beria's a fool to withdraw you; but the traitor won't survive. Comrade Captain,' he said more thoughtfully, 'you must leave Moscow immediately and return to London.'

'But Beria expects me to stay.'

Khrushchev exploded, 'What Beria wants is neither here nor there. That man's as dead as the bear I shot last month in the Ukraine. Tomorrow morning at dawn we arrest him and all his aides. If you don't want to get caught in that net you'd better leave tonight. I'll give you a note of authority in case anyone tries to stop you.' Khrushchev took a sheaf of paper from the cabinet, pulled down the flap and wrote clumsily in an untidy hand made worse by the movement of the car.

'There, Comrade Captain, take this and get back to London. I will need to use you there one day so you must save your skin now. Believe me Beria's people will be skinned alive in the next few weeks,' he chuckled, 'you'll be well out of it.'

Before the car reached the Kremlin it pulled over to let Orlenko out at an underground station. The crowd milling at the entrance stared at the limousine in respectful silence as Orlenko strolled through. It was important to move quickly. He went directly to his quarters to collect his things and although he remembered that he had left the Ministry car at Khrushchev's, he rejected it as unimportant. It was vital to get on the overnight train to Leningrad en route to Finland and Stockholm. He was relieved not to be sucked into the maelstrom of Moscow. For all its faults capitalist London was a more tranquil place.

CHAPTER 38

As a member of Churchill's inner Cabinet, rated as number four in the hierarchy, the Right Honourable Charles Baring, M.C., M.P. had much to celebrate on his fifty-sixth birthday. Lady Anne had fully recovered from her various illnesses and was playing her part as a political hostess with grace and charm. Few of the many guests who enjoyed the dinner parties at Sussex Square or the weekends at Amesbury would have suspected that relations between the Barings were formal and frigid. In company they treated each other with the considerate care which comes with an intelligent understanding of the crude value of a marriage's appearances. They each had an investment in an asset they could not afford to lose. For Lady Anne it was respectability, acceptance by the Conservative establishment and most important, an entry to the circles surrounding the Queen. For Charles it was all of that, plus the prospects of the highest office, which was not likely to go to a man with a scandal in the cupboard.

In November Winston Churchill invited the Barings to his eightieth birthday celebrations at Number 10 and in a frank moment he said to Charles, 'I feel like an aeroplane at the end of its flight, in the dusk, with the petrol running out, in search of a safe landing.' Clearly the old war horse was getting tired and his resignation was expected but later in the evening after the enormous cake had been cut and the Champagne toasts drunk, he took Baring into a corner of the large sitting room and plonked him down in an armchair, brandishing a cigar in his right hand. 'Sit down there,' he commanded, 'I want to tell you my secret.'Baring bent over so the Prime Minister could speak without shouting against a background of cocktail cackle, but Churchill still boomed in a voice everyone within three feet could hear. 'I've decided to hang on until next April before I resign, dear Charles. I know Anthony's expecting to take over but I doubt that he's ready for it yet. Frankly I'd prefer you to be my successor but the Party expects Eden, so I'll have no alternative but to recommend him to the Queen, unless his illness becomes obvious during the next few months.'

'Illness?' said Baring. It was news to him.

'A rare nervous complaint,' Churchill cautiously moderated his voice. 'It affects his judgement. Naturally we have to keep it quiet for the sake of the Government, and,' he smiled, 'I've had to be kind to him since he married Jack's daughter.'

Next year on 5th April Baring attended the last Cabinet presided over by Churchill. It was a moving occasion as members took turns in order of seniority to pay tribute to the leader who had led the nation to victory in war. There were few compliments about his contribution to the peace, but Baring in his remarks drew attention to the Prime Minister's noble stand against the Bolshevik menace. Sir Anthony Eden's suave voice during his short speech had the confident tone of a man who knew he was about to be called to Buckingham Palace to take over the seals of office fulfilling an ambition long denied.

Baring was offered and accepted the renewal of his post in the Eden government and this was confirmed after the General Election which Eden soon called and which the Conservatives won with a handsome majority.

Within a few days of the appointment of the new Cabinet Yuri Orlenko called on Baring at Sussex Square. Alone together, as Lady Anne was in the country and the resident servants were downstairs in their quarters, they were able to talk freely.

'Khrushchev is very anxious for you to take over the

Foreign Ministry. We are facing trouble with Poland and Yugoslavia. America with Dulles as Secretary of State is trying to redraw the agreed map of Europe. He's involved with groups who see a divine mission in converting communists to capitalism. If you were British Foreign Secretary you could redress the balance. We wouldn't want you to withdraw from NATO. It would be better to sabotage it from within while we're going through this crisis.'

'Eden likes running foreign policy himself. The chap he's got there at the moment suits him because he's a cypher.'

'A cypher?'

'Does what he's told. I would be too independent for Eden. Behind that elegant and charming exterior he's a very vain and arrogant man.'

'So we've noticed,' said Orlenko.

'Is Khrushchev firmly in control?' asked Baring.

'Yes, Malenkov was too weak. Nikita is a crude peasant type but he has a firm grip on policy. I report to him now. I was made one of the five most senior K.G.B. officers in recognition of my work. We each have direct access to the first Secretary of the Party. It's a device to prevent the K.G.B. Chairman getting too much personal power as Beria did.'

'What about Bulganin?'

'He's a makeweight figurehead. Khrushchev has the power.'

Baring collected the bottle of Courvoisier cognac from the cabinet and poured a generous tot into Orlenko's balloon glass.

'I find this more intoxicating than vodka,' said Orlenko, 'maybe it's because I've preferred to let my hair down here than in Moscow.'

'Are you more relaxed than at home?'

'There is the feeling in Russia that one is being watched all the time. Always one has to be on the alert. It can be wearing on the nerves.'

'I wouldn't like it I must say,' said Baring, as Orlenko went on.

'It's not as bad in England. When you reach a certain status in this country it's assumed you're loyal and the special branch leave you alone. Take Maclean and Burgess. Because they held high positions in the F.O. and came from the right backgrounds they were beyond suspicion. Same with Philby. In Russia it's the other way round. The higher you get the more suspicions are aroused. All the top people spy on each other. It's crazy . . .' but before he could continue Baring's mind cleared momentarily and he interrupted.

'What did you say about Philby?'

'Philby, oh Philby. He's our man in the Foreign Office. When you become Foreign Secretary you'll work with him. He's expected to become head of the MI6.'

'Really,' said Baring making a mental note, 'are there any others I should know about?'

'There are a dozen in the F.O. but I'm not supposed to tell you about them. You know our policy. We keep our agents' identities secret from one another to protect them from defectors.'

'You're not expecting me to defect surely?' said Baring.

'No, I'm not expecting you to sign your own death warrant.'

Baring remained silent for a full minute and then said pathetically

'I should have thought I've established my loyalty by now.'

'I've no doubt of it, Comrade,' said Orlenko, 'and nor has Khrushchev. During your election I was in Moscow and I gave him a full report. He is very pleased.

'That's good. So maybe you could begin trusting me' said Baring.

'Of course we trust you,' said Orlenko, misunderstanding the meaning of Baring's remark, 'in fact I had your office and home bugged so we could check on you and you came through with flying colours.'

'I thought you said there was no surveillance here.'

'I meant by your Government. My people did a search and

there wasn't a single device located. You're clean.'

'That's good to know,' Baring said sardonically, 'but what do you mean by "your people"?'

'I use a few of the G.P.O. engineers who service your telephones to plant our bugs and check for others. They're experts those chaps and they do it for a few pounds, no questions asked. They're unlikely to tell anyone they're fiddling the income tax; and of course,' he added 'they get into every office in the country.'

'The Prime Minister's?'

'Of course; that's been bugged for some time. The others we do from time to time to make sure we know their secrets.'

'You sound very efficient.'

'We have to be.'

'But you're not bugging me now?'

'No, Colonel.'

'That's nice to know.'

'About the Foreign Secretaryship; Khrushchev particularly asked me . . .' Baring felt his anger rising; he did not like being spied on.

'Khrushchev can bluster until he's as red as a Ukrainian beetroot but he can't expect me to become Foreign Secretary just like that. It depends on the P.M. and frankly I'd prefer to take over that job from him than be his dogsbody.'

'Take over?' said Orlenko in surprise, 'but you're the same age as Eden. He won't retire in a hurry and some of your Prime Ministers go on until they're eighty.'

'Eden's not a well man. Churchill told me that; if I play my cards right I can edge Eden out. The trick will be to find an issue on which his health will completely break. Tell your friend Khrushchev to be patient; I can be more than Foreign Secretary.'

'Just as you say,' said Orlenko, re-lighting his cigar slowly. 'You're the Colonel to my Captain so you have the last word.'

When Bulganin and Khrushchev came to London in the following year, Baring met them at an official reception at

Claridges. Khrushchev was extremely affable but did not betray a hint of recognition during the evening but as Baring left the reception, following Eden, the First Secretary of the Soviet Communist Party grabbed him warmly by the hand, and said, 'Give my warm greetings to Erik Andersen won't you Minister.'

In June Charles took Anne to the 400 Club in Leicester Square to a party to celebrate the club's twenty-first birthday. Lady Anne was with friends, the Duchess of Argyll, Lord and Lady Derby, the Duke of Devonshire and other luminaries from the aristocracy, but Charles found their company insufferable, bearing it bravely as a way of thanking his wife for her understanding over the difficult past five years. He was happy enough with his marriage which provided everything he needed apart from sex. He was happy too with the way the Cabinet was shaping, especially as he felt certain he had found a way of toppling Eden. Life was better than he had known it for a long time.

Gamal Abdel Nasser's threats to take over the Suez canal were providing just the excuse he wanted to push Eden into a Middle Eastern adventure which would almost certainly go wrong.

At Baring's next meeting with Yuri Orlenko he also picked up some valuable information which fitted in with his developing plan. Orlenko said, 'I've seen the text of Nikita Khrushchev's speech to the Twentieth Congress; it's devastating. What's worse is that reports of the speech have leaked to other communist countries and they're getting restive.'

'I've heard the rumours,' said Baring.

'The speech is supposed to be secret but, of course, we've got it in the K.G.B. Khrushchev has attacked Stalin bitterly. We all know that Stalin and Beria were guilty of terrible crimes but revealing the truth is having the opposite effect to that intended. Khrushchev expected greater unity and loyalty with this burst of honesty but, instead, the sudden sense of freedom to criticise is making many people restless — especially the Poles. They're the most difficult of all as Catholicism and Communism don't mix.'

'What is Khrushchev doing about it?'

'He wants you to help, Colonel,' said Orlenko, 'the First Secretary much admires your political skill and he says that meeting you was the highlight of his London visit. He prefers Conservatives to the likes of George Brown and you're his favourite.'

'He'd read my file.'

'Yes and he knows you're totally reliable. He says the present situation in Eastern Europe is extremely dangerous so he needs Britain and France to get involved in a war in the Middle East to produce a distraction. We're working on Mollet and that's going well but we must have Britain involved too.'

Baring smiled. 'I seem to be on the same wavelength as Khrushchev; I was thinking on the same lines.'

'That's good. What we need is a full blown crisis to keep the West out of our hair while we deal with the Poles and the others who are falling for the Dulles propaganda. If we can get a war going it would also destroy the West's credibility with the Arabs. Khrushchev is certain that the Arabs are a coming force with their oil production and we can make them our allies if the West backs Israel.'

'But how can Arabs be communists? They're mostly devout Moslems and the Royal families have the power everywhere except in Egypt.'

'Egypt is the key,' said Orlenko, through Egypt we can take over the rest of the Arab world.'

'Tell me though,' asked Baring, 'how can you be hostile to Israel with your Jewish blood?'

'It's Jewish blood, not Zionist blood. That's the difference.'

During 1956 the crisis gradually worsened as Gamal Abdel Nasser followed up his threat to seize the Suez canal, the building of which he claimed, had cost 120,000 Egyptian lives in forced labour. In the frequent Cabinet meetings called to discuss Britain's reaction to the crisis, Baring argued vigorously for armed force to be used to put down Nasser who was, he argued, another Hitler. The despatch of a few battleships to Alexandria and Port Said would bring the mad dictator to his senses. It was an international crime for Nasser to seize the canal, which was owned by an international company, and the law would be on Britain's side if Britain went in.

Baring's arguments found receptive ears around the Cabinet table and Eden, hesitant at first, took up the cause with enthusiasm. The threatening ogre of Nasser became an obsession with the Prime Minister.

When Baring next met his controller he found Orlenko in a state of great excitement. 'The news from Hungary is devastating,' said the Russian, 'it's even worse than Poland. The Poles are getting rid of Rokossovsky so they can have command of their own armed forces. That's bad enough but the Hungarians are demanding the return of Imre Nagy as Premier and he's the symbol of their independence from Russia. He will have to be crushed.'

'By force?'

'Of course by force. The Red Army will go in but Khrushchev is worried about America's reaction. Allen Dulles is trigger-happy and the *Voice of America* is broadcasting appeals to the Hungarians inciting them to revolt. Khrushchev desperately needs that war in Egypt to give him a free hand in our own sphere of influence.'

'I think I can push Eden into an agreement with the French,' said Baring, confidently, 'the Foreign Secretary is not very keen but he'll have to go along with the inner Cabinet's decision.'

'Selwyn Lloyd?'

'Yes, Selwyn is the reluctant one. He's been at the Security Council trying to work out a settlement which is exactly what we don't want.'

'It would be a disaster if an agreement were reached. There must be intervention and war,' Orlenko said, 'everything depends on it. The French are ready to back the Israelis if Britain will come in. Can you push for Selwyn Lloyd to go to France secretly. If he does the Israelis will also go and Britain can be committed to action before there's time for second thoughts.'

'Good strategy,' said Baring thoughtfully. He knew the fragility of the British decision-making process. The least pressure from the Americans and Eden's nerve could collapse. If it did the intervention would be off, Eden would survive as Prime Minister and his own hopes of the succession would be dashed. He knew it was vitally important that the meetings with the French should be kept secret from the Americans.

As the crisis worsened Baring encouraged Eden to believe there was no alternative but collusion with both the Israelis and the French for an armed attack on Egypt which would destroy Nasser and win back the Suez Canal for international control. In the Cabinet meetings the Prime Minister adopted Baring's arguments as his own and a small Suez committee was set up to co-ordinate the plans for the invasion. The three Chiefs-of-Staff were told to prepare for the war. Only Earl Mountbatten, the First Lord of the Admiralty, raised any objections but he was soon overruled in the mad, angry mood that had overtaken Whitehall.

A few wiser heads within the Government advised caution and consultation with the United States, but the only outspoken ones were a couple of junior Ministers who, Baring advised, could easily be jettisoned without harming the Party.

Foreign Secretary Lloyd was despatched to Sèvres, near Paris, on the 22nd October for a secret meeting with French Ministers and with Ben-Gurion, Moshe Dayan and Peres who had flown in from Israel. Only two of Selwyn Lloyd's senior officials knew where he had gone. The others, including his junior Ministers, were told he had a cold at home and was not to be disturbed. Baring, as a member of the Suez committee, knew and told Orlenko who immediately sent a coded message to Moscow.

It was in this way that the Russians received the green light to crush the Hungarian patriots who were on that very day demonstrating for reforms. As the secret Sèvres agreement, between Britain, France and Israel, was being signed on the 24th October the Red Army moved on Budapest with ten thousand troops, tanks, artillery and armoured cars. Soviet aircraft strafed the barricades put up by rebels.

Before the week was out Israel attacked Egypt, closely following the Sèvres plan, and Anglo-French forces prepared to land at Port Said.

Opinion in Britain was confused and divided. The Labour Party called a protest meeting in Trafalgar Square with the slogan 'Law not War' and Aneurin Bevan told the crowd, 'We are stronger than Egypt but there are other countries stronger than us. Are we prepared to accept the logic we are applying to Egypt? If nations more powerful than us adopt this anarchistic attitude and launch bombs on London, what answer have we got?'

Demonstrators surged down Whitehall towards Downing Street and police on horseback rode into the crowd to control them. A few miles away, Baring sat in his study at Sussex Square quietly drinking afternoon tea. The front door bell rang. It was Orlenko. The policeman on guard duty recognised the famous millionaire Mr. Morgan Lewis, whose photograph had often appeared in the newspapers, and saluted politely. The butler let him in.

Once on their own the controller and the K.G.B. colonel spoke frankly. 'Just as we planned,' said Orlenko, smiling broadly.

'Not quite,' said Baring, 'I was at the Cabinet this morning and Head, who's been in Cyprus, reported that he's cancelled the plans for the attack on Cairo. The attack is now to be only on the canal zone.'

'Head, the Defence Minister?'

'Yes.'

'That's hardly good enough,' said Orlenko, 'we need an all-out war. The Red Army moved two hundred thousand troops and four thousand tanks into Budapest this morning. We don't take half measures and nor should you.'

'I expect I can get the plan developed once our action starts. We invade tomorrow morning.'

'The timing is perfect,' said the Russian, 'it could not be better from our point of view but what about the Americans?'

'Eisenhower's been told we're involved in a police action to separate the combatants.'

'He won't believe that. The C.I.A. already know what the British and French are up to,' said Orlenko.

'But it's too late for them to do anything about it and our duplicity will break the Anglo-American alliance.'

The butler brought in a tray with the silver tea service and a plate of thinly cut brown-bread cucumber sandwiches and retreated silently.

'Milk or lemon?' asked Baring.

'Have you forgotten?' Orlenko said in some surprise. 'I always take milk in England.'

The British invasion of Egypt caused a crisis in the international money markets. There was a rush to sell sterling and British gold reserves fell by £100,000,000 in a week. The United States increased the economic pressure by opposing Britain's request to withdraw capital from the International Monetary Fund.

At the Cabinet meeting called to discuss the worsening crisis Baring was amazed to learn that Harold Macmillan who, apart from himself, was the most vociferous supporter of the Suez operation had changed his mind and was now arguing for a ceasefire. It was the condition the United States had imposed for allowing a £300,000,000 loan from the I.M.F. and the Chancellor had no alternative but to accept it. The battleship diplomacy had been superceded by the superior power of the cheque book.

Baring was disappointed that his plan for an all-out war had been thwarted but he had achieved most of his objectives. Most of the Arab countries had become bitterly anti-British and Britain had been totally humiliated in the eyes of the world. It would now be easier to accelerate the dismantling of the Empire. In addition, as he had expected, Eden's health deteriorated rapidly and, despite a short holiday in the Jamaica sun, the Prime Minister returned to a sullen and unhappy House of Commons a gaunt and broken man. By January the growing evidence of ill-health and pressure from insistent doctors forced a reluctant Eden to retire.

When a Prime Minister resigns in mid-term the Queen sends for the leader of the largest party in the Commons. As there had been no time for a leader to emerge it fell to the Lord Chancellor and Lord Salisbury to canvass opinions in the Cabinet about who the leader should be. A majority of the Conservative Members of Parliament would probably have supported 'Rab' Butler, or Harold Macmillan, but they were not consulted. As a result it was Baring's name that was submitted to the Palace.

As the most respected elder statesman Winston Churchill was summoned to give his opinion. He distinguished himself by going in morning dress and in the same shabby top hat he had worn thirty years before. His advice corresponded to the majority opinion in the Cabinet.

The decision was made.

The Queen's Secretary telephoned Sussex Square.

The Right Honourable Charles Baring, M.C., M.P., who was already wearing his morning suit, left immediately for his audience with Her Majesty the Queen and accepted the office of her First Lord of the Treasury and Prime Minister of the United Kingdom of Great Britain and Northern Ireland.

FIRST EPILOGUE
1957

Six months after his move to Number 10 Downing Street, the Prime Minister was sitting in bed at midnight glancing at the first editions of the newspapers which were always brought to him before he went to sleep. There was nothing of serious consequence in the *Times* or *Telegraph*, but the *Daily Express* had an exclusive front page story by Chapman Pincher. It gripped the P.M.'s eyes. 'MILLIONAIRE SEIZED BY REDS' screamed the headline and the story read 'Morgan Lewis, the brilliant Welshman who built a fortune by exporting to Eastern Europe and who wrote the bestseller *Exporting is Fun* has been arrested in Russia and accused of spying for the British. Whitehall's MI6, tight-lipped as ever, would make no official comment but my sources in the Intelligence Service told me that there is more to the Lewis story than meets the eye. The P.M. has ordered a full investigation.'

Baring, who had not previously been informed of the story, gave an involuntary wry smile at the thought of Pincher's intelligent anticipation and quickly read the rest of the article which was largely a rehash of Lewis's career.

In the morning, after a breakfast eaten alone as Lady Anne was in the country, Baring was startled by the sudden arrival of his Principal Private Secretary.

'You're early,' said the Prime Minister, 'what brought you in?' as he glanced at his Piaget watch showing 7.31.

'It's the Lewis crisis, Prime Minister. S.I.S. called me at five this morning. They're sending a top man to brief you.'

'Why the panic?'

'They're afraid Pincher may have the full story and they want you to know before you read it in tomorrow's *Express*.'

'What's that?' Baring asked, pulling on his coat and feeling a shudder of apprehension down his spine.

"Hubbard of S.I.S. is downstairs,' said the secretary, not wishing to be drawn into an embarrassing area, 'where would you like to see him, Prime Minister?'

'In the sitting-room,' said the P.M.

Hubbard, the deputy head of S.I.S. a man in his late forties and greying, opened the conversation gingerly. 'We understand Lewis was an acquaintance of your's Prime Minister.'

'That is correct,' said the P.M. firmly, 'I first met him when I was in business just after the war. I made him Chairman of the Export Advisory Board when I was at Trade. Is it true he's been apprehended by the Russians?'

'It's more involved than that Prime Minister. We now know that Morgan Lewis was killed fourteen years ago during the war. The man you knew was an imposter using the Lewis identity.'

'Good gracious,' said Baring trying to sound shocked, 'who was he then?'

'We're fairly sure he was a Soviet agent. Routine surveillance three months ago showed Lewis meeting Embassy personnel who were known as K.G.B. operatives.'

'Was he one of our's too?' asked the P.M., hoping his expression did not reveal his inner anxiety.

'He was once recruited as a low-level courier. Fortunately he was never given much information about our operations but the loss of some of our agents in Eastern Europe added to our suspicions about Lewis, or whoever he is.'

'So you don't know his real name?' the P.M. said with undoubted relief in his voice.

'No Sir. We wondered if you had ever entertained doubts about him or whether he ever gave you any clue as to his true identity.'

'None whatsoever,' said the Prime Minister with
authority.

SECOND EPILOGUE
1959

In the General Election of 1959 Baring led his Party to success. It was recognised as an outstanding feat as under his leadership the country's economy had deteriorated seriously.

For Charles Baring himself the taste of victory was made bitter by the aftermath of his wife's sickness. Lady Anne, confined to a hospital bed with a malignant stomach cancer, had been unable to participate in the campaign. Baring visited her as soon as the results were known, thinking the news would cheer her, but he found her condition worse than ever. Her emaciated body was propped up but it hardly made any dent in the pillows. Her face was already like that of a day-old corpse with dead, leathery skin drawn tightly over the bone structure and under the hospital head-cap he could see she had lost almost all her hair.

Surprisingly her mind was as alert as ever. He told her the result and she replied in a slow careful voice as if every word counted towards her demise. 'That means nothing, Charles. Your success is worthless. You have ruined the Britain I love.'

'Don't be silly, darling. I've done my best. Conditions have been difficult,' he said earnestly.

'Conditions.' The word as she repeated it sounded more like a slow, tired excuse, 'con-di-tions, no Charles, your conditions were all of your own choosing. I know you have been working for the destruction of my country. I've watched you. I watched your K.G.B. friend Lewis. I knew much more than you thought. Allow me one question, Charles. Why did you do it?'

The supreme effort of the speech exhausted her, but she summoned enough strength to withdraw her thin hand from her husband's as a mark of her distance from him.

For five minutes Baring sat speechless. Lady Anne had closed her eyes and was no longer aware of his presence.

That night she died without regaining consciousness.

THIRD EPILOGUE
1982

The State funeral for the Earl of Amesbury attracted the biggest congregation of world leaders since Sir Winston Churchill's in 1965.

Europe was represented by Mitterand of France, Schmidt of West Germany, Honecker of the D.D.R. among others. The Commonwealth was represented by Mugabe of Zimbabwe, Fraser of Australia, Ramgoolam of Mauritius and many others.

The United States was represented by President Ronald Reagan and the U.S.S.R. was represented by President Leonid Brezhnev.

Sitting in the rear row of seats at St. Paul's Cathedral were Sir Peter Chambers, the head of MI6, and one of his retired predecessors the seventy-three year old Sir Phillip Hubbard. As the coffin was slowly carried in from the gun carriage by the Royal Marines for the journey down the aisle the congregation stood.

'Strange,' whispered Sir Peter, 'Brezhnev being here. As an excuse to meet Reagan, I suppose.'

'No,' said Sir Phillip.

Later when the organ played, Sir Peter asked 'Why "no" so definitely?'

'No Soviet leader has ever left Russia for a State funeral in the West. They sent only Marshall Koniev for Churchill's. Brezhnev has come because Baring was their agent. I've suspected it for twenty-five years and now I'm certain.'